THE
CRYSTAL
...

By Julia Gray

ICE MAGE
FIRE MUSIC
ISLE OF THE DEAD

The Guardi
THE DAR
THE JASPER FORES
THE CRYSTAL DESERT

THE
CRYSTAL
DESERT

Book Three of
The Guardian Cycle

JULIA GRAY

www.orbitbooks.co.uk

An *Orbit* Book

First published in Great Britain by Orbit 2001

Copyright © 2001 by Julia Gray
The moral right of the author has been asserted.

A CIP catalogue record for this book is available from the British Library.

ISBN 1 84149 093 8

Typeset by Palimpsest Book Production Ltd,
Polmont, Stirlingshire
Printed and bound in Great Britain
by Mackays of Chatham PLC, Chatham, Kent

Orbit
A Division of
Little, Brown and Company (UK)
Brettenham House
Lancaster Place
London WC2E 7EN

PROLOGUE

Mlicki was the only one who still believed they would hear the music of life again. Every morning, when he woke, he would lie under his chilouk and listen. The darkness brought many sounds to him – the rustle of wind-blown sand, the scratching of insects, Erardi's rasping snores – but never the music.

Each morning was the same. After a while, he would be able to stand it no longer. Even though the day had not yet begun, he would get up and quietly leave the house, then make his way down to the river bank. And each morning he would be greeted by a moonlit scene that came from a nightmare from which there was no escape. It was unnatural – *wrong* – and all the more so because Mlicki knew what it *ought* to look like. Alone among the inhabitants of Bahriya, he had seen beyond the wind to a time when the music of life would ring out again. It had been as real to him as the outer world, but his visions had brought him trouble in the past, and so he had told no one of what he had seen.

The river will come back, he told himself stubbornly, as he did each morning. It will!

Mlicki was the only one who still believed, though even he felt his faith beginning to dry up now, just as the mud of the river bed was drying – becoming a cracked pavement of desiccated clay, like a million shards of crude, broken pottery. The water *would* return, but he had no way of knowing when this would happen. Or whether by then it would be too late.

The ominous silence crowded in upon him, and he looked up, sensing the weight of the moons upon his thoughts. The White Moon was full, riding majestically across the star-sprinkled plain, but there was something else that was influencing his mood this morning. Neither the Amber nor the Red Moon was in sight above the horizon, and although they were both waxing and close to full, Mlicki wasn't able to identify their power. Which meant that what he was feeling must come from the Invisible. The unseen moon had changed its pattern recently, so that no one was really sure when or where it would appear within the dome – and this had had an unsettling effect on the people of Misrah. It seemed as though there was nothing left for them to rely upon. Such a change was supposed to be impossible – though Mlicki didn't understand why this should be so – and many people were saying that if there was chaos above, then there would soon be chaos in the world of men. Mlicki couldn't follow that logic either, but just at that moment he would have been willing to wager a great deal that the Invisible was at its most potent. The idea made him feel unaccountably nervous.

'Did you do this?' he asked aloud, searching the sky for the tell-tale emptiness that marked the passage of the Invisible. The moon presented exactly the same aspect whether it was 'full' or 'new', and the only way to 'see' it was when it blotted out the stars beyond, or occasionally eclipsed the other moons or the sun itself.

The dome brought Mlicki no answer, and when he looked down again, the eastern sky behind him was illuminated by streaks of pink and pale gold. The pre-dawn light was enough to confirm that his earlier impressions had not been mistaken.

There had been droughts before – when the river had shrunk to a muddy trickle, the fertile plains that lined its banks had begun to shrivel up, and even the wells had become unreliable – but there had never been anything as bad as this. The process had always been gradual before, and – to some extent – predictable, allowing those who lived along the Kullana's shores to hoard a little water in their underground reservoirs and ensure that they had enough to last until the following year. This time disaster had struck with incredible speed. One day the river had been running strongly, and then four days later it had gone, as if it had never existed. In full spate the Kullana was over a hundred paces wide, and at its centre the water rose to more than twice the height of a tall man. All that had vanished almost overnight, and now the only thing left was an arid gully, where even the air was without a trace of moisture. The river bed had become a patchwork of death. The music had gone, and it was not even close to the dry season. The meltwaters from the distant mountains – mountains that Mlicki had never seen – should still have been in full flow, but there was nothing.

Although no one could understand what had happened, what could have caused the drought, the catastrophe that had befallen them was undeniable. Misrah was an unforgiving land at the best of times, but this latest disaster threatened to destroy the lives of even those people who had believed themselves to be secure.

Mlicki felt the heat of the newly-risen sun on his back, and watched the first rays slanting over the desolate terrain before him. As the sunlight leached away the last drops of water, even the stones that had once shone from the depths of the stream seem to have been bleached. Where once there had been blue and green and flashes of gold, orange and black, everything was now the same lifeless colour of pale umber.

Even as he watched, a sluggish breeze was enlivened by the warmth of the new day. This raised a series of kwei, spirals of sand and dust that whirled and swayed like living creatures. Some people called them sun devils, the refuge of lost souls. Mlicki's mother had taught him to appreciate the beauty in their shimmering movements – to see how they sometimes spun in different directions so that two would seem to dance together like a pair of lovers – but he took no pleasure in watching them now. Their very presence in such a place, where once water had swirled and eddied, was just another omen of dread.

On the bank, the picture was similarly unpleasant. Tamarisk bushes, which would normally have been a mass of pink and green at this time of year, were turning brown, parched by the sudden drought – and it would not be long before the villagers' precious crops were affected in the same way.

As the morning brightened, Mlicki's gaze fell upon another dispiriting sight. The wild chirkewa plant, which had seeded itself at the top of the bank, was deep-rooted, and had defied the devastation for several days, clinging to life so that its delicate green foliage still gave off the healing scent that made it such a cherished weed. Now it was drooping, the tips of its leaves turning black, as if scorched by fire. The imminent end of the herb's resistance felt like a sign – and the last of Mlicki's confidence began to drain away.

He was about to walk over to the plant, to see whether it was worth trying to salvage any of the leaves, when he jumped violently and almost cried aloud. He managed to stop himself, however, and forced a smile onto his face as he turned to look at his sister. It had been her hand, slipping into his own, that had startled him and, as always, he was amazed at the way she had been able to approach so silently.

Kalkara was eight years old now, four years his junior, but there were times when she seemed even younger still. Her bright blue eyes looked up at him with a mixture of love, concern and trust. It was that trust which he found hardest to live up to. She was his responsibility, his burden – but one he would not have relinquished for the world. There was also a constant sadness buried deep within her solemn gaze, and he would have given anything to be able to replace her sorrow with genuine contentment.

'You made me jump, Kala,' he told her, his smile more natural now. 'Why do you sneak up on me like that?'

There was no reply. Kalkara had not uttered a single word since the day they had been orphaned.

'I'll have to tie a bell around your neck, like a goat, so I know when you're coming,' he added, squeezing her hand and grinning to make sure she knew he was joking.

Kala grinned back, the expression lighting up her dark elfin face, and by unspoken agreement they turned and began to walk back towards the settlement. Even then, had Mlicki closed his eyes, he would not have known there was anyone else there. Whatever had stolen his sister's voice seemed to have made her weightless too; she appeared to float like a ghost, her feet making no sound as they touched the ground. It was just one of the things that made other people regard her as peculiar.

As they made their way back to the village, Mlicki could not help looking back at the river once more, just in case. Hope was a hard emotion to shift. But nothing had changed, and there was no point in denying it. The music was gone. But it would come back. He had to believe that. Otherwise he might as well accept that Bahriya was doomed – and he knew who would get the blame then.

It had taken Mlicki a long time to get used to living within walls and a roof that didn't move gently in the night breezes, when the erlik came to watch over their sleep. Even after four years, he and Kalkara were still outsiders, accepted for the most part, but some people regarded them as strangers, and found it hard to trust them. In truth he could not blame the villagers for thinking them odd – his appearance and Kala's silence were bound to unnerve most people – but the lack of trust rankled. They had always worked hard for the inhabitants of Bahriya, and there were several who had benefited from his gift, the talent even he did not understand. The siblings had done nothing to betray the community, and yet their place within it was still suspect. Then again, they *had* been taken in and given shelter. Destitute strangers arriving now would be offered no more than token hospitality – and this had been the case for some time even before the river vanished.

When Mlicki and Kala got back to the house, Erardi and the rest of his family were up and eating breakfast. But there was none of the chatter that usually accompanied their meals, and Mlicki felt a sense of foreboding. His unease intensified when Erardi rose and took him aside. There was anger and misery in the old man's eyes, but there was something else too, something much more worrying. It took Mlicki a few moments to recognize it for what it was, but when he did his heart sank. Buried beneath the other emotions was resignation. If there was to be a battle, Mlicki's only certain ally was already assuming that defeat was inevitable.

'There's trouble brewing,' the old man said quietly, confirming the boy's fears.

'Because of the river?' It was not really a question.

Eradi nodded.

'People are getting desperate.'

Looking for scapegoats, Mlicki thought bitterly, but he said nothing.

'This is your home,' the old man said. He looked very uncomfortable now. 'I'll do what I can for you, but I have to think of my own family first.'

Mlicki nodded. He knew that Erardi was a good man at heart. He was simply telling the truth as he saw it.

*

'Harsh measures are necessary now that water is so scarce,' Taybi declared.

'But surely two children will make little difference,' Erardi protested.

'Every mouthful is precious,' his adversary retorted. 'We must put our own first.'

The confrontation had come swiftly, within an hour of Mlicki's return. It had taken the form of an impromptu gathering in the open space in front of Erardi's house, with Taybi acting as spokesman for the villagers – most of whom seemed both angry and frightened. A few people looked ashamed, but they were the silent ones, looking at the ground.

'They're nomads by birth,' Taybi added. 'They don't belong here.'

It had only been a matter of time until Mlicki and Kalkara's origins were brought into the argument, and others quickly took up the cry.

'Let them go back to their own people!' someone called.

'Their people are dead!' Erardi responded angrily. 'Murdered! Have you all forgotten that?'

'We only have their word for it,' another onlooker muttered.

'There are other wandering tribes,' Taybi stated calmly. 'One of them—'

'And how are they supposed to find these tribes?' Erardi cut in.

The old man was standing in front of his home, his family ranged behind him, while the subjects of the dispute stood a little to one side. Kalkara was trembling, her eyes flicking back and forth as she listened to the war of words. It was for her sake alone that Mlicki stood tall, facing their accusers with as much dignity as he could muster, even as his emotions veered wildly between rage and despair. At times he had wanted to scream and shout, at others to beg for mercy – but he had remained silent, knowing there was little hope in either course. If Erardi's advocacy was not successful, he and his sister were doomed.

'Nomads are full of tricks,' someone else commented.

'They're thieves too. Everyone knows that.'

'That's not—' Mlicki began, provoked beyond endurance by such bigotry.

'We're not talking about nomads in general,' Erardi declared, overriding the boy's interruption. 'These two—'

'Are you saying they're normal?' Taybi demanded, cutting in in his turn.

'Just look at them!' another villager cried.

'And what about his so-called visions?' a woman asked.

'Many of us have benefited from Mlicki's othersight,' Erardi countered.

'But it's not natural. We want no part of such sorcery.'

'He's been taken by the burning winds.'

'How do we know *he*'s not the one who's taken the music away? He's—'

'Don't be absurd!' Erardi exclaimed angrily.

'Maybe his magic angered the winds,' Taybi suggested.

'Or he brought the unclean upon us, to drink the river dry.'

Mlicki listened to these ridiculous and spiteful accusations, and each one pierced his heart like a sword of fire. He knew there was no defence against such unreason, and the outcome of the debate was already a foregone conclusion. The only person who had ever been able to explain what he did in a way that others could understand was his mother – and she was not there to defend him.

'Do you have any idea—' Erardi began, but he fell silent when Mlicki stepped forward, taking his sister's hand in his own.

'We'll go,' the boy said, his voice strong and clear.

There was a moment's silence as everyone looked at him in surprise.

'We'll go,' he repeated.

'Are you sure?' Erardi asked hesitantly. There was genuine concern on the old man's face, but Mlicki was not surprised to see a measure of relief in his eyes too.

The boy nodded, keeping his expression carefully neutral. The wind took him beyond then, and for a moment everyone vanished and he saw Bahriya as the collection of abandoned ruins it would become. Their going wouldn't save the village, but there was no point in trying to tell them so.

When he came back to his own time, Kala was looking up at him – and to his astonishment, she was smiling.

An hour later, having packed up their few belongings, Mlicki and his sister crossed the dry river bed and set out into the endless desert.

PART ONE

THE TOMA

CHAPTER ONE

'It's usually only for three days,' Mlicki said. 'We call it the bond of salt.'

'Only three days?' Terrel exclaimed.

'And that was before the troubles began,' the younger boy confirmed. 'Nowadays the laws of hospitality are being broken all the time. Not all the tribes are as honourable as the Toma, and even they have to be careful now.'

'Then why have they let us stay so much longer?' Terrel asked. He had been travelling with the nomads for close to a short month now – and there had been no indication that he had outstayed his welcome. Mlicki and his sister had been with the Toma for much longer.

Mlicki shrugged.

'Actually, it's obvious why they're letting *you* stay,' he said. 'Just ask the family of that baby you saved, or any of the others who aren't in pain any more. A true shaman is welcome anywhere.'

'I'm not a shaman.'

'Shaman, healer, what difference does the name make? One way or another, you help people. On the other hand, the only reason they accepted me and Kala is because Vilheyuna insisted on it. Not that having us around has done *him* much good.' Mlicki glanced at the figure lying on cushions in the centre of the tent. The old man's face was perfectly still, and his eyes were closed. Only the barely noticeable rise and fall of his chest showed that he was still alive.

'He must have seen something important in you,' Terrel commented.

'My talents?' Mlicki responded derisively. 'Much good they've done *me*.'

Terrel could sympathize with that sentiment all too easily, but he didn't say so.

'I think Vilheyuna chose wisely,' he insisted. 'Who else would have looked after him this well?'

Mlicki blinked in surprise at Terrel's words.

'I've been given some of the credit for keeping him alive all this time,' he said, 'but I haven't *done* anything. He's being protected by something none of us understand. I mean, he's had no food or water, and yet he hasn't wasted away. It makes no sense.'

'No, it doesn't,' Terrel agreed. 'But without you the Toma might have left him for dead. When he wakes up he'll need help coming back to the world.'

'*If* he wakes up.'

'He will.'

'You sound very confident for someone whose healing skills can't even begin to help him,' Mlicki commented dryly.

Terrel thought about telling the boy of all the other sleepers he'd seen – some of whom had been in a coma for more than a decade, and yet were still virtually unchanged – but decided that this was not the right time. It would be too complicated. He would have to explain his connection with Alyssa then – and he wasn't ready to do that. The very thought of her threatened to tear him apart. It had been so long . . .

'This is beyond my healing,' he admitted simply, 'but the fact that he *is* still alive is important. It'll make sense in the end.'

Mlicki looked doubtful.

'Maybe if I'd been with him when he collapsed, I could have . . .' His voice trailed away.

Terrel could have told him that it would have made no difference. He had been there when Ysatel fell, and he hadn't been able to help her.

'When did you say it happened?' he asked instead.

'The summer of the year before last, in the Binhemma-Ghar. If it had been anyone else they'd have left him at one of the monuments, but they weren't prepared to abandon their shaman while there was still breath left in him. As it was, it's a wonder he survived the journey back.'

Terrel knew that the Binhemma-Ghar was a desert within a desert. Its name, translated literally, meant 'go in and you won't come out'. It was apparently a forbidding place, and he was aware of the awe in which it was held by the nomads.

'But he *did* survive,' Terrel pointed out. 'And he'd chosen you to be his assistant, to look after him, even though you were an outsider. That should mean a lot.'

'It does,' Mlicki replied. 'But if I can't do more than

make sure he isn't harmed when we move camp, or wipe the dust from his skin, then what's the point? What good am I doing?'

'You're doing all you can.' Terrel had just watched Mlicki wash Vilheyuna's face, arms and feet. The boy had been so gentle, so attentive, that it had been an oddly moving sight. Perhaps because he was an outsider, Terrel was the only person Mlicki allowed inside the tent when he tended to the shaman in this way. 'Sometimes all you can do is wait.'

'Until he wakes up?' Mlicki asked quietly.

'Or until he lets you know that you're to be his successor.'

'No!' the boy responded fiercely. 'I'm no shaman.' He glanced at Vilheyuna's ceremonial headdress, which hung from one of the tent poles, waiting for its old owner – or a new one – to claim it.

'He chose you as his assistant,' Terrel reminded him.

'And anyway, how *could* he let me know?' Mlicki asked, looking back at the unmoving figure.

'Perhaps in a vision.'

'The winds control those.'

'Maybe Vilheyuna is now in a place where he can talk to the winds.'

Mlicki was obviously surprised by this suggestion. Then he shook his head, dismissing it.

'There's more chance of the elders making *you* the tribe's shaman,' he said. 'They can't wait for ever, and at least you can heal, even if you can't lead the wind-dances.'

'Not with this leg,' Terrel agreed, glancing down at his twisted limb. 'Besides, you're not without talents yourself. We both know that.'

The two young men regarded each other steadily. Mlicki was the only person Terrel had ever met whose eyes were perhaps as strange as his own. The irises of Terrel's eyes were like pale diamonds, their only colour coming from brief flashes buried within their crystalline depths. But although his eyes were frequently the cause of amazement and alarm when he met someone for the first time, at least they were perfectly matched. Mlicki's were completely different. His good eye was a deep, soft brown. His left eye, however, was surrounded by a patch of very pale skin, which ran diagonally across the bridge of his nose and his cheekbone, and enclosed most of his left temple and part of his forehead. Within its distinct boundary, the flesh seemed to be stretched tight, distorting the shape of the eye into a sloping crescent, and the eyebrow was pure white. Most disconcerting of all, the half-hidden iris was a delicate shade of rose pink.

From an earlier conversation, Terrel knew that Mlicki was practically blind in that eye, and could only sense blurred outlines and shifting patches of colour – except when he went 'beyond the wind' and saw into another time or another world. Then his sight was perfect. He had no control over what he saw and when, and it was something he was reluctant to talk about. The fact that he had discussed it with Terrel after such a short acquaintance was testimony to the kinship the two had felt right from the beginning. And that had begun with a connection between two minds.

When Terrel had first encountered the concept of psinoma – invisible words – he had treated it with great suspicion. The idea that he could listen to another's thoughts, or even plant suggestions in another mind –

without the recipient being aware of it – had struck him as dangerous and wrong. However, in the years since his exile from Vadanis, he had come across many strange languages, and although he still felt guilty about such prying, he had used psinoma to enable himself to learn those tongues in a relatively short time. During his journeyings, the ability to communicate with those around him had been vital – sometimes a matter of life or death – and so he'd set aside his scruples until he was fluent enough to speak normally with the local people.

When Terrel had joined the Toma, he had realized almost immediately that Mlicki shared his ability to use psinoma – albeit unwittingly at first. After the boy's initial fear and suspicion were overcome, Mlicki had been able to assist actively in the learning process, the first time this had ever happened. Although they no longer needed their instinctive telepathic link, the knowledge of its existence tied them together in a bond of mutual regard which was fast maturing into a genuine friendship.

'Why are you here, Terrel?' Mlicki asked now.

'Why are any of us here?' he replied, deliberately misunderstanding the question.

'I mean why did you *come* here?' Mlicki said patiently. 'You could have gone anywhere.'

'Perhaps it was so I could meet you,' Terrel replied, knowing that his companion wouldn't take his answer seriously – in spite of the fact that it was quite possibly true.

'Very funny,' Mlicki said. 'I've never met anyone from outside Misrah before, and I don't know why anyone would want to come here. Especially now.'

'The truth is, I don't know what brought me here.' Trying to explain the vagaries of his fateful bargain would have been much too difficult.

'Is your home very far away?'

'Yes,' Terrel replied heavily. He was not even sure he *had* a home any more. The Floating Islands had begun to seem like a distant memory. Then he thought of Alyssa, lying motionless in a basement cell of Havenmoon, and knew that no matter how comfortless the notion was, that dismal place was the closest he had to a home. The oath he had sworn to return to her still bound him – even though the possibility of his ever getting back there seemed a remote prospect at the moment.

'Is it true you crossed an ocean to get here?'

'Actually I crossed two.' Terrel recalled both the ship which had brought him to the southern shore of Misrah and the makeshift raft on which he had been exiled from Vadanis.

Mlicki was staring at him in awe.

'Two?' he breathed. 'I can't imagine so much water, so much life.' He seemed lost in a kind of reverie. 'Is it true that seawater is full of salt?'

'Yes. If you try to drink it it only makes you more thirsty. Or sick.' Terrel spoke from painful experience.

'That happens to some of the wells here,' Mlicki said thoughtfully. 'The camels can drink it, but we can't.'

This information did not come as much of a surprise to Terrel. When he had first set eyes on a camel, all he could think of was what a ridiculous looking animal it seemed. However, he was beginning to appreciate just how remarkable the creatures were – and how valuable to the nomads. Being reminded of them now jogged a vague memory, something he could not place but which nagged at his subconscious.

'Of course some of the wells are completely dry now,' Mlicki went on. 'Since the river disappeared . . .' His voice died away, and Terrel saw painful memories reflected in his mismatched eyes.

Terrel knew the story of Mlicki and his sister – or at least as much of it as the boy had chosen to tell him. He and Kalkara had once been part of a different nomadic clan, but after a ferocious raid upon their camp – part of a tribal dispute, apparently – when their parents had been killed along with the rest of the clan, they had been left alone to fend for themselves. Through a combination of luck and resourcefulness that was remarkable in one so young, Mlicki had led Kalkara to a riverside village called Bahriya, where they had been taken in. Later, as events in Misrah took another turn for the worse, they had been banished from there, and had eventually joined up with the Toma.

'That changed everything,' Mlicki said softly.

Terrel guessed that the boy was still talking about the mysterious disappearance of the Kullana River, and decided against asking any further questions. He concentrated on the present instead.

'You and Kala are part of the Toma now though, aren't you? This is your home.'

'Yes,' Mlicki conceded. 'For the time being. But life is getting harder for them – us – too. If it gets too bad, who's to say they won't turn their backs on us? Especially as Vilheyuna was the one who adopted us. He's not in any position to defend us, is he?'

Terrel could understand the nature of Mlicki's argument, but he believed there was little chance of the siblings being forced into exile once more. He was about to say as much when his companion spoke again.

'You never told me why you left your family. What happened to your parents?'

Even though this question had been asked and answered – albeit mostly with evasions or outright lies – several times during his travels, Terrel was never prepared for the emotions it raised within him. It had been almost three years now since he'd learnt the truth about his parentage, and he still could not come to terms with it. Even if he had done so, no one – not even Mlicki – would have believed his tale.

'I never knew my parents,' he said, coming as close to the truth as he dared.

Mlicki regarded him thoughtfully, obviously aware that Terrel was holding something back. For a moment it seemed as though he would want to know more, but then he evidently thought better of it. Even so his next question was almost as discomforting.

'Do you have any sisters or brothers?'

Terrel was about to shake his head, no, but memories of the mocking laughter that haunted his dreams – and his waking mind if he let himself become vulnerable – made him change his mind. He would not grant Jax that small victory by denying his existence.

'I have a brother,' he replied, 'but I've never met him.'

'That's sad.'

'It wasn't my choice.'

'I'd be dead now if it wasn't for Kala.' As always, Mlicki's face softened when he spoke of his sister.

'I thought you were the one who looks after her,' Terrel remarked, glad of the chance to change the subject.

'I am. The point is, without her, I'd've given up any number of times. My bones would've been picked clean by hubaras by now, somewhere out there. But I can't let her down, can I?'

Terrel had already seen how devoted the brother and sister were. He envied them their closeness.

'I've been thinking,' he said. 'Is it possible Kala doesn't speak because something's wrong with her throat? Would you like me to see if—'

'No,' Mlicki stated, shaking his head. 'She's not ill. It's just who she is. Just as this is who I am.' He gestured towards his strange eye. 'Healing can't change that.'

'But you were born like that,' Terrel said. He did not think he could 'heal' such an affliction, and he felt that Mlicki would not even be willing to let him try. 'Kala used to talk when she was little, didn't she?'

'Yes. All the time.' Mlicki smiled for a moment at the memory. 'But that . . .' His face resumed its habitually solemn expression. 'It's who she is,' he repeated. 'The only one who can change that is her. She's happy as she is.'

Terrel nodded, accepting the decision with some relief.

'Thank you for the offer, though,' Mlicki added. 'Most people don't think she's worth bothering with.'

'Well, that's certainly not true. Besides, I like her.'

Mlicki smiled with genuine pleasure.

'She reminds me of someone I know,' Terrel added, wishing with all his heart that that someone would visit him soon – no matter what shape she chose to adopt.

CHAPTER TWO

'Are you going to be in there all day?'

Terrel and Mlicki both recognized the impatient voice that called from outside the canopy – and they both felt some misgivings about facing its owner. However, there was nothing more they could do for Vilheyuna, and they would have to leave his tent sooner or later.

'What does *he* want?' Mlicki wondered aloud.

'Maybe he needs some advice,' Terrel suggested quietly.

His companion half smiled at this patently absurd notion, but he too had realized that Zahir still had enough respect for the shaman to prevent him from entering the tent uninvited.

'I doubt that.'

'Let's go and find out.'

They pulled the flap aside, and stepped out into the open. The air was clear and cold, but the sun's glare was blinding after the relative gloom of the tent. Terrel could feel its power on his face, promising the warmth that would soon come with the beginnings of spring – and also promising the scorching heat that made the desert summers potentially lethal. When their eyes had adjusted to the sudden brightness, they saw Zahir staring at them intently. He was flanked, as always, by his self-styled 'captains', three other boys on the verge of manhood.

'Well?' he demanded.

'There's no change,' Mlicki reported.

'I need him awake. Soon!' Zahir's shaven head and prominent ears, one of which was decorated with a thick gold ring, gave him a belligerent look, and in this instance appearances were not deceptive. He was the youngest son of Algardi, the most revered of all the Toma's elders, and he wore his eminence like a crown. In fact, one of his many nicknames was 'the prince' – although no one would have been foolish enough to use it in his father's presence. The Toma were a democratic community, and the tribe's elders would never have countenanced any claim to 'royal' status.

'I'm doing all I can,' Mlicki said nervously.

'And what is that, exactly?'

'What do you mean?'

'What are you actually *doing*?' Zahir clarified. 'Besides wringing your hands and whining,' he added sarcastically.

'I . . . I . . . attend . . .' Mlicki stammered.

'Vilheyuna must wake in the next few days,' Zahir said, looking at the shaman's assistant in disgust.

Terrel could have told him that that was not going to happen, but he saw no point in doing so. Unlike most of the rest of his clan, Zahir could be arrogant and aloof, and did not bother to conceal his disdain for outsiders. He obviously considered Terrel an intruder, and regarded his presence with some suspicion. Terrel's demonstration of healing skills had done little to change this situation. If anything, it had made Zahir even more wary.

'What about you, Ghost?' he said now, turning to face Terrel directly. 'Isn't your magic up to this?'

Terrel was aware of the name he had been given when he'd first joined the nomads, and knew the reason for it. He had the palest skin that any of the Toma had ever seen. However, Zahir was the only one who ever used the name to his face.

'This is beyond my healing,' he replied, wondering why their interrogator's need for the shaman was so urgent.

'Then you'd better think of something else. We can't wait for ever,' Zahir said, echoing Mlicki's earlier statement.

What's changed? Terrel wondered. After all this time . . .

'Your kappara-tan will still go ahead, whether Vilheyuna is awake or not,' Mlicki said, evidently divining the reason for their visitor's impatience.

'I know that!' Zahir snapped. 'That's not the point. Without a proper shaman—' He broke off abruptly, and glared at Mlicki with utter contempt. 'What's the point in trying to explain it to you? You have no clan. You might as well join the unclean.'

Terrel sensed the cruel barb strike home, but he knew better than to try to defend his companion. That would only make Zahir even more spiteful. Nevertheless, he decided to divert his attention if he could.

'What's a kappara-tan?' he asked. In spite of all Terrel's efforts, there were some words in the desert language that he could not understand. For a start, the nomads distinguished between eight different degrees of thirst, culminating in 'ak-saydath' – a vehement thirst – which was also a synonym for passionate love. He had not come across 'kappara-tan' before, and the sense he had got from Mlicki's thoughts when the boy used it had not been specific.

'Trust a *foreigner* to ask that,' Zahir responded scornfully.

'It's when—' Mlicki began, then fell silent as Zahir glanced at him again.

'It's something neither of *you* will ever know,' Zahir told them, and his three allies grinned. 'But you'll soon see what it is for someone to become a man. To be chosen.'

Terrel had it now. The kappara-tan was a rite of passage, a ceremony that marked the change from boy to man. Zahir would be sixteen years old in a few days' time, and he obviously felt that the ritual marking this occasion would not be complete without a shaman present to oversee the event. It was another indication of how the elder's son viewed his own importance.

Terrel was about to ask another question when something attracted Zahir's notice.

'What's that?' he demanded, pointing to the four circles printed on the back of Terrel's left hand.

'A tattoo,' he replied, taken aback by the sudden change of subject, but glad that he, and not Mlicki, now appeared to be the focus of their inquisitor's attention.

'Only women have tattoos,' Zahir stated.

And lunatics, Terrel thought. The tattoo had been applied at Havenmoon, permanently marking him as an inmate of the madhouse.

'Not where I come from,' he replied evenly.

'And where's that?'

'An island called Vadanis,' Terrel said, aware that Zahir already knew the answer to his question.

'On the other side of the ocean?'

'Two oceans,' Mlicki put in.

'Two?' Zahir exclaimed scornfully. 'You really believe that?'

'Why would I lie?' Terrel asked.

'The winds know why you would do anything. Did you live in a house on this barbarian island of yours?'

'Yes.'

'Houses tie you down, imprison you. We take our homes with us. The only true life is the nomad way.'

'I've become a traveller too,' Terrel pointed out.

'But you'll go back, won't you? To your prison.'

Terrel did not answer, knowing that nothing he could say would change the other's opinion of him.

'At least your eyes come from the desert,' Zahir stated mysteriously.

Terrel didn't get a chance to ask him what he meant, because at that moment Kalkara ran up to join them, moving as quietly as a feather blown on the breeze. The sudden movement behind them startled the captains, and they glanced round. When they saw who it was, one of them stuck out a foot so that the girl tripped over it. It was a deliberate but almost casual act of cruelty. Although Kala fell headlong onto the sand and stones, she did not cry out. Mlicki yelled in protest, and hurled himself forward, intent on exacting revenge – only to find that Zahir had beaten him to it. He turned to the offender and dealt him a heavy blow to the chest with the heel of his hand – half punch, half push. The other boy fell to the ground, and Zahir stood over him, a look of poisonous rage on his face.

'You're a cretin, Marrad,' he growled. 'You *never* treat a woman with such disrespect.'

'She's not a—' the fallen captain began.

'Shut up!' Zahir shouted, cutting off the feeble protest. 'Get out of my sight.'

As Marrad scrambled to his feet and ran off, Zahir turned back to face Mlicki, who had gone to kneel beside his sister. Kalkara was sitting up now, and seemed more shocked than hurt by what had happened. Even so, she was wide-eyed and tearful. Terrel expected Zahir to offer some apology for his companion's thoughtless actions, but he did not. He clearly felt that it was beneath him to do so. For a few awkward moments no one spoke.

'If that's an example of manhood in your clan,' Mlicki declared eventually, 'then I'd rather be one of the unclean.'

For once Zahir had no instant retort, but the studied indifference in his dark eyes turned to anger once more. Violence hung in the air like the stillness before a thunderstorm.

'Be careful what you say, boy,' Zahir growled.

'Why sh—'

'Enough!' Terrel cut in forcefully. 'It's done. Finished.' He moved forward and put a restraining hand on Mlicki's shoulder. 'Leave it at that.' He felt ill-suited to the role of peacemaker, but his words seemed to calm the nerves of both protagonists. After a few moments Zahir simply turned on his heel and stalked away, followed by his remaining cohorts. Mlicki balefully watched them go, as if wanting to be sure they would not return, while Terrel took one of Kalkara's hands in his own and pulled her to her feet.

'Let's have a look at you,' he said, inspecting her thin limbs. 'Just a few grazes. We'll soon sort that out.'

'Why don't you speak, Kala?' Terrel asked quietly. He was talking to himself as much as to her, neither expecting nor receiving an answer. 'I think you could if you wanted to.'

While he'd been checking to see that she had suffered no more than a few superficial scrapes, Terrel had let his intuitive senses reach out. He had found nothing physical that would prevent her from using her voice, but her mind – unlike her brother's – was closed off. Terrel doubted that he could have invaded her private thoughts, even if he'd wanted to. As it was, he found the idea of even trying to do this utterly repugnant.

On occasion, when her needs required it, Kalkara would respond to a direct question with a nod or shake of her head, and she was adept at using signs and gestures if she wanted to convey anything more complicated. She rarely needed to do this, though, as her brother usually anticipated her requests. She was a self-contained creature, and even though it was clear that she could understand the speech of others, she seemed to have no reason to use it herself. But that didn't stop Terrel from wanting to understand why anyone should voluntarily cut themselves off from communicating with her fellow human beings.

'I'm sure you could tell me some amazing stories.' And some awful ones too, he added silently. He could only imagine what it must have been like for a four-year-old to witness the murder of both her parents. 'I'd like to hear them one day.'

Kalkara glanced at him, but the expression in her brilliant blue eyes was unreadable.

The two of them were sitting at the crest of a sand dune, a little way beyond the edge of the encampment. They had gone there after Mlicki had returned to Vilheyuna's tent to calm down. The girl seemed none the worse for wear after her fall, and appeared to have forgotten all about the incident.

'I'd like us to be friends, Kala. Can we be friends, do you think?'

Kalkara thought about this for a moment, then gave the slightest of nods. It was the first time she had responded directly to anything Terrel had said, and he grinned. Her answering smile transformed her normally serious little face, and Terrel laughed, genuinely delighted. But then her smile faded, leaving only the memory of its sudden glow. Kala's moods were as light and mercurial as the movements of her slender body.

'You remind me of Alyssa,' he told her. 'You don't look like her, but . . .' He paused, gazing out over the desert that stretched away into the sunset. 'She's sleeping now, like Vilheyuna, but she'll wake up one day. When I go home.'

Although Kalkara did not react to his words, he was aware that she had grown very still. Unlike many of the nomads, Terrel felt quite at ease in the girl's company, and he was able to talk to her readily enough – even about subjects he normally kept to himself. Part of the reason for that, he knew, was because he could be certain she would not repeat anything he said. But there was more to it than that. There was a connection between them that he couldn't explain.

'I think I'm finally where I'm meant to be,' he said thoughtfully. It was a feeling that had been growing within him slowly for some time, and he could only hope his instincts were right. He had already travelled further than he could ever have imagined, and had been away from Vadanis for an unbelievable length of time – and he was beginning to despair of ever fulfilling the bargain that had driven him on. Since he'd joined the Toma there had been some hopeful signs at least – but he was not given time to dwell upon them now because Kalkara suddenly sat up straight and stared over to the west. It took Terrel a few moments to spot what she had seen – and when he did, he did not understand her evident alarm.

The camel train was evidently moving at some speed – the dust raised by their passage making a small cloud behind them – and they were heading directly towards the Toma's camp. Such haste and purpose were unusual, and as soon as he had worked this out, Terrel realized what was bothering Kala. Was this how it had begun on the day her parents had been murdered? He stood up and gazed intently across the sun-burnished terrain, wondering if the newcomers really were raiders.

'Come on,' he said, after a few moments. 'Let's go and warn Algardi.'

They set off, running down the slope. Even as his

thoughts were preoccupied with the possible approach of danger, Terrel could not help but compare his own awkward, lopsided gait to the girl's fleet progress. But although her sandals barely seemed to graze the sand, there was no mistaking the urgency in her flight.

CHAPTER THREE

Long before Terrel and Kalkara reached the elder's tent,
it became clear that their warning would not be needed.
The alarm had already been raised, and the entire camp
was bustling with activity. Most of the women and older
children were rounding up the camels, while the younger
children were gathering in one of the larger tents under
the supervision of some of their mothers. Meanwhile, the
men were arraying themselves for battle.

Terrel had always thought that the Toma seemed like
a peaceful people. Their concerns were their families,
their camels, and the never-ending search for water and
food. They appeared to have little time for thoughts of
war, and even their storytellers preferred romantic tales
of love or daring to heroic feats of arms. Although most
of the men wore daggers in their belts, these were generally encased in beautifully decorated scabbards, which
made them seem more like ceremonial items of jewellery
than weapons. Nonetheless, the curved blades within were

razor-sharp and could be deadly, and Terrel was amazed to see the variety of other weaponry that had now been produced from the nomads' tents. Men carried long spears, leather slings, swords, throwing axes, and the short bows that they normally used for hunting birds. And Terrel could see, from the fierce, determined expressions on their faces, that they would put all these weapons to effective use should the need arise. Even Medrano, whose role within the clan was as an artist, was holding a staff topped by a fearsome metal hook. The man who could produce extraordinary pictures using nothing more than a few handfuls of different coloured sand – and whom Terrel had thought to be the gentlest of spirits – now had a murderous gleam in his eyes and wore a sword at his side.

'Is this as bad as it looks?' Terrel asked.

'It's a raiding party,' Medrano replied, his tone betraying a mixture of dread and excitement. 'We think it's the Shiban. But we're ready for them.'

Terrel had no idea who the Shiban were, but it was clear that they represented a real threat.

'This is all happening so fast,' he murmured. He wasn't sure if there was anything he could do to help.

'We had look-outs posted,' Medrano told him. 'Sign of the times, eh? Not so long ago—' He broke off as a loud call overrode the general hubbub. 'They're coming.' He ran off to join his comrades in arms.

Knowing he would be of little use in a fight, Terrel stood where he was for a few moments, trying to decide on his next move. A tug at his sleeve reminded him that Kalkara was still there.

'Go to Vilheyuna's tent,' he told the terrified little girl.

'That's where Mlicki will be. You'll be safe there.' As safe as anywhere, he added to himself.

Kala shook her head violently, pulling at his arm again, but before she could make her wishes plain, she was swept up into the arms of one of the Toma's matriarchs and carried towards one of the central tents. Kalkara struggled, but to no avail, and Terrel was glad to see her taken out of immediate danger. His only decision now was to work out what role – if any – he could play in the coming encounter.

In the end he found himself a mere spectator to the confrontation, which – much to his relief – did not take the form of immediate violence. To his surprise, the raiders left their mounts a few hundred paces from the camp and crossed the intervening ground on foot. He had expected them to use their height advantage, but soon worked out what must have happened. The Shiban had obviously realized that they had lost the element of surprise, and against a well-prepared enemy their camels could be a liability as well as an advantage. The inelegant creatures were belligerent enough, but they were vulnerable to steel – and in desert conditions even quite minor wounds could prove fatal. They were also very valuable animals, being not only a means of transport but also a measure of a tribe's wealth and prestige, and would not be wasted lightly in battle. And so – as if by mutual agreement – the two clans walked towards each other, coming to a halt only a few paces apart.

Both ranks bristled with weaponry, but many swords had not yet been drawn. Even from Terrel's position to the rear of the battle lines, it was obvious that neither side really wanted an all-out conflict – which would mean both clans sustaining heavy casualties that they could ill afford. It was a stand-off, but it seemed that honour had to be satisfied before any peaceful solution could be reached.

'Is this the hospitality of the Toma?' a young man asked, stepping forward from the raiders' line. He had the face of a predator, and an air of natural authority that marked him as their leader.

'Leave all your weapons here in the sand,' Algardi suggested, moving forward in turn to assume his role as his clan's spokesman. 'Then come into our camp. We'll have a feast in your honour.'

It was a hollow offer, and both sides knew it, but the ancient laws had been respected.

'You're carrying a few blades yourselves,' the young man pointed out. 'Should we disarm in the face of such a threat?'

'We have every right to defend what is ours, Kohtala,' Algardi responded. 'It is you who walk against the winds by approaching in this way.'

The raider's face registered surprise that his adversary knew his name. Then he smiled, as if proud of the fact that his fame was spreading.

'You would be right if this was yours to defend,' he said, waving a hand to indicate the camp and the land surrounding it.

'You would deny that?' the elder exclaimed, as the rest of the Toma muttered angrily.

'This vale and the well in it are within the boundaries of our territory,' Kohtala explained. 'If you are to drain the life from our land, then we expect your tribute in return.'

This statement provoked several cries of outrage from among the nomads, but Algardi waved them to silence.

'The life of this place belongs to no man and to all men,' he said. 'We have been coming here by ancient right for generations.'

'Then it seems you're behind on the rent,' Kohtala commented, to the amusement of his followers.

'We do not pay for what is already ours.'

'The Shiban are masters of all this region. Opposing us would be a mistake. I propose that you pay us one adult camel for each day you remain here.'

Once again the Toma voiced their opinion of this suggestion.

'I have it on good report,' Kohtala went on, raising his voice over their objections, 'that you've already been here for three days, so you owe us three camels.'

'No,' Algardi replied flatly.

'More if you intend to stay longer,' the raider added implacably. 'And do not think to palm us off with lame or sick beasts.'

'We will pay no tribute, because none is due,' Algardi declared. 'Your father would never have countenanced this.'

'Times change,' Kohtala observed. 'You should stop living in the past, old man.'

The raider's insolence incensed many of the nomads. Terrel saw the fury in Zahir's face, and was glad when some of the older men held him back. Although the Toma were angered by Kohtala's words, they would wait for the outcome of the debate before taking any action.

'You would do well to agree to my terms,' the raider said. 'They are more than generous. If you don't, we'll take what's due to us – and more.'

'You would do well not to wrong us,' Algardi countered. 'The Toma bear a grudge for a long time.'

Kohtala laughed.

'You're not likely to be *around* for a long time if you deny us,' he remarked. 'Even if you run away like cowards, the outer wells are drying up. You might as well try to ride the Road of Hope.'

This comment caused more amusement among the raiders, but only roused the Toma to an even greater level of indignation.

'Our curse will follow you even if we cannot!' Algardi cried.

'Oh, now you're really frightening me,' Kohtala mocked, pretending to tremble with alarm.

'You *should* be afraid,' the elder spluttered.

'Really? And just who will place this curse? Your shaman's been asleep for years, as good as dead. Your empty threats carry no weight.'

'The dome will not look down on law-breakers. Withdraw or be judged.'

These brave words were directed at Kohtala from behind the nomads' ranks, but their overall effect was rather spoilt by the wavery, high-pitched tone in which they were delivered. Everyone turned to see who had spoken, but Terrel, who was closer than most, knew immediately. Mlicki had come out of Vilheyuna's tent, and was walking towards the centre of the conflict. In itself that meant nothing, and the interruption would have been seen as an undignified breach of custom were it not for the fact that he had donned the shaman's headdress.

Because the woven cap had been made to fit another head, it sat low on Mlicki's forehead, and his face was partially obscured by the many strands of twine that bore the eyes and ears of legend. In reality these were an eclectic mixture of dried leaves, seed pods, slivers of bone, feathers and colourful pieces of cloth, but they represented the shaman's ability to see and hear things that other men could not – including the past and the future, the thoughts of the winds, the memories of sand and the approaching fury of storms.

As Mlicki passed by, Terrel could see that his friend was trembling and, even though it was half hidden, the boy's face was a mask of fear. Even as murmurs of surprise ran through the gathering, Terrel wondered what had given the shaman's assistant the courage to put on the symbol of his master's power.

By now several of the Toma were showing signs of outrage at Mlicki's presumption. To proclaim himself a shaman, especially in such fraught circumstances, was a very serious undertaking, and there were clearly many who felt that the outsider had no right to do so – even if Vilheyuna *had* chosen him to be his apprentice. Even so, the automatic reverence inspired by the headdress meant that no one was prepared to stand in the boy's way, and the crowd parted to let him through.

When the raiders saw who it was, most of them burst out laughing, but Kohtala was obviously insulted by this latest development, and his face distorted into a snarl of rage.

'What's this?' he roared, the tone of his cry silencing the mirth of his followers. 'You send a *child* to threaten me?'

Mlicki came to stand beside Algardi, and fixed the Shiban's leader with his unnerving stare. None of the

Toma spoke. Even Algardi had been struck dumb, and it was left to Mlicki himself to answer.

'Our shaman lives in spirit,' he declared. 'Through me.' His voice was a little stronger now, though it was clear he was still very nervous.

'A one-eyed brat?' Kohtala exclaimed, refusing to meet the boy's gaze and glaring instead at Algardi. 'Is this the best you can do?'

The elder's expression changed then, and Terrel knew that an important decision had been made.

'He has been chosen,' Algardi stated clearly. 'You risk much, doubting the words of a shaman.'

This unexpected endorsement made Mlicki stand taller, and the uncertainty on the faces of many nomads was replaced by growing defiance. Terrel wasn't sure whether Algardi really believed that Mlicki now wielded a shaman's power, or whether he was just going along with the boy's foolhardy bluff, but either way, he had chosen his stance. It was up to Mlicki to back up his claims – if he could.

'He is no shaman!' Kohtala shouted, but some of his earlier confidence had deserted him now. 'We risk nothing in doubting him. He can't even heal his own disfigurement.'

'My eye sees beyond the winds,' Mlicki claimed. 'Why would I wish to heal such a gift?'

'Quiet, boy!' the raider yelled. 'Go back to your mother, and leave this to men.'

His tone was dismissive, but by including the boy's mother in his insult, Kohtala had unwittingly made a serious error.

'I can see your future,' Mlicki said, pride and anger

giving his voice an edge of steel. 'And I can curse your days. You will not mock me then.'

Make them believe it, Terrel thought, remembering his own first lesson in the use of curses. That had come from a swindler on Vadanis, but he'd had reason to heed Babak's advice many times since then. Truth, Terrel knew, was rarely stronger than belief.

'You're lying,' Kohtala claimed, though some of his followers did not look so certain.

'Do you want me to *show* you?' Mlicki asked.

Kohtala tried to laugh this off, but he couldn't do so – and Terrel knew that half the battle was won. The raiders' doubts were growing. Algardi sensed it too, and returned to the fray.

'Leave now,' he commanded, 'and all this will be forgotten. You have no claim on us.'

Terrel held his breath, hoping, as Kohtala hesitated before replying.

'No,' he decided eventually. 'We will have our tribute. Show me this curse, *if* you can.' He had decided to call the bluff.

In response, Mlicki shook his head once so that the eyes and ears flew out around him in a flurry of movement, and at the same time he raised both arms. Nothing more happened, but several raiders flinched as if expecting sorcery. Mlicki grew very still, and Terrel sensed that the boy was indeed seeing beyond the winds. But that would do him little good unless he could somehow reveal what he saw to the onlookers.

'Darkness comes,' the boy intoned.

'Well, there's a revelation,' Kohtala observed sarcastically. 'The sun will set soon.'

'From below,' Mlicki went on, his voice sounding hollow and unnatural. 'The earth rises up.'

A slight breeze arose, swirling sand at the boy's feet so that it seemed to dance around him. There was some muttering at this, but Kohtala was again quick to respond.

'I've seen better mirages,' he said scornfully. 'Stop this mockery now.'

Mlicki's arms were shaking, his own determination faltering.

'This is your curse,' he whispered.

'Your words are futile,' Kohtala declared, drawing his sword. 'You have shown us nothing. Pay us what we are due, or face the consequences.'

There was a rustle of movement as weapons on both sides were removed from their scabbards. Terrel sensed Mlicki's helplessness, and wanted to do something – anything – to help him before the situation got out of control. However, just at that moment he began to experience a premonition of his own. It began as a queasy feeling in the pit of his stomach, grew quickly to the internal trembling that he remembered only too well, until he *knew* what was coming. Fear mingled with calculation in his mind. Surely there had to be a way he could use this? He was about to cry out aloud, when a better idea occurred to him.

Mlicki? Mlicki! Can you hear me? Terrel put all his effort, all his hopes, into the psinoma, and was rewarded by seeing his friend start violently. *Tell them an earthquake is coming*, he implored him. *Tell them it's a punishment, that the winds are angry with them.*

But . . . Mlicki's internal confusion was evident.

Trust me on this! Terrel urged. *There's an earthquake coming. Quickly!*

'Put your blades away!' Mlicki shouted. 'Or we all die.'

That got everyone's attention, though few seemed to be taking him seriously.

'The ground will shake,' the boy added desperately, 'to mark the truth of my words. It is the sign of the curse upon you if you break the laws!'

'The ground—' Kohtala began disdainfully, but fell silent as a low rumbling groan rose from the dunes around them.

The tremor struck. Sand shivered and slid, pebbles jumped as though they were alive, and men staggered on legs that suddenly provided no support. It lasted only a few moments, but the change in mood was emphatic. Fear and bewilderment registered on the faces of all the raiders – including that of their leader – while the Toma were caught between awe and triumph. Mlicki's legs gave way beneath him, and he sat down with a bump.

But that was not the end of the afternoon's wonders. Even though the sun still hung above the western horizon, the entire scene was plunged into a sudden gloom. At first Terrel thought it was an eclipse, but soon realized that it had been much too quick for that. Not even the Dark Moon could have brought about such a rapid change. Many of the nomads were shielding their faces, thinking that they had been enveloped by a sandstorm, but the Shiban were close to panic, many of them shouting about birds or insects, as though they felt themselves being engulfed by swarms of flying creatures. Only one thing was clear; whatever the reason, the darkness Mlicki had promised had arrived.

And then it was gone, and the orange light of the setting

sun returned to paint the desert. Algardi was the first to recover his wits.

'You have your answer,' he told Kohtala. 'Go now. And think twice before you threaten the laws – or the Toma – again.'

None of the raiders was in any mood for fighting after that and, although Kohtala tried to put a brave face on his defeat, he could not disguise his own humiliating dread. He led his men away without another word.

CHAPTER FOUR

'I'd been thinking about what you said,' Mlicki explained. 'About Vilheyuna letting me know when he wanted something from me.'

'And you thought the Shiban's coming meant you were supposed to become the Toma's shaman?' Terrel guessed.

'Winds, no!' Mlicki exclaimed. 'I just knew I had to do something. Perhaps if I could fool them, distract them for a while, it would buy us some time if nothing else. Putting the headdress on was the only way I could think of to make people take any notice of me. I didn't really know what to do after that.' He shook his head slowly, as if to clear it.

After the raiders had gone, Mlicki had lain unconscious on the ground, and no one had been able to rouse him. Some of the nomads had feared that he had fallen into a stupor like Vilheyuna, but Terrel had been able to reassure them. Mlicki, he knew, was simply exhausted by his own efforts – both mentally and physically – but he would wake up in due course.

The boy had been carried back to the shaman's tent and, although some of the elders had remained there for a while in the hope of speaking to him, it had eventually been left to Terrel to revive him. For a time he had shared the tent with three perfectly silent figures – Mlicki, Vilheyuna and Kalkara, who had slipped inside unnoticed while her brother was being tended to. Terrel had comforted the little girl, reassuring her about Mlicki's health, but she seemed quite at ease, her earlier terror apparently forgotten.

It had been late in the evening when Mlicki finally came to. By then his sister was asleep behind a screen in one corner of the tent, so the two young men talked quietly.

'Well, whatever you did, it worked,' Terrel commented.

'Better than I'd expected,' Mlicki agreed, shaking his head again, this time in disbelief.

'How did you do it? The darkness, I mean.'

'I didn't. I've no idea where it came from.'

'Are you serious?'

'Completely. I thought *you* did it.'

'Me?' It was Terrel's turn to be taken aback. 'No. I . . .'

'You knew the quake was coming,' Mlicki pointed out.

'Yes, but . . . I don't think the two things were connected.'

'But how *did* you know?'

'I don't know how it happens,' Terrel admitted.

'You mean you've done it before?'

'Yes.'

'Do you have any more useful talents you haven't told us about?' Mlicki enquired.

'Oh, lots,' Terrel replied, grinning to cover the memories that leapt into his mind.

'Well, all I can say is I like your timing.'

'We were lucky,' Terrel agreed, wondering whether the fortuitous timing really *had* been a coincidence, or whether some other forces were involved.

'Even so, I'm not sure we'd have stopped them fighting if it hadn't been for what happened afterwards.'

'But you didn't create the darkness?'

'No,' Mlicki confirmed.

'But you did see beyond the winds, didn't you?'

'Yes. I saw . . .' He hesitated, obviously puzzled. 'I saw *something*. A kind of darkness . . . But I didn't bring it here. I wouldn't even know how to try. I've never been able to show my visions to anyone else, even if I'd wanted to. Besides, it was . . . different.'

'Yet we all saw it,' Terrel said.

'I know. I saw it too, from the outside. It was separate from my othersight.'

'The curious thing is, we all seemed to see it differently.'

'What do you mean?'

'At first I thought it was an eclipse,' Terrel explained. 'But most of the nomads felt as if they were in the middle of a sandstorm. And the Shiban seemed to think they were being attacked by swarms of insects.'

Mlicki thought about this for a few moments before responding.

'Well, I've no idea what it was,' he said. 'I've never experienced anything like that before.'

They were silent for a while, each trying to put their memories in order.

'I half expected something to happen here, though,' Mlicki added eventually. 'I'd hoped it would be Vilheyuna waking up, but perhaps that's not supposed to happen yet.'

'Probably not,' Terrel agreed. 'Why here? Is there something special about this place?'

'Vilheyuna thought so. He has a theory about certain places in the desert – nodes, he calls them – where magic is strongest.'

'And this is one of them?'

Mlicki nodded.

'He'd always try to be at one of the nodes whenever there was an important ceremony to perform. But the timing was crucial too, because the magic also depended on where the moons were in the dome. He said that whether they were full or new or in between made a difference to the sources of power.'

The theory sounded familiar, and Terrel recalled the methods of the seers in his homeland and the sharaken in Macul. They too timed their various rituals by the movements of the four moons and, one way or another, the multiple lunar influences affected the lives of everyone on Nydus – from emperors and kings to the humblest peasants.

'They're not in a particularly interesting configuration at the moment though, are they?' Mlicki went on.

'Not really,' Terrel confirmed. 'The Amber was new two nights ago, but you'd think that would make it weaker rather than stronger. The other three are all waxing, but they're several days from being full. The closest is the Dark Moon – the Invisible – which will be full in two days' time, unless it's changed orbit again.'

'Do you think it could have?'

'I don't know. Two days would be a huge difference, so it probably hasn't.' Terrel felt some sort of unexplained affinity with the Dark Moon, and he was reasonably sure that he would have known if it had been full ahead of time.

'That doesn't help much then, does it?' Mlicki remarked.

'Did you feel anything when you put the headdress on?' Terrel asked.

'Nothing much. Why?'

Terrel glanced at the unmoving figure of Vilheyuna, and shrugged.

'You think his spirit might have helped me?' Mlicki wondered.

'I'm just trying to work out what happened,' Terrel replied, thinking of the other sleepers he had known – and the sometimes surprising ways they had played a part in his life.

'I think I'd have known if he was there,' Mlicki said thoughtfully.

'So we're back to the same question,' Terrel concluded. 'Vilheyuna didn't produce the darkness. Neither did you, or me, or the node. So who *did*?'

The night passed with no further alarms. No one really expected the Shiban to return so soon after what had happened, but equally no one liked to think about what might have happened if the raiders had come upon a camp that was unprepared, and so even more look-outs had been posted for the hours of darkness.

When Terrel finally got to sleep, after first ensuring

that Mlicki was settled for the night, he dreamt – for the first time in many months – about the crystal city that rose from the waters of a moonlit ocean. He took this as a good omen, because that was where Alyssa lived in his dream-world, and it might mean that he would be able to see her soon. However, the ephemeral contact was ended prematurely by a sudden screaming that woke him with a start.

At first he thought that Mlicki was having a nightmare, but his charge was sleeping peacefully, and Terrel was already certain that the noise had not come from Kalkara or Vilheyuna, so it must have originated outside their tent. But the sound was not repeated, and there was no activity within the camp as far as Terrel could tell, so he dismissed the interruption and went back to sleep, hoping – in vain – to return to his dream.

Algardi and several of the elders came to visit Mlicki early the next morning. Like Terrel, they had many questions, and the shaman's apprentice was obliged to recount his side of the story all over again. He repeatedly denied that he was the new shaman, but in spite of this many of the Toma now regarded him with a new respect. The nomad's first reaction to the events of the previous afternoon had been one of disbelief, but they could not deny the evidence of their own senses. Nor could they set aside the fact that Mlicki's intervention had saved them from a potentially disastrous battle. Like it or not, the boy was a hero. Even when he tried to explain Terrel's role in what had happened, so that the credit could be shared more fairly, it was his own actions that still drew the most praise.

'Vilheyuna obviously knew what he was doing when

he chose you,' Algardi concluded. 'We have much to thank you for. I trust we can count on you to help us until he returns.'

'I'll do what I can,' Mlicki replied earnestly. 'But I won't put his headdress on again. I'm not worthy of it yet, and I may never be. I only wore it yesterday to try to help. It was all I could think of. I didn't really believe I could . . .' His voice died away.

'Our debt to you still stands,' Algardi said, then looked around at his fellow nomads and smiled. 'Unlike our debt to the Shiban.'

His companions' laughter was fuelled as much by relief as by their new-found confidence.

'Do you think they'll come back?' Mlicki asked.

'I doubt it,' the elder replied. 'Besides, we were going to move on soon anyway. We'll be beyond the boundaries of their so-called territory within a day or two. Assuming your patient is fit to travel, of course,' he added, glancing at Terrel.

'He just needs a little more rest,' the healer assured them.

'Excellent. We'll leave you in peace then.'

As the elders trooped out, Kalkara emerged silently from her sleeping place and walked over to her brother. Sitting down beside him, she slipped her arm through his and smiled contentedly.

'Were you listening to all that?' Mlicki asked, then answered his own question. 'Of course you were. Don't worry, though. Whatever happens I'll always look after you first. You know that, don't you?'

Kala nodded, then glanced at Terrel.

'You think I should look after him too?' Mlicki guessed.

'I'll do my best, but I think it's probably going to be the other way round. He can do all sorts of things I can't.'

Don't be so sure, Terrel thought. He had the distinct feeling that one of the reasons he had joined this group of nomads was because he had been meant to meet Mlicki. We may have more in common than you realize, he added silently.

Terrel looked up to find Kalkara grinning at him. He found the unwavering gaze of those luminous eyes a little unnerving. Even though he'd been careful to keep his recent thoughts private, he couldn't help wondering if she, like her brother, was adept at psinoma.

'I knew you were special,' Mlicki told him. 'It's not many people who win Kala's seal of approval.'

'I'm honoured,' Terrel replied – and he meant it.

Another piece of the seemingly endless puzzle of his life had just fallen into place, and the feeling that he was – at last – in the right place had matured into near certainty. All he had to do now was work out what he was supposed to do there.

'I wonder what our next adventure will be,' Mlicki said, echoing both Terrel's thoughts and something another friend had once said to him.

'I suspect we'll find out soon enough,' he replied.

CHAPTER FIVE

Looking back, Terrel could not identify any single decisive moment that had led him to the desert. His progress seemed to have been driven by chance, a series of endeavours brought about by circumstance rather than any recognizable sense of purpose. He had taken advantage of the various opportunities that had presented themselves, hoping that this was what he was meant to do, that each day's travelling would take him closer to his elusive goal. On several occasions he had been offered a way of turning back, of heading towards the Movaghassi Ocean again, but he had not done so, even though the temptation was enormous. He had convinced himself that his only chance of eventually returning to Alyssa was to complete the tasks that fate – and his bargain – had burdened him with. Even if he were at her side now, it would have done them no good. Her long sleep had already lasted for more than three and a half years, and while he was reasonably certain that she had come to no harm, he knew that her fate – including the chance of her ever waking again – was inextricably linked to his own destiny.

After the extraordinary events that had taken place in Talazoria, Terrel had begun to believe that certain aspects of his life really were preordained. But as the long months since then had dragged on into years, his doubts had returned again. After so much time spent on the road – so much apparently aimless travelling – the very idea of prophesying the future seemed far-fetched, almost laughable. He had no idea what he was supposed to be doing, or where he should be going.

To make matters worse, there had been spells when he hadn't seen Alyssa – or the ghosts – for months at a time, and it had been hard then not to imagine that he was lost or had been abandoned once more. Only the joy and relief he felt whenever she appeared again convinced him that their pact still held. And on each occasion she had been able to persuade him that he was indeed doing the right thing in going on, and that he shouldn't even think about trying to get back to Vadanis yet. But with each of her absences – and the present one was the longest he had ever known – his doubts and fears returned in full measure, and it took all his courage to overcome them.

The one idea he clung to, whenever everything else seemed uncertain, was that there was surely another elemental somewhere on Nydus. There had to be; otherwise what was the point of his bargain? But because he didn't know where it was, and in the absence of any solid advice, he could only hope that he would be drawn to it by signs and omens, just as he had been directed to Talazoria. Tracking down such a creature was never going to be easy. After all, it was not something he could simply ask about. Most people would have regarded him as insane if he'd even tried, so he was forced to rely on gossip and rumour, and any tales of unusual activity. Such sources were inherently unreliable – and Terrel had no doubt that he'd have been led astray if he'd listened to all the peculiar stories he'd heard – so he had come to rely on his own intuition when deciding what was important and what was not. He was also acutely aware that he shouldn't necessarily trust everyone he encountered – the sharaken's duplicity had seen to that – and this made sifting fact from fiction even more onerous. However, because he usually had *nothing* to go on – nothing that could be considered even remotely relevant to his quest – he was left to his own devices in deciding what he should do next. It often seemed that his only guiding principle was to head away from where his heart most wanted him to go.

At least now he had become reasonably adept at making his way through foreign lands. His travails had made him physically strong, although his deformities ensured that he would never be truly dextrous or athletic. He was taller than when he'd been cast adrift from Vadanis, but he was still thin, and his apparent frailty was emphasized by his twisted leg and withered right arm. In fact Terrel now possessed a dogged stamina that belied his skewed frame, but his growth recently had been in mind rather than body. He had been forced to mature, and had learnt to be self-reliant. Coping with most of the practical difficulties that faced a traveller now came as almost second nature, and for all the rest he was able to fall back on his one marketable skill. A true healer could always be reasonably sure of a good reception, even among strangers. Once he was able to demonstrate that his abilities were real, and not the mere boastings of a charlatan, he was usually made welcome. In return for his ministrations he accepted whatever gifts his hosts could offer. In this way he'd been able to keep himself fed and clothed. He had even been able to barter for several new pairs of boots along the way – all of which had to be specially made or altered to fit his upturned right foot.

This same healing talent was generally enough to overcome any aversion caused by his strange appearance – especially by his disconcerting eyes. Terrel was glad of this, because his only alternative was to disguise them by using the glamour – another technique bequeathed to him by Babak – and he disliked doing this because it made him vulnerable to Jax's malevolent influence. Fortunately, most people accepted him as he was, and this acceptance was greatly aided by his ability to learn languages quickly. The fact that someone who was obviously a foreigner was able to converse with them in their own tongue often caused both surprise and pleasure in those he met – and even though the methods he used to become fluent would have alarmed most of them, Terrel believed that what they didn't know wouldn't hurt them. He swallowed his guilt, reminding himself that the alternative was endless confusion and possible hostility.

Everywhere he went he was the object of considerable curiosity, and he was forced to tell different versions of his story – with varying degrees of truth – about his reasons for travelling. He told as few outright lies as possible, preferring to remain silent when he had no other choice. The fact that he was actually an imperial prince, albeit disowned, didn't seem relevant, or even believable – even to himself. As it was, his censored tales often provoked amazement and interest, but that was mostly because he was so very far from home.

Everywhere Terrel went he came across many things that surprised and intrigued him. Each country, each society, had its own customs, beliefs and taboos, many of which he found incomprehensible. The only constant was a certain reverence for the moons, the stately pageant of the sky – and even there the interpretations of what various lunar configurations actually meant varied wildly. This was especially true with the many different theories he had heard about the apparently impossible changes to the movements of the Dark Moon.

There were still times when the fact that he'd been born and raised in the Floating Islands coloured Terrel's thinking. He had long since grown used to the fact that land did not *have* to move to be a viable place for people to live. Indeed, it had become clear to him that the islands were the exception rather than the rule, and that many of the places he'd visited were no less civilized than Vadanis itself. More and more of his preconceptions and prejudices were gradually being overturned. He had learnt that most bigotry stemmed from ignorance, and as a result he tried hard not to condemn anything until he'd at least learnt something about it. He had seen a great deal that he could never have imagined during his earlier life at the haven – where the only travelling he had done had been in his imagination, inspired by the old books he'd read in the abandoned library. Even so, nothing could have prepared him for the land of Misrah – and he'd never met anyone like the Toma before.

The vast land was like none he had seen or even dreamt of. It held unsuspected horrors that he was still not even close to understanding. But there was wonder there too. And beauty.

The Toma's beliefs were as bizarre as anything Terrel had ever encountered, and their way of life was equally strange. And yet he already felt comfortable among them. Even the way he had joined their caravan had come about because of a peculiar coincidence, which had led Terrel to wonder if he had somehow been *meant* to join them. He had hoped that this was the case, and hoped so still. He'd begun to despair of ever being able to fulfil his bargain, but since he'd been travelling with the nomads he had regained at least a glimmer of hope. Recent developments had made that glimmer glow even brighter, but there was only one sign that would convince him he was on the right track at last.

That sign was to come the very next day.

At first Terrel could not tell what Kalkara was pointing at. She had come to find him while the Toma were busy breaking camp. This was a practised operation, and Terrel had soon learned that he should keep out of the way and let the nomads get on with it. On this occasion he had simply been watching as the tents and all the other belongings were wrapped into bales to be loaded on to the camels, when Kala, who was similarly unemployed, had come up to him and taken his hand. She had led him over a low line of dunes, then motioned for him to be quiet as they looked over the dry gully beyond.

'What is it?' Terrel whispered, as he tried to follow the line of her pointing finger. 'I don't see anything.' He couldn't imagine why she wanted to show him what appeared to be just another stretch of barren sand and soil.

Kalkara made no attempt to answer his question, merely waving him into silence again. Then she took hold of his sleeve and pulled him down to sit beside her. She obviously intended him to wait for something, but Terrel had no idea what it might be.

After a little while a light wind began to blow, and Terrel shivered. The nights were still bitterly cold at this time of year, and the sun had yet to warm the day properly. Kala was oblivious to his discomfort, and seemed as though she would be content to sit there all day, her gaze still fixed on the far side of the gully. Faint noises from the activity in the camp drifted to them on the breeze, but otherwise the silence of the place was complete. It was an aspect of the desert that Terrel found both enticing and occasionally oppressive. Such silence could be utterly peaceful, but it was also a reminder that the place was devoid of life.

He was about to get up, to stretch his chilled limbs if nothing else, when he felt Kalkara grow tense beside him. Only then did he see what she had been staring at. There was life here after all.

A tiny movement alerted him to the existence of several small holes in the far bank. He had taken the darker patches for shadows, but now realized that there was some kind of burrow only a few paces from where they were sitting. Kala's insistence on their being still and quiet made sense now, but Terrel couldn't imagine what kind of creature could possibly live there. There was no way rabbits could have survived in such terrain, and he didn't know of any other animals that dug communal warrens. According to the Toma, some of the more mountainous regions of Misrah supported foxes, bears, gazelles and even a much revered beast known as a snow-leopard, but the only wildlife Terrel had seen since he'd left the coastal plain had been a few birds, snakes and scorpions. Clearly, none of them were responsible for this excavation.

Kalkara's fingers tightened on his arm as movement showed again. This time he was waiting for it, and caught a glimpse of a small head with large ears. The creature's fur matched the colour of the sand almost exactly. After looking round for a few moments, the animal emerged into the daylight. It looked rather like a brown rat, except for the size of its ears and the fact that its hind legs were very long, out of proportion to the rest of its body. Terrel had no idea what the creature was, but it looked faintly comical, especially when it moved off in a series of rapid bounds. Its bouncing progress brought it closer to the two onlookers, though it did not seem to have noticed them.

Taking his lead from Kala, Terrel kept very still, but he couldn't resist glancing at his companion. Her face was shining with pleasure, a sight that made his heart swell. He wondered how she had known where to look, then forgot such speculation as a sudden rush of movement brought his attention back to the burrow. As if in answer to an invisible signal, more of the animals emerged. Soon the gully seemed to be filled with them, all leaping about in apparently random directions, as though they were celebrating their release from confinement by being as energetic as possible. Terrel was entranced, and had to fight hard to keep from laughing out loud. As it was, his smile now matched the expression on Kalkara's face. He wanted to thank her for enabling him to witness such a delightful spectacle, but knew that he would have to keep quiet or risk frightening the animals.

After a while the frenetic activity died down and the creatures settled into more leisurely pursuits, some of them basking in the increasing warmth of the sun, others grooming one another, while a few began digging with their forepaws in the sand. Terrel and Kala watched, their presence apparently having no effect upon the activity below. Eventually, however, Terrel began to worry about the length of time they'd been away from the camp, and he decided they should get back before someone had to come looking for them.

'Come on,' he whispered to Kala. 'We—'

He broke off as she gave him a quick frown, but it was too late. Ears had pricked up at the sound of his voice, and many of the creatures were now looking in their direction, their noses twitching. Terrel froze, but the wind caught at the loose material of his sleeve and the flapping cloth was obviously seen. One of the animals responded by thumping its back feet on the ground, and in a flurry of bouncing and scurrying, the entire group fled to the various holes and disappeared underground. Within a moment or two they had vanished – all except one.

This creature stayed out in the open, squatting on its hindquarters, staring directly at Terrel – and his heart lurched with sudden hope.

Alyssa? he queried tentatively.

Shut up! she replied. *How can you ever listen to anything if you all keep talking at once?*

CHAPTER SIX

By the time Terrel realized that Alyssa had not been talking to him, he had been further confused by Kalkara's reaction to this latest development. Whether she had heard something of the exchange, or was just unnerved by the creature's unnatural behaviour, the little girl had leapt to her feet, her mouth open in a silent scream, her eyes wide with fear. A moment later she flew off, her feet skimming over the dunes as she ran. But Terrel was too delighted by Alyssa's long-anticipated return to worry about this for too long.

I don't care, Alyssa declared. *You can be whole without me.*

As her voice sounded silently in his mind, Terrel wondered whether he ought to use psinoma. Although it seemed as though she were talking to someone else, he couldn't be sure. Alyssa often began conversations in the middle, blithely assuming that her companions had followed her earlier train of thought. In the past he'd been quite good at guessing what she meant, but occasionally her statements had simply been incomprehensible – as they were in this instance. However, all that paled into insignificance compared to the fact that she was here at last. Terrel was in no doubt that he would be able to talk to her soon.

I can run to darkness, Alyssa protested. *I just don't want to. Leave me alone, or she'll never come back.*

What's going on? Terrel ventured. *Alyssa?*

What? she responded. *I know he's not part of the circle. But there's no need to be afraid. Stop it. Stop it! You're driving me crazy.*

Under any other circumstances this statement coming from Alyssa would have made Terrel smile, but she was clearly distressed, and that was something he couldn't bear. Even so, he'd already guessed that his earlier interruption had only made matters worse, so he kept his thoughts to himself for the moment, restraining his need to talk.

Alyssa was clearly coming to terms with the body of her latest host, and the creature began to move along the gully in a series of lurching hops. As Terrel scrambled to follow, he heard her muttering about having to get away. Her flight became more rapid, each jump longer, as she gained in confidence, and it was only when she stopped on the far side of another dune that he was able to catch up with her. He was breathing heavily when he slumped down beside her, and was glad he did not have to use his voice to speak.

Is it all right now? he asked. *Is this far enough?*

Alyssa was sitting upright, her ears twitching as if she was straining to hear some faint sound, but she didn't answer him immediately. As he regained his composure, Terrel was able to study the animal, looking for her ring. He had made it from one of his own hairs and from pieces of thread, and although it had begun as a joke between the two friends, it was vitally important now. It was the link that bound them – and their worlds – together, enabling her to find him even when he was so very far away. He saw it eventually, half buried in the soft fur of one of her forelegs.

Who was she?

It took Terrel a few moments to realize that she was actually speaking to him this time.

The girl who ran away? That's Kalkara. She's the sister of a friend of mine.

She had flames in her eyes, Alyssa commented, sounding puzzled, but before Terrel could ask what she meant, she'd moved on. *What took you so long?*

Me? So long to do what?

To let me know where you were, she replied, as if this should have been obvious. *It was bad enough crossing another moat, but this* . . . Her rodent eyes swept over the surrounding terrain.

I thought . . . Terrel began, then abandoned any attempt to try to understand. She was here now, and that was all that mattered. *It's good to see you, Alyssa.*

It's not me you're seeing, she pointed out.

You know what I mean. It's been such a long time.

It's not always my choice, she replied. *Just because I don't come for a while, it doesn't mean I don't love you.*

Terrel was stunned by her words. He had known for a long time that he was in love with Alyssa, and he hoped that she felt the same way about him, but this was the first time they had spoken about it. Their friendship was beyond question, and they shared the certainty that one day they would be together again – in mind and body – but was there more to it than that?

You love me? he said quietly.

Of course I do, you idiot. Why else would I put up with looking like this to see you? She lifted one ridiculously large rear foot and glanced at it ruefully.

Terrel smiled, then grew serious again. What kind of love? he wondered, taking care to keep the thought private. Like a brother? He was thinking of Kala and Mlicki. That was not what he felt – or wanted.

I love you too, he said.

I know, she replied dismissively. *Why are you here?*

It was not the reaction he'd hoped for, and he was left still wondering.

I'm not sure, he replied, trying to collect his thoughts. *But I think I might be in the right place at last. Or getting closer, at least.*

Have you heard anything about another Ancient?

Rumours in both Vadanis and Macul had led Terrel to the alien creatures there, and he would have recognized anything similar easily enough.

Nothing specific, he admitted. *At least I don't think so. But I . . . It feels possible.*

I'm surprised you can think at all in this place, with all this chatter going on.

What . . . he began, then realized what she meant. *The other animals? Can you still hear them?*

Can't you? Alyssa asked, then reconsidered. *It's not so bad here, I suppose. It's as if they're all part of one big mind,* she went on, shuddering slightly. *It wouldn't be so bad if any of their thoughts were actually interesting. But being assaulted by so much banality is awful. And what's worse, they seem to think that taking my host here away from the rest of the group will make a terrible difference. Moons! I thought cats and horses were bad enough, but these things . . .*

What are *you?*

I've no idea, and I don't think I want to know. I won't be able to stay too long or the entire tribe will go mad. Doesn't bear thinking about. Anyway, you'd better not waste time. Why do you think this place is important?

Terrel struggled to marshal his thoughts. He'd been wondering about this very topic a lot recently, and welcomed the chance to discuss it with someone who would understand. However, before he began there was something else he needed to ask.

Where are the others?

I don't know. They're being rather secretive at the moment.

Even Elam? Terrel's boyhood friend had rarely been able to keep a secret, and even as a ghost his personality hadn't changed.

I haven't seen much of him recently, Alyssa replied. *And Muzeni and Shahan seem to spend all their time complaining about the seers' lack of progress with the Tindaya Code. Not that they're much further ahead, as far as I can tell. Anyway, they're not likely to be here any time soon, but I can try and pass a message on to them.*

This news dismayed Terrel. The three ghosts had helped guide him in his earlier exploits, and he was distressed by the fact that they all felt they had more important things to do. Even so, he knew Alyssa would convey his report to them if she got the chance. And in any case, she was his closest and most important ally – the only one who had been able to stay with him when he'd faced the elementals.

All right, he said, trying to put the points he wanted to make in a rational order. *Even before I crossed the Iron Sea—*

That's where I lost you, she cut in. *When you were on the moat.*

Well, even before that, I had no real idea where I was heading, and when I got to Misrah – that's this place – it was even worse. The first thing that made me think I was on the right track was the way I met the Toma.

Who?

Terrel explained briefly about the nomads and their way of life. Alyssa seemed amazed that anyone would choose to live in such a way, but she did not interrupt again.

I'd been working my way east, along the coastal plain, Terrel went on, *waiting for inspiration. Then I was told about an old hermit woman, who was supposed to be an oracle. She lived in a cave in the hills outside the town I was in, so I set off to look for her. But I must have got lost on the way, because I never found any caves. Instead I came across an encampment on the edge of the desert. It was evening by then, and there were fires burning and drums beating – the most incredible sound I've ever heard – but I couldn't see any sign of people, not even those playing the drums. It was all absolutely still, and it felt quite eerie.*

Alyssa began fidgeting, and Terrel took this as a sign of impatience.

To cut a long story short, he said quickly, *when I reached the camp, I saw that there was an open space inside the ring of tents, with shapes marked out on the ground with pebbles. They looked like crude mosaics. Each one represented a moon, and they all matched the phases of the moons that night. Then I realized the White Moon was full, and that this must be some sort of ritual, though I still couldn't see anyone. But I could still hear the drums. I called out – I don't remember what I said – and the sound stopped in an instant. It was a bit of a shock, but for some reason I wasn't afraid. It felt welcoming, somehow. I called out again, and this time someone answered. They said, 'The voice of rain', and then it did rain.*

That was quite a coincidence, Alyssa commented dryly.

It only lasted a few moments, Terrel went on, *but when it was over I was surrounded by people – all staring at me as if I'd done something amazing. I still don't know where they all came from.*

You took this as a sign?

Wouldn't you? I've been with them ever since. The next day we headed north, into the desert. And there've been any number of things since then that have made me think I'm doing the right thing.

Such as?

Well, one of the Toma is a sleeper, like you and Ysatel. He's called Vilheyuna, and he's their healer – they call him a shaman – so when they found out I was a healer as well as 'the voice of rain' they made me welcome. They were disappointed that I couldn't heal Vilheyuna himself, but I did enough with others to gain their acceptance.

The spirit world is getting busier, Alyssa remarked quietly.

Do you think you or one of the others would be able to contact him? While he's wandering? Terrel asked.

We're all connected to the elementals somehow, she said, but did not answer his question. *What else?*

There's someone here who might be another Mentor.

Really? For the first time, Alyssa seemed genuinely impressed. *Muzeni and Shahan will definitely want to hear about that. Who is it?*

His name's Mlicki. He's the brother of that girl you saw.

And what makes you think . . . ?

He reminds me of me, Terrel said. He went on to explain about Mlicki's odd appearance, his partial blindness, his talent for psinoma and othersight. *He's an outcast too*, he added. *The more I learnt about him, the more I realized we had in common, and I think I was meant to find him.*

That's a big jump, Alyssa pointed out.

I know, but Shahan did say there could be more than one Mentor. And I could use some help. Besides, there's more.

Tell me quickly then. I don't think I can stand this much longer. Her ears were twitching almost constantly now.

There's the river, Terrel said, feeling slightly flustered.

What river?

It disappeared. I thought it might have been because of an elemental. You know how much they hate water.

It's possible.

And then I remembered the dream I had ages ago, when I saw the hospice floating on the water. That turned

*out to be an accurate premonition, and in the same dream
I saw the desert too – though I didn't know what it was
at the time – and a camel—*

A what?

I'll show you later, he promised, grinning as he imagined Alyssa 'borrowing' the body of one of the ungainly
creatures. *I also dreamt about a woman with tattoos on
her face – and some of the women in Misrah have markings just like I saw.*

Have you found the actual woman herself?

No. But I think maybe I'm meant to try.

Fair enough, Alyssa said, nodding her host's pointed
head.

*That's not all. Two days ago, something very strange
happened.* He told her about the raiders, and the way in
which violence had been avoided.

So Mlicki produced this illusion? she queried.

That's just it, Terrel replied. *He says he didn't. He
saw it, but he had no way of showing it to anyone else.
Which means it must have been conjured up by some
outside power.*

By an elemental? Alyssa wondered.

It could be, he agreed eagerly. *Everyone saw it differently, but the most interesting thing is how Mlicki himself
described it. He said it was a kind of darkness, and that
he couldn't see it properly. You remember what the
elemental looked like? All that swirling, never being able
to see straight or focus on it . . .*

Dark where it should be light . . . Alyssa added. *You're
right. It could be.*

*And now there's another reason why I think I may be
getting somewhere at last.*

What's that?

You're here. That means the unknown road is about to turn, doesn't it?

Maybe, she conceded, displaying less certainty than Terrel would have liked. *Have you actually asked anyone here about the Ancients?*

How? he responded. *What would I say? Oh, by the way, have you seen this thing that you can't really see, but looks like a shadow that shouldn't be there? It has no body, no substance, but it can cause earthquakes and make rivers flow uphill. They'd think I was mad.*

Would that matter? The important thing is to get the information.

I'll think about it, Terrel said – although he felt uncomfortable at the thought of such a direct approach.

The circle will break soon. I have to go.

No! Please. Not yet. You haven't given me any news. What about—

I'll come back as soon as I can. In something better than this, she added vehemently. *Digging can't be that important.*

Terrel was about to protest again, but knew straight away that it was too late. He watched as the ring melted away before his eyes, and felt the loss of separation as Alyssa's spirit left. The animal beside him blinked once, then bounded away in terror. As he watched it disappear over the ridge on its way back to the burrow, Terrel heard someone calling his name, and stood up to see who it was.

'I'm here!' he shouted, and began to make his way back towards the camp.

Zahir came over the top of the dune at a run.

'What happened here?' he gasped, as soon as he was close enough to talk.

'Kala and I were watching the animals,' Terrel told him. 'They came out of holes over there, and ran about. Then—'

'You saw the djerboas' dance?' Zahir exclaimed in disbelief. 'No wonder strange things are happening.'

'What strange things?'

'It still doesn't explain what happened to Kalkara though,' the nomad said. He was obviously very worried about something.

'What happened to her?' Terrel demanded, frightened now.

'Her face and arms are all burnt,' Zahir replied. 'It's as if she walked into a fire.'

CHAPTER SEVEN

'What did you do to her?' Mlicki rasped, his voice hoarse with anger and worry.

'Nothing!' Terrel replied, taken aback by his reception.

There was quite a gathering outside the shaman's tent, and Zahir had helped Terrel push his way through until they reached the flap that served as a door. As soon as he'd stepped inside, Mlicki – who had been kneeling next to his prostrate sister – stood up and barred his way. Algardi and his wife, Bubaqra, were also there, their faces betraying shock and concern.

'I didn't do this, Mlicki,' Terrel exclaimed, trying to see past him to the girl. 'Kala's my friend. You both are.'

'Then how did she get burnt?' Mlicki demanded.

'I have no idea.' Even as he spoke, Terrel could hear Zahir telling those outside the tent about him and Kalkara witnessing the djerboas' dance – and could hear the incredulity that greeted this revelation. He was still none the wiser as to why it should be considered so sensational, but he had no time for speculation now. 'We'd been watching some animals,' he went on. 'Then Kala jumped up and ran away. I don't know why. But she wasn't hurt when she left me.'

Terrel's evident sincerity was making an impact on Mlicki, who clearly no longer knew what to believe.

'Let me help her,' Terrel pleaded. 'I can—'

'No! Stay away from her!'

'I swear I'd never harm her. If she's hurt I can save her some pain at least.'

'What do you mean, *if* she's hurt?' Mlicki shouted. 'Look at her!' He stood aside so that Terrel could see Kalkara. The little girl was lying on her back, and her eyes were shut, her face screwed up in agony. She was trembling, and her face and arms were covered in livid red weals. It did indeed look as if she had been badly burnt. The genuine horror that registered on Terrel's face inadvertently aided his case.

'I don't think Terrel had anything to do with this,' Algardi told Mlicki.

'And the salves I've tried aren't doing any good,' Bubaqra added. 'Let him try to help her.'

'He *is* a healer,' the old man pointed out. 'We've seen that. Let him do what he can now, for Kala's sake.'

Grateful for the elders' support, Terrel turned to Mlicki in mute appeal, and saw that suspicion still lingered in his friend's mismatched eyes.

'All right,' Mlicki said eventually. 'But if you harm her, I'll kill you.'

Terrel was in no doubt that this was a serious threat.

'I won't harm her,' he promised, then moved forward

quickly to kneel beside the girl. Mlicki stayed close by, watching him like a hawk.

Terrel reached out and gently took one of Kalkara's hands in his own. She did not flinch, for which he was grateful. Indeed, she didn't even seem to be aware of his presence. Such physical contact – a simple touch – was usually all it took for Terrel to establish some sort of link with his patient. His first experiences of healing had been unconscious; he had literally not known what he was doing. Later, when he'd tried to make deliberate use of his supposed talent, it had been a journey into the unknown, in which instinct was his only guide. Initially he'd been aided by the advice of Babak, the self-styled apothecary, who had told him that if someone *believed* they were going to get well, then they usually would. The human mind was a wonderful physician. For a long time Terrel had been convinced that he was merely helping people to heal themselves, but he'd eventually realized that there was more to it than that. He'd helped in several cases where the sick person had had no faith in him to start with – or was even unaware that he was trying to help them. At the beginning he had not truly believed in his healing powers, but then results had made him reconsider. His talent, it seemed, was real.

Even so, his powers were limited. Some diseases and injuries were beyond the scope of his abilities. He could not make a broken bone whole again – but what he *could* do was help control the associated discomfort, and make sure that the patient suffered as little as possible, and had the best possible chance of an eventual recovery. There were even those who claimed that his ministrations speeded up the natural healing process, by removing the anxiety and weakness that pain caused. In a way, this made sense to Terrel, who had been in pain his whole life – from a time even before he was born. He could recognize its sources in others, and trace its patterns. He *understood*. But this time it was different.

Whenever he made a connection with someone, it was like falling into a waking dream, into a realm where everything looked and felt different. Terrel would see beyond himself, into a landscape of mystery and raw sensation. He had never been able to describe this alien landscape properly, but in some way it corresponded to the patient's state of being, the unseen systems and balances within their body. In this way the healer actually shared their symptoms, burning with the heat of a fever, feeling the lethargy induced by a long illness or the pain of an injury. And in sharing the symptoms he was able to control them, to make even the worst torment bearable – and was then able to pass on this knowledge to his patients. With experience had come confidence – and expectation. Moving into the waking dream was now a process Terrel took for granted, usually finding that the touch of a hand and simple readiness were enough to set him on his way. But with Kala he found himself floundering like a novice again.

The dream was there. He could sense it. But it was remote, and it spurned his increasingly desperate efforts to enter its preserve. Shields within shields protected Kalkara, so that his instincts were of no use. Terrel closed his eyes and concentrated, the outside world fading as his struggle continued.

Deliberately, he took a mental step back, trying to see why she had erected such defences against him. But it did no good. There was simply no way in.

Kala, please. I want to help you.

There was no response. Ordinarily, Terrel would have avoided using psinoma – which he considered an invasion of privacy – as part of the healing process. But he was at a loss now, and was willing to try anything.

'Mlicki?' he whispered aloud. 'Help me.' He raised his right arm, and felt his friend's hand close over the clawed fingers. His left hand still held Kalkara's.

'What should I do?' Mlicki asked anxiously, his voice seeming to come from very far away.

'She needs to feel someone she trusts absolutely,' Terrel replied, then was silent, concentrating once more on the inner struggle. He thought he heard Mlicki speak again, but the words fell on deaf ears as the healer tried to relax and seek out the dream again.

Let him help you, Kala. Mlicki's silent voice was gentle, but his fear imbued every word. Even so, his intuitive contribution proved effective. Terrel felt himself falling at last – into a world that was unlike any he had ever encountered.

It was not like the dreams of the unborn babies in the fog-bound valley – those dreams had been terrifying, quite beyond his healing. It was not the unreachable isolation of the sleepers. Nor was it the final surrender of the dying, those who Terrel had not been able to save but whose passing he had eased. There was nothing here to match the malice of poison or the malevolence of disease. This was different because he could find *nothing* wrong.

Kalkara's pain was real enough, but there was no reason for it. Terrel could find no source of her torment, no pattern to its assault. Her body was whole, unharmed. How was he supposed to heal a non-existent injury?

His confusion made the dream-world seem a place of chaos, when it should have been perfectly ordered. His instincts were still useless; they were leading him nowhere. He realized that what he needed to do was apply logic. If the burns were not real, then they must be imaginary. If her body was whole, then perhaps it was her mind that was hurt? Was it possible to apply Babak's theory in reverse? If someone *believed* they were going to be harmed – even if it was not really the case – would they fall ill? That was how curses worked, after all. But who, or what, could have put a curse on Kalkara? And why? There was only one chance of finding out.

Terrel hesitated, but only for a moment. He felt guilt at even the thought of deliberately prying into the secrets of her mind, but knew he had no choice. He had promised to help her, and Mlicki was standing over him should he fail, like an avenging spirit.

Tell me what happened, Kala, he said tentatively. *What hurt you?*

There was no response, but the dream shifted uneasily.

Please, Kala, he persisted. *I don't know how to help you unless—*

Terrel broke off abruptly as her reply came, not in words but in flashes of memory. He was back in the desert now, looking over the gully as the animals relaxed and went about their usual business. He experienced the eerie sensation of sitting next to himself, and knew that he was seeing through Kalkara's eyes. Contentment and wonder seeped through him as he remembered the earlier dance, but that suddenly changed when he heard his other self whisper, and all but one of the creatures fled.

His perspective lurched as Kala leapt to her feet, and

as he saw what she had seen, terror flooded through him. The last remaining djerboa was surrounded by a blinding sheet of flame that blazed and then flared out so that he was engulfed. Heat, pain and panic assaulted him simultaneously, but he fought against it, telling himself that it was only an illusion, willing himself to believe it. Defeated, he turned and fled. And the memory released him.

Terrel clung to his own sanity, searching for an explanation. Kalkara had seen something that was not of the real world. Had she somehow been able to sense Alyssa's presence within the creature? That seemed unlikely, given that not even Terrel was able to do that in any visual sense. And in any case, why would she think that Alyssa – of all people – would want to hurt her? Why would that have invoked the false flames that had scorched her skin? The only interpretation that made any sense was that Kala *had* somehow seen Alyssa's spirit, but that she had mistaken her for someone or something else. Something so evil that her fear had been strong enough to produce her injuries.

Kala, listen to me, he begged. *What you saw was my friend. She meant you no harm. You only imagined the flames.*

Again there were no words in reply. Kalkara's response came in the form of stark disbelief. What she had seen had been real to her.

It wasn't real, Terrel went on urgently. *Her name is Alyssa. She wouldn't hurt you. She* didn't *hurt you. I know her, and she's the gentlest person I've ever met. The flames weren't real. There's no need to torture yourself like this.*

The child's resistance was wavering, and Terrel persevered – repeating his assurances and hoping that his sincerity, his own *belief*, would eventually register.

When she comes to visit me again, I'll tell you, he added. *So you can meet her properly.*

This idea produced a spasm of fear, and he worried that the offer might have been a mistake, but in the next moment he knew that Kalkara had finally been convinced. The pain began to retreat.

Terrel released his grip on her hand, feeling faint from exhaustion. He opened his eyes long enough to see that the ugly weals were fading to nothing, leaving Kala's skin smooth and brown again. Before he passed out, he just had time to hear Mlicki cry out for joy.

CHAPTER EIGHT

A dozen or more voices intruded into the last fragments of Terrel's dream. As the crimson sea released him, his fear retreated too, leaving him alone again. He realized gratefully that he was no longer blind, that all he had to do was open his eyes to see where all the voices were coming from, but he decided to lie still for a while and simply listen. He felt almost unbearably weary, and the thought of actually moving any of his lead-weighted limbs was out of the question. Eventually, however, because he could make little sense of what was being said, he couldn't resist opening his eyes.

He found himself looking up into a pair of deep brown eyes, and for one heart-stopping moment he thought they belonged to Alyssa. He hadn't seen her in her own form for more than three years now – and his longing to do so had been growing more acute in all that time. Even on the rare occasions when Alyssa appeared in his dreams, it was in the guise of one of her animals, or simply as a disembodied voice.

An instant later he was brought back to reality. This girl was beautiful, but her oval face was full, her skin dark and, unlike Alyssa's uneven crop of short blonde spikes, her hair was a mass of lustrous black curls. Even her eyes, now that he saw them properly, were older, without the child-like wonder that marked Alyssa's gaze. Her smile was familiar, but for the moment his sleep-fogged brain could not recall her name.

'He's waking up!' she called, and immediately the hubbub of voices fell to an expectant hush.

Terrel forced himself to lift his head and glance around. He was in Algardi's tent, one of the largest in the camp. Several generations of the elder's family lived under its woven roof, and it appeared that most of them were there now. It was certainly very crowded.

'Are you all right?' Bubaqra asked as she came to sit beside him.

'I'm just tired,' Terrel replied, struggling to sit up. 'Is Kala all right?'

'As right as rain,' Algardi reassured him, coming to join his wife. 'You'd never know there'd been anything wrong with her. She's sleeping now.'

'And Mlicki?'

'He's with her,' Bubaqra said. 'We thought it better to bring you here. There are already too many patients in Vilheyuna's tent.'

Terrel sighed with relief.

'Thank you.'

'Thank Ghadira,' the matriarch said, smiling. 'She's the one who's been watching over you.'

Terrel remembered the girl now. She was Algardi and

Bubaqra's eldest granddaughter. She was exactly the same age as Zahir, even though he was her uncle.

'Thank you.'

'I was glad to help,' Ghadira told him, with a cheeky grin. 'I might get burnt myself one day, and then you can look after me.'

'Stop flirting, girl,' Algardi admonished her. 'And go and fetch some food for our guest.'

Flirting? Terrel thought in bewilderment. With me? What was the old man talking about? The elder's words had been spoken in a good-natured, teasing tone, but Terrel fought hard to suppress a blush – which of course only made matters worse – and he couldn't help noticing that Ghadira was still smiling as she went to obey her grandfather's command.

'How long have I been asleep?' Terrel asked.

'Several hours,' Bubaqra replied. 'Whatever you did obviously exhausted you. It's close to dusk now.'

'In view of the circumstances,' Algardi added, 'we thought it best to delay our departure. We'll leave at first light tomorrow.'

'What about the Shiban?'

'We have look-outs posted, just in case, but I don't think we'll see anything of them for a good while yet.'

'Do you feel up to telling us what happened?' Bubaqra asked.

'I'm not sure I can,' Terrel replied, wondering just how much he should tell them. But he was saved from having to say any more when Ghadira returned with a wooden plate of curds and bread, and a cup of water. He accepted them gratefully, trying not to meet her gaze. After taking a long draught of water, he began to eat, and realized that he was very hungry. Having his mouth full had the added advantage of making it impossible for him to speak.

'You're the only one who can explain today's events,' Algardi pointed out. 'Tell us what you can, when you're ready.'

'Mlicki was beside himself when Kalkara came back like that,' Bubaqra added, watching with approval as Terrel ate. 'And no one knew where you were. Then someone remembered seeing the two of you go off together, so a few of the boys went to look for you. What were you doing out there in the first place?'

Terrel swallowed his latest mouthful.

'Didn't Zahir tell you?'

'Our youngest son is prone to exaggeration,' she stated dryly. 'We'd like to hear it from you.'

Terrel hesitated. He was aware that although some of the bustle inside the tent had started up again, it was quieter than it had been before, and many of its occupants were probably trying to listen to the conversation.

'Kala took me to see some animals,' he said eventually. 'They're called djerboas, I think.' As he went on to tell them about the strange, almost comical dance, the tent became quieter still, but Terrel found that he was now ready – even eager – to talk. This part of the story was relatively straightforward, and he wanted some information from his listeners in return. 'What's so special about what we saw?' he asked, once he'd finished his description.

'There are many legends connected to the djerboas' dance,' Algardi told him, 'but nothing that would explain

Kalkara's plight. Generally witnessing it is thought to be a *good* omen.'

'For a woman it means she will be blessed with many healthy children,' Bubaqra explained.

'For a man,' Algardi went on, 'it means good fortune. "Full wells and many camels", as the saying goes.'

'And for a man and a woman to see it together means they're each other's true love,' Ghadira added, keeping a straight face for once, but raising her eyebrows in a silent question.

'Our granddaughter has a romantic nature,' Bubaqra said fondly, 'which probably explains her almost complete lack of common sense.'

Ghadira pretended to take umbrage at this remark, but a moment later her smile was back.

'These are only examples,' Algardi said hurriedly. 'There are all sorts of ridiculous tales.'

'But why is it so remarkable?' Terrel asked. 'Anyone could have gone to watch their burrow.'

'Djerboas are usually nocturnal creatures,' the elder explained. 'It's rare to see them in daylight, and even more surprising to see them in the morning. And it's said that each clan only dances like that once every three years, so the chances of anyone witnessing it are very slim.'

Terrel nodded. Now that he understood the nomads' reaction, he wondered whether Kala had just been lucky – or whether she had somehow known what was going to take place. But in the end that didn't really matter, and he was still left with the problem of what had happened next.

'But none of the stories mentions fire of any kind,'

Algardi went on, 'so we still don't understand how Kalkara came to be burnt.'

'Nor does it explain how you healed her so completely,' his wife added. 'We were hoping you could enlighten us.'

'I'm not sure I understand it myself.' Terrel knew that in a sense Kala had brought the injuries upon herself – but he couldn't really tell them that. In any case, he had no idea why she had imagined the flames. So what was he supposed to tell them? 'I didn't even know there was anything wrong at the time,' he said eventually. 'It was only when I was trying to heal her that part of what happened became clear.' He paused again, deciding to stay as close to the truth as he could. 'Kalkara *did* see a fire, but it was an hallucination, a mirage. There weren't any flames, but she thought there were. To her they were real, and that was enough to cause the burns. I didn't really heal her at all. I just had to convince her that the flames *hadn't* been real, and then she was all right again. In a sense, she had never been burnt.' He looked back and forth between the elder and his wife, wondering whether they would accept his version of events.

'A mirage, you say?' Algardi said after a short silence.

'I don't know how else to describe it.'

'We've all seen plenty of mirages in the heat of summer,' the old man commented, 'but I've never known one to have that sort of effect.'

'Kalkara is a singular girl in many ways, dearest,' Bubaqra said. 'Who knows what goes on inside that pretty head of hers?'

'And she's not likely to tell us, is she?' Ghadira remarked.

'How did you convince her the flames weren't real?' Algardi enquired thoughtfully.

'I . . . I just pointed out that I'd been there too, and I wasn't burnt,' Terrel improvised.

The old man nodded, apparently satisfied.

Terrel was left in peace then to rest again, but once he was alone with his own thoughts he knew that sleep would be a long time coming. Various ideas had occurred to him – none of which were pleasant – and even though he knew he'd have to face them eventually, he was trying to put that moment off for as long as possible. He told himself this was because he was tired, and not because he was a coward, but the argument didn't even come close to being convincing.

To try to take his mind off his troubling thoughts, Terrel watched the bustle within the tent. Although there were several children of both sexes inside the dwelling, most of the adults present were women. When Terrel had first come to live with the Toma, all but the youngest and oldest females had worn veils over the lower part of their faces. He had assumed that this was simply part of their normal attire, perhaps designed to protect them from the rays of the sun, which could be fierce even in the cooler seasons. Later he had realized that the coverings were being worn because there was a stranger in their midst – himself. He had found that odd, and it had made him feel uncomfortable – especially as some of the women also seemed reluctant to talk to him. Even if he discounted Alyssa's intermittent presence, it was undeniable that women – especially Ysatel and Esera – had become his closest friends during his travels. To find his newest acquaintances hidden away, as if he were a potential danger to them, seemed unnatural. However, after only a few days, when it became clear that he had been accepted as an honorary member of the clan, the veils were put aside and all reticence had since disappeared. The fact that the women in Algardi's tent were all more or less ignoring his presence, and going about their business as normal, made him feel almost like one of the family.

Some of them were busy mending the woven curtains that divided the interior of the tent and allowed a certain measure of privacy. Others were sewing saddlebags and cushions. One of the older aunts was telling stories to a group of small children, while several of the older girls, including Ghadira, were preparing food. However, most of the activity – as well as laughter and a good deal of ribald banter – was centred on a young wife who had recently produced the newest member of the clan. Her son had been born four days earlier and, much to Terrel's relief, it had been an uncomplicated delivery which had not required any assistance from him. The baby was currently being washed in camel urine before being rubbed with salt. He would suffer this indignity every evening for the first sixteen days of his life – half a cycle of the White Moon – and he was clearly enjoying the attention of so many of his relatives, if not the process itself. When Terrel had asked the purpose of this apparently disgusting ritual, he'd been told that it would protect the child agaisnt infection while he was at his most vulnerable. It seemed an unlikely theory, but it appeared to be working because the baby was indeed thriving.

Algardi's family – and the Toma as a whole – seemed

to be able to function as a close-knit team in conditions that would normally produce a great deal of friction, and Terrel could not help but admire them for it. His own experiences of being part of a family had only come when he'd been forced into exile – and even then most of what he'd learnt had done little to counteract the cynicism he harboured as a result of having been abandoned at birth. Even when he'd seemed to become part of an apparently stable household, something had always happened to undermine the hopeful beginnings of his newly acquired faith. He could only hope that the same thing would not happen here.

Terrel was keenly aware that, to some extent at least, his own presence had been responsible for the problems he'd encountered – and that, inevitably, led him back to wondering about his role within the tribe and, in particular, to the disturbing events of the morning.

His joy at Alyssa's return had been at least partially overshadowed by what had happened to Kalkara. He had convinced himself – and subsequently Kala too – that Alyssa had meant her no harm, but how could he be absolutely sure that was true? Was it possible that Alyssa *had* somehow been antagonistic towards the little girl? And if she was, could that have contributed to what Kala saw – or thought she saw? Terrel still refused to believe that Alyssa would have hurt the child deliberately, but what if she had done so inadvertently, by displaying an antipathy that Kala had mistaken for something much worse? *Who was she?* Alyssa had asked, and Terrel tried to remember the tone of her voice. She had sounded both curious and dismissive when she'd commented about Kalkara having 'flames in her eyes', but that didn't prove

much. In fact, why would Alyssa feel *anything* towards
the other girl? She didn't even know her. Had she just
been in the way, making the exchange between the two
friends more difficult? Another possibility occurred to
him then, prompted by what he'd learnt about the djerboas' dance. 'And for a man and a woman to see it
together . . .' Could it be that Alyssa had felt an irrational and quite unjustified surge of jealousy, because of
his friendship with the little girl? She had, after all,
accused him of falling in love with Esera. Don't be
absurd, he told himself. That's a ridiculous idea. Kala
had simply mistaken Alyssa's presence for something else
entirely.

Nevertheless, for the first time ever, Terrel found
himself suffering a few qualms about when and where
Alyssa would next appear. And his promise to introduce
Kalkara to her now seemed rather unwise.

'So what's outside the dome?' Terrel asked.

'Fire,' Mlicki replied.

The two boys were walking beside one of the pack
camels, near the centre of the long line that made up the
Toma's caravan. Kalkara rode high above them, atop the
bundles tied to either side of the animal's saddle-harness.
She seemed to have no fear of heights, and occasionally
even stood up to get a better view ahead – in spite of the
fact that the camel's lurching gait would have sent most
people tumbling to the ground.

'Fire?' Terrel repeated, trying hard not to laugh. He
had to remind himself that every creed should be
respected, no matter how peculiar or misguided it seemed
to him. 'So what's beyond that?'

Mlicki gave him a strange look.

'The First Fire,' he said patiently, as if his companion simply hadn't heard what he'd said. 'The fire that gave birth to the land, to the winds, to the music of life, to everything. There *isn't* anything beyond that. How could there be?'

Terrel had no answer to this. He had come across many odd beliefs on his travels, but this was the most bizarre yet.

'Have I got this right? The world, all of Nydus, is surrounded by a revolving copper dome. The stars are holes through it, to the fire beyond, and the sun is just a bigger hole.'

Mlicki nodded, choosing to ignore his friend's faintly sceptical tone.

'What about the moons?'

'They're inside, of course, hanging on chains.'

Although Terrel was tempted to ask why these chains couldn't be seen, he knew that Mlicki would have what – to him at least – was a plausible answer. The chains would be hidden on the far sides of the moons. Or they would be too thin to be visible from below. Terrel might think the idea ludicrous, but it apparently made sense to the Toma.

'If the dome is made of copper,' he asked instead, 'why is the sky blue?' Even as he spoke, he recognized that this was an unfair question. He saw the sky, and everything in it, very differently, but he had no idea why it was blue either. He'd always thought of it as empty space, but surely that would be black, as it was at night. So how did the sky turn it blue?

'I've forgotten,' Mlicki replied, unconcerned. 'One of

the storytellers will know. You can ask them at the kappara-tan.'

'When will that be?'

'Four days from now, when the White Moon is full. We should reach the well at Chlendi before that, and I'm pretty sure that's where Vilheyuna would've chosen at this time of year. The elders, and Zahir, have agreed.' There was a certain pride in his voice now.

'They must trust you, if they're taking your advice on such an important matter.'

'They think I learnt what to do from Vilheyuna,' Mlicki confessed, sounding less confident now, 'but I'm just guessing really.'

'I'm sure it'll go well,' Terrel assured him, but wondered how Zahir would react if it did not.

They walked on in silence for a while, and Terrel's thoughts returned to the events of the previous day. He was half relieved, half disappointed that Mlicki didn't seem to have been aware of the silent, one-sided conversation between Terrel and Kalkara. Naturally enough, the two friends had talked about what had happened, but Terrel had simply repeated the tale he'd told Algardi and Bubaqra, and Mlicki had accepted this at face value, giving no hint that he might have heard anything more.

As far as Terrel could tell, his healing of Kalkara had restored Mlicki's faith in him. And although Terrel had not been able to explain how Kala had been hurt, Mlicki recognized that his friend had no motive to cause the girl any harm. His sister was well again, and that was all that really mattered.

Kalkara herself seemed to have forgotten about the entire episode, and was treating Terrel exactly as she had before. He couldn't help wondering if she was able to simply block out unwanted memories. Glancing up at her now, he could only guess at what was going on behind those clear blue eyes.

'We should be stopping soon,' Mlicki said, interrupting Terrel's thoughts.

'Is there a well near here, then?'

'Not a permanent one. Between here and Chlendi we have to find what we can.'

'But there isn't anything!' Terrel exclaimed, looking round at the parched, dusty terrain.

'There might be,' Mlicki replied. 'Beneath the surface. Algardi will have sent scouts to spot the most likely places to dig.'

'How do they do that?' The search for water was central to the Toma's existence. In their language the word for it was indistinguishable from the word meaning 'life'. Wells and oases were vital to their wanderings, but this was the first time Terrel had thought about what would happen when they couldn't reach such a place.

'They look for where the white crystals shine.'

'Salt?' Terrel guessed.

Mlicki nodded.

'It forms a thin crust on top of low-lying sand.'

'But surely any water below that would be undrink-able?'

'Sometimes, but not always. Even if it *is* salty, at least the camels can drink.'

'But what do *we* do?'

'The same as if we don't find any crystals,' Mlicki replied. 'We go thirsty. We survive on what we're carrying with us, and go on until we do find water.'

An hour later, the site for their temporary camp had been chosen, and the nomads sprang into action, gathering their camels and unloading tents, food and other necessities for an overnight stop.

'There. Look,' Mlicki said, indicating a nearby hollow.

Terrel turned to where the boy was pointing, and saw the faint glitter of crystals in the light of the lowering sun.

'Looks like your eyes, doesn't it,' Mlicki remarked.

CHAPTER NINE

Medrano had enlisted the aid of several children to collect the many pebbles he needed for the ceremonial mosaics. Apart from the full circle of the White Moon, both the Amber and Red Moons were about three-quarters full, and only the fourth member of the quartet would be represented by a smaller crescent shape, matching its unseen presence in the sky above.

Kalkara was among the artist's helpers but, unlike all of the others – who obediently brought only stones of the appropriate colours – she chose to bring an assortment of different hues, simply because she thought they were pretty. Some of the other children scoffed at her stupidity, but Medrano knew better and accepted them graciously. Rather than discard them, he put them aside and in due course – once the four moons were complete – he incorporated the girl's offerings into the sand picture that lay at the centre of the square marked out by the mosaics. This picture showed an infant surrounded by childish things – toys, a feeding spoon, a wrapping cloth, and so on. At the end of his kappara-tan, Zahir would destroy the picture, symbolically demonstrating all that he had left behind now that he was a man. The fact that the picture would only last for a few hours did not mean that Medrano would take any short cuts in its creation. Like all that he made, this would be a true work of art, and – watching him as he dribbled sand between his fingers, then shaped and shaded it with his thumbs – Terrel could only marvel at the nomad's skill. He would not have believed that such beautiful depictions, with all their subtle variations of light and dark, were possible using such basic materials. Kala watched too, and was clearly delighted with the results of her own labours.

As dusk drew in, fires were lit both to provide warmth and light and to start the cooking for the feast that would follow the ritual. The nomads usually existed on a nutritious but monotonous diet, based almost entirely on the milk from their camels. However, they also ate bread – which they baked on curved metal sheets balanced on stones over their fires – and supplemented this with the small purple onions and various herbs that grew in a few places in the desert. Wolf-berries and dates were a welcome addition to any meal whenever they could be obtained. And for special occasions, there was also meat. Camel raisers usually looked down on those who herded sheep and goats, but they were not above trading for these animals when necessary. Hot stones had been put into metal cauldrons to cook mutton stew, and several goat carcasses were being roasted whole over the campfires, filling the air with mouthwatering scents.

As Terrel wandered through the camp, observing the evening's preparations, he felt slightly out of place. The fact that everyone else seemed to have some task to complete made it all too obvious that he was an outsider.

The Toma were all wearing their finest attire, the robed men carrying their best daggers in colourful belts, the women in dresses and cloaks of the most ornate weaves and patterns, with remarkable arrays of jewellery around their necks and wrists. Many of these adornments were valuable as well as beautiful, crafted in talismanic designs that often depicted one or more of the moons. Bubaqra had told Terrel that in the past women and children had been immune to the depredations of war. Not even the most depraved raiders would have thought to harm them or steal from them – and this was one reason why many nomads had stored up much of their wealth in gold and gemstones for their wives and daughters. In recent years, however, this code of honour had not always been adhered to. What had happened to Mlicki's tribe was proof enough of that. As a result, such finery was now only worn on special occasions – and this was obviously a matter of regret for the nomads' matriarch. Seeing her now, proud and smiling at the heart of her clan, Terrel couldn't help wishing that, in some things at least, time could be reversed. He also wished he had finer clothes to wear, so that he too could have dressed in an appropriate manner for the celebrations.

The air of excitement intensified as darkness drew in, but Terrel could sense an underlying uncertainty too, a nervousness that hung in the air like the smoke from the fires. At first he thought this was because the nomads were afraid of raiders coming upon them while they were preoccupied with the ceremony – though sentries had been posted as usual – but it wasn't long before he understood the real reason. He had already gathered that this night was significant for the Toma, over and above Zahir's coming of age. No one would talk about it openly, but it was clear that certain decisions were to be made, decisions that would affect the nomads' future. And the man who should have played a central role in making these judgements was, to all intents and purposes, absent.

The serious nature of this absence was brought home to Terrel shortly before the ritual was due to begin, when Vilheyuna was carried out of his tent and brought to the ceremonial arena. The shaman's headdress lay on his chest; Mlicki had remained true to his word and refused to even countenance putting it on again – but the fact that he had allowed his comatose master to be moved, when it was not strictly necessary, was testament to his understanding of just how important the presence of the old man was. If Vilheyuna could not play an active role in proceedings, at least he might be able to watch over them in spirit.

Once the shaman had been settled in his place of honour, Mlicki retreated into the shadows, determined that his own role should be as an onlooker and nothing more. Terrel saw the anxiety on his friend's face, and went over to stand beside him. Mlicki glanced at him and gave a slight smile, grateful for the company, but they did not speak until the ceremony began. The sound of the drums seemed to come from all around them, an insistent thunder rolling out of the darkness. Terrel found that his heart was beating faster, keeping time to the central rhythm, while the drummers wove a dozen patterns of sound around it – creating a whole that was both hypnotic and invigorating.

'Where are they?' Terrel asked, looking round in a vain attempt to see the musicians.

'Beyond the firelight,' Mlicki told him. 'Each one alone and blind. They don't need to see each other, or even their own hands. That way they become one with their drums.'

'That's amazing.'

Mlicki nodded, then turned his head again and cupped a hand over Terrel's ear so that he could be heard over the growling thunder.

'The dance will begin soon,' he said, pointing to a group of men who appeared to be dressed in rags and feathers.

'What are they eating?'

The men were all chewing vigorously.

'Qard,' Mlicki replied. 'The food of the pure.'

'It looks like leaves.'

'It is. Chewing them makes you feel dizzy and excited. The dancers believe it helps them to fly on the winds and experience pleasure in all things. Qard can bring dreams and even visions.'

'Have you ever tried it?'

'No! I have quite enough visions as it is.'

And I have enough dreams, Terrel thought, resolving to follow his friend's example and avoid the leaves at all costs. The memory of the last time he'd ingested a similar substance still had the power to bring him out in a cold sweat, and he had no intention of ever allowing Jax to take control of him again.

The dance began slowly, each man moving in a circle

around the square of the moons. Their movements varied from the expressive to the frenetic, steering individual courses through the complex labyrinth of sound. As they passed by, Terrel could see that the dancers' eyes were glazed, as if they were all quite unaware of their surroundings. Their world seemed to be defined by the rhythms of the drums, and by their own motion.

Gradually, the beat at the core of the music grew faster and louder, the embellishments less important, and these changes were reflected in the dance. Each man still followed his own course, but their movements were becoming more and more alike, until – just as it seemed that they must succumb to exhaustion – they became perfectly synchronized. Although none of the dancers seemed to be paying attention to the others, it was as if they were all in the grip of an identical compulsion – each foot stamping at precisely the same moment, each hand waving in the same sweeping gesture. They even began to cry out in unison, wordless calls that seemed more avian than human.

As the drums roared to a crescendo, Terrel found that he was holding his breath, drawn into the knife-edged tension of the moment. The sweat-slick dancers leapt and whirled, nearing their own climax. Then with one last joint bound, they challenged the starlit sky and fell back to the ground as one just as the drums fell silent. For a few heartbeats everything was deadly quiet. Nothing moved except the shadows thrown by the flames of the campfires.

Finally, as the Toma came back to life, Terrel was able to let out a long breath and fill his aching lungs again. Groups of people moved forward, surrounding each of the now motionless dancers. Terrel heard the whisper of several conversations and then, as the performers were led away, he saw the look on the faces of both the dancers and their attendants. The air of disappointment was palpable.

'What's happened?' he whispered to Mlicki.

'None of them went beyond. Not to the past or the future.'

'No visions?'

'Vilheyuna should have led their quest. Without him the trance was bound to fail.'

Terrel wasn't sure what had been expected, but he found it hard to believe that such a spellbinding perform- ance could be considered a failure. But before he could ask Mlicki about this, a new set of players entered the stage and he was forced to rein in his curiosity. The kappara-tan was about to begin.

The ceremony opened with a series of incantations in a language Terrel did not understand, and which seemed to be addressed to the night sky. One after another all the men of the Toma came forward to speak. Some uttered only a few words; others delivered complicated and obviously long-winded orations that made even those who could understand them fidget with boredom. However, there were no interruptions. In spite of the fact that the tribe relied heavily upon their elders for advice on many matters, Terrel knew that it was a matter of principle for the Toma that every man had the right to speak his mind on any topic – and on such an occasion it would have been considered unacceptable to deny anyone his moment at the centre of the ritual.

It was only as the last of the speeches ended that the leading actor in the play appeared on the torchlit stage. Zahir was dressed in a plain white robe that hung loose from his shoulders to his ankles. His head, arms and feet were bare. The expression on his face was both stern and proud, as if he was aware of the audience but didn't care to acknowledge them, accepting their attentiveness as of right.

Immediately behind him came Ghadira, dressed in her finest clothes and jewellery. She moved with a graceful, casual elegance, but her slight smile betrayed the fact that she too was well aware of being the object of the spectators' gaze. Because she was a girl she had come of age some time ago, but as she'd been born on the same day as Zahir, she was the obvious choice to act at his guide and partner in the symbolic journey he was to undertake. Behind her came several more women, some old, some young, each carrying various objects in their hands. Try as he might, Terrel couldn't make out what these were, and in the silence that held the camp in its grip, he did not like to ask.

Reaching the mosaic of the White Moon, Zahir walked slowly round it three times, while Ghadira and the other women looked on. Then, still without a word being spoken, Zahir strode across to the depiction of the Red Moon and repeated the process around its incomplete circle. Having finished his third orbit, he knelt on the ground beside the stones and waited until Ghadira came to stand over him.

'May the sky's fire give you strength,' she said in a clear voice that rang out in the silence, carrying easily to everyone present. 'Strength in war. Strength in love.'

Some things don't change, Terrel thought. In his homeland the Red Moon was thought to control the realms of violence, fire and passion – and it seemed that the same was true here. He could not help recalling the festival at Tiscamanita and his own alarming brush with the potency of the Red Moon, but then he turned his attention back to the drama unfolding before him. Ghadira had turned to two of her followers and taken the objects they carried. These were a small brush and a pot of crimson paint, with which she deftly outlined several shapes on Zahir's left cheek. The markings glistened like blood in the flickering light, and it was hard for Terrel to see what – if anything – they represented. He guessed that they might be intended as flames, but they reminded him of something else. It was a few moments before he realized that they looked like the decorations on the red dome of the sharaken's fortress, and his sense of wonder deepened. It seemed that certain aspects of reverence for the moons were indeed universal.

Ghadira finished her handiwork and passed the materials back to her attendants. Zahir then got to his feet and made his way to the Amber Moon. Once more he made three circuits of the mosaic, then knelt.

'May the winds watch over you,' Ghadira said. 'In the hours of waking. In the hours of sleep.'

For Terrel the Amber Moon was linked to the spirit realm – to intuition and dreams – and it had also held a special significance for the sharaken, the 'dream-traders' of Macul, so he was not really surprised by Ghadira's reference to sleep. What did surprise him was the golden symbol that she painted at the centre of Zahir's forehead. It was a crude but unmistakable outline of an eye, echoing the sleepless tattoos that the sharaken wore on their eyelids.

Before he could work out the implications of this new parallel, the procession moved on to the crescent shape of the Dark Moon – and Terrel felt a stirring of unease. This was the moon most closely bound up with his own fate, and it was also the most mysterious, not least because of its recent erratic behaviour, but also because of its connection to the invisible forces of the world – and to death itself. Even its name in the nomad tongue – 'the Invisible' – was a reflection of its ominous and enigmatic nature.

'May the black light shine for you,' Ghadira intoned. 'In motion. In stillness.'

This time, having received the necessary implements from her companions, she anointed the right side of Zahir's face with another emblem. After what had gone before, Terrel was not surprised that he recognized it – but he still found himself growing excited and a little afraid. He had seen the design of the dark star before, at the ruined temple near Tiscamanita and on the mountaintop at Tindaya. He also knew that it appeared in several places in the Tindaya Code, and that it had some uncertain connection to the Ancients, but he was unable to guess the significance of its use here. Looking at its five points, each extended in tapering wavy lines, like tentacles, he was aware that he had begun to tremble.

He was still shivering when Zahir returned to the White Moon, completing his journey around the square, and Ghadira's words and the final symbol that she painted did nothing to set his mind at rest.

'May the bringer of change grant you good fortune. As one life is ended, so another begins.'

This was obviously a reference to Zahir's transition from boy to man, but Terrel felt as if Ghadira were talking to him too, and he couldn't help but wonder what his own future held. When he saw the smaller, white star that she painted on Zahir's chin, he felt another surge of anxiety. Without thinking, he looked down at his left hand, but the amulet – the bright star that he carried within him – was not visible. It could only be seen during an eclipse, or when he was *inside* one of the elementals. At any other time there was nothing to mark its presence.

Terrel forced himself to concentrate on the ceremony. He saw that Zahir was standing now, and had loosened the collar of his robe to expose the upper part of his chest. And there, over his heart, Ghadira was placing her final image; four concentric circles, one in each of the colours of the moons. Terrel had seen that before too; in the jasper of the fog-bound valley – and on the back of his own hand. His own tattoo was permanent and of a single dark colour, but the symbolism was the same.

'Only the moons have eternal life,' Algardi stated, stepping forward and looking around at the entire clan. The implication of his words was obvious. The moons might live for ever, but men do not. 'Time does not touch them. Their changes are constant.'

Or they used to be, Terrel thought, instinctively glancing up at the sky.

'This is a turning point,' the old man declared. 'For the White Moon, and for my son, Zahir.'

At these words, the audience broke into cheers and applause, and Algardi's face creased into a smile of delight. Zahir's answering grin was equally broad as the two embraced, and the Toma took up an insistent chant.

'A child no more! A child no more!'

Taking this as his cue, Zahir strode over to the sand picture, then hesitated, milking the drama of the moment.

'A child no more!'

Zahir began a manic dance, stamping and kicking with glee, until the picture was gone and he had said goodbye to his childish past.

More cheering greeted his performance, and the tension vanished from the atmosphere. Now that the formal part of the ritual was over, even Terrel was able to relax a little as he watched Zahir receive the more worldly trappings of manhood. A wide belt was fastened around his waist, with a sheath and a splendid curved dagger attached. New sandals were put on his feet, and a band of colourfully embroidered material was tied round his head, so that the amber eye was covered. All this was accompanied by a great deal of good-humoured noise, as everyone seemed to want to chatter at once now that the enforced silence had ended. Only Terrel remained quiet, too astonished by what he had witnessed to ask any of the questions that were now teeming inside his brain.

After a short interlude, the feasting began. Everyone ate their fill – and then, at the urging of their fellows, they all ate more, as if their appetites were suddenly being used as a measure of their self worth. Terrel soon abandoned the attempt to keep up, marvelling at the nomads' capacity for devouring such enormous portions of food. The atmosphere was cheerful now, almost rowdy, and even though he was still conscious of being an outsider, Terrel felt his spirits rising at the evening progressed.

Even the fact that some of the revellers were chewing qard leaves no longer concerned him.

Several hours later, as the feasting came to an end, he watched as the remnants of the gargantuan meal – which, for some reason he didn't understand, were called 'the snow-leopard's portion' – were cleared away. After an evening of excess, the Toma's frugal ways were reasserting themselves; nothing would be wasted. However, Terrel could not understand why several clean mutton bones were placed into a fire to bake.

'Why are they doing that?' he asked Mlicki.

'When the bones crack,' his friend replied sleepily, 'the shaman reads omens in the patterns.'

'So who'll do it this time?'

'I don't know. It won't happen for a while yet.'

'Why not?'

'We have the storytelling next,' Mlicki replied, sounding eager now in spite of his obvious tiredness.

'Who tells the stories?'

'Medrano will start. After that, anyone who can make themselves heard and keep the audience's attention! It'll probably be dawn before it's finished.'

Terrel already knew that the Toma were fond of story-telling. Having no written language, they kept a record of their history – as well as myths and legends, jokes and parables – in their heads.

'It sounds as if it's going to be an entertaining night,' he commented, feeling a little of his friend's excitement himself now.

Eventually, Medrano got to his feet. He waited for the general rumble of conversation to die down, but it gave no sign of abating – and Terrel couldn't help feeling that it would take an earthquake or something equally devastating to quieten the boisterous gathering. But he was wrong.

While Medrano waited patiently, Zahir stood up and, setting his fingers to his lips, let out a high-pitched, piercing whistle. Even then the noise did not stop, but at least it fell in volume.

'Before the storytelling begins,' Zahir shouted, his face flushed and his eyes shining, 'I have something to say! Soon you'll be telling stories about me! I'm going to be the Toma's champion in the Race of Truth.'

The silence then was absolute, with shock and outrage frozen on the faces of all the elders. Terrel was taken aback by their response. He had no idea what Zahir's announcement meant – or why it should have provoked such a stunned reaction.

CHAPTER TEN

'Sit down, b—' Algardi caught himself just in time. Calling his son 'boy' on this of all nights would have been an insult too vile even for Zahir's crime. 'This is neither the time nor the place.'

Taken aback by his father's anger, Zahir was about to respond, but Algardi did not give him the chance.

'You have no right to make such a claim. The winds—'

'The winds failed us!' Zahir burst out, finding his voice at last. 'We have to do this on our own.' But there was uncertainty in his eyes now, in spite of his defiance. He was in the wrong and, deep down, he knew it.

'Even so,' Algardi replied, tacitly admitting the truth of his son's words, 'this decision is to be made by the Toma as a whole, not by any one man. And not now.' The finality of this statement silenced Zahir.

No one else spoke. Most people kept their eyes averted from the protagonists, and even though he did not fully understand the reasons for it, Terrel shared in the general mood of embarrassment.

'Sit down,' Algardi repeated, quietly this time.

As Zahir obeyed, swallowing his pride, his father turned to look at Medrano. The artist had been as shocked and dismayed as anyone else by what had happened, but he understood what was needed now.

'This is the oldest story of all,' he began. 'So old that it was once written down!' His voice was a little uncertain at first, but it quickly gained in confidence. His audience recovered too, glad to be able to return to the proper events of the evening, to something they understood and enjoyed. Most looked up at Medrano, their faces displaying a mixture of relief and anticipation.

'It was carved into the stones of the forbidden city of Y-Harah,' the artist went on, 'which the nomad scholar Zayla found during the years of his wanderings. It's thanks to him that this story is still told, because he committed it to memory and it has been passed from father to son for countless generations. Listen then, and carefully, for Zayla's tale is all we have left from that ancient time.'

Medrano paused, looking round at the eager faces before him. Terrel glanced around too, and realized that he was the only one surprised by the nature of the artist's opening. The rest of the gathering had obviously been expecting nothing else. Most people were nodding, or smiling in recognition of familiar words. Tradition evidently decreed that the oldest story of all was also the first to be told at such important gatherings.

'Long ago, in a time before the burning winds came, when life flowed freely across the green plains of Misrah, the city of Y-Harah was ruled by an evil tyrant called Hargeysa, a man so insane he always chose to ride a horse rather than a camel!'

This comment drew more smiles and some laughter from Medrano's audience.

'Hargeysa called himself the Sentinel, and claimed to watch over his people with the eyes of the moons – and because Y-Harah was a prosperous city, its inhabitants were content to believe him. Of course, their faith might have been influenced by Hargeysa's army of loyal body-guards, who enforced their master's every wish. Anyone who disagreed with the Sentinel was liable to vanish mysteriously in the night, never to be seen again. But for most life was good, even though Y-Harah was cut off from the outside world. The city had its own language. Their clothes, their music and dances, even the way they cooked their food, was quite unlike anywhere else – which was the way Hargeysa wanted it. None of his subjects was allowed to leave. Those allowed to work outside the city walls were watched by the soldiers, and anyone caught trying to escape was publicly tortured before being put to death.

'What was worse, Hargeysa saw all foreigners – he called them nonbelievers – as a threat, because an oracle had once told him that if such a heretic ever entered the city walls, then the inhabitants of Y-Harah would all be doomed. Because of that, any stranger found within a day's march of the city was executed on the spot, so that there was no chance of breaking the spell that protected them.'

By now the Toma were engrossed, their earlier disappointment set aside. Terrel had the feeling that even

Zahir's egotistical presumption was already being viewed in a more forgiving light, as the hot-headedness of a very young man. The humiliation of the public rebuke by his father had been punishment enough – and now it was time to enjoy the rest of the night's entertainments. Medrano's initial nervousness had vanished now, and he knew that he held his audience in the palm of his hand.

'Hargeysa's actions became known far and wide, and for many years no outsider even tried to approach Y-Harah. So the Sentinel slept easily beneath his chilouk, which was woven from threads the colours of the four moons. Many tribes looked from afar upon the city's riches and were envious, but even when such people were suffering from terrible droughts, the citizens of Y-Harah refused to share any of their plentiful crops. And none dared raid Hargeysa's lands, because his reputation was now that of an invincible ruler, a king. It was said that the walls of Y-Harah were lined with weapons no army could withstand, sorcerous devices that spewed forth fire and smoke to choke a man to death, or hurled spears of metal and stone that could tear man or beast apart before they had even come within sight of the city's towers. It was said that Hargeysa could make the ground open up to swallow his enemies in pits of scalding tar, and that the trees in his orchards grew vines that would snake around any foe and strangle him as he attempted to pass by. Many people thought such tales were ridiculous, but no one was prepared to risk their life to discover the truth. No one except Soofarah the Meddler, that is.'

The mention of this character drew another round of smiles, and this was followed by laughter as Medrano went on to describe her. He told of how, as a girl, Soofarah had been wilful and inquisitive, always poking her nose into things that did not concern her, so that even among her own clan she became the cause of much friction. However, she also learnt many things, including the 'gift of many faces'. Years later, having satisfied her curiosity about the ways of men on her wedding night, she divorced her husband and set out alone to travel wherever the winds took her. After many adventures, she met a sorceress who told her that she would only meet her true love if she journeyed to Y-Harah.

'True to her nature,' Medrano continued, 'Soofarah set out immediately, heedless of the dangers. Eventually she reached the borders of Hargeysa's land, where she came across the body of an ancient goatherd who had died while tending his flock. Ignoring the rank smell that infused the coarse material, Soofarah dressed herself in the old man's clothes, and used her gift to take on his likeness. Then, having hidden the corpse in the under-growth, she made her way towards the city. When she was in sight of the walls she began to hobble, crying out in a feeble voice and feigning illness. The tale she told was of raiders who had driven off her animals and left her for dead, and although this sounded incredible – who would dare to do such a thing? – no one questioned her identity and she was taken inside the city.

'There she stayed for seven days and seven nights, changing her appearance wherever necessary so that her disguise fitted her purpose. She visited every part of Y-Harah, including Hargeysa's palace, as she searched for her true love.'

After a suitable amount of embellishment, Medrano revealed what everyone in the audience, except Terrel, already knew. Soofarah's true love was a cat, a creature who was as endlessly curious and as selfish as she was. They escaped from Y-Harah together and remained inseparable for the rest of the cat's long life.

'And there it would have ended had it not been for the fact that, on her continuing travels, Soofarah came across the caravan of the great hero, Zorn.'

This name was clearly familiar to the nomads, and there were murmurs of appreciation as Medrano went on to describe the fabled warrior – whose destiny was to defend his land and his people from all evil. Terrel, who had been enjoying the story as much as anyone, found himself frozen in disbelief when he learnt that, according to the legend, Zorn had been born on the night of a lunar confluence, when all four moons had been full and perfectly aligned. Terrel and his twin had been born on such a night, and it had been prophesied that another hero – the Guardian of the Tindaya Code – would be born at the time of one confluence and fulfil *his* destiny at the time of the next. The seers had originally thought that this would be seventy-five years later, but the changes to the orbit of the Dark Moon meant that the timing was now uncertain. However, Terrel had little opportunity to wonder whether Zorn was Misrah's equivalent of the Guardian; he didn't want to miss any more of Medrano's story.

'While Soofarah was in Zorn's camp, there was a night of storytelling, and she chose to relate the tale of her visit to Y-Harah. At first no one believed her, but when she changed her appearance to that of the old goatherd and demonstrated how she had entered the forbidden city, even Zorn began to take notice. Soofarah's description of the place was so detailed that in the end no one doubted her, and she proved more than willing to answer the warrior's questions about the strength of the walls, the layout of the gates and the streets within, as well as the nature of the city's weapons and fortifications. In doing so she gave the lie to many myths that had grown up about the Sentinel's impregnable stronghold.'

Terrel could see where this was heading. He'd read an account of the fall of another forbidden city in the library at Havenmoon. The names and many details of the story had been different, but in that version, just as in Medrano's, the fortress had been brought down by a single interloper. Were *all* legends universal? he wondered. How could that be? The Floating Islands had been cut off from the rest of Nydus since time began.

Returning his attention to the artist, he heard how, armed with this intelligence, Zorn decided to invade Y-Harah. His success was aided by a sudden eclipse, which the defenders took as an ill omen, and in due course the city was ransacked and Hargeysa killed. Soofarah's adventure had indeed broken the Sentinel's spell, and brought the oracle's curse to fruition.

'But that was not all,' Medrano added. 'After the city had been plundered, a great shaking of the earth shattered every building until the place was in ruins. And these remains were buried the following day, by the greatest karabura the world had ever seen. The evil that was Y-Harah was gone for ever.'

Terrel knew that a karabura was a 'black sandstorm', the worst, most violent kind of desert whirlwind. To him even the idea of a yellow sandstorm – a sarik-buan, which the nomads had told him was easier to survive – sounded terrifying. He fervently hoped he would never encounter either of the dreadful phenomena.

'Some say that Y-Harah reappears for one day every ten thousand years,' Medrano went on. 'Others claim that it will rise again when the world is coming to an end. But if either of those auguries is true, the evil will not return alone. For Zorn is not dead but sleeping – perhaps within the ruins of Y-Harah itself – and he will return to the land of the living to protect us when he is needed. And the signal of his rebirth will be another alignment of all the moons.'

As the artist's tale came to an end, he looked up to the night sky where the White Moon hung like a pale echo of the desert sun, dazzling and beautiful but cold. Most of his audience followed his gaze, and then – as Medrano sat down – they shouted and whistled their approval, banging hands and feet upon the ground.

After that, Terrel was sure that none of the other stories would be as dramatic, or seem so relevant to his own concerns – and he was right – but many of them came close. As the night drew on, he listened to tales of lakes that wandered from place to place; of desert dreams in which lost souls tried to lure unwary travellers to the deathly wasteland; of the caravan of a thousand men and camels that had been swallowed by a karabura, never to be seen again. One man recited a long poem, with the entire tribe chiming in on the final few words of each verse; another painted so vivid a picture of the erlik, the desert spirits of the night, that Terrel could almost see these creatures above them, watching over the encampment. There was humour too, with the tale of the lazy camel who lay down and refused to get up – until its resourceful handler thought of lighting a fire under the animal's hindquarters!

Many of these stories were obviously as familiar as Medrano's had been, and yet the nomads' rapt attention did not waver – and knowing about the good bits to come often seemed to add an enjoyable element of anticipation. Terrel marvelled at the dramatic skills of the storytellers. These lay in the nuances of presentation, the subtle variations of words or phrases – and even though they were working with old material, each speaker held the audience spellbound. If any had failed to do so, Terrel suspected that they would have been rapidly forced to give way to another, but none did – and he began to wonder whether the seemingly endless store of tales would ever come to an end. More to the point, he wondered if the Toma would expect *him* to contribute to the night's entertainment. The prospect of trying to match their efforts made him feel quite sick with nervousness.

In due course, Algardi rose to his feet, and the clan instantly gave him their full attention.

'An old person who doesn't tell stories does not exist,' he said, evidently quoting a well-known saying. 'So here is mine.' He paused, apparently deep in thought. At first Terrel believed that the elder was choosing between the many tales he knew, but then realized it was simply a device Algardi was using for dramatic effect.

'Sand and flame is a dangerous combination,' the old man declared, provoking several murmurs of surprise. If this was not a new tale, then it was certainly a new beginning. 'There is magic in the movement of sand, when the wind takes it and reshapes the desert floor. Ancient augury tells us how to read the patterns of such movement, how to see the snakes swirling within or to hear the echoes of another time, but that is commonplace magic. To see beyond the memories of sand, to the flame beyond, requires a refinement of the senses, of the spirit. It requires us to move beyond the realm of certainty, beyond the world of dreams. For it is there that the tiarken live.'

At this the audience let out a communal sigh of understanding. They were back on familiar ground. Algardi went on to explain that these creatures of fire and light had been given birth by the eternal blaze beyond the dome. He told of their infrequent forays into the world of men, and of the disruption their appearance usually caused. The tiarken had no conception of honour or responsibility, of life or death, of good or evil.

'But they can also bring great joy,' he added. 'If any man is able to capture one of them and keep it in a box or a sealed jar, the tiarken will be obliged to grant him his greatest wish. Yet even here there are risks, and you must be careful what you wish for. Be true to yourself – and those you love – or you may get more than you bargained for.

'And the risks of even trying to trap such a creature are great. While free they can be more blinding than a karabura, hotter than the summer sun, and deadlier than the bite of the nachar crystal-snake. They can command the spirit of an animal to depart, and use its empty body as a plaything.' Algardi lowered his voice to a sepulchral whisper. 'And it is possible for unwary humans to suffer the same fate.'

Many of the nomads shuddered at this idea, but Terrel was too absorbed in his own speculation to notice. Could it be that Kalkara had misinterpreted Alyssa's presence in the djerboa as one of these flame-spirits? That would certainly explain her terror – and her belief that she had been burnt. Looking at Mlicki, who was sitting beside him, Terrel saw that Kala was there too, but she had finally succumbed to the lateness of the hour. The little girl was asleep, nestled against her brother. Terrel was glad she had not heard Algardi's tale. It might have reawakened her fear.

'And now,' the elder announced in a more cheerful tone, 'I think it's time we heard from the voice of rain.'

The nomads roared their agreement, but it was only when Terrel found almost every eye turned towards him that he realized who the voice of rain was.

'Come on, Ghost,' Zahir added jovially. 'Give us something new.'

Terrel got slowly to his feet. Now that the moment he'd dreaded had come, he found that he was able to regard it as an opportunity rather than an ordeal.

'I want to tell you about the Bringer of Earthquakes,' he began.

CHAPTER ELEVEN

'Moons! That was some story,' Mlicki whispered. 'Is it true?'

'As true as anything we've heard tonight,' Terrel replied.

During the course of the evening, he'd come to realize that the Toma made little or no distinction between history and myth. He had no idea whether the nomads had believed his tale and, in a sense, it didn't matter – to them or to him. His only concern was to see what reaction his words provoked, and theirs was simply to judge whether he told a good story or not. In the end Terrel had been disappointed; the nomads had not. Even when he'd been part of Laevo's troupe of actors, Terrel had never performed before such an attentive audience. He hadn't even considered using the glamour – his version of Soofarah's gift – to enhance his performance, and yet they'd hung upon his every word, openly marvelling at his inventiveness. When he'd finished, the applause had been as enthusiastic as any that night. But that was all it had been; appreciation for a good story, well told. Terrel had hoped for something more.

'Do you have any more like that?' Mlicki asked, keeping his voice low so as not to disturb Zahir, who had taken up the challenge of following Terrel, and who was now telling a convoluted tale of thwarted love and treachery.

'A few.'

'If they're all as good as that, you're never going to get any peace,' Mlicki told him. 'They'll want you to tell stories every night.'

Terrel smiled but shook his head, indicating that they ought to honour the spirit of the occasion and listen to Zahir. Mlicki took the hint and fell silent, even though it was obvious he was bursting with questions, but Terrel found it harder to heed his own advice. Ever since his conversation with Alyssa had been cut short, he'd been trying to think of a way to find out whether the Toma had heard anything that might indicate the existence of an elemental in their country – without them thinking he was completely insane. Belatedly, he'd realized that the kappara-tan had provided him with the perfect opportunity.

And so he had related part of his own history, changing the name of the 'hero' of course – calling him Aylen, in honour of the friend who had been with him at the time – but otherwise it had been an accurate, albeit abbreviated, account of real events. He'd described the jewelled city of Talazoria, its mad king, and the magical dome that had surrounded Ekuban's palace – the dome that had been intended as protection, but which in the end had trapped an earthquake *inside* its boundaries. The hero's escape from the doomed palace with the help of a giant, otherworldly bird, had been one of the highlights of his performance, but he had concentrated on the 'monster' responsible for the devastation. Painting a verbal picture of the Ancient was almost impossible, but Terrel did his best, hoping that the nomads would respond with some sign of recognition, no matter how slight. But there had been none, only the wonderment caused by something entirely new to them. If there was an elemental anywhere in Misrah, it was clear that the Toma were not aware of its existence.

The disappointment brought many of Terrel's earlier doubts flooding back, but he told himself that one setback was not enough to discount the other omens. He was still in the right place. That feeling had been reinforced by Medrano's tale, and Terrel now listened to the other storytellers in the hope that he would learn something more. The prophecies of the Tindaya Code had been engraved in stone; if anything similar existed in Misrah, it would surely be contained within the nomads' oral myths and legends.

In that respect, Zahir's contribution was a disappointment. It was an overblown and melodramatic romance, which he presented in deliberately flamboyant style. The fact that he obviously recognized the nature of the tale, and was able to take himself less than seriously for once, seemed out of character. Terrel's opinion of Algardi's son rose as he watched him coax laughter from the audience, sometimes at his own expense. Zahir seemed at ease, his earlier humiliation forgotten, and there was no doubting his flair for dramatic gestures. Was this a new-found confidence, now that he was officially a man and no longer felt the need to prove himself? Or was it simply that the storytelling tradition within the clan was so strong that anyone could defy their own nature within its scope, without fear of ridicule or loss of dignity? Either way, this was a side of Zahir that Terrel had not seen before, and he couldn't begrudge the young man his time as the centre of attention. It was his night, after all.

When Zahir eventually sat down, to a prolonged round of applause, Terrel saw Ghadira thread her way through the crowd to bring her uncle a drink. She stooped to kiss his cheek, and they exchanged a brief private joke before he drank gratefully.

'I could do with some water myself,' Terrel muttered. His throat was still dry from his own performance.

'You only have to ask,' Mlicki told him. 'Just raise a hand and one of the women will bring you something. That's one of the privileges of taking a turn as a story-teller.'

Terrel hesitated. It seemed arrogant to presume that any of the Toma should wait on him.

'Go on,' Mlicki urged him.

'Can't I just go and get some myself?'

'No. That would be rude. We stay where we are until all the stories are told.'

Another elder had just stood up, and was beginning to tell the legend of how the snow-leopard got its spots. The old man's voice was resonant and warm, but slow, as if he were savouring each syllable, and it was clear that it would be some time before he finished.

Half expecting that no one would notice, Terrel raised his good arm into the air. He felt foolish, and quickly lowered it again, but almost as soon as he had done so, a metal cup appeared before him. Looking round, he saw that it had not been brought by one of the women, but by Nadur, one of Zahir's captains.

'Thank you,' Terrel whispered, wondering if this was a peace offering.

'Good story,' Nadur replied, grinning, then moved silently away.

Terrel was about to drink when Ghadira appeared at his side.

'I was about to ask what you wanted,' she said, smiling, 'but I see someone's beaten me to it. Is there anything else I can get you?'

Terrel didn't know what to say, so he just shook his head. Ghadira gave a slight shrug of disappointment and slipped away again. Terrel turned to watch her go, admiring the grace of her movements, and when he turned back he noticed that Kalkara had woken up. She was watching him, a sly smile on her face. For some reason he did not understand, Terrel blushed as she looked away.

Taking a sip of his drink, he tried to concentrate on the snow-leopard's tale. The water was cold and slightly bitter, but at least it was not salty. Any such taste still brought back horrible memories of his first sea voyage, when he'd almost died of thirst. He drank again, and the tiredness that had been creeping up on him began to drain away.

'The snow-leopard called down from the mountains to his love,' the elder intoned, 'but it was too late. By then . . .'

Terrel found his attention wandering. The White Moon was no longer visible from where he sat, and the scene before him was illuminated solely by the red glow of the dying fires. It made the night seem warmer than it was. Swallowing the last of the water, Terrel set the cup down on the ground next to a stone the size of his fist. A moment later the stone uncoiled, and slithered away in a fast zigzag motion.

Terrel was so astonished that he didn't even think to cry out. He knew he ought to warn others about the snake, but he seemed unable to make his tongue work. The strange thing was that none of the nomads seemed to have noticed the creature as it sped past.

'Each grey ring is a mark of the smoke from that fire, and these marks have remained on the soft fur of the snow-leopard from that day to this,' the old man concluded.

The applause that followed sounded hollow in Terrel's ears, and he wanted to laugh without knowing why. The flames of the nearest fire had grown brighter, but they looked odd somehow, as if they were burning too slowly.

He was thirsty again and glanced down at the cup, only to find that it was now lying on its side and the last few drops of liquid had spilled out on to the sand. He couldn't remember knocking it over. Then he noticed that the side of the goblet was decorated with a familiar sign. It shone gold against the iron grey, and reminded Terrel of the eye that had been painted on Zahir's forehead. He stared, wondering why he had not noticed it earlier. It was beautiful. Like the eye of a snow-leopard. He had no idea where that thought had come from, but it seemed a perfect description.

The eye blinked.

Terrel blinked himself, then stared again, wondering

for the first time what was going on. He felt warm, but far away – in another world – a sliver of ice was forming in his heart.

Looking round, he saw a blur of faces, but couldn't recognize any of them. A hand reached out of nowhere and the cup vanished. The world began to spin as Terrel felt himself fading away.

Hello, brother, said a voice that Terrel knew only too well. *This is a surprise. I thought you'd left me for good.*

CHAPTER TWELVE

When Terrel woke up, his head was pounding as if the Toma's drummers had taken up residence inside his skull. Pain was nothing new to him, but the nausea that accompanied the headache made him feel dreadful, and he lay where he was, making no attempt to move. He tried to open his eyes, but the glare of the sun directly above him was far too bright, sending burning needles into his brain, so he quickly abandoned that idea. But although getting up was clearly out of the question – even thought was difficult – some of his senses were still working.

He was lying on his back, which felt cold and clammy, while his face and chest were comfortably warm in the sun's rays. He could hear a rustling in the breeze and, further away, several voices, though he couldn't make out what they were saying. There was an unfamiliar smell in the air. If the idea had not been so ridiculous, he would have said it was a mixture of damp earth and

flowers. Intrigued, he tried to open his eyes again, but
without success. The pounding in his temples grew
worse and he groaned, finding that his tongue was
swollen and his lips felt numb. The noise that emerged
was no more than a croak, but it was enough to draw
someone's attention.

'Are you awake?'

'I'm not even sure I'm alive,' Terrel replied, but the
words came out as a broken – and probably unintelligible
– hissing sound.

Mlicki laughed, which seemed grotesquely unfair to
Terrel. There was nothing funny about his plight. A
moment later he felt water trickling on to his lips and he
opened them, accepting the drink gratefully.

'Better?'

'A bit. Thanks.'

Finally Terrel was able to raise his good arm and shade
his face, so that he could open his eyes a little. What he
saw made him think he was dreaming and, in spite of the
swirling discomfort in his head, he forced himself to sit
up to get a better look. The entire valley floor around the
well of Chlendi was carpeted with an incredible array of
brilliantly-coloured flowers. There were swathes of red,
pink, yellow and purple, and each bloom was surrounded
by lush green foliage. The desert floor was a riot of
verdant growth where previously there had been only
sand and arid rock.

Terrel was thunderstruck by this astonishing sight, and
for a while he could only stare in disbelief, but other
details gradually began to register in his beleaguered
mind. Although he had no memory of how he'd got there,
he found that he was lying on a woven mat in the midst

of this fragrant profusion of colours. Both the mat and
his clothes were steaming gently in the sun. Nearby,
Vilheyuna lay unmoving on another rug. Further away,
Terrel could see several nomads moving among the
plants, apparently collecting various petals and leaves.
Beyond that, camels and people were milling about, but
he could see no sign of the camp. Even the contours of
the valley seemed different. Bewildered, he looked back
to Mlicki, who was kneeling beside him.

'What happened?'

'You don't remember?' The nomad's strange face was
alight with excitement.

'No.'

Mlicki nodded, his expression becoming thoughtful.
He offered the water bottle to Terrel, who drank gratefully.

'If you'd told us it was coming, we'd have been better
prepared.'

'Told you what was coming?'

'The rain, of course.'

Terrel's blank look convinced Mlicki that he needed
to explain further.

'It's amazing. I mean, look at all this!' He waved an
arm at their transformed surroundings. 'It's just that it
was all so sudden. When the storm broke, the rain just
poured down. No one's ever seen anything like it, especially this late in the year, and I've never heard thunder
that loud. But the ground was too dry to absorb so much
life all at once, so there were several flash floods. We had
to abandon camp and move as much as possible to higher
ground. Some of the tents were damaged, and a few people
were injured, but no one was drowned, thank the winds.'

'Drowned!' Terrel exclaimed. 'There was that much water?' He was still finding it hard to come to terms with what he was hearing.

'Oh, yes,' Mlicki confirmed. 'But we were lucky. We were even able to get Vilheyuna to safety before his tent was washed away. And now everything's wonderful. The well's overflowing. We've filled every container we could find, and these plants will replenish our stocks of herbs and essences for a year or more.' He plucked a succulent leaf from a nearby growth and held it to his nose. 'We have a lot to thank you for.'

'You think I . . . ?' A horrible suspicion germinated in Terrel's mind, as the implications of what his friend was saying finally sank in.

'The most amazing part is, I knew what you were trying to do,' Mlicki went on, appearing not to notice Terrel's confusion.

That's more than I did, Terrel thought.

'You didn't *say* anything,' Mlicki added. 'Even in here.' He tapped the side of his head. 'But I just knew.'

'How?'

'I'm not sure. I just did what you told me.'

'What was that?'

'You really don't remember?'

'I don't remember anything between drinking the water last night and waking up just now.'

'It was more than water,' Mlicki said.

With those words Terrel's suspicions turned to unpleasant certainty.

'Qard,' he whispered.

Mlicki nodded.

'It seems that either Nadur or another of Zahir's

captains had the brilliant idea of squeezing some juice from the leaves and putting it in your cup.'

'Moons!' Terrel muttered. 'How could I have been so stupid?'

'It was a nasty trick,' Mlicki said, 'and they're in a lot of trouble – but it worked, didn't it!'

'How do you mean?'

'You really were the voice of rain.'

Not me, Terrel thought. It wasn't me. 'Tell me exactly what happened,' he said.

'Well . . .' Mlicki hesitated as he collected his thoughts. He had clearly not been expecting such a request. 'Raheb had just finished his story about the snow-leopard when you reached out and knocked the cup over. I picked it up – that's when I smelt the qard – but you'd got to your feet by then. People were looking at you, thinking you were going to tell another tale. That's not normally allowed, but I think they would've made an exception in your case. But you didn't say anything, just looked around as if you hadn't seen any of us before. Then you walked over to the fire where they'd put the mutton bones and looked down at that. No one else knew quite what to do at that point, but I followed you.'

'Because I told you to?'

'Yes. You wanted one of the bones, so I got it for you. I burnt my hand, but it was worth it.'

Terrel looked in horror at the hand Mlicki was holding up. There were blistered weals across the palm and the fingers. How could his friend have believed he wanted him to injure himself in that way?

'Everyone thought you were going to read the cracks and see beyond the winds,' Mlicki went on, 'but you just looked at it. You didn't say anything. By then someone had brought some water to cool the bone, and you picked it up. But instead of studying it, you threw it up into the sky. That's when the thunder started.'

'Are you recovered?'

Terrel and Algardi were alone in the elder's tent, which was one of the first to have been dried out and re-erected well away from the ravines gouged out by the floods. Without the usual family bustle it seemed huge, like a man-made cavern.

'I'm well enough,' Terrel lied. His headache had receded a little, but he still felt weak and shivery.

'I'm afraid that after you collapsed we had little time for niceties,' Algardi said. 'In our haste we may have handled you roughly.'

'Better that than letting me drown.'

The old man looked surprised at this, then nodded.

'Life should not bring death,' he commented. 'Especially to the voice of rain.'

'I'm not sure I deserve that title.'

'Everybody saw what you did.'

'But I don't remember any of it.'

'Qard has that effect sometimes. Your memories will return.'

I doubt it, Terrel thought ruefully. His greatest fear now was that having been confirmed as the voice of rain in the eyes of the Toma, he might be expected to produce a repeat performance the next time water was desperately needed. Even in such circumstances, he had no intention of doing so – but he couldn't tell the nomads why.

They talked for a while about the events of the night, but when it became clear that Terrel knew nothing other than what Mlicki had told him, Algardi's questions took an unexpected turn.

'Do you know someone called Elam?'

Terrel's surprise was so great that the elder must have seen the answer on his face even as he hesitated.

'I used to,' he said eventually.

'In your homeland?' Algardi queried, obviously hoping to prompt further clarification.

'He was my friend. But he's dead now.'

Algardi nodded, as if this explanation made sense to him.

'And do you want his spirit to stop following you?' he suggested.

'No!' Terrel exclaimed, without thinking. 'What makes you say that?'

'You were shouting during the storm,' the elder told him. 'It was in a language none of us could understand, but you sounded very angry, and kept waving your arms as if you were trying to ward off an invisible foe. The name was the only thing I could pick out.'

That gave Terrel a new set of ideas to worry over, none of which made much sense as yet.

'Do you remember anything I said?' he asked. 'Anything at all? It could be important.'

Algardi thought for a while before answering.

'No. I'm sorry. As I said, you spoke in a strange tongue. And I had a lot on my mind at the time,' he added dryly.

Terrel was disappointed, but recognized the validity of the elder's answer. They sat in silence for a few moments, each lost in their own thoughts.

'If you feel up to it, there are a few people who were injured in the flooding,' Algardi said eventually. 'Your healing skills would be appreciated.'

'Of course.' Terrel had already done his best to ease the pain of Mlicki's burns which, unlike Kalkara's, had been entirely real. 'I'll get started straight away.'

'Before you do,' Algardi said quickly, 'there's another matter I wish to deal with.'

What now? Terrel wondered. The elder's voice had become stern and businesslike.

Algardi turned away and called out.

'Bring them in!'

The tent flap opened and Zahir and his three captains trooped in, all except their leader looking fearful and ashamed. Each of them glanced at Terrel, then quickly looked away. Only Zahir was able to meet his gaze for more than a moment, his face an expressionless mask.

'Qard is sacred,' Algardi stated bluntly. 'Its misuse, in any way, is not merely misguided but inexcusable. To claim that this was a joke only brings dishonour upon all of us, especially as this so-called joke was directed against a guest of our clan.'

The four miscreants remained silent, their eyes downcast, squirming under the impact of the elder's words. Terrel began to feel sorry for them.

'That my own son should be involved is a matter for shame,' Algardi went on, turning back to Terrel. 'I beg for your forgiveness on behalf of my family and of all our tribe.'

Terrel could have pointed out that Zahir had been busy telling his own story at the time, and so could not have been actively involved in the prank, but he sensed that Algardi was in no mood to accept excuses.

'I don't know who conceived this reprehensible plan,' Algardi went on, 'nor who carried it out, but these four do not act alone. They all share the responsibility, and all owe you an apology.'

Terrel was about to declare that he neither wanted nor needed any such thing, but he was forestalled by Zahir, who looked up to face him squarely and spoke without hesitation.

'I apologize for my thoughtless actions, and offer whatever recompense you think fit.' Zahir's pride was still there in his voice, but it was tempered with true regret – through Terrel couldn't tell whether this was genuine remorse or simply that Zahir resented having to utter such a demeaning statement.

After that Nadur and Marrad took their turns, repeating their leader's words in quieter, less formal tones. Finally, Redin, the youngest of the four, did the same, adding 'I'm sorry' at the end. He seemed close to tears.

When they had finished, Algardi looked at Terrel, as if expecting some response.

'From what I've been told,' he began awkwardly, 'no great damage has been done, and some good may even have come from this. I want no recompense.'

'Then we remain in your debt,' Zahir replied, while the others simply looked relieved.

'Your generosity does you credit,' Algardi said.

'I would like us to be friends,' Terrel added on impulse. The fact that the four had stuck together and had not tried to divert blame on to one another was to their credit.

Redin smiled briefly at this offer, but there was no reaction from the other three.

'Leave us,' Algardi commanded them. 'You have much work to do before you earn *my* forgiveness.'

Soon after this, various members of Algardi's extended family began returning to their home. One of the first to arrive was Ghadira. She brought Terrel a bowl of fresh milk, which he accepted gratefully.

'It's just milk,' she told him, smiling. 'Nothing extra in it this time.'

'Good,' he replied, drinking some of the frothy liquid.

'Mind you,' she said quietly, 'I think you should have qard more often.'

'Why? Because of the rain?'

'That, and other things,' she said mysteriously, and went away again, leaving Terrel free to tend to the first of the injured nomads who were now being brought to see him.

Even though he had much to think about, Ghadira's words had an unsettling effect on Terrel, and he couldn't put them out of his mind. When he next had the opportunity of a private conversation with the girl, he took his chance.

'What other things?'

'You don't remember?' she replied. 'That's not very flattering, you know.'

'Did something happen? Between us?' he asked, wondering how many more complications the events of the previous night would bring.

'Nothing happened between us,' she told him, her smile restored, 'but it wasn't for the want of trying on your part.'

'I'm sorry.' Terrel felt horribly embarrassed, but he

had no way of explaining what had happened.

'I'm not,' she said, grinning. Ghadira was clearly not at all embarrassed. She seemed to be enjoying the situation.

'You haven't . . .' He hesitated, feeling even more awkward.

'Told anyone?' she guessed. 'No. It'll be our secret.' Fluttering her eyelashes in exaggerated fashion, she left him alone once more.

It was early evening by the time Terrel was at last given the chance to think in peace, so that he could put everything that had happened into perspective. He knew now that the qard had so unhinged his brain that it had allowed Jax to take over, and he was still disgusted with himself for letting that happen. Once Jax had taken control of Terrel's body, he had amused himself – as he always did – and the fact that he was a weather-mage had enabled him to initiate the rain storm. The ironic thing was that, on this occasion, the prince's destructive impulse had actually brought a positive result. The benefits of the rain had outweighed the inconveniences, and in spite of the dangers posed by the flooding, the nomads were genuinely grateful for what had happened. What was more, Terrel's status within the community had risen as a result – which was something his twin would never have intended. By itself this would have been almost laughable, but there were several aspects of Jax's intervention that were anything but funny.

Terrel quickly realized that the prince's ideas were limited by the weather of the Floating Islands – hence the rain. However, if he ever discovered the potential weapons at his disposal in Misrah's climate, the results did not bear thinking about. The prospect of him directing the fury of a sandstorm made Terrel shudder.

His other main concern was what had happened to Mlicki. Jax was also an enchanter, and as such was able to direct susceptible minds for his own ends – even to the point of his victim committing suicide or murder. In the past this had only applied to people he'd come into direct contact with, but if he was able to do the same thing when inhabiting Terrel's body, the implications were horrifying. More specifically, if Mlicki was one of those vulnerable minds – and Terrel could think of no other reason why the boy would have picked up the scalding hot bone – then the consequences of any future contact could be disastrous. It was another reason for Terrel to be determined that such a lapse would never occur again.

Fortunately, it seemed that Ghadira's defences were stronger than Mlicki's. Whatever Jax had tried to do – and given his previous exploits it didn't take much imagination to guess what that was – she had had the physical and mental strength to reject his advances. The most confusing thing about her subsequent reaction was that Jax's attentions seemed not to have been entirely unwelcome.

Not wanting to dwell on that point, Terrel turned his thoughts to what was perhaps the most mystifying element of what he'd been told. A long time ago, Elam had said that he would keep an eye on Jax. As a ghost he was able to do that while remaining undetected, but from what Algardi had said, the prince appeared not only to have been aware of him but to have been actively annoyed by his presence. That reminded Terrel of his time in the fog-bound valley in Macul, where neither Alyssa nor the ghosts could reach him. On that occasion the remote contact had been in a dream – one that Jax had invaded – but Elam had still been able to use it to pass on a message, albeit in somewhat cryptic form. However, it seemed that this time – if Elam had been trying to do the same again – Terrel's consciousness had been entirely absent, and no one around him had been able to understand what had been said. That in itself was frustrating, but worse still was the thought that if Elam was desperate enough to attempt such a means of communication, it meant he'd had no other option. Which implied that Terrel was unlikely to see the ghosts – or Alyssa – any time soon.

On that discouraging note, Terrel fell to brooding about his brother. Jax had been the bane of Terrel's life since before their birth. His twin had crippled him while they were still in their mother's womb and, in spite of the fact that they had never met face to face, Jax had dogged his footsteps ever since. In one sense – a sense that Terrel did not want to think about – they formed a team, and whether he liked it or not, their fates were inextricably linked. It seemed unlikely that Terrel would ever be free of his brother's malign influence.

'You know,' Mlicki said, 'if you think about it, the story about Y-Harah doesn't make much sense.'

Terrel nodded. He had come to much the same conclusion. 'I know. Zayla was supposed to have found the tale carved into the stones of the city, but according to Medrano, the city had already been destroyed, and then buried! So how *could* it have been carved into the stones?'

'And even if it was,' Mlicki added, 'how could Zayla have found them?'

The two friends were sitting in Vilheyuna's restored tent. Kalkara was already asleep in her corner, exhausted after the night's excitements and a day picking flowers. Terrel was tired too, and his brain was already over-loaded before he'd begun to consider the strange parallels between Y-Harah and Tindaya. Other elements of the story had also featured in the Code – eclipses, earthquakes, a hero born at a lunar confluence – and Terrel would have liked to discuss it with the seers. But there seemed little chance of that. He would just have to try to work it out for himself – when he felt strong enough.

'Y-Harah doesn't even sound as if it was all that evil,' Mlicki remarked. 'I mean, Hargeysa was obviously vicious and bigoted, but most of his people seemed to do all right. There are worse leaders around today. I don't see why Zorn was so keen to destroy the place.'

'Me neither,' Terrel agreed. 'Did it really deserve to be annihilated like that?'

'Still, it makes a good tale, I suppose,' Mlicki commented. 'Though I preferred yours. At least that made sense.'

'It's just a story,' Terrel said, not really wanting to discuss it any more.

'I'd like to see one of those Ancients.'

I'm not sure you would, Terrel thought, but he was saved from having to respond by a voice from outside the tent.

'Come and look at this,' Medrano said when they had answered his summons.

'What?' Mlicki asked.

'You'll see.'

The artist led them back to where the tribe had been camped before the storm. Most of the central area, where the moon mosaics had been, had been washed away by the flood waters, leaving the surface of the valley deeply rutted and uneven. However, a small portion had escaped unscathed, and it was to this area that Medrano was heading.

The slender crescent of the Dark Moon was undisturbed, but that was not all. The rest of the circle was now complete, but the stones that had been used to fill it were not black. These crystals made up a rainbow array of colours, arranged in a swirling pattern that seemed to move about as they looked at it. It was as though the pebbles themselves were alive, shifting with each flicker of light from Medrano's torch.

'I only came across it by chance. Amazing, isn't it?'

'It's beautiful,' Mlicki breathed.

'No one saw anything, or knows who did it,' the artist told them. 'Or at least they won't admit as much to me.'

'You mean it wasn't you?' Mlicki said in surprise.

'Me? No. It's a mystery. I haven't a clue what it means, but I'd like to meet whoever did it. Do either of you have any ideas?'

Mlicki shook his head. If, like Terrel, he had a suspicion of who might have been involved, he was keeping it to himself.

'It wasn't me,' Terrel said. He knew that Jax would never have had the time or the patience for such an undertaking.

'It'll just have to stay a mystery then,' Medrano said.

Looking at the fanciful representation of his moon, Terrel found himself thinking that perhaps the most important question was not *who* had created it, but *why*.

CHAPTER THIRTEEN

'As I see it, the most important consideration is not who is going to be our champion, but whether we should even be going to Qomish in the first place,' Raheb stated.

'That's a bit extreme, isn't it?' another elder said, giving voice to the general surprise.

'I don't think so.' Raheb looked round the gathering with a belligerent air. 'What exactly is the point? All that effort for the chance of one day's bragging? Our resources would be better used in trying to help ourselves in more practical ways.'

'You think honour and glory are worthless?' one of the younger men asked. 'Does tradition count for nothing?'

Raheb bridled at the impertinence of this suggestion, and Algardi intervened quickly before the argument could become personal.

'Raheb's sense of honour is not in question,' he declared, 'and in times of change even traditional values are not above scrutiny.' This was the first time the Toma's most revered elder had spoken in the debate, and his comment gave the other nomads pause for thought. Both Raheb and his young accuser remained silent.

'If we don't go to Qomish, we'll miss out on hearing the latest news,' Bubaqra pointed out. 'Surely we can't afford to do that, even if we've no intention of entering the race this year.'

Women rarely spoke during the clan's discussions, but this was usually because of their own reticence rather than any disregard for their views. And everyone recognized that Bubaqra had made a valid point.

'Trust a woman not to want to miss the chance of some gossip,' Raheb remarked, but he was smiling as he spoke and the matriarch did not take offence.

'I seem to remember several of you men talking the hump off a camel last year,' she said, glancing at Raheb. 'If it hadn't been for all the mint tea you drank, you'd have lost your voice altogether.'

This exchange defused some of the tension that had been building up, and the ensuing banter lightened the mood still further. Terrel was as relieved about this as anyone. To him, the Toma were like an enormous family, and conflict within any such group distressed him.

He had been watching and listening from his position at the edge of the gathering and, although he didn't understand everything that was going on, it was obvious that these proceedings were very important. He had seen various groups of elders meet before – and ask the advice of others – but this was the first time the entire clan had come together to exchange views, which was a clear indication of just how significant the decisions they were there to make would be. It was also evidence that the Toma relied upon consensus, rather than the views of any one man or faction, in planning their future.

Terrel had been aware that the debate was imminent, but because he already had so much to think about, he'd paid little attention to the topics that were to be under discussion. He knew that the timing had been hastened by Zahir's brash declaration on the night of his kapparatan, but it was only when the meeting had actually begun that he tried to make sense of what was being said.

'It's true that the Festival of the Winds is not just about the race,' Algardi observed, bringing the group back to the matter in hand. 'Knowledge is always valuable.'

'It can be dangerous too,' someone put in.

'That's right,' Raheb agreed. 'With everything that's happened recently in Misrah, there are bound to be disputes and feuds. We're a small tribe. We can't afford to take sides.'

'Even if one side is clearly in the right?' Bubaqra queried mildly.

'Would being right be enough for you if it led to your sons being killed?' he replied.

'You're surely not suggesting that any of the tribes would break the ukasa?' Algardi said.

'Probably not,' Raheb admitted, 'but who's to say violence won't occur *outside* the oasis?'

'Raheb's right,' a young man said. 'Ever since the river disappeared, there's been madness everywhere. Look at the Shiban. And they're not the only tribe that's ruled by a warlord now. Life's never been more scarce – and even Qomish may not be immune to such a threat.'

The idea that even the greatest of all the desert oases

might be affected by drought silenced the nomads for a few moments.

'I don't see that we have any choice but to go to Qomish,' Medrano said eventually.

'Even with all the dangers we face?' Raheb asked.

'The Toma have never fled from danger—'

'I never—' the elder began, in outrage.

'Nor do I think that is what you're suggesting,' Medrano responded quickly, holding up his hands in a placatory gesture. 'My point is we can't afford to avoid any possible conflict. Apart from the fact that not going would cut us off from the flow of news, leaving us ignorant, we have a duty to do what we can to ensure that the ukasa is not broken. If that pact is set aside, then chaos beckons. Ours is a voice of reason, and deserves to be heard before it comes to that.'

There were murmurs of agreement from all around, and even Raheb did not argue the point.

'Perhaps we can't afford to take sides in a dispute between larger tribes,' the artist went on, 'but we may have a role to play even so. There is honour in acting as peacemaker.'

'Only if the warring parties are willing to listen to reason,' Raheb's young ally pointed out.

'That's true,' Medrano responded, 'but even if they do not, we will at least have tried.'

'This is all a matter of speculation,' Algardi said. 'We can't tell what will happen at the festival. Not even the winds can show us that.'

'But we'll never know, if we don't go,' Medrano replied. 'That's the point I've been trying to make. And what about trade? Where else but at Qomish are we likely to get value for our wool? Where else will we obtain what we cannot make for ourselves?'

'For an artist you have a remarkably practical turn of mind,' Raheb commented with grudging admiration.

'I may not require much to follow my calling,' Medrano answered, 'but I still have to eat. None of us can live on sand and stones, and my work is pointless unless there is someone to appreciate it. We need to trade.'

Terrel had seen the bales of wool that Medrano was referring to. As the worst of the cold weather came to an end, the camels shed their winter coats and, after the nomads had used what was needed for their own purposes, anything left over was carefully gathered.

'There are other markets,' someone said.

'Agreed,' Medrano responded. 'But are there any where we have such a good chance of receiving a fair trade? It's already been pointed out that these are uncertain times. We don't know what we'll find elsewhere. The very size of the gathering at Qomish will give us the chance to barter properly.'

Terrel knew that the nomads prided themselves on driving a hard bargain. He'd already witnessed them in action on several occasions, and Medrano's argument had the advantage of challenging their trading skills. The artist's intervention had changed the mood in the camp, and it was soon obvious that the first of the tribe's decisions had been made. No formal vote was taken, but when Algardi put the general feeling into words, no one raised any objections.

'So, we go to Qomish. The next question is whether we take part in the race.'

This statement provoked some voluble arguments, and

for some time the debate descended into chaos. Terrel could make neither head nor tail of what was being said and now, more than ever, he was frustrated by his own ignorance. Just what *was* this race? Zahir had called it 'the Race of Truth', but that meant nothing to Terrel. He was still looking round for someone he could ask when Algardi managed to bring the discussion under control once more.

'You'll all get your chance to speak,' he said, as silence fell at last, 'but to make a wise decision we must also listen. Raheb?'

Raheb nodded to his fellow elder, then addressed the clan as a whole.

'I ask again, what would be the point? We will go to Qomish in search of news and trade, but to do more is to risk much to no purpose. Even if we were to win – and let me remind you, we haven't done so in more than a decade – what do we gain? We can brag of our success for the next year. But we are the Toma! We don't need to win a race to know we're the best of the desert travellers. And one of the reasons for us being the best is because we know when *not* to attempt a foolish journey. The Binhemma-Ghar does not forgive fools. It will be drier and even more forbidding than ever this year. Not even Zorn himself would be keen to venture there now. Many men and camels could be lost. Do we want ours to be among them?'

There was some subdued muttering at this, and Terrel could see Zahir biting his tongue, but no one spoke up.

'Thirty-five years ago,' Raheb went on, 'I was in Algardi's party when he was the first to reach the summit of Makranash, and I rejoiced in his victory as much as any man, but those were simpler, less violent days. Times have changed, and even if our champion did become King of the Desert for one day, what would that really mean? The homage the others tribes would pay him would be no more than an empty ritual duty. It means nothing. And the king's decrees are equally worthless. In the face of Misrah's problems, the whole thing is a trivial waste of time and resources.'

'But what if for once the king's decrees did *not* deal with trivial matters?' Zahir asked. The question burst from his lips as though he was physically unable to remain quiet any longer. The assembly reacted with surprise and disapproval. Several elders, including his own father, frowned at his words.

'The winds would never allow such a blatant disregard of the spirit of the race,' Raheb answered. 'And such misuse of the day's power would bring down the wrath of the other tribes.'

'If you *wanted* the ukasa to be broken,' another elder added, 'that would be as good a way of going about it as any other.'

'But—'

'Be advised in this, Zahir,' Algardi said firmly, cutting off his son's objection. The old man stared at his youngest heir as if daring him to continue, and Zahir bowed his head in submission. The message implicit in his father's warning was that if the young man still harboured any hopes of being chosen as the Toma's champion, then he had better keep his mouth shut.

Once again it was Medrano who chose to counter Raheb's argument.

'Aren't we forgetting something?' he said. 'The Race

of Truth has *always* been pointless. It's *always* been dangerous. That's never stopped us before. I too have accompanied a champion into the Binhemma-Ghar, and although I've never been part of a successful team, as Raheb was, I have felt the wonder and the worth of challenging that fearful place. Is it not true that in dark times we have an even greater need of heroes and heroic deeds? Such things inspire us. Glory – even *trivial* glory – cannot be set aside so easily. I for one would gladly risk my life on such an enterprise.'

The artist's heartfelt declaration clearly struck a chord with many of the nomads, and several voices were raised in his support. Others remained more sceptical, and waited for Raheb's response.

'Your passion is admirable,' the elder said respectfully. 'I just hope it's not misplaced.'

Most people expected him to say more, but the old man fell silent, and Terrel could see the memories behind his eyes. In spite of everything that had gone before, Medrano's words had obviously touched him.

'What do you say, Andriyet?' Algardi ventured. 'You were the last to plant the Toma's banner on the mountaintop. Are those days gone for ever?'

Of all the Toma, Andriyet was the last person Terrel would have picked as a successful champion. The nomad's legs were bent, and his face wore a permanent scowl. Terrel had been able to ease his pain on occasions, but the injuries were so old that there was not much more he could do. The idea that Andriyet could have won any sort of race seemed absurd. You of all people should know better than to judge by appearances, Terrel berated himself, as Andriyet struggled to his feet.

'I hope not,' the nomad said gruffly. He'd looked surprised at having been brought into the debate, but now a new determination seemed to settle upon him. 'You don't ever forget an adventure like that. It wasn't just me. It was all of us. Together. I could tell you of the efforts of every man who came with me. That we won was a great joke of the winds, but I wouldn't exchange the memories of what we went through for anything. If that wind-blasted camel hadn't fallen on my legs a few years back, I'd be the first to volunteer to go with our champion this time.' Having said all he had to say, Andriyet say down abruptly and lowered his head so that his face was hidden. His wife put a consoling arm around his shoulders as a thoughtful silence descended on the meeting.

Having weighed up the new mood of the clan, Algardi glanced at Raheb, who nodded, conceding defeat.

'Do we race?' Algardi asked quietly.

'We race,' Raheb confirmed.

Terrel found Medrano looking out over the expanse of shrivelled brown remains that covered the valley floor. Now that the weather had returned to normal, the flowers had faded almost as quickly as they had arrived; only the memories of their scents and colours were still fresh. Terrel had been told how the desert could bloom, how seeds lay dormant – sometimes for years – beneath the surface, requiring only a little rain to let them rise in full glory. Even so, had he not seen it with his own eyes he would never have believed the astonishing effect that water could have. It was no wonder the Toma called it life.

'I suppose we'll be moving on now,' Terrel said. The nomads had stayed longer at Chlendi than anticipated.

Medrano nodded, but didn't say anything.

'Tell me about the Race of Truth.'

The artist turned to look at him. There was a melancholy in his gaze that made Terrel think there were sad stories from his past that Medrano had never told.

'What do you want to know?'

'Everything.'

'You don't want much, do you,' Medrano laughed, his smile dispelling his earlier sadness.

'I worked out some things from what was said at the gathering,' Terrel said, 'but there's still a lot I don't know. Like when it was first run, or why a champion needs a team with him, or—'

'All right,' the artist cut in. 'Point taken. No one knows when it was first run, but it was hundreds, perhaps thousands of years ago.'

'And it's happened every year in all that time?'

'In one form or another, yes. It's said that one year Zorn himself returned to take part.'

'Did he win?'

'No. He disappeared, along with the whole of his team, and they were never seen again.'

'Odd thing to happen to a hero,' Terrel commented.

'Yes, isn't it? But myths are like that. You have to look beneath the surface for any vestiges of truth.' Medrano fell silent again, and Terrel had to prompt him into continuing.

'The race goes from Qomish to Makranash, which is in the Binhemma-Ghar?'

'Yes.'

'How far is that?'

'About twenty days' march.'

'What!'

'You really don't know much, do you?' Medrano observed, then decided to give Terrel the information he wanted. 'The Race of Truth is a trial of strength and stamina, but mostly of willpower. Stubbornness, some would say. It begins at the mid-season full of the White Moon each summer, when the weather can be so hot you don't need a fire to cook your food, so it's not something to be undertaken lightly. Each tribe enters a champion, to represent their clan and carry the emblem. Every contestant is accompanied by a team of supporters, with camels to carry supplies. These men tend to their champion overnight, when no travelling is permitted, but between sunrise and sunset he must walk alone, unaided and without food or drink. The victor is the first to plant his banner at the summit of Makranash and return with the winner's emblem from the previous year as proof of his achievement.'

Terrel was so astounded by the savage nature of such an ordeal that it took him a few moments to frame his next question.

'The winner has to return to Qomish to claim his prize?'

'Yes. But he can ride on the way back, and drink whenever he wants to – provided his team hasn't run out of life, of course. Then he's proclaimed King of the Desert for one day, and the festival ends for another year.'

Terrel was beginning to see Raheb's point. It did indeed seem like an awful lot of trouble for very little reward.

'And what makes the race so important?'

'The challenge,' Medrano replied. 'History. Faith. Sometimes I think it's only in the pointless things we do that we prove ourselves, find out what it is to be a man. The Race of Truth defines us. It's as much a journey of the spirit as it is of the body.'

Such philosophical musings meant little to Terrel, but he could tell that his companion felt strongly about this.

'Does anyone ever cheat?'

'No!' Medrano looked genuinely shocked by this suggestion. 'No one would ever dare break the code of honour.'

'But who would know if you walked at night, or had a drink during the day?' Terrel persisted.

'A victory gained in such a manner would be worthless,' Medrano replied with steadfast conviction. 'The winds would see what happened, even if no one else did. There is nowhere to hide from them, especially near Makranash.'

'What's so special about this mountain?'

'It's where the winds first came down from the dome,' the artist replied. 'Where all life began, and where it will all return when humanity comes to an end. "Makranash" is an ancient word. Translated literally it means "the holy presence", but that's just a title, really. The mountain's true name is forbidden to men. It lies at the heart of the desert, the centre of the world. It is our place of destiny, but no man may go there except in his quest to win the Race of Truth.'

Medrano's description sounded almost reverent, and Terrel realized that the race was no mere contest. It was, in part, a pilgrimage – an extreme demonstration of faith

– and, as such, it must be surrounded by a degree of fanaticism. The thought of this made him feel uncomfortable.

'Do you think Zahir has a chance to be the Toma's champion this year?'

'If he can keep his tongue in check,' the artist said, 'there's really no other choice. Just don't tell him I said so.'

The gathering had broken up before the tribe had even begun to discuss this possibility. Although Zahir had been visibly disappointed, Terrel had overheard Algardi reassuring his son that there would be time for that later. Now that he knew the race would not take place until mid-summer, Terrel could see the sense in waiting. It would give all the Toma – especially those with misgivings – the chance to accept that they really were going to be a part of the race, and to forget Zahir's rash outburst.

'You said that the champion had to walk unaided,' Terrel added, as another question occurred to him. 'What happens if he gets into trouble during the day?'

'There's nothing his followers can do,' Medrano replied. 'It's not unknown for contestants to collapse and die while their fellow tribesmen can only look on from a distance. The code of honour forbids them to go to his aid before sunset.'

'That's barbaric!' Terrel exclaimed, without thinking.

'That's the meaning of the Race of Truth,' the nomad told him. If he had taken offence at the foreigner's outburst he gave no sign of it. 'The competitors all accept the risks. In fact there are several monuments in the Binhemma-Ghar which have been erected in honour of those who perished in that manner. Whenever a team passes one of these shrines, they always stop to pay their respects. You'll see that for yourself.'

'Me?' Terrel gasped.

'You're a healer,' Medrano told him. 'Vilheyuna can't go, can he? Whoever we choose as our champion, they'd be foolish not to pick you as one of their team.'

CHAPTER FOURTEEN

'Look, Kala, I know it was you. Who else would've done something like that? I'd just like to know *why* you wanted to do it.' Terrel paused, hoping for some reaction, but as was so often the case Kalkara gave no sign of even having heard him, let alone of giving the answers he sought. 'It must have taken you ages to collect all the crystals,' he went on, still watching her out of the corner of his eye. 'And they made a beautiful pattern, all that shimmering light contrasting with the black. The Dark Moon – the Invisible – is important to me. Is it for you too?'

For a moment he thought she nodded, but it was just the rocking motion of their camel, and her expression gave nothing away. The double saddle, which allowed them to sit one on each side of the animal's hump, made travelling easy and secure but not exactly comfortable. Terrel was already looking forward to dismounting and setting up camp for the night. It had been a long day, and although he'd hoped that talking to Kalkara might help him set his own thoughts in order, it had not. Even direct questions had produced no response. If he hadn't known better, he would have thought that the little girl was deaf as well as dumb. She was the most enigmatic person he had ever met.

Several days had passed since the Toma had left Chlendi, and already the sunlight was noticeably warmer, though the nights were still cold. Spring was apparently a short season in Misrah, and it would not be long before the last remnants of winter gave way to the first harbingers of summer. The Festival of the Winds was still four median months away and the nomads had a long way to go before they reached Qomish, but their course was set now. Once the decision had been made, the entire clan – even those who'd had misgivings – behaved as if they were wholly in favour of the plan. The way they worked together, with no recourse to second guessing or furtive dissension, was one of the things Terrel most admired about the Toma. Differences of opinion were aired openly, disagreements settled and then forgotten. In the desert cooperation was vital – the nomads' very survival depended upon it – but that didn't make it any less remarkable in practice.

However, while no doubt existed as to where they were headed, the Toma had still made no move to choose their champion for the race – and no one had said anything to Terrel about becoming a member of the team. In many ways he was glad of that. He'd discovered that it was not only the contestants themselves who sometimes died; whole teams had been lost on occasion. Inexperienced as he was, Terrel could not help but be frightened by the prospect of venturing into the Binhemma-Ghar, and for the time being at least he was prepared to let the future take care of itself. A lot could happen in four months.

Glancing now at Kalkara, he saw that she was smiling at something only she could see, and his frustration at being unable to find out what went on inside her mind welled up again. *Does she ever worry about the future?* he wondered.

Although Terrel normally enjoyed Kala's apparently carefree spirit, and found that talking to her often eased his own anxieties, there were also times when a deep sadness showed in her eyes, and he wondered how happy she really was.

'Do you ever see beyond the winds, Kala?' he asked quietly. The question had only just occurred to him. Was it possible that she shared some of her brother's talent? And if so, did she see into the future or the past?

Kalkara did not react and he was not even sure she had heard him, so he raised his voice for his next question.

'Do you see another time in your dreams?'

This time she did respond – and the startled look she gave him was as eloquent an answer as he could have hoped for.

'Have you ever seen beyond the winds, Terrel?' Mlicki asked as they were preparing to go to sleep that night.

Coming so soon after his one-sided conversation with Kalkara, the question took Terrel by surprise. Mlicki's sister was already asleep, but was it possible that her intuitive link with her brother had allowed her to influence his thoughts?

'I mean, I know you don't go about it in the same way,'

Mlicki added. 'Your winds are different from ours. But prophecy is possible, don't you think? Under the right conditions?'

'I suppose it is,' Terrel replied. 'The seers in my home-land certainly think so.'

'But have *you* ever done it?'

Terrel thought about it.

'Not really,' he said eventually. It was a half-truth, but he didn't feel capable of explaining about all the premon-itory dreams he'd had in Macul. Those dreams had shown him certain phases of all four moons, which had allowed him to foresee the date of the earthquake in Talazoria. But they had been more of a warning than a prophecy – a *possible* future, and one he'd been able to avert. 'Augury is not an exact science,' he added, quoting one of the seers' favourite axioms.

'It's difficult to see how the future could be fixed,' Mlicki said, 'when there are so many different things we could do tomorrow, let alone next month.'

'That's right. And anything you see is open to mis-interpretation,' Terrel agreed, recalling another dream. 'I had a vision once where I saw the Dark Moon's surface covered with diamond-bright swirls. That was a mad idea, but it might just have meant I was going to see the mosaic back at Chlendi.'

'That sort of thing's happened to me too,' Mlicki said, but Terrel had been distracted by his own thoughts.

There'd been another time when he'd seen beyond the winds, something he'd forgotten until now. On that occasion it had been a genuine vision rather than a dream, which somehow made it more ominous. In it Terrel had been transported to the summit of Mount Tindaya, where two worlds – or two times – had been superimposed upon each other. And he had seen the moment of his own death.

Remembering that eerie sensation again now, Terrel had to struggle to keep from becoming completely disorientated, and it took a considerable effort for him to recognize that Mlicki was still speaking – and to make himself listen to what his friend was saying.

'On the other hand, there have been some things I've seen that seemed so clear, so definite, that I never had any doubt they would actually happen.'

It took Terrel a long time to fall asleep that night, and before he did, the silence of the desert was shattered briefly by a scream of fear. Someone was having a nightmare – and Terrel knew just how they felt.

The next day brought a sight that made Terrel realize that, no matter how uncomfortable his life became, there would always be others who were infinitely worse off.

The long line of camels had been trudging along for most of the morning when some of the advance scouts returned, and the caravan changed direction for no apparent reason. The first indication of why it had done so came not to Terrel's eyes but to his nose. The rank smell of filth and decay reached him on the sultry breeze that drifted over the line of dunes they were skirting around, and Terrel wondered what could possibly be on the far side. Curiosity made him leave the caravan and climb to the crest of the ridge. It was an arduous ascent, and he almost gave up several times as the sand slid beneath his feet with each step, but when he finally reached the top the view that greeted him knocked what little breath he had left from his lungs.

The encampment in the valley beyond was nothing like the Toma's. It was huge, a sprawling mass of people and makeshift dwellings. Terrel was too far away to make out much detail, but it was clear that none of the tents was sound – most were little more than a collection of rags – and the huddled groups of men and women didn't appear to be doing anything. Even if the awful stink that permeated the air was set aside, the place still had an atmosphere of listless despair.

'What are you doing?'

The breathless voice behind Terrel sounded both anxious and indignant. Turning round, he was surprised to see Marrad, one of Zahir's captains. Not far behind him were Nadur and Zahir himself.

'Get down!' Marrad shouted, waving as he struggled up the slope. 'They'll see you.'

Terrel stood where he was, looking back and forth between the camp and his pursuers. When Marrad finally came up beside him, he grabbed Terrel's arm and tried to pull him to the ground. Terrel shook him off angrily, and the boy thought better of trying anything more until Zahir arrived.

'Who are they?' Terrel asked.

'The unclean. Can't you tell?'

'But what are they doing here?'

By then Zahir and Nadur had joined them, and it was the boys' leader who repeated Marrad's warning.

'You should stay out of sight.'

'Why?'

'They'll attack anyone for a few scraps of food, or for

the clothes you're wearing. The unclean will steal anything. They have no honour.'

'Why do you think the caravan was diverted?' Nadur added. 'You're putting us all in danger.'

'These people are no danger to us,' Terrel said. Even from a distance he'd seen enough to know that was true.

'You can't be sure of that.'

'My father sent us to bring you back,' Zahir said.

'Would you drag me back against my will?'

'The safety of my tribe is more important than your will.'

'They're quite safe. Even if anyone in the camp has seen me, no one's coming this way. And you're in my debt,' Terrel reminded them. 'At least tell me who these people are.'

'I told you—' Marrad began, but Zahir cut him off.

'They're exiles from the lands of the far north.' He too had decided that there was no immediate threat, and so was prepared to give Terrel the explanation he wanted.

'What are they doing here?'

'There's been war in the north for several years, and many of them have been driven from their homes. The lakes there have been shrinking too, and their crops withering. They've been forced to make their way down here, to take the Road of Hope.'

Terrel had heard that expression before, but it was a few moments before he realized when and where. Kohtala had mentioned it in passing, but in the aftermath of the aborted raid, Terrel had forgotten all about it.

'And that road brings them here?' he queried.

'It used to run all the way to the coastal plain,' Zahir explained. 'In this region it kept just outside the inhabited lands, on either side of the Kullana River, but since its music died the local people are either unwilling or unable to offer any help to outsiders.'

'Why should they?' Marrad commented. 'They've enough problems of their own.'

'And things are getting worse,' Zahir agreed. 'There's war here too now, and these people' – he waved a contemptuous hand towards the camp – 'haven't the strength for a fight. Most of them don't even know the ways of the desert.'

'They can't go on, and they can't go back,' Terrel concluded.

'And if they stay here they'll die,' Nadur added. He at least sounded as though he felt some pity for the refugees.

'Good riddance,' Marrad muttered.

'That's not a very hospitable attitude,' Terrel said.

'There's nothing we can do,' Zahir responded. 'There are too many of them, and their needs are too great. We could give them all our food, slaughter all our camels, and it still wouldn't be enough. It would just condemn the Toma to extinction.'

'They're not even real nomads,' Marrad said, his disgust plain. 'Look at them.'

Terrel looked, and knew he could not leave it at that, in spite of the logic of Zahir's argument.

'We should get back to the caravan,' Nadur said nervously.

'I'm going down there,' Terrel countered.

'No!' Zahir exclaimed.

Terrel stared at him, consciously using the strangeness of his eyes to unnerve his opponent in their battle of wills. The other two would go along with whatever their leader decided. Zahir was the one who mattered.

'You might never get back to the camels,' the elder's son pointed out. 'Do you want to be left behind?'

'I'll take that chance.'

'Why? What can you hope to achieve?'

It was a good question, and one Terrel couldn't really answer.

'I have to see for myself,' he said defiantly.

'You could be killed.'

'Then come with me, as my bodyguards. You said yourself they're no fighters.'

'But there are hundreds of them!' Marrad objected.

'A lot of them are women and children,' Terrel replied pointedly.

'That's—'

'I'll understand if you're afraid, though.'

'I'm not afraid!' Marrad shouted angrily, glaring at Terrel. 'But it's—'

'Enough!' Zahir cut in.

'Come with me,' Terrel repeated. 'As soon as I've seen what I need, we'll go back to the caravan.' With that he turned and set off down the slope without waiting to see whether his appeal had been successful. He was glad when a slithering of sand to either side of him told him that it had.

'If this goes wrong, we'll be in a lot of trouble,' Zahir said quietly as he came alongside.

'I'll take the blame,' Terrel assured him.

'It's not as simple as that. You don't know my father as well as I do.'

For a moment the two young men grinned at each

other, and Terrel felt for the first time that their natural enmity might eventually be overcome. But then all thought of such trivialities was driven from his thoughts.

As they drew closer to the encampment, it was easy to understand why the exiles had come to be called the unclean. The Toma were always meticulous in burying their waste and leaving their campsites in as near a pristine condition as possible. Although the desert was often their enemy, it was also their home, and they treated it with respect. It was clear that these refugees either had no such scruples or lacked the energy to make a similar effort. The entire area was strewn with rubbish, and little attempt had been made to dig even rudimentary latrines. The thin smoke from a few small fires did little to disguise the appalling stench, and clouds of flies swarmed around the pitiful, ragged tents.

But worse by far was the condition of the refugees themselves. Skin was stretched tight over stick-like limbs and cadaverous skulls; bellies were either hollow or unnaturally distended. The older people seemed to have withered away to dry husks, and even the younger adults looked like walking skeletons. The numerous children were more pitiable. They did not seem real to Terrel. They were too thin, too quiet and too fragile to contain a human life. And worst of all was the way each of them looked at the newcomers.

Their eyes were dead, indifferent, beyond even despair. These were people who were already defeated, able to do nothing but wait for death. Terrel knew he had been right; they posed no threat. Their apathy was too deeply ingrained. They watched the strangers' progress without expectation. No one spoke. The only sound in the camp was the buzz of insects; not even the babies had the strength to cry. Whatever optimistic impulse had brought them to this awful place, it was long forgotten. The route they had chosen should have been called the Road of Despair – and it was clear to Terrel that it had only been taken when there was no other choice. It was the last resort of the truly desperate, and now, it seemed, the road led nowhere. Even that forlorn promise was being denied the refugees by circumstances quite beyond their control.

Terrel had thought the stews outside Talazoria were bad, but this was beyond even that nightmarish slum. If he had not known that a simple lack of food was at the heart of the problem, he would have assumed that these people were the victims of some diabolical plague. As it was, he could see that disease would soon claim many lives. He wanted to try to heal them. Every one of his instincts cried out to do something – but there were just too many of them, and their suffering was too great. And their lethargy and despair meant that there was no chance of them healing themselves, even with his guidance.

As Terrel walked among the exiles, Zahir and his captains stayed at his side, looking about warily, their hands on their knives. But they need not have worried. Their presence – and their eventual departure – was accepted with a complete lack of curiosity. As Terrel made his way back up the sand dunes, he felt chastened and sick to his stomach. He knew that he would never be able to forget the empty expressions on the faces of the unclean.

CHAPTER FIFTEEN

Terrel looked down at the black lake, and wondered if he had taken leave of his senses. Not only was the surface of the pool the most unnatural colour he had ever seen, but it was also *moving*. Bulbous mounds rose up like slow, solitary waves, as though some humpbacked creature was rising from the depths only to subside again. Even on the hilltop where Terrel stood there was hardly a breath of wind, and in the valley below the air must have been quite still, so that could not be the cause of the peculiar undulations. Elsewhere, mostly around the edges of the lake, there were patches that reflected the sunlight differently, as though a second, paler liquid was layered over the dark substance. What was more, the smell that rose from the place was like nothing Terrel had encountered before. It reminded him a little of the acrid smoke of the smelting fires at Betancuria, but this had a different, pungent odour that caught at the back of his throat and made him want to gag.

'I don't think I'd want to drink from that lake,' he muttered, 'no matter how thirsty I was.'

'Me neither,' Mlicki said, laughing. 'There's no life there.'

'It's not water?'

'No,' the nomad replied, realizing that his friend was serious. 'You've never seen a tar pit before?'

Terrel shook his head.

'What is it?'

'Tar bubbles up from under the ground,' Mlicki told him. 'No one knows how or why. It's nasty stuff, because it's usually hot enough to take skin from flesh, and it sticks to anything. It makes the air close to it poisonous too.'

'Moons!' Terrel breathed.

The two friends stood and watched as another sluggish wave rose and fell. This time a small plume of smoke was expelled as the bubble subsided, as if the lake were sighing.

'Why would anyone want to build a town near something like this?' Terrel wondered aloud.

'Black tar has its uses,' Mlicki replied. 'You'll see that when we get to Triq Dalam. But they didn't build here because of the lake. They chose this place because there's life here. There's an oasis on the far side of the valley.'

Terrel looked in the direction Mlicki was pointing, and saw a distant patch of green.

'What's the lighter stuff?' he asked, returning his attention to the pool.

'That's neft. When you get clear patches like that it can look like water, but it's not. One spark and it bursts into the fiercest flames you've ever seen. The poets call it walking fire.'

*

As the caravan circled around the southern end of the valley and drew further away from the tar pit, the air grew fresher once more. They were following the line of the ridge, heading north again now, and the town of Triq Dalam was coming into view.

In Vadanis it would have been considered no more than a village, but here it seemed like a city. It was the first permanent settlement Terrel had seen since entering the desert, and the sight of the cluster of mudbrick buildings made him realize why the Toma were excited about the prospect of getting there. Such a community would present a stark contrast to the endless miles of sand dunes and barren rock, and would provide new sights and sounds, opportunities for trade and entertainment, news and gossip. The fact that Triq Dalam was also an oasis promised a few days of relative ease, and the chance to replenish their dwindling reserves after the hardships of the desert. However, when the caravan turned to follow a winding trail down into the valley, Terrel saw that Mlicki was frowning.

'What's the matter?'

'It's not as green as usual for this time of year.'

Compared to the terrain they had passed through in recent days, Terrel thought it looked positively verdant. There were bushes and even a few trees among the houses – the largest growing things he had seen yet in the desert – and on the far side of the settlement he had glimpsed cultivated fields. And, unless it was a mirage, there was also a small lake – a real one, this time – to the west of the town.

'Is that a problem?' he asked, reacting to the worry in his friend's voice.

'It could be,' Mlicki replied. 'Even the lake looks smaller than last year. If they don't have enough life for their own needs, we may not be able to take as much as we want. We haven't had much luck in the last few days, and it's a long way to the next reliable well. Not that *any* of them are particularly reliable these days,' he concluded gloomily.

'Where does the lake come from?' Terrel asked. There was no river or stream anywhere as far as he could see.

'No one really knows for sure,' Mlicki told him. 'Some people say it comes from the ice that lies at the heart of Nydus. Others reckon there are underground rivers that flow all the way to the northern mountains, which only come to the surface at oases like this. But it doesn't really matter where it comes from, does it? As long as there's enough.'

By the time the caravan reached the low ground, they were close enough to Triq Dalam for Terrel to be able to make out individual buildings. The most striking aspect of the town were several curiously shaped towers, which rose far above most of the roofs.

'What are they?'

'Wind-catchers,' Mlicki replied. 'The openings at the top trap the slightest breeze and bring it down to cool the inner chambers. Otherwise they'd be like ovens in the summer.'

'How do they know which way to make them face?'

'They don't. But there are adjustable panels at the top, and they're moved round according to which way the wind is blowing.'

'Clever.'

'It's still not as good as a tent,' Mlicki commented.

Spoken like a true nomad, Terrel thought. He was about to say as much, but then the camel they were walking beside let out the loudest rumbling roar Terrel had ever heard, and began to move a little faster. It was accompanied by several other animals – without any prompting from their herders.

'What's happening?' Terrel asked, caught between amusement and alarm as more beasts gave vent to their uniquely raucous cries.

'They can smell the life,' Mlicki explained.

'But it's on the other side of the town.' The lake had been out of sight for some time.

'They still know it's there.'

'I could do with a drink myself,' Terrel remarked. Most of what little water they had found recently had been brackish, better suited to camels than men.

'Let's hope there's enough to go round,' Mlicki replied as they hastened to match the caravan's new pace.

Shortly after that the head of the procession came to an unexpected halt, and as those behind began to catch up there was soon a milling throng of nomads and animals. Terrel and Mlicki made their way to the front, to try to find out what was going on, and discovered that all was not well. The inhabitants of Triq Dalam had evidently decided to set conditions before offering their usual welcome, and the group who had come out to meet the Toma were now in discussion with Algardi and some of the elders. Terrel was too far away to hear what was being said, but as he moved closer he was able to make out more details of the town. What he saw was unsettling. Although Triq Dalam was not enclosed by a continuous wall, squat towers were set at regular intervals around the perimeter. Judging from their solid construction and narrow slit windows, the towers had been built for defensive purposes. As Terrel watched, he saw several men armed with bows moving about on the upper battlements. Many of the nomads had also become aware of these guards, and the mood among the Toma had swung from anticipation to a mixture of puzzlement and anger.

'But you *know* us,' Algardi was saying, as Terrel eventually came within earshot. 'When have we ever done you harm?'

'There are others whom we once considered friends,' the leader of the town delegation replied. 'They have betrayed us.'

'Are we to be punished for another's crime? Do you doubt the honour of the Toma?'

'These are uncertain times. Even our neighbours can no longer be trusted. Triq Dalam has been attacked by both the Shiban and the wanderers of the Mgarr. When such men are without honour, can you blame us for fearing treachery?'

'We come to trade,' Algardi stated. 'Not to fight or steal.'

'I believe you,' his opposite number admitted. 'But when the safety of my wives and children – and all of my people – is at risk, I owe it to them to be certain.'

'How *can* you be certain, if honour is no longer enough?'

'You will camp over there,' the townsman replied, pointing to a low hillock that the caravan had already passed. 'Where we can see you. If you wish to trade, you will come in separate groups of no more than ten men at a time. And you will come unarmed. Access to the lake for you and your beasts will also be in groups, and for a limited time only. We've learnt a harsh lesson from our own generosity to outsiders, and we won't make that mistake again. The life was already below normal levels, but since the unclean were here, the lake has shrunk even more. We waited too long before driving them off.'

'We are not the unclean!' Algardi declared angrily. 'We will respect the life, as we always do.'

'Those are our conditions,' his adversary said. The man looked uncomfortable, but stuck to his argument. 'Obey them, and our hospitality is yours. We would welcome the chance of honest trade.'

Algardi appeared to be about to say something else, but thought better of it. After a hurried consultation with his fellow elders, he turned back to the townspeople.

'It seems you give us no choice,' he said. 'We will accept your conditions.' The tone of his voice made it clear that, although an agreement had been reached, the Toma felt betrayed and offended.

'Since when do the Toma camp at a site chosen for them by others?' Zahir exclaimed. 'This is an insult.'

'What would you have us do?' Bubaqra enquired, calm in the face of her son's bluster. 'Fight them? That would make us no better than the raiders they fear. Or perhaps you think we should leave without the chance to trade or to benefit from the life here.'

'At least we would leave with dignity.'

'As we will this way,' she replied patiently, 'at a time of our own choosing. We will prove our honour – and gain from our stay.'

'Their *conditions* make us beggars.'

'My son,' Bubaqra told him, 'you have a fierce spirit and a good heart, but you don't yet have the mind to match your father's. Let us hope that such wisdom will come with age.'

Zahir was about to make an angry retort, but he caught the warning look in his mother's eyes and decided against it. Instead he turned on his heels and left the family tent.

'He's just annoyed because he wasn't chosen to go with the others to the town,' Ghadira remarked. 'It's the first chance he's had since he became a man, and he wanted to show off in the market place.'

'Don't be too hard on him,' Bubaqra advised. 'None of us likes what's happened here, and it's his nature—'

'It's his nature to be a sixteen-year-old male,' Ghadira interrupted. As she spoke she turned to look at Terrel, and grinned mischievously.

'I'm seventeen,' he found himself saying, before he had time to think. 'Nearly eighteen.' As soon as the words were out of his mouth he wished them back. He had no idea why he had felt the need to say anything at all.

'That explains a lot,' Ghadira commented.

'Leave Terrel alone,' her grandmother told her. 'Haven't you anything better to do with your time?'

The girl shrugged and walked off, looking distinctly unrepentant.

'Don't mind her,' Bubaqra said fondly. 'She's just as young as Zahir.'

'But not as stupid,' Ghadira remarked over her shoulder in parting.

Terrel was grateful to Bubaqra for intervening, but hated the fact that she had had to. There was something about Ghadira that he found disconcerting. He knew the girl was flirtatious by nature, but he still couldn't believe that she was attracted to him. Which meant she was teasing him. And he found that hard to deal with, especially as he still didn't know exactly what had happened between her and Jax.

'There. That should be fine enough, don't you think?' Bubaqra said, looking at the results of Terrel's latest efforts, and releasing him from his uneasy train of thought.

'I suppose so,' he replied, glancing at the herbs he'd been mixing.

After the nomads had set up camp, Bubaqra had commandeered Terrel's help in making more of her salves and potions, using the remains of the unexpected harvest from Chlendi. This involved grinding roots, seeds, stalks and petals in various combinations and mixing them with oils or boiled water. He had been glad to help – though his clawed hand made wielding a pestle and mortar awkward – not least because his healing had its limitations and he was always keen to learn about alternative treatments.

'This is good for shortness of breath and pains in the chest,' Bubaqra told him as she took the bowl and sniffed its contents.

'Do you really think Zahir is being stupid?' Terrel asked. He'd been an unwilling witness to the earlier argument, and his thoughts returned to it now of their own accord. He couldn't let it go, because he'd felt sympathy for both sides of the dispute.

'A little,' Bubaqra replied. 'I could wish the world was different, but that won't change what is. Sometimes we just have to accept that, however much we dislike the idea.'

'This is going to happen more and more, isn't it?'

'Probably.' She set the bowl aside, realizing that Terrel needed to talk. 'While there are tribes like the Shiban, and with all the unclean where they don't belong . . .' She shrugged.

As always, mention of the exiles brought back disturbing memories. Terrel had spoken to Algardi about them, but the elder had made much the same points as Zahir had done. Even so, Terrel had been unable to dislodge their suffering from his mind, and nor had he been able to accept that there was nothing that could be done to help them. He had tried to tell himself that their plight was none of his concern – he was just an outsider, a mere witness to another example of the world's capacity for hideous cruelty – but the argument didn't work. His compassion had been aroused by the faces of strangers – and the fact that he couldn't do anything about it only made it more painful.

'I hate to think of all those refugees' – he couldn't bring himself to call them unclean – 'being driven out into the desert.'

'What else were they supposed to do?' Bubaqra said. 'If the oasis here dies, so does Triq Dalam and everyone in it. First and foremost, each tribe is responsible for its own people.'

'So we all just leave them to die?' he asked quietly. 'Who *is* responsible for them? They're exiles, like me.'

'But you made your own way. You've taken responsibility for yourself. They must do the same.'

'It's too late for that.'

'The conflicts that are preventing them from reaching the coast are not of our making,' the old woman pointed out. 'The road was never meant to carry so many people.'

Terrel had learnt that, in places, the Road of Hope actually was a paved track, originally built to carry produce from the oases and river farms to and from the coastline. He had even seen part of one such stretch, and had found it hard to comprehend the labour that must have been involved in such a massive undertaking. However, most of the road was now either buried under shifting sands or broken beyond repair.

'How have you avoided being drawn into the wars?' he asked.

'By knowing when and where it's safe to travel, and keeping to ourselves when necessary. For the most part, the places we use aren't worth fighting over, and we have the reputation of breeding fierce warriors, so people leave us alone. But it's getting harder,' she admitted. 'You've seen that, with the Shiban and with what's happened here. Which is another reason why we can't waste our time trying to help the unclean.'

Terrel nodded resignedly. The demands of self-preservation would always override those of simple humanity – and he couldn't blame the Toma for that. Their way of life was already balanced on a knife edge.

'Maybe if the Kullana began to flow again . . .' Bubaqra murmured.

'If the world was different . . .' Terrel added.

They looked at each other for a few moments, knowing that their wishful thinking counted for nothing, then returned to their salves.

A short while later, the tent flap was thrown aside as Zahir returned in a rush.

'Terrel!' he called. 'You're needed in the town.'

'Me? Why?'

'The daughter of one of their elders is sick, and their shamen don't know what to do. Algardi offered to let you treat her.'

Moons, Terrel thought, as the implications of the summons sank in. If I make a mess of this, we'll be more unwelcome than ever. On the other hand, if I *can* heal her, it could really help things.

'Go on,' Bubaqra said. 'This is your chance to make a little difference in the world.'

Terrel nodded, grateful to the matriarch for pushing him into action.

'I'll come with you, show you the way,' Zahir added eagerly.

Terrel saw Bubaqra and Ghadira exchange amused glances as he went out, but then all he could think about was the task ahead.

'What's the matter with the girl?' he asked.

'If they knew that they wouldn't be sending for you, would they?' Zahir answered. Seeing the look of alarm on Terrel's face, he added, 'Don't worry. I'm sure you'll figure it out.'

CHAPTER SIXTEEN

The first thing that struck Terrel about Triq Dalam was the manner of its construction. Many of the buildings had several levels, both above and below ground, which seemed to be used either for habitation or storage at random. However, the one thing the houses all had in common was that they were solidly built. The rough, ochre-coloured bricks were held together with a viscid dark brown substance that Terrel assumed must be tar. Apart from the wind-catcher towers, there were a few odd domed structures, which looked like shrines of some sort, and several water tanks and cisterns. Some of the narrow lanes were even covered with solid roofs, turning them into darkened tunnels, presumably to protect the people below from the summer sun. In all it was a fascinating place, but there was no time to explore. Zahir was leading Terrel through the streets at a rapid pace.

Several locals glanced at the two strangers with suspicion, and some were obviously startled when they saw

Terrel's eyes. He was used to that, but when he heard someone mention crystals, he wondered if his unusual appearance might have a particular significance for the people of Triq Dalam. To his surprise, almost all the adult women in the town had tattoos on their foreheads and chins – white dots and lines in a variety of intricate patterns. He couldn't help wondering whether one of them might be the woman from his dream in Tiscamanita – and whether he would recognize her if he glimpsed her in passing.

As they made their way through one of the tunnels, the air became unusually cold, and Terrel glanced into a doorway where steps led down into darkness. The unnatural chill seemed to emanate from there and he hesitated, wanting to know what it meant.

'They keep blocks of winter ice in the mattamore,' Zahir explained impatiently. 'If they store it properly, the last of it won't melt till late summer, but there's nothing much to see. Come on.'

Emerging from the covered alleyway, they threaded their way through the market square, which Terrel guessed was near the centre of town. He recognized much of what was for sale on the various stalls – dried fish, goat's milk cheese, cloves and other spices, woven carpets, filigree silver jewellery, and much more. There was also some beautiful cloth, which Zahir told him was called silk, and an array of vegetables he couldn't put a name to. It seemed that the market was thriving, but the elder's son remarked that there was less produce than usual.

'Some merchants are obviously still coming this way,' he observed, 'but the warlords have started to control many of the trade routes now, so it's not as easy as it once was. We're nearly there,' he added, as they left the square.

The door of the house Zahir led them to was guarded by two massive hounds, whose broad, flat faces were distinguished by prominent yellow brows. From a distance, this made them look as if they had an extra pair of eyes. The beasts were chained to the wall, but they rose to their feet and growled menacingly as the visitors approached.

'Four-eyed dogs,' Zahir muttered. 'Charming.'

'Aren't they expecting us?' Terrel asked as they came to a halt, safely beyond the range of the tethers.

'They're supposed to be,' the nomad replied, 'but I'm not going to argue with these monsters.' Raising his voice, he shouted a greeting.

A few moments later the door opened and Algardi appeared, in the company of a man whom Terrel took to be the town elder. At a word from him the dogs sat down, and they remained docile as the newcomers were beckoned inside. Algardi gave his son a questioning look, as if to say 'What are *you* doing here?', but chose not to make an issue of it. Instead he introduced the two young men, then turned to their host.

'This is Tyoka, an old friend of mine.'

'You are welcome to my home,' the elder stated formally. He had not been one of those in the town delegation.

'Can I see your daughter now?' Terrel asked, not wanting to be delayed by any social niceties. He was nervous enough as it was.

'Of course.' Tyoka was obviously preoccupied, and did not seem to have noticed the healer's eyes – or if he had, he did not find them unusual. 'Come with me.'

Leaving Algardi and Zahir in the hallway, Terrel followed their host into the house. After living in the nomads' tents for several months, it felt as though he was walking into a dark labyrinth, and that impression was reinforced when they entered the patient's room. The air was still and stuffy, and the only light came from a partially shuttered skylight. Terrel had difficulty making out the small figure who lay on the bed, and the woman who sat beside it.

'I'm sorry it's so dark,' Tyoka said, 'but light hurts her eyes. Should I bring you a lamp?'

'No. It doesn't matter.' As Terrel's eyes adjusted to the gloom and he moved closer to the bed, he saw that the girl's attendant was obviously frightened, but he didn't know whether she was afraid of him or the disease. He still couldn't see much of the invalid.

'You may leave us now, Hera,' Tyoka said. 'Thank you.'

From the way he'd spoken, Terrel assumed that the woman was a servant, rather than the elder's wife, and this was confirmed when she had gone.

'I've been sitting with her myself most of the time,' Tyoka said quietly, 'but I don't know that I'm doing any good. Elodia's mother would have known what to do, but she died a year ago. I don't think I could bear it if I lost my little one too. She's the only family I have.'

'I'll do what I can,' Terrel replied, trying to sound confident, but inwardly somewhat daunted by the task that lay before him.

'The shamen here can't even identify her ailment,' the townsman added. 'At first she just complained of feeling unwell, but then the fever came and she began to have periods of madness when she shouted and screamed and threw herself about. It was impossible to calm her, but the fits never lasted long, and in between times she's been falling into a deepening torpor, as she is now. The worst thing is she won't eat or drink anything. Her throat seems to close up if I try to make her, and she's starting to waste away.'

Terrel was only half listening to the whispered description of the girl's illness. His attention had been caught by the sound of her laboured breathing.

'She won't let anyone wash her or even cool her brow,' Tyoka went on. 'A damp cloth seems to send her into convulsions.' The elder sounded ashamed, and Terrel wondered if this was because of his own perceived failures, or because he was being forced to let a stranger see his daughter in such a reduced state. The musty odour of stale sweat grew stronger as he approached the bed.

'Do you need anything?' Tyoka asked anxiously.

'No.' Terrel could see now that although the girl was not covered by any bedclothes, she wore a long dark robe, and the lower half of her face was covered by a veil. Her eyes were closed but moving within their sockets, as if she was dreaming. Her limbs twitched occasionally in response to events in the unseen realm. 'May I hold her hand?'

'Of course.'

Terrel reached out and gently took her hand in his. The skin was hot and damp, and she muttered something in her sleep as he fell, unresisting, into the waking dream. Unlike Kalkara's, this was close to the surface, but like Kalkara's, Elodia's illness stemmed primarily from fear. Terrel sensed it instantly, recoiling from the impact while trying to fight against it. But he soon realized that this was not the same kind of terror that Kala had faced. This wasn't an imaginary event that he could negate by persuading her that it wasn't real. What was making Elodia ill *was* real – and so was her fear.

In some ways it reminded Terrel of how the unborn babies in the fog valley had been inexplicably terrified of the outside world. But Elodia's fear was less vague, more focused. And he couldn't identify its source; every time he thought he was about to track it down, his vision shifted and it slipped away, like water through his fingers.

After a while Terrel abandoned his attempt to find the cause of the disease, and concentrated instead on its symptoms. He found that he was able to ease the dull ache that filled her entire body, and could reduce the effects of her fever as well as helping her to breathe more easily. At that point Elodia suddenly opened her eyes, looking at him with a mixture of horror and curiosity.

'It's all right, my sweet,' Tyoka said quickly. 'This is Terrel. He's a shaman.'

The girl seemed to calm down as she heard her father's voice, and the veil lifted gently as she sighed deeply. Terrel could tell that she was feeling better, but knew it was probably only a temporary respite.

'Will you take something to drink now?' Tyoka asked hopefully, picking up a cup from a side table.

'No!' It was half shriek, half croak – and Terrel saw the agony it caused her as her neck muscles went into spasm. 'Take it away!'

Her father stepped back quickly and Terrel fought to calm her again, showing her how to relax her taut muscles and combat the pain. With her free hand, Elodia reached up and pulled the veil away.

'What are you doing?' she whispered.

'I'm trying to help you. What are you afraid of?'

'You have crystal eyes,' she breathed, then fell asleep again.

'What's happening?' Tyoka asked.

Elodia's dream shifted and swirled, and Terrel withdrew, letting go of her hand. He had done all he could for now. And his last glimpse of her inner world had revealed its secret.

'She's sleeping,' he said, hoping his voice did not betray his sense of shock.

'She looks a little better,' the elder remarked hopefully. 'Her breathing's easier, and there's more colour in her cheeks.'

'I've helped her a little, I think.'

'Do you know what's wrong with her?'

I do, Terrel thought, but you wouldn't believe me.

'Not really,' he said. 'I've treated her symptoms, not the underlying cause.'

'Well, it's a start,' Tyoka commented. 'Will you stay with her? What should I do now?'

'I'll stay. You should get some rest.' The townsman looked haggard, and Terrel assumed that he hadn't slept properly for several days.

'Shall I send Hera in to sit with you?' Tyoka was obviously desperate to get some rest, but was still nervous about leaving his daughter alone with a stranger.

'Whatever you think is best,' Terrel replied. 'Elodia has nothing to fear from me.'

'No. Of course not. I didn't mean . . .' For a moment, the elder's embarrassment got the better of him, but he recovered quickly. 'I'll leave you to it. If you want anything, just call. My servants will bring whatever you need, and they can wake me at any time.'

'I don't suppose it'll be necessary, but thank you. I'll call if I need anything,' Terrel promised.

'Good.' Tyoka hesitated as he stood by the door. 'Thank you, Terrel. I am already in your debt. If you can bring my daughter back, you may ask anything of me. Anything.'

'Her recovery would be reward enough.'

Tyoka nodded solemnly.

'May the winds blow gently for you,' he said, then went out into the corridor.

Terrel turned back to the sleeping child. She seemed peaceful enough now, but he knew that was deceptive. He hadn't been able to discern the cause of her malady at first, even though the clues had been plentiful, but now he knew what it was. Something – or someone – had made her mortally afraid of water. And that, in the desert, was to be afraid of life itself.

As he watched her, Terrel was still trying to work out the implications of his discovery. Alyssa had always disliked water, and to some extent was even afraid of it – but not to the point of making herself ill if any was nearby. Elodia's fear was as irrational as the curse that had affected the babies in the fog valley, but that did not make it any less potent. And Terrel knew the origin of that curse.

Was it possible there was an elemental near Triq Dalam? And if so, could its hatred of the magic in water have somehow been transferred to the girl? Was this where he was supposed to be, the place where the fates decreed he should meet the latest terms of his bargain? Terrel had no idea how he was supposed to find the answers to any of these questions.

But why would the presence of an Ancient – if there really was one nearby – affect only one of the town's inhabitants? Terrel assumed that he would have been told if there were others suffering from the same malady. Why should Elodia be vulnerable when no one else was?

He was about to take the girl's hand again, hoping to seek out the answers to at least some of his questions, when he was disturbed by a sudden clamour in the hallway outside. Moments later Zahir burst into the room.

'We have to get out of here,' he gasped. 'The town's under attack!'

CHAPTER SEVENTEEN

'Come on!' Zahir exclaimed as Terrel hesitated, horrified by this latest development. 'There's no time to—'

'I can't leave her like this,' the healer protested.

'She's already dying,' Zahir told him, coming over to the bed and grabbing Terrel's arm. 'And this isn't our battle.'

'No.' He tried to shake off the nomad's grip. 'She's helpless. If—'

The decision was taken out of his hands then as Tyoka ran into the room. He took his unconscious daughter into his arms and fled through the open doorway, the look of terror on his face making any words unnecessary.

'*Now* will you come?' Zahir demanded, tugging at the healer's arm again.

This time Terrel did not resist, and followed Zahir out into the corridor and thence into the street. He hardly had time to notice that the guard dogs had gone and that darkness had fallen before his guide set off down an unfamiliar alleyway. Terrel stumbled after him, wondering how he had stepped into this nightmare. Even as he ran, he realized that both the Amber and White Moons were new, and that the only visible moon in the sky would be the Red – which was only half full. Was that just a coincidence? Or had the raiders chosen this night specifically because of its lack of light?

Moments later he had no time for such speculation. As Zahir rounded a corner, he came to an abrupt halt – and then threw himself back, flinging them both to the ground in a tangled heap. With the breath knocked out of him, Terrel wasn't able to ask what was going on, but in the next instant the reason for his companion's alarm was made all too clear when bright orange flames suddenly roared through the street they'd been about to enter. Terrel felt the intense heat of the conflagration at the same time as he smelt the acrid scent of the tar pit.

'Winds!' Zahir gasped. 'They're using neft.' He scrambled to his feet and pulled Terrel up, as the smoke grew thick around them. 'Keep low,' he whispered as they set off back the way they had come.

Terrel was not a good runner at the best of times, but when he was bent double he became even more awkward, and had difficulty in keeping up with his guide. Knowing that he'd have no chance of finding his way out of the maze of streets alone, he limped on, hoping that Zahir would not outdistance him. Other sounds were registering with him now; voices shouting and the clash of weapons, as well as the crackling of flames. It seemed as though half the town was on fire, and the air was becoming hard to breathe.

Zahir granted him a few moments' respite as they took

shelter in a doorway, and Terrel saw vague outlines moving through the smoke, ghost-like puppets in a deadly shadow-play.

'Who's doing this?' he whispered.

'I don't know,' Zahir replied. 'And right now I don't care. In this mess we could be killed by either side, so our only chance is to get out of here. If we can reach our camp we'll be safe enough.'

Terrel wasn't sure how his companion had reached that conclusion – and finding their way out of Triq Dalam seemed an almost impossible task – but he didn't have the breath to argue.

'We'll circle round,' Zahir muttered, 'then cut across the southern quarter. Ready?'

Terrel nodded, and they set off again.

Afterwards, Terrel found it hard to believe that they had actually managed to escape. Their route had seemed so convoluted that he'd begun to think Zahir must be lost, but he had no choice but to trust the nomad's sense of direction. On several occasions Terrel had been convinced that they were about to die – either at the hands of the invaders, or in the furnace-like heat of another fiery onslaught – but on each occasion Zahir's quick reactions had helped them get away.

When they finally emerged into the open, leaving behind the deadly, choking air, the screams and the collapsing buildings, their sense of relief was immense. But even then Zahir did not relax his guard. He knew that the attackers – whoever they were – would be expecting the inhabitants to flee, and would be waiting for them. So he and Terrel lay down in the dirt, where they remained perfectly still for some time. Sure enough, they soon spotted patrols of armed men circling the town. As they watched, hoping to remain undetected, a group of fugitives ran out between two houses. Terrel was about to yell out a warning when Zahir put a hand across his mouth and shook his head violently. Terrel was forced to watch as the dazed and wretched townsfolk were cut down by their pitiless enemies.

Eventually, in a gap between patrols, the two young men made a dash for freedom and managed to reach the relative safety of ground further from the light of the fires. As they made their way round to the Toma's campsite, it became clear that the whole of Triq Dalam had become one giant inferno. Whoever had decided to destroy the town was making a thorough job of it.

The nomads were out in force, forming a complete ring around the tents, their weapons at the ready. The newcomers were challenged as soon as they got close, but once they identified themselves, suspicion turned to joy. The return of the elder's son and the tribe's healer was greeted with equal measures of relief and delight, tempered only by the knowledge that three others were still missing. Zahir was soon reunited with his parents and, once they had reassured themselves that he – and Terrel – had suffered no more than a few bruises and some scorched clothes, they wanted to know exactly what had happened. Terrel was happy to let Zahir do the talking, glad that Algardi had not been trapped in the town.

As the Toma waited, the Red Moon climbed in the sky above them, looking as though it was reflecting the light that now filled the valley. The nomads were obviously concerned that, having sacked the town, the raiders might turn their attention to their camp, and they were prepared to defend themselves if necessary. However, even though the attackers must have been aware of the nomads' presence, they made no move to approach them, and the tribe was left to watch and wait, still hoping for the return of the missing men. As the night wore on, the chances of that actually happening grew increasingly remote.

'Shouldn't we go and look for them?' Zahir asked eventually.

'We can't,' Algardi replied. 'If we're seen to be taking sides in one of these wars, it will be the end of us. Our neutrality is our only safeguard.'

'But we'd only be trying to help our own people!'

'Others may not see it that way. Besides, I'm not willing to risk greater losses for the sake of three men who in all probability are already dead. I would say the same even if you were one of them,' the elder added grimly.

Zahir nodded, his youthful face grave, reluctantly accepting his father's unrelenting practicality. Standing beside him, Terrel wondered what such a decision would have cost the old man, but he said nothing. It was not his place to interfere in such matters.

'So much for our role as peacemakers,' Medrano commented. The artist had joined them and was now gazing at the burning town, his dark eyes troubled.

'There was no peace to be made here,' Algardi told him. 'This was a well-planned and ruthless attack.'

'What dispute could possibly justify such a massacre?' the artist wondered. 'They're sparing no one.'

'We may never know,' the elder replied, 'but the Toma would do well not to make enemies of such men.'

'Didn't anyone see who the raiders were?' Zahir asked.

'You two probably got a better look than anyone else,' Medrano said. 'So if you couldn't tell . . .' He shrugged.

'Could it have been the Shiban?' Mlicki asked, as he came to stand beside Terrel.

'I've no idea.'

'Well, whoever they are, I'm glad you got away from them.'

'I only got out because of Zahir,' Terrel admitted. 'He's more than repaid any debt he owed me.'

Zahir looked pleased at this, and his parents both nodded their approval, but no one spoke. All eyes were still focused on the destruction of the town.

'Is Kala all right?' Terrel asked eventually.

'She's asleep,' Mlicki replied. 'At a guess, she's the only one in the whole camp who is.'

'Maybe that's for the best.'

'I thought so. She was asleep before the attack began, and I didn't see any point in waking her.'

Mlicki did not need to add that the raid would have brought back unhappy memories for his sister.

The Toma waited until the following morning before they approached the ruins of Triq Dalam. By then it was clear that the raiders had gone, disappearing into the night as stealthily as they had come, and leaving behind them a scene of utter devastation. The flames had all died down now, but many of the smouldering remains were still much too hot for anyone to approach too closely. Near the centre of the town, the fire had burned so fiercely that in places it seemed to have melted stone, and many of the mud bricks had been reduced to powder. More flammable materials – wood, straw and cloth – had simply vanished.

Terrel went with the first group of nomads to explore the debris, though they had no hope of finding anyone alive and in need of his healing skills. Those who had escaped the fury of the blaze had been butchered by the waiting patrols, and their bodies lay where they had fallen. Inside the town, the dead had been reduced to just a few scraps of charred flesh, clinging to blackened bones. It would have been impossible to identify any of them.

There was no sign of life anywhere. The raiders had driven off some of the town's animals, but others had been slaughtered and left to rot in a wanton act of barbarism that seemed to shock the nomads as much as anything else they had seen. In the desert, such wasteful behaviour was unconscionable. For Terrel it typified the malicious pointlessness of the attack. What could the people of Triq Dalam have possibly done to warrant such a fate? The massacre was a work of evil, of true madness, without conscience or any remnant of human feeling. The attackers had obviously taken some booty, but their departure when so much was still left behind was evidence that robbery had not been their primary motive. The crops in the fields had not been touched, other stores had either been burnt or ruined indiscriminately, and in the gutted market place, small pools of melted silver proved that they had not even been interested in valuable jewellery. And it seemed that the raiders had simply ignored the most precious commodity in all of Misrah – the lake and the spring that fed it.

As appalled as he was by what had happened in purely human terms, Terrel also felt a personal loss. He would never know now if one of the tattooed women of Triq Dalam had been the figure from his dream. Nor would he get the chance to ask anyone about the possible presence of an elemental. And, as Elodia and her father were presumably among the dead, he would not be able to investigate her illness any further. It was a setback he could not simply discount as one of the vagaries of destiny.

For the Toma, the most important reason for investigating the ruins was to determine the fate of the three missing nomads. Two had been found quickly enough, among the dead outside the town. The raiders had apparently had no quarrel with the travellers, so it was assumed that these two had been mistaken for locals. That, of course, did nothing to assuage the grief of their families, nor of the tribe as a whole, but the close relatives of the third man were left in an even more invidious position. No trace of his body was found and, although he was presumed to be dead, a tantalizing sliver of hope remained. Not knowing his fate was the worst torture of all – and so the hunt went on in spite of the dangers faced by the searchers. Terrel and Bubaqra were both called to tend to those whose efforts had left them with burns, or who had been weakened by the effects of smoke and fumes.

Towards the end of the day, when the nomads were on the point of giving up their hopeless task, the search party was joined by a new and unexpected member. Kalkara came running through the ash and rubble, heedless of the perils around her, and ignoring the warning shouts of those nearby. Terrel was one of those who tried – and failed – to stop her, and as he stumbled in her wake, he wondered what had made her act so recklessly. He did not have to wait long to find out.

Kalkara came to a halt near a hollow in the ruins, which marked where some part of an underground chamber had evidently collapsed. Clambering down into the hole, she began to pick up the tumbled stones and hurl them aside.

'What are you doing?' Terrel asked breathlessly.

Kala ignored him, and carried on digging as other nomads – including her brother – arrived at the scene.

'There's someone down there,' Mlicki stated.

At that several men climbed down to take over from the little girl. Although she struggled, she was lifted out and had to be content with watching the excavations from above.

'I hope you're right about this, little one,' Mlicki murmured. 'If they do all this work for nothing . . .'

'What's going on?' Zahir asked, as he arrived from another part of the devastated town. 'Is someone in the mattamore?'

'The ice-house,' Terrel said, belatedly recognizing the uncovered stone stairway.

'They'd have a better chance down there than anywhere else,' Zahir commented, as he began to help with the digging.

Such was the urgency of their progress that it was only a quarter of an hour later when the rescuers uncovered a heavily reinforced door that had survived the inferno. Zahir pounded on it with his fist, and called out, but there was no response from inside. The men set to again, and eventually managed to force it open. As a gush of dirty water soaked their feet, Zahir peered through the narrow gap, and sensed movement within. As the others continued to pull the door open, he slipped inside – only to reappear a few moments later.

'Terrell!' he called. 'We need a healer. Get down here!'

Terrel responded quickly, wondering what sight would greet him in the former ice-house. Some of the nomads helped him climb down, and as his eyes adjusted to the gloom of the underground chamber, and the door was forced a little wider to allow more light in from above, Terrel felt his heart lurch.

Staring back at him from the darkness were at least a dozen pairs of small, frightened eyes.

CHAPTER EIGHTEEN

Over the next few days, the ice-house children were inte-
grated into the life of the Toma with the minimum of
fuss. There had never been any question of them being
left behind. Once the nomads had buried their dead, the
caravan resumed its long journey towards Qomish, but
before they left they collected whatever they could use
from the ruins of the town, and harvested some of the
crops in the abandoned fields. The fact that the tribe had
benefited indirectly from the death of Triq Dalam and
its inhabitants did not alter the nomads' belief that wasting
resources in the desert was a crime. They saw their actions
not as looting but as a practical necessity of their way of
life. The raiders' actions in not making use of the valley's
water supply had raised some doubts about its purity, but
the Toma's camels obviously sensed nothing wrong,
drinking greedily from the lake, and so the nomads made
sure that every container was full before they left. The
temptation to remain at the oasis, with its plentiful supply

of life, was very great, but no one wanted to look at the blackened remains of the town for any longer than was absolutely necessary.

The tribe took with them the fourteen rescued children. The nomads soon discovered that the newcomers had not been raised as citizens of Triq Dalam, but were from the north. In spite of their recent ordeal, the children were in better health than any of those Terrel had seen in the refugee camp, but they were still exiles – and there were those among the Toma who were uneasy about adopting some of the unclean. However, simple compassion soon overrode such feelings, and before long the children – both individually and collectively – began to win over even the doubters. As Terrel had seen, nomad children grew up fast in the desert. They were expected to do chores from an early age, and responsibilities bred toughness. Such considerations applied to the exiles to an even greater degree and all of them, even the youngest, proved willing to do whatever was asked of them.

As far as anyone could tell, their ages ranged from four to nine years old. All their parents were either dead or lost somewhere along the tortuous journey south. As orphans, the children had apparently been taken in by the people of Triq Dalam when it became clear that the other refugees were either unable or unwilling to care for them. That they had survived long enough to be in a position to benefit from such help was a testament to their resilience. Some of them were frequently miserable – which was hardly surprising – but although they had become hardened to their situation, they were not imbued with the terrible apathy that Terrel had witnessed earlier. The kindness they'd received at the oasis town, and subsequently from the nomads, had restored some of their wellbeing – mental as well as physical. Even so, they were still undernourished, and several were suffering from the aftereffects of injuries or illness. Terrel did his best for them. His first priority had been to negate the effects of heat, smoke and the lack of good air that could so easily have turned the mattamore into their burial chamber. But the chill of the ice and the strength of the sealed door had enabled them to survive – although the terror of waiting there in complete darkness, knowing nothing of the events unfolding above them, scarred their dreams still.

For their part, the children seemed to accept their absorption into the Toma without question. They had lost any control over their own fates a long time ago, and had learnt to live each day, each hour, as it came. They were a mixed group, coming from several different tribes, but they banded together now in a tightknit alliance. With the Road of Hope reduced to chaos, none of them had any way of telling where their own clans were – or even if any of them were still alive. Triq Dalam had taken in only orphans. Everyone else had been moved on.

Terrel had spent as much time with the newcomers as anyone, partly because of his responsibilities as a healer, and partly because even the nomads had difficulty understanding their harsh northern dialects. Terrel's intuitive grasp of languages meant that he could act as an interpreter when necessary, and this earnt him a good deal of respect. In fact, the exiles regarded him with the kind of awe normally reserved for great shamen, often staring into his light-filled eyes as if secrets were hidden there. He felt awkward about such adulation, and tried to play down his talents. He wanted friends, not followers. At the same time, he couldn't help feeling a little pride in being able to help the young refugees. Fate had dealt them a bad hand, and anything he could do to improve their lot was very definitely worthwhile.

'It seems to me,' Medrano said, 'that whoever attacked Triq Dalam must have believed that the town had offended the winds somehow. That was no ordinary tribal skirmish. It was a punishment – and a terrible one.'

Terrel nodded. He had come to much the same conclusion. The cold-blooded slaughter of the entire population, coupled with the destruction of property, rather than theft, had made the raid unusual. It bore all the hallmarks of religious mania.

'I've been wondering if they chose that night because of the lunar significance of the two new moons,' Terrel said. 'Not just for the lack of light.' He was aware that the White Moon in particular was important to the nomads. Most of their rituals and ceremonies were planned to take place at its full, when it was said to 'watch over' them.

'No one was watching,' Medrano replied quietly, echoing Terrel's line of thought.

The pair were sitting near the campfire, waiting for the evening meal. Terrel hadn't seen much of the artist recently, and it seemed natural now to compare their speculation over the brutal destruction of Triq Dalam.

'What could they have possibly done to deserve it?' Terrel asked, returning to the question that puzzled him the most. 'They didn't seem to be doing anything unusual.'

'I doubt anyone ever *deserved* that,' Medrano

remarked grimly. 'It's still hard to believe it happened before our eyes.'

'Might it have had something to do with the refugees?'

'Because they helped them, you mean?'

'Yes. The children were hidden away. Were they being concealed because the town was ashamed of their presence? Or because they knew they might be the cause for an attack?'

'I don't see why it should be either,' Medrano answered. 'It's clear enough the townspeople tried to help the unclean, and it was only when their numbers became overwhelming that they drove them off. I can't believe they paid such a price simply because of their generosity to a few children.'

'It doesn't make much sense, though,' Terrel said. 'Why would they try to protect the exiles, and not their own children?'

The raiders had spared no one – man or woman, old or young.

'I don't know,' the artist said, shaking his head in bewilderment. 'I don't understand any of this. The Shiban and the Mgarr have done some pretty vile things at times, but never anything as bad as this. But anyone else would have had to travel a huge distance just to get there, and you'd need a very good reason to do that. It's madness.'

'There is another possibility,' Terrel said hesitantly.

'What?'

'You remember the girl I was treating?'

'The one who was afraid of water?'

'What if the raiders thought there was plague in Triq Dalam? Would they destroy the place to stop it spreading?'

'But there was only one case!'

'Perhaps they didn't know that.'

Medrano thought about this for a few moments.

'I suppose it's possible,' he admitted, 'but it still seems an insanely drastic solution.'

'It would explain why the raiders didn't touch the water supplies,' Terrel added. 'Perhaps they thought it was infected.'

In fact, the water seemed fine. They had been drinking it for some time now, with no sign of ill effects.

'Or perhaps they thought the unclean carried the plague,' Medrano suggested. 'And because the town had taken some of them in, it had become a danger to the entire region.'

'None of the children were ill,' Terrel stated. 'If they had been, they couldn't possibly have gone down into the mattamore. It was full of frozen water.'

'Maybe that's *why* they were the only ones down there. The others didn't want to get close to the ice, even though it offered some hope of safety from the fire.'

'You mean Elodia might *not* have been the only case? Just the most advanced?'

'It makes as much sense as anything else in this whole sorry business,' Medrano observed.

'I would have sensed something like that,' Terrel said uncertainly. 'I think.'

'We'll probably never know now,' the artist said fatalistically. 'Just like we'll never know how Kalkara knew the children were there.'

That indeed was another mystery. The refugees owed their lives to Kalkara. Terrel suspected that it might have been her dreams that had guided her, but he had no proof of that – and was never likely to.

The two men fell silent as the food was passed round and they began to eat. Terrel found himself brooding about another mystery – a personal one this time. When he and Zahir had been trapped in the burning town, he had been in grave – possibly mortal – danger. In the past, that had often been the trigger that brought Alyssa to his side. And yet this time she had not come. Had she known that Zahir would be able to keep him safe? Or was there another reason for her having stayed away? A month had passed since her last brief appearance, and the hopes that had raised were fading now. Terrel felt lost again. Life with the Toma had its purpose and its pleasures, but in the past all his journeyings had been a means to an end – and that end had never seemed as remote as it did now.

'My father told me that when I was born our lake was ten times as big as it is now,' Hamriya said. 'It used to take us less than an hour to carry our boats to the water's edge then. Before we left it was taking four days – and when we got there the air was so thick with insects you couldn't see the sky.' She shuddered at the memory.

'It was the same at our village,' Luleki said. 'Sand blew over the fields, making them so dry that nothing would grow, and burying our houses.'

Even allowing for youthful exaggeration, it was plain that the girls' northern homeland was in the grip of a horrendous drought.

'The only place we could grow anything was in the mud where the lake used to be,' Hamriya added, 'but the maggots ate everything. That's why we had to take the Road of Hope.'

The two girls were the oldest of the refugees, and the most voluble, often acting as spokesmen for the younger ones. They were a tough pair, old beyond their tender years, and as close as sisters. They retained a little pride, claiming that they could have managed on their own, and that they wanted to resume their journey south when the rest of the children were up to it. However, they were realistic enough to know that their best hope lay in staying with the Toma, in spite of the fact that the tribe was travelling in a northwesterly direction.

It was clear from what the children said that they didn't really understand the true nature of the journey their tribes had taken. The Road of Hope was still a potent symbol for them – a road that would lead to a wonderful, almost mystical place of plenty, by the great sea of life. They knew nothing of the politics that had led to war and famine, and they had a touching – and probably misguided – belief that they would eventually be reunited with their families. It had proved hard to get any of the exiles to talk about the events that had led to them being separated from their parents. In fact this was one of the rare occasions that they had been coaxed into talking about the past. It was all too easy to raise painful memories.

'You've come a long way,' Bubaqra said. Other than Terrel, she was the only one who seemed to have gained the girls' complete trust and respect. Having had only sons herself, the matriarch had always taken a keen interest in her granddaughters, and she'd taken the two girls under her wing.

'We would've been further south if we hadn't had to go round the Sorcerer's Mouth,' Luleki said.

'What's that?' Terrel asked.

'You don't know?' Hamriya exclaimed in surprise.

Terrel shook his head and glanced at Bubaqra, who was looking equally mystified.

'It's where Nydus swallowed the great river,' Luleki explained. 'The earth split open when the Sorcerer opened his mouth, and the river disappeared inside.'

'You saw this happen?'

'No. But we heard it,' Hamriya replied. 'The ground shook and groaned, and then all that was left was a roaring canyon a day's march wide, full of rainbows.'

Like many of the tales they told, this sounded like a garbled version of a story they had heard from adults. It was clear that it referred to the Kullana River – and might explain why it had dried up with such dramatic speed – but Terrel couldn't see how such an enormous chasm could have been created by a normal earthquake. It must have been a massive upheaval, and that would surely have devastated the entire land. What was more, if it had 'swallowed' the river, it must have happened two years earlier. This meant that if Hamriya's claim to have heard it were true, then she had been on the road even longer than anyone had suspected.

'Did you really hear it yourself?' Terrel queried. 'Or did someone tell you about it?'

'We heard it ourselves,' the girls replied together.

'It only lasted a few moments,' Luleki added, 'but it was very loud.'

Terrel believed that such an upheaval would have lasted days, if not months, but he decided not to pursue the subject. Bubaqra was about to ask another question when the conversation was interrupted by the arrival of

Mlicki with one of the youngest exiles, a thin-limbed boy who rarely spoke at all.

'There you are,' Mlicki said, looking at Terrel. 'Bakhi wouldn't give me any peace until we'd found you. Well, go on then,' he told the child, who was obviously nervous. 'Give it to him. That's what we came here for.'

Bakhi stretched out a small hand and slowly uncurled his tightly clenched fingers. On his palm lay a flawed but translucent crystal.

'Is that for me?' Terrel asked gently.

The boy nodded once, his gaze flicking back and forth between the stone and Terrel's face.

'He said it matches your eyes,' Mlicki informed them. 'And he's right.'

Terrel reached out and took the gift.

'Thank you. I shall treasure it.'

Bakhi smiled briefly, then glanced seriously at each of the others in turn, as if seeking their approval. When he came to Bubaqra, he became very still, staring.

'You're old,' he announced solemnly.

'I am,' Bubaqra replied, laughing.

'No pictures,' Bakhi said, touching his own chin.

'Toma women don't wear tattoos,' she told him, realizing what he was talking about.

'My mother had one,' Mlicki said gently.

'Mine was going to be done soon,' Hamriya claimed. 'I'm old enough now.'

'Me too,' Luleki said, not to be outdone, 'but the one who paints them went away.'

She sounded sad, and Terrel wondered just how many people in her young life had 'gone away'.

'We could ask Medrano to paint them for you,' he

suggested. 'It wouldn't be a real tattoo, so you could wash it off again if you didn't like it.'

The excited smiles on the girls' faces let him know what they thought of his idea.

'Can we do it now?' Hamriya asked eagerly.

CHAPTER NINETEEN

'Up there?' Terrel asked.

'Yes,' Medrano told him. 'At the top, next to the obo.'
He was pointing to a rough pile of stones ahead of them,
which marked the highest point of the pass between two
hills.

'But there's nothing here,' Luleki objected, her face
mirroring Terrel's surprised expression.

'Doesn't the oracle need to eat?' Hamriya asked.

'Of course she does,' Medrano replied, smiling.

Ever since he'd agreed to paint the girls' faces, the
artist had become something of a hero to the two exiles.
He'd been reluctant at first, pointing out that for the
women of many tribes tattoos were a serious business,
and that he had no skill in such matters. However, his
doubts had been overcome by the enthusiasm of Hamriya
and Luleki, and he had eventually done as they wished,
ceremonially daubing their foreheads with white paint.
He had later confided in Terrel – whom he blamed for

making the suggestion in the first place – that he had no idea what the markings were supposed to signify, and that he hoped he'd done the right thing. But the girls' obvious delight had soon assuaged the artist's misgivings.

Now, several days later, the 'tattoos' had faded so that they were barely visible, but both refugees still spent part of each day with Medrano if they could, perhaps hoping that he would repeat the process. The girls were inquisitive, frequently asking questions and begging the artist to draw pictures for them whenever there was time. For his part, Medrano accepted their intrusive presence in good spirit, calling them his acolytes, and was almost always willing to share his knowledge on any subject. The exception to this rule had been the oracle, about whom he had been annoyingly mysterious.

Terrel was as confused as the girls. Ever since he'd learnt that the caravan was altering course so that they could consult the oracle of the Senglea Hills, he had assumed that the prophet was a woman, like the hermit he'd been told about when he first came to Misrah. Medrano had done nothing to disabuse him of this notion, referring to the oracle as 'she', but Terrel was beginning to have his doubts. The hills were rocky and completely arid. No one, not even the most determined ascetic, could survive in these surroundings for long. And the rough cairn was certainly not a dwelling of any kind.

'The oracle actually lives here?' he asked.

'As much as she lives anywhere,' Medrano replied enigmatically.

The artist walked on, obviously enjoying his companions' puzzlement. The foursome had left the rest of the tribe setting up camp for the night. Ordinarily, Medrano would have chosen to complete his journey alone, but the other three had all begged to be allowed to come with him.

'Is she there now?' Luleki asked.

'No. We'll have to wait until the White Moon rises tonight. Then she'll come.'

The White Moon, Terrel knew, would be full that night.

'So why are we going there now?' Hamriya asked.

'There are some preparations I have to make.'

'What?'

'Wait and see,' Medrano replied, and would say no more.

When they finally reached the heap of stones – or obo, as Medrano called it – there was still no indication as to why the prophetess had chosen this place as her 'home'. The artist picked up a small rock and added it to the cairn, then walked slowly round the structure three times.

'You must do the same,' he told the others. 'To honour the spirits of the hills.'

The girls did as they were told, taking the duty seriously, and Terrel followed suit, feeling rather foolish as he paced round in a circle. When they had finished, Medrano nodded his approval.

'Now you must let me work,' he said, indicating that they should go and sit on a nearby boulder, a few paces away.

Like the girls, Terrel had several questions he would have liked to ask, but Medrano's earlier amusement had now given way to a grave air of concentration which none of them felt able to disturb. Instead, they watched in silence as the artist moved around the obo. He was staring at the ground, and after a while he knelt down and smoothed an area of dusty soil with his hands. Then, using a carved wooden pointer, he began to outline something in the flat space. The onlookers were too far away to see what he was drawing, but they overcame their curiosity and stayed where they were. Once he was satisfied with his efforts, Medrano stood up and moved on, beginning the process again in a nearby patch of sand. In all he scraped out seven pictures, spaced out in a circle around the obo. Having done that, he came over to join the others.

'Now all we have to do is wait,' he said.

'Can we go and look?' Luleki asked.

'Yes, but don't disturb the pictures or go inside the circles.'

The girls ran off and Terrel, curbing his own impatience, walked more sedately beside the nomad. When he saw the first of the incised symbols, he felt a shiver of recognition. He had seen something similar carved into one of the jasper touchstones of the fog valley – two wavy lines next to a five-pointed star.

'That's the river in the sky, isn't it?' Hamriya exclaimed. By then the two girls had already made a complete circuit of the pictures.

'Where the rain comes from,' Luleki added knowledgeably.

'That's one of its meanings,' Medrano agreed.

As Terrel studied the rest of the marks in the soil, he felt a growing sense of anticipation. Some of the other signs also seemed vaguely familiar, and he wondered where he might have seen them before. Tindaya? The sharaken's fortress? In the books of Havenmoon's lost library? Surprisingly for a land where water was so scarce, two of the depictions were of fish. Another was a stylized representation of a bird – Hamriya informed Terrel that it was called 'the eyes of the wind' – but the next was an unrecognizable angular shape that he found somehow threatening.

'Is that the crooked arrows?' Hamriya asked, sounding unsure of herself for once.

Medrano nodded.

'The dome sends sky-fire to punish our misdeeds,' the girl said quietly, and Terrel had the feeling that she was quoting something an adult had once told her.

'Or to warn us,' Medrano added.

Terrel had never thought of lightning as either a punishment or a warning, but he could easily see how it could be interpreted that way. It was frightening and inexplicable, even when you knew it was a natural phenomenon.

The next picture was of a circle with a set of four branches spreading out from one side, like the antlers on a stag's head.

'The horned dancer,' Luleki said, confirming Terrel's intuition.

'That's the way of the shamen,' Hamriya told him, in case he hadn't seen the connection to the ritual headdress. The two young exiles had been eager to display their expertise, vying with each other to show off to both Terrel and Medrano, but they were both baffled by the last symbol in the ring.

'What is it?' Luleki asked.

To Terrel it looked like some sort of bulbous insect, or perhaps an animal of some kind.

'I've never seen that one before,' Hamriya admitted.

'That's the double-headed man,' Medrano told them. 'The one who carries a star in his hands.'

Without thinking, Terrel glanced down at his own left hand, remembering the glow of the invisible amulet that he carried. Was *he* the double-headed man?

'What does he do?' Luleki asked, unaware of Terrel's confusion.

'He brings wisdom from our ancestors,' Medrano answered.

'From the spirits of the dead?' Hamriya exclaimed, wide-eyed.

'I've never seen a ghost,' Luleki said, sounding regretful. 'Have you, Terrel?' She was teasing, aware of the nomads' nickname for him, but he was unable to answer her, even in jest. He'd been enveloped by a sense of foreboding that made it hard for him to think, let alone speak.

'Your tattoo's like ripples spreading out in a pool of life,' Hamriya observed.

Terrel realized that he was still staring at his left hand. In the fog valley, the four concentric circles had been called the 'circles of life'.

'Like the circles here,' Luleki added, pointing to the ground.

For the first time, Terrel took in the fact that the ring of pictures had been enclosed by four lines, two inside, two outside, each of them a circle with the obo at its centre.

'I think we were right to come here, don't you, Terrel?' Medrano said. 'I have a feeling you may be the one the oracle speaks to.'

*

'Do you ask the oracle questions?'

'No.'

Terrel had recovered his wits as the little group had made their way back to the camp. There was a lot he didn't understand – and a lot more he wasn't sure he *wanted* to understand – but his own curiosity, combined with a reluctant sense of duty, made him go on with his enquiries.

'Then what's the point?' he asked. He wanted information from the oracle on a lot of subjects – if only he could be certain that he'd like what he heard.

'She may give us some answers anyway,' Medrano said.

'How?'

'You'll see.'

Two hours later, when the White Moon rose, brilliant in the crystal clear air, Terrel was sitting on one side of the pass, looking down on the obo. Almost all the Toma had made the climb up from the camp, and knowing that so many people were there, all perfectly still and silent, invisible except as moonlit shadows, made the night seem even more eerie.

Time passed with agonizing slowness, and the waiting began to grate on Terrel's nerves, but the nomads seemed quite at ease – which only made him want to fidget all the more. The temptation to speak to Medrano or Mlicki, who were sitting to either side of him, was almost overwhelming, but he forced himself to stay quiet, and tried to keep believing that the oracle must surely come soon. The White Moon was now well up in the sky, casting its 'cold light of logic' across the hills. In the Floating Islands, the White Moon was associated with destiny as well as reasoning, and in Macul it had been said to bring news from afar. The prospect of the oracle speaking to him about either was distinctly unnerving.

Glancing once more at the face of the moon, Terrel was amazed to see a small piece of it break off and fall down towards the ground. He soon realized that the illusion had been created by the movement of a bird, which was now heading for the pass. A slight susurration – indrawn breaths and the muted rustle of movement – told him that the nomads had seen it too. As it drew closer, Terrel could see that it was a bird of prey, its sleek lines emphasizing its swift and powerful flight. But it was like no hawk he had ever seen. Its plumage was pure white, and its eyes, beak and talons were the palest shade of pink. In the matching moonlight it shone as if it were luminous, and Terrel knew that this was no mere harbinger of the oracle's arrival. This *was* the oracle.

The bird alighted on the cairn amid an expectant hush. After looking about for a few moments, as if inspecting her silent audience, the white hawk hopped down to the ground and strutted about, at times seeming to perch on the sand, at others flexing her wings or preening herself. Terrel couldn't tell whether she visited all the pictures, but she certainly seemed interested in some of them, and he assumed that whatever the bird was doing down there would result in the messages the oracle chose to pass on.

After what seemed like an age, the hawk gave a single rasping cry and rose into the air. Only when its retreating form had vanished from sight did the nomads move, flowing down from the slopes like a human tide to see what the prophetess had to tell them. Nobody went too close to the outer circles, and when Medrano and Terrel arrived, the crowd parted in deference to let them through. Some torches had been lit, and their wavering flames contrasted with the serene moonlight.

The first thing Terrel noticed was that several pebbles – all but one of which matched the colours of the four moons – had been laid on some of the pictures. Two white stones and two orange ones lay next to the horned dancer; four more ambers were immersed in the river in the sky; four red pebbles, one of which was only half the size of the others, marked the corners of the crooked arrows; and a single clear crystal lay on the eyes of the wind.

'What does it mean?' someone asked softly.

'Vilheyuna would normally be the one to interpret such things,' Medrano replied, 'but even I can read such a message.'

'What is it?' Terrel asked.

'It means we must beware the time of storms,' the artist said.

The nomads were clearly disturbed by the oracle's portent, and this increased Terrel's own sense of unease. As the Toma muttered and whispered, he continued to study the pictures. At first he thought that the other four signs had not been affected, but as he walked around the circle, he saw – to his dismay – that this was not the case. Several of Medrano's designs had been scuffed by the passage of the bird's feet, though their outlines were still clear enough. But one picture had clearly come in for special attention.

The double-headed man had been completely obliterated. And in his place was a single black stone.

CHAPTER TWENTY

'It's coming!' Terrel yelled, and heard his warning being echoed down the line of the caravan.

As the earthquake struck, camels bellowed with indignation, staggering drunkenly on their gangly legs. Several people were caught off balance too, and some fell to the ground, while a few of the smaller children – those who didn't understand what was happening – began to cry. The nearby sand dunes began to sing and hum, vibrating as if they were hollow. The quake was over in a few moments, with no serious damage done, but as always the silence that followed a tremor was full of doubts. Several of the nomads near Terrel glanced at him, and he was glad to be able to reassure them.

'It's over.'

There had been several tremors – of varying strengths, and each a few days apart – since they had left the Hills of Senglea. Terrel's internal sensors meant that he could predict their arrival, but beyond being able to warn those around him, his talent was of little practical use. If the caravan happened to be on a steep-sided dune at the time, sandslides were a problem, and the disorientation for both humans and animals was always unpleasant. But the Toma coped well enough. Of more concern to the tribe was the fact that such tremors were known to affect the patterns of subterranean water supplies in the desert, the wells and springs on which they depended. Now that summer had arrived, the permanent oases were more vital than ever – and if they were to become unreliable, even greater hardship would follow. The distances between such places were further than ever now, which meant that the travellers had to husband their resources much more carefully, rationing the amount that both men and animals were allowed to drink. After such a period of abstinence, each approach to a possible source of water was fraught with tension – which would give way either to great relief or even greater disappointment. When the tribe found a good well, they would camp there for several days before moving on, and this made their progress towards Qomish somewhat sporadic. When they were not on the move, their camels were allowed to roam freely to forage for what sparse vegetation there was, returning of their own accord to be watered and milked.

Because he was still not used to the desert's climate, Terrel suffered more than most from the heat and thirst, and so the nomads allowed him to ride more often than before. Zahir, perhaps thinking ahead to the Race of Truth, was especially concerned about the foreigner's welfare, but others kept an eye on him too. Apart from his closest friends, who looked after Terrel for his own sake, many of the nomads had a vested interest in keeping him strong and active; in times of deprivation, a healer's skills were essential to the wellbeing of the tribe. In such conditions even minor illnesses or injuries could easily become serious, and Terrel was kept busy trying to make sure that did not happen.

Once the tremor had subsided and order had been restored, the caravan set off again. Although a wind sprang up, the air was so hot it had little or no cooling effect. The relative comfort of winter and early spring was fast becoming a distant memory, and it was only at night – when the temperature dipped rapidly under clear skies – that Terrel was able to feel some ease. Ironically, he often woke shivering, glad of the early warmth of the newly-risen sun, only to long for the cool of the night again an hour later. He couldn't believe that it could possibly get any hotter than it already was, but midsummer's day was still more than a long month away.

As they crested one of the huge sand dunes, Terrel looked up from his seat atop one of the baggage camels and saw an isolated cloud in the distance. This was such a rare sight that he stared at it longingly. For a brief, insane moment, he wished Jax were there, so that the weather-mage could bring it closer and provide the nomads with some shade – perhaps even a little rain. The cloud cast a purple shadow over a small patch of the seemingly endless desert, and as Terrel watched, a slowly forming rainbow glimmered beneath the base of the formation. But it faded quickly, the brief shower evaporating before it reached the ground.

Even the river in the sky is drying up, Terrel thought dismally.

*

Discussions concerning the possible interpretations of the oracle's message had continued for a long time. Without their shaman to provide definitive answers, the whole tribe had been free to put forward their own theories. Most people agreed with Medrano's view of the warning. 'The time of storms' usually referred to the latter half of the summer, when the dry winds from the east were at their most violent – and it had not been lost on anyone that this would begin during the course of the Race of Truth. However, this had not altered the Toma's determination to take part. They had all faced storms before.

Other ideas were put forward, but none of them gave Terrel much comfort. He had told no one about his suspicions concerning himself and the double-headed man. He'd learnt that Medrano's picture had been a version of a traditional oracular symbol, but it fitted Terrel too well to be a coincidence. The fact that, in a sense, he carried a star in his hand, and that he was able to talk to ghosts, made the comparison all too obvious. But as the talisman only became visible during an eclipse, and because no one else could see or hear his spectral colleagues, he saw no point in revealing these things to the nomads. Even if they believed him, it would only make them think he was even stranger than they suspected. In any case, if the double-headed man *did* refer to Terrel, he had no idea what the oracle's actions meant. The black stone had presumably been some sort of reference to the Dark Moon, but beyond that it meant nothing. And although it seemed ominous, the erasing of the sign itself could mean anything.

Eventually, Terrel had no choice but to try to put the entire episode from his mind.

*

'When's your birthday?' Ghadira asked.

'I don't know for certain,' Terrel replied. 'Why?'

'You said you'd be eighteen soon.'

'I will,' he agreed warily. 'I might be already. It must be around now.'

'Then we'll celebrate tomorrow night,' Ghadira decided.

Terrel tried to dissuade her, not wanting any fuss, but she ignored his protests and, to his surprise, she found several allies for her plan among the other nomads. Zahir and Bubaqra expressed their approval, and Algardi decided that the tribe's morale would be improved by a little merrymaking. Preparations for the celebration began that night, though Terrel wasn't allowed to know what was being planned.

The mood in the camp became buoyant. As luck would have it, they had reached a strongly-flowing spring that afternoon and, knowing that the following day would bring them a rest from travelling – and with a celebration to look forward to in the evening – the nomads' spirits had risen already. Eventually Terrel set aside his trepidation, and began to wonder what was in store for him.

The only discordant note was struck by something quite beyond the nomads' control. The sunset that night was spectacular, the western sky streaked with bands of orange, gold, and deepening shades of pink. Watching it with Mlicki and Kalkara, Terrel was in awe of such beauty, but he soon become aware that his companions felt some disquiet at the sight.

'Don't you think it's amazing?' he asked.

'It is,' Mlicki replied, 'but a display like that generally means there's a lot of dust in the sky.'

'Is that bad?' Terrel asked naively.

'It means there must have been a sandstorm,' his friend said. 'A big one.'

The next day dawned clear, with no sign of further storms on the horizon. Terrel spent the morning with the refugees, tending to a few minor ailments. The children seemed to be adapting to their new situation, and although they still tended to gather together at night, many of them spent their waking hours with their new Toma friends.

In the afternoon, Medrano, Mlicki and Kalkara persuaded Terrel to go for a walk with them. The ostensible reason for this was that they wanted to show him something in a nearby cave, but he suspected that Ghadira wanted him out of the way so that she could prepare some sort of surprise for his 'birthday'. However, he went willingly enough, especially because Kala in particular seemed to be excited about the expedition.

His friends led him to something that was indeed fascinating. The cave had obviously not been inhabited for some considerable time, but on a wall just inside the entrance there were several paintings of deer, horses, and men with spears. Although these were crudely drawn, they still captured all the movement and brutal magic of the hunt.

'How old are they?' Terrel asked.

'No one knows,' Medrano replied. 'But animals like that haven't existed in this region for a very long time. For hundreds, perhaps thousands of years.'

'So there were artists even then,' Mlicki commented.

'Mine is an ancient craft,' Medrano agreed, deliberately pompous.

'Venerable, in fact,' Terrel said, laughing.

'Precisely.'

'Did they paint like this to tell a story?' Mlicki asked.

'My guess is it was supposed to bring them luck when they went hunting,' the artist said. 'If they picture themselves having success, then it made it more likely to happen.'

'So it was like an oracle?'

'I suppose so, yes. But one with a very specific purpose.'

This turn in the conversation made Terrel feel uncomfortable, because it reminded him of the possible significance of the double-headed man. At least the symbolism here is obvious, he thought, as he turned away.

'Have we been away long enough, do you think?' he enquired. Now that the mood of the excursion had been spoilt, he wanted to leave.

'What do you mean?' Mlicki said innocently.

Terrel began to make his way towards the mouth of the cave, but he was prevented from escaping by Kalkara, who caught his hand and pulled him back. Having captured his attention, she drew him a little further into the cave and pointed to two smaller paintings that he hadn't noticed earlier. In the shadows it was hard to make out much detail, but the outlines were easy to recognize. One painting was of a bird in flight, and the other was a djerboa in the act of leaping into the air, its absurdly large hind legs fully extended. Kalkara touched the bird and then tapped Terrel's chest in a deliberate gesture which he could not interpret. Then she looked back to the other picture.

'Like the ones we saw,' Terrel realized, and she

nodded, and grinned, before hopping wildly out of the cave.

'My sister's finally gone mad,' Mlicki remarked, laughing at her antics as they followed her outside.

'She's being a djerboa,' Terrel told him. 'There's a picture of one of them in there.' He was glad the memory of the earlier encounter no longer seemed to bother the little girl.

When they were only a few paces outside the cave, a shadow fell across the earth. Looking round, they saw a yellow mist rolling across the ridge behind them. It was moving in absolute silence but at a rapid pace.

'Chilouk ta'kwei,' Medraño muttered.

It took Terrel a few moments to work out what the artist meant – and it wasn't at all reassuring. The 'blanket of dust devils' did not sound as if it would be very comfortable – but they were about to be covered by it nonetheless.

The mist enveloped them with an eerie stealth, reducing his companions to shadows and making the landscape vanish. The last time Terrel had been in a similar situation was in the fog valley, where he'd blundered on, half blind, navigating only by judging whether he was going uphill or down. The mist there had been damp, but this was literally as dry as dust – and yet it was also pleasantly cool. Had it not been for the fact that it stung his eyes and throat, he would have enjoyed the novel sensation. Talking was impossible – when he tried to open his mouth, his teeth and tongue were instantly covered with grit – but he did not want to lose touch with his companions. Even though they were not far from the camp, it would be all too easy to lose his bearings and head off in entirely the wrong direction – with potentially disastrous consequences.

Terrel stumbled towards the nearest shadow, only to find it shifting and slipping away like a mirage. Fighting panic, he tried to call out, but all that emerged from his throat was a muffled croak. He stood still, wondering if he'd be better off staying where he was and waiting for the mist to pass. He told himself that this must be the remnants of a distant sandstorm, probably the same one that had produced the dramatic sunset the night before. But unlike such malevolent whirlwinds, this presented no immediate danger. Even so, the fact that he could no longer see his companions was unnerving, and he was about to cry out again when he noticed something that took away what little breath he had left.

The swirling sand at his feet was now full of glittering shards of crystal, brighter and more beautiful than any he had seen before. He watched, mesmerized, as they flowed in sinuous patterns about his boots. Light spread up from below, impossible and almost blinding after the earlier gloom. He saw rainbows, and heard the rumble of thunder. The crystals at his feet shifted again, and the mist was swept away.

And now there was *nothing* at his feet.

CHAPTER TWENTY-ONE

A small part of Terrel's brain knew that this wasn't real. It wasn't a dream, but it wasn't real. It was an hallucination, conjured up by his imagination from the tales he'd been told. He was trapped by something he did not understand, some form of desert magic.

A small part of Terrel's brain knew that all this was true. The rest of him was flying.

The vertiginous terror that had gripped him subsided as he realized he was floating *on* the air, not falling through it. Far below him, a wide, silver-blue river flowed across the land. Along its banks were swathes of green and gold, trees and crops, which faded to brown in the distance as the desert fought to regain the fertile corridor for itself, in the age-old war between life and death.

Without warning, Terrel was enveloped by a gigantic rumbling sound, so vast that it had a physical presence, blurring his eyesight and threatening to collapse his lungs.

He had heard it only once before, but it was not an experience he was ever likely to forget – and this time he knew what it presaged. As the wordless roar fell silent, and the buffeting stopped, another noise took its place.

The earth cracked open, as if its surface were no more than a fragile casing around the darkness below. The land split from horizon to horizon, as though the entire country was being divided in two – and the rapidly widening crevasse cut directly across the river's course. In no more than a few heartbeats, the ravine had become broad enough and deep enough to swallow the entire flow of water from the north. To the south, robbed of its driving force, the current swirled and eddied, some of it falling back into the abyss.

Within the canyon, the newly-created waterfall roared and glittered, sending up clouds of spray that shone with rainbow arches. It was an awe-inspiring sight, but the most incredible thing about the entire spectacle was the speed with which it had come about. It was just as Hamriya and Luleki had described it.

That must be it! Terrel thought, even as he gazed in wonder. The exiles' fanciful tale must have prompted this vision. It couldn't possibly be real.

The earth stopped moving then, and the growling tremor fell away, leaving only the distant thunder of the waterfall as it plunged into the subterranean caverns of Nydus.

Terrel's attention was caught by a bird, flying below him, above the tumult in the canyon. It reminded him of something, but he couldn't remember what, and then – before he had time to think – he was enfolded by clouds that left him blind. The last thing he felt before the vision released him was the presence of the Dark Moon, looking down on him and on the fractured landscape.

The illusory mist turned to dust again, and Terrel found himself sitting on dry but solid ground. He felt dizzy and tired, but strangely exhilarated. What was more, to his intense relief, he could see that the eerie darkness was clearing. First Medrano, then Mlicki and Kalkara became visible, each of them sitting on the ground no more than a few paces away.

As the sunlight returned, Terrel found that a phrase was running through his head. It seemed vaguely familiar, but he couldn't remember when or where he had heard it. 'The memories of sand' seemed a nonsensical concept, but he could see how it might be appropriate to his experience. He was getting to his feet when Kala came bounding over, a huge smile on her face, and took his hand.

'Are you all right?'

She nodded vigorously, her eyes bright, and Terrel wondered what – if anything – the little girl had seen in the mist. By then the others had risen too, and were walking over to join them. Both Medrano and Mlicki looked distracted, their thoughts evidently far away even as they brushed the sand from their hair and clothes.

'This must be a place of power,' Medrano said as he came closer. 'I've had desert dreams before, but never as vivid as that.'

'What did you see?' Mlicki asked.

'I was a hunter, stalking a herd of deer. What about you?'

'I was running faster than a camel at full pace, but I

had hooves rather than pads. I think I might have been one of the deer you were chasing.'

Terrel listened to this exchange in amazement, realizing that he was not the only one who had experienced an inexplicable vision. At the same time, he wondered what it meant that – even in his dreams – Mlicki saw himself as a victim, the hunted rather than the hunter.

'Did you see anything, Terrel?' Medrano asked.

'I was flying, like the bird Kala showed me.' He decided not to describe what he had seen through the bird's eyes.

'So our dreams all came from the cave,' Mlicki concluded, glancing back at the opening in the rock. 'We must be at one of the nodes Vilheyuna told me about.'

'I wonder if *I'll* ever paint a picture that'll retain such potency long after I'm dead and gone,' Medrano said. The artist sounded wistful, and with her free hand, Kalkara reached out and took his in a gesture of consolation.

'I'm sure you will,' Terrel assured him.

'You probably have already,' Mlicki added.

Medrano bowed his head gratefully, and they set off to retrace their steps to the camp. As he walked, still holding Kalkara's hand, Terrel saw some fresh tracks in the sand – looking remarkably like the imprints that would have been made by the leaping of a djerboa – but he dismissed that idea as too fanciful even for one of the desert's dreams.

That night, the Toma held a feast in Terrel's honour. There was no fresh meat, but they made up for this by the imaginative use of some of their precious reserves. Strips of dried meat were softened in a broth flavoured

with herbs and onions; bread was baked to accompany
the curds and cheeses; dried mulberries were soaked in
milk; and there were even enough dates for each person
to have two or three mouthfuls. But what Terrel would
always remember was not the food – delicious though
that was – but the sense of belonging that came with his
formal acceptance into the tribe. Algardi made a speech
of welcome, praising Terrel's character, his skills and his
loyalty.

'For a foreigner, he's getting to know the ways of the
desert quite well,' the elder added, provoking some good-
natured laughter. 'He is a worthy addition to our clan.'

After that, Terrel was given some gifts – which added
to his embarrassment, but also to his pleasure in the
evening. On behalf of the men of the Toma, Zahir
presented him with a curved dagger, complete with a
decorated scabbard, which was almost as splendid as his
own. Ghadira brought the women's offering, a woven belt
which displayed one of the colourful, intricate patterns
that were a nomadic tradition. Finally, Medrano produced
a small clay tablet attached to a leather thong. On the
stone's surface was the mark of the river in the sky.

'For the voice of rain,' he said as he hung the pendant
round Terrel's neck.

By then, Terrel was so choked with emotion that he
probably would not have been able to speak, but in any
case he knew this was not the time to tell the artist that
he'd chosen the wrong symbol. He was fighting hard to
keep the tears from falling from his eyes, but everyone
was looking at him, and he knew he had to make an effort
to respond to their generosity.

'Thank you,' he began, his voice trembling.

'Enough of that,' Bubaqra stated jovially. 'We need no thanks. Tell us another of your stories instead!'

This suggestion met with universal approval, and Terrel smiled gratefully at the matriarch, knowing that she had guessed his state of mind and was trying to save him from further embarrassment.

'All right,' he agreed, his voice stronger now. 'But only if you all promise I won't have to drink any qard juice this time. I don't think I could go through all that again!'

His words were greeted with laughter and a few cries of 'Shame!'. Even Nadur, who looked mortified by this reminder of his earlier misdeed, soon joined in the merriment. When they were reasonably quiet again, Terrel began.

'There is a valley, far away from here, where the people have never seen the sun.'

Some hours later, long after his tale was over, Terrel was sitting by one of the campfires, watching a group of nomads dance. On this occasion both men and women were taking part, and the drummers were in full view, because the dance was purely for enjoyment, a social event rather than a means of augury. Their movements were rhythmic and energetic, but elegant too, conveying a sense of dignity as well as sheer pleasure.

The dancing had followed Terrel's story, which had held his audience spellbound. The desert dwellers had been stunned by his description of the white-skinned people who lived beneath a permanent roof of cloud, but had rejoiced with them when the curse upon their home was lifted. Once again Terrel had changed some facts to suit his purpose, and had not cast himself in the role of

the Messenger, but had kept close enough to the truth to
make it a convincing narrative. No one had taken up the
challenge of following him with a tale of their own. This,
Terrel suspected, was a most unusual occurrence, and he
was flattered by the fact that the nomads had left the stage
to him alone. However, there was a further surprise in
store before the evening's entertainments were over.

When the apparently tireless drummers took a well-
earned rest, the entire gathering turned its attention to
Raheb, who was making some adjustments to a curious
display that had been set out at the centre of the feasting
area. This consisted of what looked like a nondescript
collection of stones, small branches and leaves, and Terrel
had assumed it to be purely decorative. The nomads
obviously knew better, because they were watching the
elder avidly and the air of excitement was unmistakable.

'What's going on?' Terrel whispered.

'Wait and see,' Mlicki told him.

Raheb was eventually satisfied with his arrangements,
and strode off to one of the fires. There he lit a taper and
returned to centre stage. Leaning down, he set the
burning end of the taper to one of the stones, confusing
Terrel even more. But then, against all expectation, the
stone caught fire – with a beautiful blue flame!

As the elder stepped back, one of the neighbouring
rocks flared up, this time with a vivid green flare. Terrel
watched, utterly entranced, as coloured fires ignited and
died in turn, weaving a tapestry of light in the evening
air. When the trail reached the wooden branches, Terrel
expected them to burn quickly, but he was in for one last
surprise. The flames turned to sparks, like the last brightness of a dying ember – and yet they did not fade away.

Instead the sparks crawled up and along the branches, splitting and spreading along the twigs and leaves like an army of luminous insects. And along the way they changed colour several times – from red to green to orange, and back again – until at last they all came to rest, all shining white. It was as though a constellation of stars had been called down from the night sky for their wonderment, and Terrel, like many of the onlookers, found himself holding his breath until the display at last faded into darkness.

After a moment's silence, the gathering erupted into rapturous applause – and Raheb accepted their acclaim graciously.

'I've never seen anything like that,' Terrel breathed. 'Never. How does he do it?'

'I've no idea,' Mlicki replied. 'Why don't you ask him?'

Terrel got up to do just that and, as guest of honour, he was quickly granted an opportunity.

'It's a simple enough skill,' Raheb answered modestly. 'Bubaqra uses various essences from plants and from the other gifts of the soil to make her remedies. I do much the same, but for a more trivial end.'

'Such beauty could never be considered trivial,' Medrano commented.

'It was wonderful!' Terrel exclaimed.

'I'm glad you enjoyed it,' the elder said.

'That was why we had to get you out of the way,' Mlicki told Terrel later. 'So Raheb could set up his fire poem.'

'Then it was worth getting lost in the mist,' Terrel replied.

The dancing had begun again now, and the last

remnants of the feast were being passed round for those with any appetite left. When Mlicki went to check on his sister, Zahir came to sit beside Terrel.

'Have you enjoyed your evening?'

'More than you can imagine. I'm honoured to be part of this tribe.'

Zahir smiled at that, then pointed to the knife.

'You like your gift?'

'It's wonderful.'

'You deserve it.'

'The belt is beautiful too.'

The elder's son nodded.

'Ghadira made it herself, you know,' he added casually. 'She originally intended it to be a wedding gift for her husband.'

'What?' Terrel exclaimed.

'Perhaps it was a hint,' Zahir said, laughing. 'I think she'd take you, actually, but I don't suppose you could afford the dowry!'

CHAPTER TWENTY-TWO

With all the recent talk about the Race of Truth, and with
the champion due to be elected that afternoon, Terrel
found something nagging at his mind. For a long time it
would not come to the surface, but taunted him from the
dark recesses of his memory. When he finally made the
connection, he couldn't believe that he hadn't thought to
ask such an obvious question.

'Mlicki, are you there?' he called, coming into the
shaman's tent in a rush.

'I'm here,' his friend replied, rising from behind
Vilheyuna's pallet. 'What's the matter?'

'Nothing. I just need you to tell me something.'

'What?'

'You told me months ago that Vilheyuna became a
sleeper in the Binhemma–Ghar, two summers ago. Was
it during the race?'

'Yes. He was part of the team that year. Why?'

'Do you know *where* he collapsed?'

'I've no idea,' Mlicki admitted. 'I wasn't with them. I've never been there, but Medrano would know. He was part of the team too.'

'Thank you.' Terrel left the tent and ran off to find the artist.

'The place where it happened doesn't have a name,' Medrano replied, when Terrel had repeated his question.

'Was it anywhere near Makranash?'

'About two days' march under normal conditions,' the artist said. 'That was the closest we got that year. We were already well behind the leaders, and when Vilheyuna became ill no one had the heart to go on.'

'Did anything strange or violent happen when he collapsed?'

Medrano looked at him curiously.

'What are you getting at?'

'I've heard of other people who've fallen asleep like that,' Terrel explained. 'And there was often something unusual about the events surrounding them.' The two he had personally witnessed had certainly been strange.

'There are others like him?' Medrano asked, astonished.

Terrel nodded.

'In Misrah?'

'Not that I know of, but there are several in the other lands I've visited.'

'And no one's found a cure?'

'Not yet. *Did* anything odd happen?'

'It was just an accident,' Medrano told him. 'One of the waterskins we were carrying exploded. They do that sometimes. It startled Vilheyuna's camel, and he fell off.

The curious thing was that there wasn't a mark on him – no broken bones, bumps or bruises. He just wouldn't wake up. Does that answer your question?'

'Yes,' Terrel replied. 'Yes, it does.'

The Toma had stayed at the spring for five days, their longest period of relative ease for some time. The unaccustomed rest had been agreed upon partly because the White Moon would be full again on the fifth day, and that was deemed an appropriate time to choose their champion for the race – which would begin exactly thirty-two days later, once the White Moon had completed another cycle.

As Terrel waited for the gathering, wondering what form the election would take, he thought back to his conversation with Medrano. If there *was* an elemental in Misrah, then the logical place for it would be at the dead heart of the desert, as far from any water as possible. Given that Terrel believed the Ancients were somehow linked to the sleepers, the fact that Vilheyuna had fallen near Makranash – and the way in which it had happened – lent weight to that supposition. Was it possible that some of the legends and the religious reverence that surrounded the mountain stemmed from the presence of the alien creature? It seemed all too likely. But he couldn't discuss any of this with the nomads. Given their beliefs, they would almost certainly regard his ideas as sacrilegious – and he could not afford to disturb or distress his hosts now. However, if his speculation was accurate, the consequences were unpleasantly obvious. There was no alternative. Terrel would have to go with the team, into the deadly emptiness of the Binhemma-Ghar.

'Have you decided who to vote for?' Medrano asked as he came to sit on the ground next to Terrel.

'Me?'

'You're one of us now,' the artist reminded him. 'You're entitled to speak, and to make your own choice.'

Terrel hadn't considered the implications of his formal acceptance in such terms before. Being part of the tribe brought its own responsibilities.

'I thought you said Zahir was the only choice,' he said uncertainly.

'*I* think so, but others may not agree.'

'Then I'll just listen to what everyone has to say and make my mind up then.'

'Wise as well as talented,' Medrano commented with a grin.

'Will you be part of the team this year?' Terrel asked him.

'I hope so, but it's up to the champion to choose his own team. What about you?'

'I'll go if I'm asked.'

The artist nodded approvingly, then looked up and smiled as they were joined by another late arrival.

'Have I missed anything?' Ghadira asked, as she sat down on Terrel's other side.

'They haven't started yet,' Medrano told her.

'It's not going to be one of those horribly long-winded debates, is it?' she muttered. 'It's pretty obvious who we should send.'

'We have to do things properly,' Medrano replied.

Ghadira gave him a withering look, then switched her attention to Terrel, and saw that he was wearing his new belt.

'I'm glad you like your gift,' she said.

'I do,' Terrel responded, hoping he wasn't blushing too fiercely.

He did indeed like the belt, and had worn it every day since the celebration – but after Zahir had teased him about the gift's significance, he'd been prey to a confused mixture of emotions. He told himself that he had not been avoiding Ghadira for the last few days, but that was not the whole truth, and deep down he knew it. He couldn't believe that she was attracted to him in any romantic way. And yet he recognized that there seemed to be some evidence to the contrary. But why would she be drawn to him? It made no sense.

For his part, he had to admit that the nomad girl was beautiful, but every time he even thought of the possibility of there being anything between them, his thoughts flew to Alyssa and he was immediately consumed by feelings of betrayal and guilt. The fact that, after so long, he was beginning to wonder if his memory of her was really accurate only made him feel worse. He loved Alyssa – but if he couldn't see her face, and she was half a world away, what did that mean? Ghadira's presence – her close, physical presence – only deepened his confusion, so it had been easier just to keep out of her way. Of course that was not always possible, as his present predicament demonstrated.

'What are you thinking?'

'Oh . . . nothing,' he lied awkwardly, unable to meet her gaze. There were times when he wished he could tell her about Alyssa – but it was too complicated and, in any case, by doing so he would be assuming that Ghadira was interested in him. If he was wrong, it would be unbearably embarrassing.

'There's a lot going on behind those eyes of yours,' she remarked. 'Things you don't tell anyone.'

Terrel didn't know how to respond to her mild accusation. Although she hadn't called him a liar to his face, the implication was there – and he was glad when Algardi rose to his feet to begin the proceedings.

'You all know why we're here,' the elder added, 'but first, is it agreed that we have stayed here long enough? The level of the spring is falling, and we don't want to exhaust the life of this place.'

The nomads all murmured their agreement.

'Then we'll leave at first light tomorrow,' Algardi decreed, correctly gauging the mood of the clan. Then he asked the winds and the moons to guide their thoughts in the decision to be made that day, and called for the prospective champions to announce themselves.

Zahir was on his feet immediately, declaring his name and lineage, and promising to protect and enhance the honour of the tribe to the best of his abilities. As he sat down again, Ghadira leant across Terrel to whisper to Medrano.

'He's going to sulk for months if we don't choose him.'

'I don't think it'll come to that,' the artist replied quietly.

Then two more young men announced their candidacy, though neither spoke with Zahir's assurance. The discussion that followed was not as long-winded as Ghadira had feared, consisting as it did of one speech of recommendation made by an elder on behalf of each of the contestants, and then some of the tribe asking each of the three young men about their proposed tactics for the race. None of this made much impression on Terrel, but by the end of the interrogations, most of the nomads seemed to have made up their minds.

Recognizing this, the other two candidates withdrew and Zahir was chosen as the Toma's champion by unanimous acclaim. He rose to his feet, accepted his election graciously, and announced that he would be honoured to have his two rivals as the first members of his team. They both agreed readily, and Terrel assumed that this outcome had been foreseen well in advance. The debate had been a formality. Doing things properly, as Medrano had put it.

'I'll let you all know who else is to join me in the next few days,' Zahir added, then sat down again with no further ado. Only the bright fire in his eyes betrayed his inner triumph.

'We can't take them all, Kala,' Terrel said, looking at the array of pebbles laid out in front of him. 'There are just too many. The camels already have enough to carry.'

During their few days' rest, Kalkara had gathered a collection of stones she'd found near the camp. Put together they made an impressive display, glittering in the late afternoon sunlight. Terrel hadn't realized just how many splendid colours could be found amidst so much undistinguished sand, but the evidence was before his eyes now. Some of the stones were of a single hue – rose pink, lime green, peach, lilac, dark red and jet black – all polished to a jewelled shine by the constant scouring of wind and sand. Others were more varied, marked with stripes or spots of two or more colours, and there were even a few translucent crystals that seemed to conceal mysterious images within their fractured depths. They were all beautiful – Kalkara had an excellent eye for such things – and some of them would undoubtedly have been valuable in Fenduca, the mining town in Macul whose very existence was dedicated to the search for such treasures. However, here they were regarded as worthless, commonplace leftovers from the desert's endless supply of barren rock, and Terrel knew the nomads would not allow Kala to keep all her finds.

'We just have to choose a few of the best ones to take with us.'

Kalkara frowned, obviously disappointed by his suggestion, but she soon came round to the idea when Terrel pointed out that the alternative was to throw them *all* away. She was in the process of dividing her favourites from the rest when Zahir came striding purposefully towards them. Terrel's heart began to beat a little faster as he wondered if he was about to be invited to join the team for the Race of Truth, but to his disappointment, Zahir walked straight past them. But then he hesitated, and turned to look at the jumble of stones.

'What *are* you doing?'

'Choosing the ones we want to take with us,' Terrel replied. 'Beautiful, aren't they?'

'They're just stones,' Zahir stated dismissively, earning him a glare from Kala. 'What use are they?'

Terrel was about to answer when he saw that Zahir's attention was already elsewhere. He'd spotted a girl called Byaddra, who had just emerged from a nearby tent.

'Now she *is* beautiful,' the nomad said. 'After I win the Race of Truth I might make her my first wife.'

'Your *first* wife?'

'"Marry only as many women as you can treat

equally",' Zahir replied, evidently quoting a well-known saying. 'I don't see why I should stop at just one.'

Terrel was astonished. Most Toma men only had one wife, as far as he could tell. Any other arrangement seemed unnatural to him, but Zahir's arrogance was reasserting itself. Being acclaimed as the tribe's champion had clearly done a great deal for his self-confidence.

'Then again,' he said thoughtfully, 'maybe I'll get a better offer in Qomish. The King of the Desert is always popular with the women.'

Terrel chose not to point out that Zahir hadn't begun the Race of Truth yet, let alone won it. He was beginning to remember why he had instinctively disliked the elder's son when they'd first met. Nevertheless, his own personal concerns forced him to set such considerations aside, and he took the opportunity to ask the question that had preoccupied him since the gathering.

'Will you want me as part of your team?'

'No.'

For a few moments Terrel was too stunned to respond. The last thing he had expected was such a definite, flat rejection.

'Why not?' he began eventually. 'I—'

'I've thought about it a lot,' Zahir cut in. 'You're a good healer, but we've others who can deal with any problems we're likely to encounter out there. To be honest, I don't think you're up to the rigours of the journey. You haven't even *seen* the real desert yet.'

'But—'

'No foreigner has ever gone into the Binhemma-Ghar, let alone all the way to Makranash,' Zahir went on, betraying his real feelings about Terrel's place among the

Toma. In the champion's eyes, he was still an outsider.

'I'm sorry,' Zahir added briskly, not sounding at all apologetic. 'I can see you want to go, and I can understand that, but you're not ready. You're better off here.' He glanced at Kalkara and her pile of stones.

The implication was not lost on Terrel. He was more suited to playing with a little girl and her toys than to adventuring with the nomad men. Given his physical disabilities, there was some justice in that – though it didn't make him feel any better. He had only just got used to the idea of being part of the race, of actually wanting to go into the heart of the desert, and now his assumption that he had the choice of doing so had been swept aside.

'Are you sure—' he said, making one last attempt.

'We can't let anyone slow us down,' Zahir said, interrupting him again. 'That's my final decision.'

So saying, he turned and went on his way. Kalkara glowered at his retreating back, then picked up one of the lesser pebbles and threw it at him. Fortunately for them both, she missed.

CHAPTER TWENTY-THREE

Now that all the outstanding issues had been settled, the Toma were travelling with renewed purpose. Their aim was to reach Qomish as soon as possible, and they planned to get there between three and five days before the start of the race. The Festival of the Winds traditionally began on the eve of the race, but the travelling parties from many tribes came earlier, eager to begin the round of trading that would go on for more than a median month – until the winner of the race returned to claim his prize. In a year that had brought traumatic changes and frequent conflict, the success of such trade would be vital to the wellbeing of many tribes, and as nomads, with no land of their own on which to grow crops, the Toma were no exception to this. The drought had meant that many staples of the wanderers' diet might well be in short supply, with fierce competition for what was available and prices higher than ever. Even so, everyone was looking forward to the great gathering. Whatever the possible drawbacks, the festival was still the most exciting time of the year.

Several days had passed since Zahir's election, and he had advised most of those who would be making up his team. However, a few places had yet to be filled, and knowing that he still had the best part of a month in which to persuade Zahir to change his mind, Terrel had decided to bide his time. He hoped that once Zahir's euphoria at being chosen had worn off, he would be more likely to take the advice of older and wiser heads, and that the advantages of including a healer in his group would be made clear to him. Several people, including Algardi and Medrano, had already spoken on Terrel's behalf, but so far Zahir had stuck to his original decision.

As far as Terrel knew, the only other person actively campaigning to be added to the team was Marrad. He was the only one of the captains who was older than their leader, and thus eligible to participate, but in spite of their friendship, Zahir clearly had some doubts. Terrel did not find this hard to understand. Marrad was very strong for someone of his age, and seemed to deal with even the harshest conditions easily enough, but he was not very bright. In a place as dangerous as the Binhemma-Ghar, stupidity could be as much a liability as physical weakness. One mistake could lead to disaster. Nonetheless, Marrad persisted in his entreaties, and Zahir obviously felt he owed him at least the chance to prove his worth. To this end he had allowed Marrad to accompany him on what he called his 'practice runs'.

Every third day – the elders flatly refused to let him do it more often – Zahir would walk a little way from the caravan on a parallel course, taking no food or drink from sunrise to sunset. In doing so he reproduced as closely as he could the conditions he would experience during the race. Although the heat was not as great, nor the terrain as forbidding, it was still a formidable test of stamina and determination. Marrad accepted the challenge gladly, even though he wouldn't have to endure such rigours during the race itself. And, not to be outdone, Nadur and Redin joined in too, even though – having not yet come of age – they knew they had no chance of making the trek to Makranash. None of the captains would presume to give Zahir advice, but there was no doubt that they were likely to have some influence over the champion's thinking. For that reason Terrel was careful in his dealings with them. He even considered volunteering to join them on one of the practice runs, but decided against it. Zahir was unlikely to let him take part, and even if he did, the chances were that the results would only confirm his opinion of the healer. It was also likely to be an exhausting exercise – which was why the elders had set limits to the project – and Terrel wanted to save all his energy for the race itself.

His conviction that there must be an elemental near Makranash remained strong and, one way or another, he was determined to make contact with the creature. It had been more than three and a half years now since he'd encountered the first of the Ancients and, even though he hadn't been aware of it initially, his travels since then had all been directed by the need to fulfil his bargain with them. Every instinct told him that he was where he was now in order to continue this task – and that the sacred mountain was where the next stage of his destiny was due to be played out.

The very fact that he had been in exile for so long, banished from his homeland by forces he was only just beginning to understand, made Terrel feel both weary and dejected. How long would it go on like this? When would he finally be able to turn his face towards home? That thought inevitably made him wonder when Alyssa would return. He longed to see her, no matter what form she took. Just hearing her voice would be wonderful. He was also desperate to talk to the ghosts, to discuss his plans with them and, hopefully, have them confirm that he was doing the right thing. Alyssa's ominous comments about the seers' preoccupation with the Tindaya Code, and Elam's uncharacteristic secrecy, had unnerved him, and now he needed to reassure himself that they were still his allies. They hadn't visited him for an inordinately long time.

Terrel was lost in such speculation as he trudged beside one of the camels, but his train of thought was interrupted by a scream – followed by several urgent shouts – coming from somewhere over to his right. Looking up, he saw that the commotion centred on Zahir and his captains, who had been walking a few hundred paces from the caravan. One of them had fallen to the ground, two others were crouched over the prostrate figure, and the fourth – Redin – was running at full tilt across the sand, heading straight for Terrel. Realizing that someone must be ill or injured, and in need of his help, Terrel began running himself, his lop-sided gait making him slower than several other nomads who were now heading the same way.

'Quickly!' Redin yelled, beckoning wildly even as he ran. 'Quickly!'

'What's happened?' Terrel gasped.

'Marrad's been . . . stung by . . . a lurker,' Redin panted as he turned to keep pace with the healer.

'A what?'

'A sand-scorpion. Be careful . . . when you get closer . . . We don't want . . . it to sting you too.'

Terrel didn't like the sound of that at all.

'Poison?' he breathed.

'The worst,' Redin replied.

By then several people had reached the spot where Marrad was lying, and one of them lifted him up and began to carry him towards Terrel. The rest of the group, as well as Zahir and Nadur, stayed where they were. They had drawn their knives, and were searching the ground, moving very cautiously, and Terrel assumed they were looking for the creature that had felled Marrad. Then the man carrying the victim reached Terrel, and laid him at the healer's feet.

'Do what you can,' he said breathlessly. 'I have to get some spears.'

As the tribesman ran off back towards the caravan, Terrel examined his patient. Marrad's face was frozen in an expression not of pain but of surprise. His eyes were wide open, staring unseeing at the sky, and his skin was much paler than normal. He was trembling slightly, and flecks of foam were collecting on his lips. A small puncture mark above his left ankle was oozing a clear liquid, while the flesh around it was swelling visibly even as Terrel stared. He had never seen anything like this before, and had no idea whether his skills were up to the task of saving the captain.

'Don't touch the wound,' Redin warned anxiously. 'The poison can reach you even through unbroken skin.'

Terrel nodded, his thoughts whirling. He reached out
and took Marrad's hand, hoping his instincts would show
him what to do, when a voice in his head threw him into
utter confusion.

Terrel?

'Alyssa?' He didn't realize he'd said her name out loud
until Redin spoke.

'What?' The youngest captain was looking puzzled
now, as well as frightened.

The waking dream teetered on the edge of Terrel's
consciousness, waiting to engulf him once he allowed
himself to fall, but Alyssa's voice claimed his attention.

What are you doing? Who's he?

He's ill. I'm trying to heal him. Where are you?

Over here, she replied uselessly. Psinoma did not allow
him to pinpoint the direction her voice was coming from.

'Can you save him?' Redin asked, unaware of the silent
conversation.

'I'm not sure,' Terrel replied, feeling suddenly inadequate, incapable of dealing with all the demands that were
being made upon him.

There are men with knives all around me, Alyssa
reported.

Terrel knew where she was then. More to the point,
he knew *what* she was.

Don't let them see you, he told her urgently.

They can't, she replied. *Several of them have already
looked straight at me and then moved on. It's as if I'm
invisible.*

Keep still then, he advised her.

I don't know what I am, Alyssa said thoughtfully, *but
this mind is very simple, very focused.*

I can't talk to you now, Terrel told her. *We'll speak as soon as I can.* 'What are they doing?' he asked aloud, indicating the armed men.

'Trying to find the lurker,' Redin answered shortly. 'What about Marrad? Is he going to die?'

'Not if I can help it. Why can't they see the lurker?'

'Sand-scorpions can change colour,' Redin explained, 'make themselves look just like the rock or sand they're standing on. You can only see them when they move.'

Keep very still, Alyssa, Terrel told her again.

Why? she queried.

Just do this for me, he pleaded. *I have to be a healer now.*

Hoping that she would heed his warning, Terrel let himself fall into Marrad's waking dream. The poison was not hard to find. It was like an unnatural shadow, spreading through his entire being, standing out not only because it was vile but also because it was *wrong*, a blight upon everything around it. Terrel could see his patient's health shrivelling before his inner eye. He shivered, feeling chilled, then told himself to *do* something. He could not afford to be afraid.

Concentrating on the venom, the healer drew on the anger he felt at the pernicious effects of such evil, and fed that energy into heat and light, instinctively seeking ways to force the enemy back. The toxin's progress faltered at his first assault, then reasserted itself and came on, as if aware of how close it was to victory. Terrel responded by feeding all his emotions into the battle, willing Marrad's own defences to come to his aid, and flooding the dream with as much warmth and brightness as he could.

Far away, in another world, there was a voice, which he recognized as Bubaqra's.

'Where's Mlicki? We need to know the aspects of the moons. Go and find him. Quickly!'

What do the moons matter? Terrel wondered, then realized that he knew the answer. The strength of the sand-scorpion's poison varied according to the phases of the moons. Even as he continued fighting against the cold shadow, the healer tried to remember the lunar alignments, but he was too distracted. He was also starting to feel weary now, the constant effort of holding the poison back beginning to take its toll. The darkness was not advancing any further, but nor was it retreating – and he could see no end to the stalemate.

'The Invisible should be full tonight, the Amber will be full in two days' time, and the White is two-thirds full but waning.' Mlicki's voice was faint, a wavering echo from a distant realm.

'What about the Red Moon?'

'It's waning too. Just under half full, I think.'

'Waning? You're sure?' Bubaqra sounded worried. 'Both the Red and White Moons?'

'Yes.'

'Then there isn't much hope,' she concluded heavily. 'Not even Vilheyuna . . .'

Her words faded into silence as Terrel deliberately shut the voices out and focused on the battle for Marrad's life. The captain's spirit was flickering now, on the point of giving up the unequal struggle. The pain that had come as the venom invaded almost every part of his being was beginning to overwhelm his resistance. Terrel sensed the body starting to shut down, willing itself to die rather than face the continued agony.

'He's stopped breathing.'

The unknown voice was barely audible, but the under-lying sense of loss and disappointment were clear enough.

No! Terrel raged silently. I won't let this happen. Come on, Marrad. Fight! The healer fed every particle of his determination into his efforts, and was rewarded by a sudden rush of light flooding through the dream. He heard someone cough and splutter, and knew from the surprise and delight in the muted voices around him that Marrad had begun to breathe again. More! Terrel yelled, knowing that he couldn't let himself – or Marrad – relax for a moment. You can beat this. You can!

He had the measure of the pain now, diverting it, allowing his patient's shock to subside, making it possible for him to try to deal with the underlying cause. The shadows retreated a little, but that was all. Driving them out completely was another matter altogether – and it was beginning to look as though it would be beyond their combined strength. Terrel knew that without his help Marrad would already have been dead, and if he with-drew now the end would come quickly. He seemed to have been battling for the captain's life for hours, and his own resilience was fading, but he hung on grimly, earning a little more time. And through it all, he just wanted it to be over so that he could see that Alyssa was all right, and talk to her.

Marrad's resistance faltered, and there was nothing Terrel could do to prevent the poison advancing again. He was nearly spent, close to a fatal despair.

And then a new vision came into the dream, from outside their joint world – a vision of the Dark Moon, surrounded by a brilliant, shifting halo of light. It was a sight Terrel had seen before, during an eclipse, but he didn't know what it signified here. An eclipse occurred at the new moon, and yet the Dark Moon was full, at the peak of its influence. Could he use its power somehow? It was *his* moon, after all.

At this thought, his entire world grew dark, and Terrel was about to admit defeat when he realized that the darkness came not from the triumph of the shadows but from an influx of black *light*. It made no sense, but – somehow – the Dark Moon had come to his aid.

When the dream returned, the shadows were retreating, and Terrel could feel warmth returning to the unreal world – and to Marrad's hand.

'He's got a chance,' he heard someone say. 'If he's not dead by now . . .'

'Look at the wound!'

You're winning! Terrel told Marrad, watching as the shadows fell back even further. The last of the pain was being neutralized, defeated by the victim's own revitalized defences. He would live. He would be ill for a time, but he *would* live. Relief made Terrel feel dizzy as he released his grip on Marrad's hand. He almost collapsed, but managed to remain upright, kneeling beside his patient.

For the first time, Terrel was able to look around and see the crowd gathered about him. Bubaqra, Mlicki, Algardi and Kalkara were there, and he couldn't see beyond them to the place where Marrad had been attacked. That was presumably where Alyssa still was – if she had been able to stay.

Alyssa? he called silently.

I'm still here. What's going on?

You poisoned one of the people I'm travelling with.

No! I . . . It must have happened before I got here.

It doesn't matter. Just stay perfectly still.

Several nomads were now tending to Marrad, while others were trying to help Terrel, asking him if he wanted to be lifted to his feet. He waved them away, knowing that his legs would give way beneath him.

'The scorpion?' he croaked. 'Have they found it yet?'

'No, but they will,' Algardi reassured him. 'It can't hide for ever, and when it moves they'll kill it.' The elder pointed across to where several men waited, armed now with long spears.

'Marrad's not going to die,' Terrel said. 'Why risk someone else getting stung? Can't we just leave it alone?'

'We must kill it,' Algardi replied. 'Once a lurker has attacked one human being, it becomes a menace to everyone. Normally they hide from us, and they only attack if we're unlucky enough to get too close. But once a sand-scorpion has stung a man, it goes out of its way to do it again and again. No one knows why. We have no choice but to hunt it down.'

'I'm surprised it hasn't already tried to attack again,' someone added. 'That's normally when we catch them.'

Terrel was about to continue the argument when he was stunned by the appearance of the three ghosts, only a few paces away. Shahan, Muzeni and Elam all looked astonished by the scene they had entered – and by the landscape around them.

Terrel desperately wanted to talk to them, but he knew what he had to do, even though it almost broke his heart.

Alyssa! You have to leave.

But I've only just got here. And—

If they see you they'll kill you, Terrel cut in. *You have to go, then come back as something else.*

What about us? Muzeni asked. *We need—*

Later! Terrel snapped. *If Alyssa doesn't go now, we could lose everything.*

'Are you all right?' Mlicki asked anxiously.

Terrel looked at him, wondering if his friend had heard some echo of his conversation. Then he caught sight of Kalkara. She was staring, wide-eyed, at the ghosts.

'I'm fine,' Terrel said, addressing his words to the little girl. 'Everything is all right.'

Even as he spoke he saw the ghosts fading, and knew that Alyssa had gone. Moments later a cry went up from the hunters, and there was movement as the spears did their work. Kalkara's expression softened, though she still looked puzzled. Of all the nomads, she was the only one who had given any sign of noticing the ghosts.

'We got it!' Zahir shouted triumphantly, as he ran over to see how his captain was faring.

Terrel swallowed hard, hoping that Alyssa had got away in time. He wanted to lie down, to sleep, but there was something he had to do before he could allow himself any rest.

'Can I see the lurker?'

The creature was brought to him, still impaled upon the blade of a spear. It was much longer than any of the scorpions he'd seen earlier in his travels, and a drop of poison still clung to the barb at the end of its curled tail. Terrel suppressed a shudder as he inspected it closely. To his great relief, Alyssa's ring was nowhere to be seen.

'Thank you,' he whispered.

'We're the ones who should be thanking *you*,' Bubaqra said, but the healer wasn't paying any attention.

As Terrel slumped to the ground, having reached the limit of his resources, Marrad was struggling to sit up.

'What happened?' he mumbled blearily.

'You should be dead, you dumb ox,' Zahir told him. 'But Terrel saved you. I'm not sure what—'

A dark and dreamless sleep claimed Terrel then, and he heard no more.

CHAPTER TWENTY-FOUR

Terrel woke to find the world swaying around him. It was all he could do not to close his eyes again and retreat back into the sanctuary of sleep, but he forced himself to look around. By the time he realized that it was not the world that was swaying but his own passage through it, his re-emergence had been noticed.

'I was beginning to think you weren't ever going to wake up,' Mlicki remarked. He was in the other seat of the double saddle, balancing Terrel's weight across the camel who was carrying them both.

'I almost wish I hadn't,' Terrel grumbled. He still felt weary, and he was very stiff. 'Did you have to tie me in so tightly?' Bands of cloth were bound around his waist and legs, keeping him in place.

'We didn't want you to fall off,' his friend replied. 'It's a long way down.'

Terrel glanced down, then wished he hadn't. The ground was still tilting alarmingly. Nevertheless, he began to loosen his bonds.

'There's a waterskin by your left arm if you want a drink,' Mlicki informed him. 'How are you feeling?'

'I'm fine,' Terrel replied. 'More or less.' He retrieved the flagon, unstoppered it and drank gratefully. 'How's Marrad?'

'He's well. Still weak, but considering he ought to be dead, that doesn't bother anyone very much. You're a hero now, my friend.'

'Don't be stupid.'

'Actually, I think that's an understatement,' Mlicki went on. 'As far as the Toma are concerned, you're now well on your way to becoming a legend! What you did yesterday—'

'Yesterday?' Terrel exclaimed. 'How long have I been asleep?'

'A full day, and then some,' Mlicki replied. 'That's why we've set off again. The elders decided we couldn't afford to wait any longer.'

Terrel took a few moments to digest the fact that he had lost an entire day. His actions in saving Marrad had obviously exhausted him completely, but he still didn't understand why his efforts should have impressed the nomads so much. At the time, other aspects of what had been going on had seemed – and still seemed – to be more important. And now his overriding concern was the thought of when Alyssa and the ghosts were likely to come back. The fact that he had forced them to leave felt barely credible. The loss of such an opportunity, especially when he hadn't known when he might get another, was enormously frustrating. He knew he'd had no choice – the memory of the sand-scorpion impaled on the spear was proof enough of that – but that didn't help him now.

He was brooding about this when he realized that Mlicki was still talking.

'. . . is what made it so impressive. The venom's especially virulent when the White Moon is waning – one life growing weaker – and if one or more of the other moons is also waning, the effect is even worse. Not even Vilheyuna was ever able to save one of the lurkers' victims in circumstances like that. And yet Marrad's hardly showing any ill effects at all now. The swelling in his leg has gone down, and the skin's not even discoloured. Healing like that would turn *anyone* into a legend.'

'That's ridiculous.'

'All right, so maybe I'm exaggerating a bit,' Mlicki conceded. 'But not much. Seriously, Terrel, what you achieved has earned you more respect than ever, and not just as a healer. The elders are all talking about asking *you* for advice now, and Zahir's been converted too. If you're still set on going on the race with him, I don't think he'd dare refuse you a place now.'

This was good news, but just at that moment Terrel was too tired to contemplate such matters. He was still trying to remember the events of the previous day, and to work out their ramifications.

'Has Kala been all right?' he asked.

'Kala? Yes, of course. Why?'

Terrel was sure that Kalkara had seen the ghosts, but they had not seemed to bother her unduly. Although the appearance of the spectres had certainly shocked the girl, she had shown no real fear.

'I saw her there,' he said feebly, knowing that Mlicki was puzzled. 'I just thought she might have been frightened.'

'Not at all. She was more concerned about you than Marrad – she doesn't like him much – but I don't think she was too worried. Bubaqra told her you weren't hurt, just sleeping.'

Another secret then, Terrel thought. Kalkara, the girl without words, knew more about him than anyone else in the tribe.

Beneath them the camel stumbled, making the seats rock violently for a moment, and Terrel was suddenly glad that he was still tied in place.

'Steady, boy!' Mlicki called.

The camel's progress was erratic for a few paces, lurching forward and from side to side, as if its legs were operating independently of one another. Then it settled back into a steady, rolling gait. At the same time, a rumbling from deep within its body erupted from its mouth in a bubbling roar, and this was followed by a series of diminishing belches that ended in a kind of hiccup. By then both Terrel and Mlicki were laughing uncontrollably, and the animal seemed to sense that it had become an object of ridicule. Twisting its long neck around so that it could look at Terrel, it bared discoloured teeth in a nightmarish grimace – which was made even more comical when it raised its huge bushy eyebrows in apparent surprise.

I'm glad you think it's funny, Alyssa remarked, silencing Terrel's laughter in an instant. *This thing's got at least three stomachs, and it's got indigestion in all of them!*

For a variety of reasons it was evening before Terrel was able to talk properly to Alyssa. Mlicki's presence had been an inhibiting factor. He'd been intrigued by his friend's behaviour, and at one point he'd even asked if Terrel was talking to someone, tapping the side of his head to indicate that he meant by using psinoma. Knowing that his friend was also reasonably adept at communicating in this way made Terrel wonder again whether Mlicki might 'hear' some part of any silent conversation. He wanted to tell his friend the truth, but he wasn't sure Mlicki would believe him. And if he did, what would his reaction be when he learnt that Terrel was talking to their camel? As a result, his initial exchanges with Alyssa had been limited to checking on each other's welfare, and a few expressions of his pleasure at her return. She had told him that the ghosts had been very busy lately, but that they would be there soon. In the end, Terrel spent most of the afternoon simply enjoying her presence and sharing the occasional joke at the expense of her current host. He also tried – and failed – to discover the latest resting place for Alyssa's ring.

When the caravan stopped that night, the handlers were puzzled by the camel's odd behaviour. The routines of unloading and setting up camp, of feeding and foraging, were as familiar to the beasts as they were to the nomads, but this particular animal seemed to have forgotten everything it had ever learnt. At length, fearing that Alyssa might be mistreated – or do something rash – Terrel begged to be allowed to tend to the camel personally.

'I think it's probably my fault,' he explained. 'I must have unnerved him somehow. Let me calm him down.'

After his exploits the day before, the Toma were ready to believe that Terrel was capable of anything, and so his plea was heeded.

I'm getting the hang of this, Alyssa muttered as she

lowered herself to the ground, front legs kneeling first, then the back legs collapsing in turn. *It's a bit like a horse, but a lot more awkward and a lot less mad.*

We can talk properly now, Terrel said as he sat down in front of her.

About time too!

It's not my fault, he said, reacting to the critical edge to her voice.

Isn't it?

You haven't been here! And if you'd stayed in the lurker, you'd have been killed.

Well, I'm here now, she replied, her tone softening. *And so are the others.*

As she spoke, the three ghosts materialized in the air beside her, faintly luminescent in the fading light. As always, Muzeni's image was less clear than those of the other two. He'd been dead for several hundred years, and his spirit's connection to Terrel's world was not as well defined. Even so, he made a distinctive figure in his outlandish clothes. One of the few possessions Terrel had been able to keep with him during all his travels was the clay pipe that had once belonged to the ancient heretic. The other two ghosts were more recently dead, both murdered at least in part because of their connection to Terrel. He had seen Shahan killed in a dream that had been real; Elam had been stabbed before his waking eyes. Although Terrel still felt some guilt over what had happened to his friends, he was very glad to see them now.

What is this place? Elam breathed, looking round at the desert. *Couldn't you find anywhere habitable to hide?*

I'm not hiding. I—

No. Alyssa told us . . . He paused, having apparently seen the camel for the first time. *Moons! What are you?*

Alyssa had been chewing slowly, and now she spat out a wad of something indescribable. Her aim was perfect, but the missile passed through Elam's body as if there was nothing there.

It's a camel, Terrel told him. *A male.*

Which probably explains why she's in such a bad mood, Elam said, laughing. *This is your best disguise yet, Alyssa.*

Terrel suddenly realized, for the first time, that Elam still looked exactly as he had when he'd been killed. Unlike Terrel, he hadn't aged at all. He was still fifteen years old – and probably would be for all time. The thought made Terrel almost choke with sadness.

If you three have quite finished, Shahan said impatiently, *there's a great deal we need to discuss.*

There certainly is, Terrel agreed, eager to move on. *Did Alyssa tell you why I think I'm here?*

Yes, Muzeni replied. *We want—*

Well, there's more now.

Recognizing their protégé's need to talk, the ghosts fell silent and waited for him to go on. Terrel took up his story, beginning with the aftermath of Alyssa's appearance as the djerboa. Then he told them about Zahir's kappara-tan.

I gave a version of what happened in Talazoria as part of the storytelling, he said, after he'd described the ceremony itself, *but there was no reaction when I told them about the elemental. Still, that doesn't mean there isn't one here.*

Just that the Toma don't know about it, Muzeni agreed.

Exactly. Terrel told the ghosts about the trick that had been played on him, and about Jax's intervention. *Of course, that confirmed the nomads' idea that I was the voice of rain, even though it wasn't my doing.*

So that's *what was happening,* Elam said, an unusually thoughtful expression on his face.

What do you mean?

I've been keeping an eye on your brother. I'll tell you more about that later, but on one occasion his dreams got very animated. He was shouting and laughing. I knew something was happening, and that it concerned you, but it was all very confused. Especially when I tried to interfere, he added, grinning.

You tried to get a message to me, didn't you? Terrel said, remembering.

I knew I wasn't going to be able to see you in person for a while, Elam explained, *so I thought I'd take advantage of the situation if I could. I get the feeling it didn't work.*

No, it didn't. What were you trying to tell me?

I wanted to warn you that Jax has been meddling with the Ancient in Betancuria.

What! Terrel was aghast. *Why would he do that?*

I've no idea, Elam said. *He's not exactly made himself popular with the seers, or the locals, but he doesn't seem to care. There's been—*

We'll come to that later, Shahan cut in. *I'd like to hear the rest of Terrel's story first.*

For a moment Terrel thought about arguing, but decided against it. It seemed that the ghosts were going to stay for as long as was necessary, and he would learn all he needed to know in due course. So he returned to another of his concerns from the night of Zahir's coming of age.

If Mlicki is someone who's susceptible to Jax, does that make it more or less likely that he's one of the Mentors?

I can't see that it matters one way or the other, Shahan commented gravely.

It just means you'd better not turn your back on him when Jax is around, Elam remarked, then looked awkward. *Sorry, Shahan.*

The seer had been the victim of another man who'd fallen under the enchanter's spell – and had been slain by a crossbow bolt in the back. Terrel hurried to continue with his tale, describing the next significant event in his journey through Misrah. He became so caught up with the details of the massacre at Triq Dalam, and the subsequent discovery of the refugee children, that he almost forgot to mention Elodia's strange illness. When he did, Muzeni and Shahan exchanged glances, and Terrel wondered if they might have come across anything similar. However, neither of the seers said anything, and so he went on to describe the oracle of the white hawk – and his own uncanny resemblance to the double-headed man. The ghosts made no response to this either.

The four circles, he added, holding up his tattooed hand. *They were part of the oracle too. It's another link between me and this land, don't you think?*

I think we can take that for granted, Muzeni said, confirming for the first time that the ghosts agreed with Terrel about the purpose of his journey to the desert.

No one agrees on the exact interpretation, though, Terrel added, hoping that the seers might be able to shed some light on this, *except that we should be wary of the time of storms.*

You don't have to be an oracle to know you should be careful when storms are about, Elam remarked.

No one else offered any comment.

Go on, Terrel, Shahan said.

The next important thing was the sand mist. He told them about his vision of the canyon and the river, and described the sound that had accompanied it. *It was like the noise I heard at Tindaya. If the vision was accurate, then I think it's more evidence that there's an elemental here.*

Who diverted the river for its own ends, Muzeni agreed, nodding.

Then I found out where Vilheyuna became a sleeper, Terrel went on. The ghosts listened calmly as he outlined his theory about the Ancient's lair, and told them of his plan to join the Race of Truth. *I still can't work out why the elementals choose to save some people and not others,* he added, glancing at Alyssa, *but their connection to the sleepers isn't in any doubt, is it?*

Alyssa remained silent.

That's about it, Terrel concluded. *Yesterday, when you all arrived, it was in the middle of a crisis, which is why—*

Trust Alyssa to poison someone just when we finally get here, Elam teased.

The camel gave him a baleful glare, but didn't rise to the bait.

So that's all my news. Now, what about you?

There was a moment's silence before Shahan spoke.

We're worried that something important might have

gone wrong, he said. *All our certainties about the Code are crumbling, and . . .* He faltered, glancing at Muzeni for support.

Your presence here might be responsible for the outbreak of a great plague, the heretic stated.

Terrel was stunned, unable to respond.

The portents aren't good, Muzeni went on. *Even the seers in Makhaya have recognized that.*

In Makhaya? Terrel exclaimed, disbelief freeing his tongue. *Even if there is a plague here, it couldn't possibly spread as far as the Floating Islands.* He looked back and forth between the solemn, ghostly faces. *Could it?*

It already has, Shahan told him.

CHAPTER TWENTY-FIVE

That's not possible! Terrel exclaimed.

I'm afraid it is. Shahan replied. *We've seen it for ourselves.*

But what makes you think it originated here?

As you know, Muzeni said, *the Code has several apocalyptic descriptions of earthquakes, tidal waves, vast storms and the like. But there's one particularly unpleasant section that no one's ever understood – until now. It tells of thousands of people dying because of a terrible plague. The illness is said to have overrun 'a blasted land' where nothing grew, and spread from there. The seers have always assumed that the plague caused the devastation to the land, but when Alyssa told us about where you were – and now that we've seen it for ourselves – it's obvious the passage is a description of the place where the plague began. Here.*

And what you've just told us is confirmation of that, Shahan added.

Why? Terrel was bewildered now.

The plague itself – both in the prophecy and in what's currently happening on Vadanis – is characterized by a fervent and quite irrational fear of water, the seer explained. *Like the girl in Triq Dalam.*

In the worst cases, the victims die of thirst because they refuse to drink, can't even bear to have water anywhere near them, Muzeni said. *No one's been able to work out how the disease spreads. It seems to strike at random. But I'm sure you can guess where the greatest concentration of deaths has been.*

Betancuria, Terrel said, and knew he was right even before Shahan confirmed his thoughts.

It's reached epidemic proportions.

And you think the elementals are responsible?

Don't you? Muzeni replied. *Isn't it obvious?*

Terrel paused for a moment to take this in, then returned to one of the seers' earlier revelations.

But why me? Why should my presence cause the plague to begin? It doesn't make any sense.

I'll try to explain, Shahan said. *We're speculating now, but the argument makes as much sense as anything. Assuming there is an elemental in Misrah, it seems possible that when you entered its territory – after you crossed the sea that divides this land mass from the next – it sensed your presence. Because of what you've already been through, it may even have recognized you. At the same time, because of your bargain with its brothers, it may have become aware of them for the first time.*

Through me?

Exactly. Just as the creature in Talazoria became aware of the one in Betancuria.

But I had to make direct contact with it before that happened, Terrel objected.

Perhaps the Ancients have become more aware of their surroundings now, Shahan said. *Or perhaps you've changed.*

Even if that's true, I still don't see why—

It thought of you as a friend, Muzeni cut in, *but when you became the 'voice of rain', it saw that as a betrayal. It's possible the elementals understand humans better now, because of their contact with you. And you're a healer. Your instincts may have allowed it to see inside the workings of the human mind and body. But because it believed you'd deceived it – and that therefore men were the enemy after all – it decided to try to make us all hate water as much as they do.*

When it found that this worked, Shahan said, *at least on some people, it told the other two, and they tried the same thing. We know that they can communicate once they've been made aware of each other's existence, even if we don't understand how they do it. That's how the plague could spread halfway round Nydus in no time at all.*

But surely the others would have told the one here that I helped them avoid water, Terrel argued. *I helped them.*

Perhaps this creature retains a certain amount of independence, and would only trust the evidence it had seen in its own domain, Muzeni suggested. *Or perhaps their more recent experiences have made the others reconsider their views on humanity.*

Think about it, Shahan added. *In this place, humans seek out water. They spend their whole lives doing little else. You can see how that could affect the Ancient's view of them. And of you.*

Especially when you proved it right by producing rain – twice! Muzeni said.

But that wasn't even my doing.

We *know that,* the heretic conceded, *but the elemental may not be able to distinguish between you and Jax. You're connected to what it sees as evil magic and, as yet, you've had no chance to put your side of the story.*

So how do I do that?

The same way you dealt with the other two, Shahan replied. *By finding it and talking to it directly.*

And as soon as possible, Muzeni added. *Before the plague destroys the whole planet.*

By now Terrel was feeling as if he'd been physically beaten, and he desperately wanted to lie down and escape into sleep. Every part of his body hurt, and his head felt as though it were being crushed under the weight of so much unwanted knowledge. But there were questions he couldn't leave unasked.

Elodia is the only case I've actually seen here, he said, *though I've heard rumours about others. And we can't be sure she was going to die. If the plague really started here, why does it seem to be so much worse on Vadanis?*

Two reasons, Shahan replied. *Firstly, there's more water on and around the Floating Islands than there is here, so the fear of it would be more acute. And secondly, the elemental there is much closer to a large number of people. It seems that the further away you are from one of the Ancients, the less likely you are to be affected.*

So you do *think the one here is in the Binhemma-*

Ghar? At Makranash? Terrel said, picking up the implications of Shahan's words.

We're almost sure of it, Muzeni confirmed.

Have you been able to check? Terrel knew that the ghosts could return to Vadanis – their own territory from their earlier lives – of their own volition. Elsewhere, as in Misrah, they needed Alyssa's help to guide them. If there was indeed an elemental at the sacred mountain, none of the ghosts would be able to get within several miles of the place, even with her aid. They would be repelled by a force that could not be seen or felt by the people of Terrel's world, but which to the ghosts had the strength of a hurricane.

Not yet, Muzeni admitted. *We could try, I suppose. Just to be certain.*

Don't be too sure of that, Alyssa warned, entering the discussion for the first time. *There are no animals at all for miles around that mountain. I may not be able to get you close enough.*

I don't really think it's necessary, Shahan told them. *The Code mentions a 'mountain built of winds' as one of the places where the Guardian and the Mentor are supposed to interact again. There's no known connection between that section and the piece mentioning the plague, but from what you've said, it must surely be a reference to Makranash.*

So I've got to go there, Terrel concluded. *I'd more or less worked that out for myself.* I just didn't know how urgent the journey would be, he added to himself.

This Race of Truth doesn't sound like much fun, Elam commented, re-entering the conversation at last. *Isn't there any other way of getting to the mountain?*

Not unless Ysatel can come to carry me there, Terrel replied, referring to his airborne rescue in Talazoria.

I wish I could've seen that, his friend said with a grin, then became serious again. *If you're really going to have to put yourself through all that, we should at least make absolutely certain that's where the Ancient is. The seers haven't exactly been infallible when it comes to interpreting the Code so far. No offence*, he added, glancing at Shahan and Muzeni.

None taken, the heretic said, with surprising humility.

I stand corrected, his colleague said.

Although Terrel was surprised by their response, he had already sensed a subtle change in the relationships within the trio. In the past, the seers had both been dogmatic, even pompous at times, and had obviously regarded Elam as insignificant. They would certainly never have taken his criticism so meekly. Terrel was intrigued, and wondered what could have happened to produce such a change, but there was no time for that now.

We'll try as soon as we can, then, Elam decided, looking to Alyssa for confirmation. The camel nodded in agreement. No one spoke for a while.

There's something else you should be aware of, Shahan said eventually. He sounded reluctant, and Terrel braced himself for more bad news. *From the moment the race begins, you'll obviously be getting closer to the elemental.*

Assuming it's there in the first place, Elam commented pedantically.

The seer nodded, and shrugged that idea aside.

The closer you get, the greater the risk will be of the plague affecting you. If any of your companions are vulnerable, then they're likely to succumb eventually.

Your champion might fall ill, as could any member of the team. It's even conceivable that it might affect you.

This possibility had not even occurred to Terrel, and he instinctively rejected it.

No, he said. *I know the truth. I'll be all right.* The prospect of Zahir being affected was more worrying. If the champion collapsed during the hours of daylight, the chances were that he would die – even if the plague itself did not prove fatal.

You might want to see whether you can devise some way of testing for latent signs of the disease, Shahan suggested. *Try to determine who is at risk before you start.*

I'll see what I can do, Terrel promised, sighing inwardly at having yet another task added to his list.

There's something else to consider, Muzeni told him. *We've been studying the lunar aspects of your travels, and we've come up with something rather interesting. When you were in Macul, you were in the sphere of greatest influence of the Amber Moon – dreams, and so on. Here you've passed into the realm of the White Moon.*

Logic and destiny, Terrel said. *I was coming to that conclusion myself.* He was thinking of the way the White Moon – more than any of the others – seemed to dominate the nomads' lives. *What does that mean for me exactly?*

Just that you should be aware of its cycle, when it's full or new, waxing or waning, the heretic answered. *It might just have some bearing on your efforts.*

I thought my destiny was tied to the Dark Moon.

It is, Shahan replied, *but it's not just your destiny we're dealing with here.*

You will return to the Dark Moon, Alyssa stated.

Return?

Every circle returns to its beginning.

She's talking in riddles again, Elam muttered.

When I get back to Vadanis? Terrel asked, ignoring the interruption.

Perhaps, Alyssa replied.

The thought of his homeland reminded Terrel of an earlier disclosure.

Has Jax's meddling at Betancuria made things better or worse?

As far as the plague's concerned, Muzeni replied, *we've no way of telling.*

Knowing the prince, it's unlikely to have improved matters, Shahan declared sardonically.

There's no evidence one way or the other, Elam said. *Obviously it's the one place on the island I couldn't follow him, but we know for sure that he's caused several minor earthquakes and even a few tornadoes. He treats them like playthings – though nobody around him even seems to notice what he's doing!*

Unfortunately, no one at court is overendowed with great intellect, Muzeni commented sourly.

Has Havenmoon been affected? Terrel asked, remembering his last sight of Alyssa sleeping in the basement of the asylum. *By the tremors, I mean.*

I'm fine, Alyssa assured him patiently. *I've told you many times. I'm protected.*

Although Terrel did not understand how the mysterious forces that surrounded his friend could protect her if the entire building collapsed, he recognized her tone of voice and knew better than to argue.

What exactly is Jax doing? he asked instead. *Do we know?*

I'm not sure, Elam replied, *but I think he's opened up some of the sealed mine shafts. I've even heard that he's had soldiers pour water into the tunnels.*

Is he insane? Terrel exclaimed, aghast.

Good question.

Why would he want to do something so dangerous?

Mischief? Elam suggested. *Malice? Boredom?*

Boredom?

I get the feeling the prince may be jealous of you.

Of me? Terrel queried in disbelief.

While you're off having all these adventures, he's stuck at home with his doting parents and a group of numbingly dull courtiers.

Talking about the prince's parents – who were his own parents too – always filled Terrel with a powerful mixture of emotions, none of which were very pleasant. With a deliberate effort, he set aside his sadness and resentment, and concentrated again on practical matters.

More to the point, he said, *why is anyone letting Jax do all these stupid things? Why would the seers risk breaking the agreement that saved the islands?*

You're forgetting that as far as the Floating Islands are concerned, Jax is still the Guardian. Muzeni spoke contemptuously, as he usually did when he referred to the living seers. *So, by definition, whatever he does has to be good for the Empire. He can get away with anything.*

But there must be some people who have their doubts about him.

There are a few, Shahan agreed, *but not enough to overcome the fear of his supporters.*

Is A-Adina still claiming to be the Mentor? Terrel asked, stumbling over his mother's name.

She is. Privately, no one takes that very seriously, but Jax's claim is much stronger. We're the only ones who know what his real role was. The frustration of not being able to educate his former colleagues was clear in Shahan's words – and in his hard grey eyes. *While they labour under that misapprehension, there's little chance of them getting things right when they try to reinterpret the Code. It might be different if Lathan were around, but he's still a sleeper.*

At Tindaya? Terrel asked, recalling his encounter with the renegade seer.

No. His body was found and taken back to Makhaya. As far as I know it's still there.

The one thing Kamin and his cronies seem to have got right is that the Dark Moon's orbit is still changing, Muzeni said.

Really? Terrel was surprised. *I know its cycle altered, but I thought it had settled into a new pattern – a regular one.*

So did most people, the heretic said with a touch of his old smugness. *The later changes are very subtle, but they still make a huge difference to any long-term calculations.*

The next four-moon conjunction? Terrel guessed.

It's now reckoned to be due forty-one years after the last, not seventy-five, Muzeni confirmed. *That's only twenty-three years from now. However, my guess is that it'll change again before too long.*

It's getting closer, Terrel observed.

Still plenty of time, though, Elam commented. *Before we all get wiped out by the apocalypse, that is.*

You're already dead, Alyssa pointed out.

So I am, he said amiably. *Before you all get wiped out then.*

This is no joking matter, Shahan berated him.

I know that. But don't you ever think that whoever devised the Tindaya Code might have been playing a huge joke on us?

The two seers stared at him as if he was insane, but Elam held their gaze without flinching.

I mean, he went on, *wherever they are – and they're certainly not in our world, are they? – they're probably watching us run round like scalded ants, and laughing till they're sick. Look at the facts. There's an ancient prophecy written on the stones of a ruined temple on top of a mountain. Not very helpful, is it? Not only that, but it's been broken and jumbled up, and some of it's missing. And the bits that can be read are written in a language we can't always translate, and even when we do, it's sometimes so obscure it makes the average oracle seem like a model of unambiguous brevity. The two main characters in its hallowed pages are the Guardian, who's described variously as a king, a prophet, a god, as well as some sort of creature, who was born – or maybe only woke up – at a lunar confluence, and the Mentor, who's a teacher, a go-between and an interpreter, who has to guide this other bloke and teach him the difference between good and evil. You know, simple tasks for everyday folk. Oh, and just in case that isn't complicated enough, there might be one or more of either or both of them. Nobody's really sure. The only thing we are sure of is that everything in the prophecy is supposed to happen during the seventy-five years between one four-moon conjunction and the next.*

The Guardian has to fulfil his destiny then, or we all die horribly as the planet tears itself apart. Except that it turns out it's not seventy-five years after all. It's sixty-five, or sixty, or forty-one. It's crazy.

Have you quite finished? Muzeni enquired, after a moment's stunned silence.

For now, Elam replied quietly.

It was the longest speech Terrel had ever heard his friend make – and the most impassioned. Beneath the sarcasm and flippancy there had been a real sense of anger and injustice.

It's real, Elam, Terrel said softly. *We may not like it, and it's not fair. But we have to deal with it.*

I know that, the ghost replied heavily. *You've proved that already, and I've no doubt you will again before you're finished. But sometimes it helps to keep things in perspective.*

He has a point, Alyssa said, before either of the seers could respond. *Fate can take care of itself. What we have to do is focus on the immediate issues.*

I thought that's what we were doing, Muzeni sniffed.

We needn't concern ourselves with what's going to happen twenty-three years into the future, she went on. *Let's concentrate on the present.*

There was another short but awkward pause, before Shahan returned to the fray.

All right. To be specific, he said, looking down his great beak of a nose at Elam, *we've already agreed that the Code seems to indicate Terrel should go to Makranash. Let's start from there.*

Do you still think the Ancients are the Guardian? Terrel asked.

It's the best theory we have, the seer replied. *We know they can affect the land around them in ways we can't even hope to emulate, so it's more than possible that in acting together they would be able to prevent the cataclysm. If they choose to do so, of course. It's obvious they have the capacity for both good and evil.*

Which means you think I'm the Mentor.

You're certainly the go-between for our two species, yes.

But there may be others?

Possibly. The Code—

But even if there are others, Elam cut in, *Terrel's the one who's here.*

And I'm the one who made the bargain with them, Terrel concluded. *So it's up to me.*

We'll all do whatever we can to help, Muzeni promised.

And our main priority is to try to put an end to this plague, Shahan added. *Or the world won't even be worth saving.*

Terrel nodded. That had to be his most immediate goal, though there were others he had in mind. But he didn't want to share his ideas with his companions yet.

I'll do my best, he said. *The first thing I've got to do is make sure I take part in the Race of Truth.*

You have to go now, Alyssa told the ghosts abruptly. *I need to rest.*

The two seers accepted their dismissal without demur, vanishing in the same instant, but Elam stayed where he was.

I'm curious, he said. *What happens if one of the other teams in the race reaches the top of the mountain first? Do you and Zahir still go on?*

No, Terrel replied. *Once the race is over, everyone turns back to Qomish.*

Elam nodded, his image fading even as he spoke his parting words.

You'd better make sure you win, then, he said.

CHAPTER TWENTY-SIX

You will come with me to Makranash, won't you? Terrel
said, hoping Alyssa would not need to 'rest' immediately.

Of course, she replied. *I'd rather not travel in* this,
though.

You may not have much choice, he said, though he
was relieved by her positive response. *Would being a
camel for a long time be such a problem?*

Once they reached the area where the invisible forces
prevented the ghosts from going any further, Alyssa's
spirit would be trapped in whatever animal she was
inhabiting at the time. To try to leave would mean
annihilation, so she had to choose carefully. Some of her
hosts had been a lot easier to live with than others.

It might be, she replied, *but, as you say, I may not
have a choice. We'll see.*

At least I know what I'm supposed to do now, Terrel
said. *I was right about being meant to come here.*

When Alyssa didn't respond to this comment, he wondered what she was thinking about. He was just going to ask her when she spoke again.

There are some corners you can't see round, she told him. *That's the trouble with living in a palace.*

Terrel did not make the mistake of trying to link these peculiar statements to their earlier exchange. Alyssa's habit of beginning conversations in the middle annoyed many people, including Elam, but Terrel usually enjoyed the challenge of trying to work out what she was talking about. On this occasion, however, he was lost.

The worst thing is, they have perfectly good reasons for everything they do, or don't *do*, she added.

Who's she talking about now? Terrel wondered.

I'm tired, Alyssa whispered.

Do you have to go now? To rest? Terrel couldn't hide his disappointment, but knew she had to allow her spirit to return to her own body every so often.

No. Not yet, she replied. *I just wanted the others to go. I can only take them for so long.*

The ghosts? Terrel was uncomfortable at the thought of discord between his allies.

Their business here was finished anyway, Alyssa said. *For now.*

Is something wrong?

The camel, who had been slumping down as if about to fall asleep, lifted its head. Alyssa looked directly at him through the beast's eyes, but said nothing.

You can tell me, he prompted gently.

Not me. Them.

It took Terrel a few moments to realize what she meant.

The ghosts? he repeated. *Do you mean they're not telling me everything?*

We don't even know what everything is, Alyssa told him.

Not sure what to make of that, Terrel sought to reassure her – and himself. Thinking back, Shahan and Muzeni had both seemed tense and worried, and not so full of their usual self-importance. And underneath his humorous cynicism, Elam had obviously been frustrated about something, or he would not have boiled over in the way he had. But Terrel couldn't believe that they would do anything to harm him.

I'm sure they're doing what they think is best, he said. *And you said yourself they have good reasons for what they do.*

Or don't do, Alyssa repeated. *It's a matter of trust.*

I'm doing all I can.

They know that.

Then why won't they trust me?

Not you, she replied. *The moons. Or the winds. Or fate. The palace-builders have a lot of names.*

Terrel realized that he was never going to get to the bottom of this particular puzzle. Judged by the rules of the conventional world, Alyssa really was mad – at least some of the time – but that did not affect his love for her. A longing to be with her surged through him then, a longing so powerful that it made his entire body ache. It was hard to believe that Alyssa had been a sleeper for almost four years now – and harder still to believe that in all that time she had come to no harm. Terrel had seen other sleepers, who had been comatose for much longer, and who had seemed almost untouched by the passing years, but that didn't stop him worrying.

I'm going to wait for you, Alyssa said, as if she'd heard his private thoughts. *How many times do I have to tell you that?*

Terrel smiled, grateful for her intuitive reassurance – and for her implicit faith in his eventual return to Havenmoon. As he looked at the camel now, he suddenly thought of something he'd forgotten to check.

Where's the ring? he asked.

For answer the camel snarled at him again, and this time Terrel saw the ring, looped around one of its teeth.

That doesn't look very safe, he remarked, laughing.

'Ugly bastard, isn't he?'

Terrel swung round and saw that Ghadira had approached unnoticed. She was grinning.

'At least you managed to calm him down,' she added. 'I heard he was being a bit peculiar.'

As always, Terrel felt awkward in the girl's presence, and the fact that Alyssa was there too, observing the encounter, made him even more uncomfortable.

'Did you want something?' he asked.

If Ghadira was offended by the terse question, she did her best not to show it.

'We were wondering if you were going to join us for the evening meal,' she said. 'You've been out here on your own for ages.'

'No. It's all right.'

'I could bring you something out,' she offered. 'There won't be anything left if you wait much longer.'

'No. Thank you. I'll come soon.'

Is this another of your girlfriends? Alyssa enquired silently.

Terrel couldn't tell whether she was teasing him or was genuinely jealous.

'What's the matter?' Ghadira asked, obviously puzzled by his suddenly stricken expression.

'Nothing,' he replied.

'Come and eat,' she persisted. 'You look worn out, and some food will do you good.'

She's beautiful, Alyssa commented. *I—*

'Don't hurt her!' Terrel blurted out. In his confusion, he didn't realize that he'd spoken out loud.

'What?' Ghadira was obviously nonplussed.

You really think I'd do that? Alyssa exclaimed.

'Have you been at the qard again?' the nomad girl asked, frowning.

Terrel closed his eyes and willed himself to be calm.

You think I'm jealous! The camel made a rumbling sound that might have passed for laughter – or perhaps for anger.

'What's going on, Terrel?' Ghadira asked. 'Are you all right?'

'I'm fine,' he said, opening his eyes again. 'I'm sorry, Ghadira. I just need some time on my own to sort a few things out. In here.' He tapped the side of his head. 'Then I'll come and eat. All right? Will you put some food aside for me?'

'Fair enough. I know when I'm not wanted.' She turned and made her way back towards the camp, leaving Terrel to wonder whether her parting words meant that she was angry, or disappointed, or simply teasing him.

You handled that well, Alyssa remarked acidly.

I'm sorry, I never meant to accuse you . . . He faltered.

*It's just after what you said about Esera, and then what
happened to Kalkara—*

That wasn't my doing!

I know. I'm sorry. I'm an idiot. Will you forgive me?

If you forgive me, she replied quietly.

What for?

I am a bit jealous, Alyssa admitted.

But you've no reason to be! Terrel exclaimed.
Ghadira's just a friend. Not even that, really.

*I know. But she gets to be with you in person. How
can I compete with her, when I look like this?*

You don't need to compete, he assured her. *It's you—*

But I'm half a world away. And all I do is sleep.

That won't be for ever, he told her.

We've got to keep telling each other that, Alyssa said,
sounding more vulnerable than she ever had before.

We will, Terrel promised.

For the next few heartbeats, neither of them spoke.
Terrel simply gazed at the camel, hoping that something
of Alyssa would show through in the creature's eyes.

I really do have to rest now, she said eventually.

When will you be back? he asked quickly.

As soon as I can.

Good. You know I couldn't do any of this without you.

You'd better go and get some food, she told him. *Or
you'll be in trouble again.*

After he'd eaten, Terrel went to check on Marrad, who
was making good progress, and then returned to
Vilheyuna's tent to rest. But even though he was incredibly tired, sleep would not come. What he'd learnt from
his visitors had been bad enough – but it was what they

hadn't told him that worried him more. That, together with the fact that there was clearly some tension between the ghosts and Alyssa, left Terrel feeling uncertain about many things, and set him brooding.

The revelation that even the elementals with whom he'd had personal contact had turned against humanity once more made him doubt the validity of their bargain. He was doing everything he could to uphold his side of the argument, but were they? For the first time, he began to wonder about the possibility of deliberate deception. Were the Ancients simply using him for purposes of their own? Either way, his efforts to teach them the difference between good and evil didn't seem to have been very effective. On the other hand, he couldn't deny the logic of Shahan's statement that he had to go to the elemental at Makranash and talk to it directly. He just had to keep trying.

And the only way to do that was to make sure that Zahir won the Race of Truth!

Terrel finally fell asleep, still wondering how to go about 'testing' the members of the team to see whether they were likely to be vulnerable to the plague.

When he awoke the next morning, Terrel remembered hearing screams in the night, but he couldn't be sure whether they'd been real or simply part of his dreams. But he was given no opportunity to dwell on this because an enraged bellowing from somewhere near the tent drove everything else from his mind. He stumbled outside to find a female camel roaring and spitting at the men around it. They were shouting and brandishing sticks.

Alyssa?

It's about time you woke up, she replied. *Tell these idiots I'll bite them if they don't leave me alone.*

Calm down, then.

Ignoring the warning cries from the nomads, Terrel walked towards the animal, which quietened and lowered its head to allow him to pat its neck. The handlers looked on in amazement. They couldn't understand why a previously docile creature should have run amok, but Terrel's effect upon her was in some ways even more astonishing. When a camel lost its temper it could become very fierce indeed.

'Leave her to me,' he told them. 'We'll walk a bit, and then she'll be fine.' He set off without waiting for their agreement, and Alyssa followed meekly in his footsteps.

I thought a female would be easier, she said. *Turns out they're even worse.*

I'm glad you're back anyway.

I can't stay long this time.

Although Terrel was disappointed, he knew better than to question Alyssa's decision.

Is there any more news? he asked.

There's definitely an elemental at Makranash. Elam and I tried to go there during the night. He couldn't get within a hundred miles of the place.

A hundred! That's much more than it was with the others.

Perhaps because they're getting more powerful.

*Do you think—*Terrel began, but Alyssa didn't let him finish the question.

There's someone coming, she said.

Turning round, Terrel saw Zahir running towards

them from the camp. As he reached them he glanced around, as if to check that he wasn't being followed, then looked suspiciously at the camel.

'Is she quiet again?'

'Yes. Did you want something?' As had been the case the previous night, Terrel resented the interruption, especially as Alyssa could not be with him for long this time.

'I need your help,' Zahir said.

His frank admission took Terrel by surprise, but he still wanted to be left alone with Alyssa.

'This isn't a good time. Can we talk later?'

'It has to be private,' Zahir said. 'Just between the two of us. This seemed like the best chance.'

'We can—' Terrel began, then broke off as Alyssa's voice sounded in his head.

I think you need to hear what he has to say.

Why? Terrel noticed that the camel was staring fixedly at a space just above Zahir's head, where the cloud-like remnants of his dreams hung. Although these remnants were invisible to most people – including Terrel – Alyssa could see them. It was one of her more extraordinary eccentricities – and one that had often got her into trouble in the past.

His dreams are full of fears, she said.

That didn't sound like the Zahir Terrel knew.

He won't admit to them during the day, Alyssa went on, *but he can't hide from them at night. He* does *need your help.*

'We can what?' Zahir asked, obviously bemused by the healer's prolonged silence.

'Let's talk,' Terrel said.

I have to go. You're going to need his help soon. Be kind to him.

With that piece of advice, Alyssa left and the camel wandered off, quite placid now. Terrel felt a pang of loss, but forced himself to concentrate on what Zahir was saying.

'You'll keep this between the two of us, won't you?'

'If you want me to,' Terrel replied. 'It's you who's been screaming at night, isn't it?'

For a moment, Zahir looked astonished. Then he shrugged.

'How did you know?'

'I'm a healer. I have an instinct for when something is wrong.'

'There's nothing wrong with me,' the elder's son said defensively.

'Then why do you want my help?'

'I . . . I have to be as fit as possible for the race. And for that I need to sleep well.'

'But your dreams won't let you.'

'It wouldn't be a problem if it was just once or twice,' Zahir replied. 'But I keep having the same nightmare over and over again, and . . . I want it to stop.'

Admitting to such a weakness was a sign of trust, and Terrel knew that he had to prove himself worthy of it.

'Tell me about the nightmare,' he said.

Now it was Zahir's turn to hesitate.

'It's stupid,' he muttered, glancing round at the camp again.

'Dreams don't usually make much sense.'

'It's about the race. Everything's going well, I'm in the lead, and it's just a matter of time till we're the first to get to the mountain. I have the banner ready, and I know I'm going to win.' Now that he'd begun to unburden himself, Zahir's words tumbled out in a rush. 'But then, as I'm walking along, someone offers me a drink of water. Of course I refuse. I would lose the race, lose all honour, if I accepted. But this person won't take no for an answer.'

'Do you know who it is?'

'I can never see his face. It's as if the sun is directly behind him, blinding me. He keeps pushing an unstop-pered waterskin towards me, even though I tell him again that I don't want any. We go on, and it happens again – and this time I see that everyone else on the team is watching. But then it's not just my team but the whole tribe, and people from other tribes, all watching me. I still refuse, but I'm afraid they'll think I was cheating. I can't seem to move any more, and the other champions are catching up. He tells me I'm going to lose unless I drink, but the idea revolts me. Just the smell of the water makes me feel sick. I'm sweating and dizzy, and everyone's looking at me. Then suddenly he squeezes the skin and water shoots out, splashing my face and arms. Some of it goes in my mouth and I scream, because it burns my skin and my throat. And I know I've lost. That's when I wake up.'

Zahir's dark face was sheened with perspiration. It was obvious that the memory of his nocturnal ordeal was tormenting him.

'I told you it's stupid,' he added, looking thoroughly embarrassed. 'No one would do that to me.'

'Perhaps you're imagining doing it to yourself.'

'What? That's ridiculous.'

'Dreams are sometimes meant to show us things,' Terrel said, quoting Alyssa. 'But sometimes they're just a reflection of what we feel deep inside us, what we're worried about. Being the Toma's champion is a huge responsibility. You're aware of that – and it's enough to make anyone anxious.'

'You think I'm afraid I'll fail?'

'Perhaps you're just afraid of the unknown. We all are, to some extent.'

'The Binhemma-Ghar doesn't frighten me. No desert does.'

'That's not what I meant. This is a new experience for you, your first major task as a man. Anyone would find such a prospect nerve-wracking.'

'I'm only nervous when I'm asleep,' Zahir muttered, sounding exasperated.

'That's because the fears are buried deep in your mind. You hide them – even from yourself – when you're awake.'

'And these fears created the dream? Is that what you're saying? So you don't think it's a premonition, then? It's not actually going to happen?'

'I don't think so, no.'

'So how do I get rid of these fears?'

'You don't,' Terrel said. 'You have to accept them as part of you. Fear is nothing to be ashamed of. It's a very necessary emotion. Without it, you wouldn't pull your foot away when you were about to tread on a scorpion. You need to be afraid of being stung.'

'So if I accept these fears, the nightmares will stop?'

'Probably.'

'How do I do that?'

'You've already started,' Terrel told him. 'By talking

to me, you've brought them out into the open for the first time. And I think I might be able to help you go a bit further.'

'I don't want anyone else to know about this,' Zahir said quickly. 'People must have heard me scream, but no one's said anything. They don't know what it's about.'

'I won't tell anyone,' Terrel repeated. 'I'd like to see if I can help you from the inside, as I do when I'm healing someone.'

'All right.' Zahir's agreeing so readily was a measure not only of his sincerity but also of his desperation. Without further prompting, he held out his hand.

Terrel took it in his own, and allowed himself to fall into the waking dream. The process was familiar and yet disconcerting, because the ailment he was seeking lay deep within his patient's mind rather than in his body. The two were linked, of course, but it made the search a little more haphazard and time-consuming. Pain usually pointed the way, but there was none here. What was more, the hidden fears were a natural part of the inner world, rather than malignant invaders. Terrel found what he was looking for eventually – shadows within shadows – and brought them out into the daylight, where they could be seen and accepted for what they were.

Having done all he could, Terrel withdrew and let go of Zahir's hand. He felt dizzy and disorientated on his return to the real world, and when he was able to look up, Zahir was already gone, striding purposefully back towards the camp. As he walked he was rubbing at his eyes, as if some sand had blown into them. But Terrel knew better. Zahir was wiping away tears – and he hadn't wanted Terrel to see them.

It was only after his patient had gone that the healer realized, with a jolt of dismay, that there was another possible interpretation of the dream. 'Just the smell of the water makes me feel sick.' Was it possible that the nightmare was a premonition after all? And if so, did it mean that Zahir was going to be infected with the plague?

CHAPTER TWENTY-SEVEN

The nomads continued their journey to Qomish, but the pattern of their days altered dramatically. Travelling all day in the heat of summer was exhausting, and so the elders agreed that it was time to make the Toma's annual change to the hours of darkness. The caravan now moved during the night, continued until about an hour before noon, then stopped for food, water and rest until dark.

Walking or riding by moonlight was a fascinating experience for Terrel, and for the most part he was glad of the change. Like everyone else, he found adjusting to the new sleeping routine difficult at first, but he soon got used to it. Zahir worried that it might affect his team, because they would have to revert to sleeping at night during the race, but the elders reassured him that they'd arrive in Qomish in plenty of time for them to adapt once more.

Terrel marvelled at the way the Toma were able to navigate at night, using the position of the stars and moons to set their course, and recognizing familiar land-marks even when the sky was at its darkest. When one or more of the visible moons lent their radiance to the scene, the desert took on an almost otherworldly beauty that masked its unforgiving nature. It was a place of wonder, but also a place of hardship and danger – which was emphasized when the nomads' efforts to find new water supplies were not as productive as they had hoped. A spring that was usually reliable all year round was dry, and several holes dug in crystal hollows produced only meagre rewards. The tribe's reserves were running low, and the only thing that kept them from serious worry was that they were now just a few days from the great oasis.

'This is absurd,' Okan muttered angrily. 'Worse than that, it's insulting.'

His stare challenged Zahir, but the younger man's steady gaze did not falter.

'I've made my decision,' he said.

'But you chose us all precisely because we're healthy and strong!'

'And I can just as soon choose others,' Zahir retorted. 'This is *my* team.'

It was a double-edged threat, and everyone there knew it. Okan was the Toma's finest scout, an expert reader of the terrain, its sand patterns and trails. He could see the best way through a line of shifting dunes faster than anyone else, and he had the sharpest eye when it came to spotting a possible source of water – even in the most unlikely places. His absence would weaken the team considerably, but Zahir remained steadfast.

'There's nothing wrong with me!' Okan exclaimed.

'Then you've nothing to fear from the test,' Zahir responded implacably.

'I only want to make sure that all is well,' Terrel explained. 'That there's nothing that could become a problem after the race is under way, when it would be a danger to you and the rest of the team.'

It had taken Terrel some time to convince Zahir to let him monitor the health of the team *before* the race began. However, once the champion had been won over, he became committed to the idea, in spite of the objections of the others. Terrel understood their arguments, but his fears about the plague made him glad that Zahir was so determined.

'How can you see a problem that isn't there yet?' Fanari asked. Like Okan, he was in his early twenties and, outwardly at least, looked extremely fit. The two of them had been the other candidates for the role of champion on the night Zahir had been elected. They had been asked to join the team as a matter of courtesy, but they would both have been valuable members anyway. In Fanari's case, this was because he had an uncanny ability to read the weather, especially when there were storms about.

'I'm not sure I can,' Terrel admitted, deciding that honesty was his best option, 'but there are signs within us all. I can see them just as clearly as you can see the patterns in the sky.'

'Terrel's skill goes beyond that of any shaman,' Zahir claimed. 'Have you forgotten what happened when Marrad was poisoned?'

'That was a great feat,' Okan conceded, 'but this is different. None of us needs any healing.'

'You're missing the point,' Zahir said, remaining calm even though his authority was being questioned.

'Start with me,' Korioth offered abruptly. 'I'm not sure what good it'll do, but I don't see any harm in it.' He was the oldest of the group by several years, and his role within the team was as quartermaster, in charge of the vital supplies that would have to last them through the ordeal of the Binhemma–Ghar. The others all respected him, and Terrel knew that his word counted for a good deal.

'No,' Zahir said. 'I'm glad you're with me on this, Korioth, but I'll go first. The rest of you can follow in any order you like.'

Terrel looked around the group. There were eight of them in all, including himself, the latest addition to the team. Apart from Zahir, the only other person he knew at all well was Medrano. Fanari and Korioth were both familiar, but he hardly knew anything about Okan or the other scout, Cassar, who was apparently an expert at navigating by the stars. Although this skill would not be of immediate use during the race, it would be a way of checking their position at night – and could well prove invaluable on their return journey. The final member of the team was Luqa, a handler whose knowledge of camels, their habits, ailments and eccentricities, was second to none. He was a quiet young man, more at ease with animals than people, and Terrel couldn't remember ever hearing him speak – which made it all the more surprising when he was the one to ask the next question.

'Who's going to test *you*?' he said, looking at Terrel. 'I mean, you're going to be there with us too.'

'And I have a twisted leg and a withered arm,' Terrel

completed for him, knowing what they were all thinking. 'I may lack your physical strength, but I've looked inside myself many times – you have to do that as a healer – and I am strong there. I won't let you down.'

'And we're just supposed to take your word for that, are we?' Okan asked. 'Even though you refuse to accept ours.'

'I would accept your word without question if we were talking about reading the lie of the land,' Terrel replied. 'That's your skill. This is mine.'

'Satisfied?' Zahir demanded.

Okan glanced at his companions, saw that they had finally accepted their leader's edict, and nodded.

'What do you want me to do?' Zahir asked Terrel.

'I just need to touch your hand,' the healer told him, 'but before I do, I want you to drink a mouthful of water.'

'Why?' Zahir's bewilderment was echoed in the faces of the other nomads.

'It purifies the inner workings of the body,' Terrel improvised. 'It may reveal any hidden imperfections.'

'And what happens if you find any of these imperfections?' Medrano asked.

'Then *I* decide whether they represent an acceptable risk or not,' Zahir answered. 'And take action accordingly.'

'And if he finds any in you?' Okan queried.

'Then I shall withdraw as champion, and allow the tribe to choose either you or Fanari as my replacement.'

This blunt response ended the last remnants of opposition, and Terrel was able to begin.

'I'm not sure I'll be able to examine all of you today,' he said. Their meeting had taken place at noon, under the shade of an open-sided tent, and he knew that they would all need to get some rest soon, even if his own efforts didn't exhaust him first. 'We'll see.'

A waterskin was found and passed to Zahir, who drank, then came to sit next to the healer. He held up a clenched fist and Terrel placed his own fingers around it, then closed his eyes.

An hour later, feeling light-headed from fatigue, Terrel completed his task.

'Well?' Luqa asked. He was the last to have been tested.

'You're fine,' Terrel told him. 'You're all fine.'

'What did I tell you?' Okan said, but – like the rest of the group – he was smiling, glad that the healer hadn't found anything sinister.

'Better to be safe than sorry,' Medrano remarked.

'Let's get some sleep,' Zahir decided.

Terrel lay down where he was, as the others made their way to their own tents. He was too tired to move. But then a small detail from what he had seen gnawed at him and kept him from sleep. Although he had not lied to his team-mates when he'd said they were all fine, this had not been the whole truth. Deep within every one of them he had found a trace of fear, a tiny echo of what he'd sensed in Elodia. That might just be a sign of the reverence they had for water, but it was also possible that – to some slight degree – each of them was vulnerable to the plague. If that were true, the implications for the Race of Truth were enormous. It might also mean that *everybody* was susceptible to the illness to some extent – and the consequences of that for the people of Betancuria and Talazoria would be almost too appalling to contemplate.

It also implied that, sooner or later, the Ancients' curse would affect every single human being on Nydus.

Terrel was woken at dusk by a gentle hand shaking his shoulder.

'I let you sleep as long as you could,' Ghadira told him, 'but we need to break camp now.'

Terrel sat up, blinking. He had expected his dreams that afternoon to be full of ominous imagery and fearful perils, but he could remember nothing of them at all.

'I brought you some breakfast.'

'Thank you.'

Ghadira sat down beside him as he began to eat and for once, rather than feeling awkward, he was glad of her company. There was something warm and reassuring about the girl's presence, which came from her being so at ease with herself. Terrel still found Ghadira's attitude to him baffling at times, but he envied her down-to-earth nature. He had the feeling that nothing in her life was truly complicated, because she wouldn't let it be.

'What have you done to Zahir?' she asked. The accusation in her tone was tempered by a smile.

'What do you mean?'

'He's been different lately. More considerate. Less full of himself.'

'He's growing up. He has responsibilities now.'

'It's not just that,' she said thoughtfully. 'It was after he'd talked to you that his nightmares stopped, wasn't it?'

'He told you about that?'

'Winds, no! He'd never discuss anything like that with me.'

'That's a shame,' Terrel said. 'You'd probably have given him the same advice I did.'

'And what was that?' she asked, smiling at the compliment.

'I gave him my word it would remain between the two of us.'

'How very honourable.'

'How *did* you know then?'

'Just a guess,' she replied. 'I know he trusts you. Otherwise he'd never have made the rest of the team take that test of yours. Who else was he likely to go to? Everyone knew about his nightmares, but no one dared mention it. We all thought he'd be ashamed.'

'There's nothing wrong with being aware of your own vulnerability,' Terrel said.

Ghadira gave him a measuring look.

'I suppose not,' she conceded. 'But maybe a champion needs to think he's infallible. Zahir used to be like that, but he's changed.'

'He still has the confidence to be a good leader,' Terrel said.

'Better than before, if you ask me,' she agreed. 'I hate to admit this, but he might just become the sort of man that others would follow to the ends of the world.' She paused, then grinned. 'Which is just as well really, because that's exactly what you're going to have to do.'

'We're going to win,' Zahir declared. 'So the question doesn't arise.'

'I'm sure we will,' Terrel responded, 'but it's absolutely essential that I go to Makranash. Will you take me there, even if we don't get to the summit first?'

'No! There would be no honour in that – and anyway, we're going to win. I don't want anyone on this team who doesn't believe that.'

'I just—'

'Why is it so important for *you* to reach the mountain?' Zahir demanded. 'I'm the one who'll be carrying the emblem.'

Terrel had considered what answer to give to this obvious question before he'd broached the subject.

'There's a power there that controls our fate,' he said earnestly. 'Including that of Vilheyuna and all the other sleepers in the world.' This was true at least, but the inference that by going to the mountain he would be able to help the shaman wake up was *not* true. Terrel had decided not to point this out to Zahir, and could only hope the elder's son wouldn't ask him that specific question.

'You want to talk to the winds?' the nomad queried incredulously.

'Yes. In a way, I suppose I do.'

'We can't even *try* to do that unless we win,' Zahir stated firmly. 'We can't afford to anger them. If we win the race, you can do what you like. If we don't, you'll turn back with the rest of us, even if I have to put a knife to your throat myself.'

CHAPTER TWENTY-EIGHT

Terrel had seen birds of prey before, but never from so close.

'She's beautiful,' he whispered.

'This is a saker, the best of all hunting birds,' Johari told him proudly. 'Her name is Isptar.'

The falcon perched calmly on her owner's arm, her deadly talons gripping the leather sleeve that was strapped around his wrist. Huge black eyes, ever alert, watched everything around her. Johari turned so that Terrel could see the bird's long tail feathers.

'The longer they are,' he said, 'the better flyer the bird is – and the more valuable. I would not sell Isptar for gold or camels.'

Johari was one of a group of three hunters who had joined the caravan the previous day. They had brought with them an offering of fresh meat, and had asked to join the Toma on the last leg of their journey to Qomish. The nomad elders had welcomed them gladly, as much for the news they might bring as for the gift of food.

'I wish I could show her in action,' Johari went on, 'but the season is more or less over now. It's too hot here for birds to hunt effectively.'

'I'd like to have seen her in flight,' Terrel admitted.

'You would not believe her swiftness in the kill,' the hunter told him.

Until now, Terrel had not had any chance to speak to the newcomers, but he'd already learnt that during the season they travelled even more widely than the Toma. Each man owned a camel, but it was from their falcons that they made their living, feeding themselves and trading with the meat and pelts of the animals they caught. However, it was not their way of life that made Terrel eager to talk, but the information they might be able to give him.

'Raheb said you saw what happened to the Kullana River,' he prompted.

'I did,' Johari confirmed, his expression grave now. 'It was over two years ago, but I can still see it as if it were yesterday.'

'Will you tell me about it?'

At first Terrel thought his companion was about to refuse, but then Johari overcame his evident reluctance.

'If I hadn't seen it with my own eyes, I wouldn't have believed it.' He went on to describe an exact replica of Terrel's sand-mist vision. Almost every detail corresponded with what the healer had experienced, from the enormous noise that had preceded the opening of the crevasse, to the clouds of rainbow-threaded spray.

'Isptar was flying directly overhead as all this

happened,' Johari concluded. 'I thought I'd never see her again.' He stroked the bird's silken neck feathers.

'Being so close must have been terrifying,' Terrel commented. 'I'm amazed you weren't hurt.'

'I'm amazed we weren't all killed!' the hunter replied. 'It was like no earthquake I've ever known. It was vast, horrifying, and it should have destroyed everything for miles around – but it didn't. There were some houses only a few hundred paces from the ravine, and they didn't even collapse. There was something controlled about the movement of the earth – almost as if it was deliberate.' Johari shook his head. 'Now I'm sounding like a madman.'

No, you're not, Terrel thought. What the newcomer had done was confirm that Terrel's vision *had* taken him beyond the winds, but his journey had taken him into the *past*. And now, more than ever, he was certain the elemental had been responsible for the canyon's spectacular creation.

'Everything changed after that,' Johari added. 'I don't need to tell you the effect it had on life in the desert. It might even have been the start of that plague people are talking about.'

'The water-sickness?' Terrel queried, glad of the chance for more information about the mysterious illness.

'It seems to be getting more serious. And apparently it's everywhere. You're lucky it hasn't affected the Toma yet.'

'I've been told it's worst in the north. Is that right?'

'Seems to be. And it seems to affect children mostly. Some people are saying the onset of the disease is affected by the moons, especially the Invisible.'

This was news to Terrel, but it didn't really surprise him. The moons influenced every aspect of life on Nydus.

'We've had contagions before,' Johari went on, 'but this is different. It used to be that you could treat them with an antidote from the leaves of the saxaul tree, but that doesn't even touch this new sickness.'

'Does anyone know how the plague might have started?'

'At first people thought it was passed on by fleas, as usual, but now they're talking about it being from tainted water supplies. Others are saying it's carried by the unclean.'

'I don't think that's true,' Terrel said. There had been no sign of the illness in the refugee children.

'Neither do I,' Johari said. 'But in times of trouble people look for scapegoats. And there was enough trouble with them even before the plague began.'

His remark made Terrel think of what had happened at Triq Dalam. Had the raiders who had burnt the town been trying to stop the spread of the plague – because of a single case? Or could they have heard that the townspeople were harbouring some of the northern exiles, and decided that was sufficient reason for the massacre? Either way, it was an insane overreaction. However, if fears about the plague *were* behind the attack, it might explain why the raiders had avoided the lake. If they'd believed the water to have been tainted, nothing would have induced them to drink there.

'Still,' Johari added, 'such things are in the hands of the winds, not men.'

This fatalism sat uneasily with Terrel's own beliefs.

'We have to try to help people though, don't we?'

'When we can,' the hunter replied. 'But right now no one knows what to do.'

'Let's hope we find out at Qomish,' Terrel said.

Johari nodded, though he did not look particularly optimistic.

That evening, as the nomad camp began to stir again after their time of rest, Terrel sensed a new presence in the open-sided tent. Looking round, he saw a falcon perched on one of the luggage bundles. It wasn't Isptar, but a smaller, darker bird. However, that didn't matter at all to Terrel, because he knew instinctively that Alyssa had returned. He was about to speak to her when he realized she was staring fixedly at Kalkara, who was stretching and yawning on her mat. Alyssa's concentration was so fierce that Terrel didn't like to interrupt her, though he couldn't understand her intense preoccupation. He could only hope that she was not feeling jealous again.

By then others were stirring, and the falcon had been noticed.

'What's that bird doing here?' Mlicki mumbled, his voice still thick with sleep.

'I don't know,' Terrel replied.

Abruptly, Kalkara got up and ran off, disappearing into the maze of tents. Mlicki watched his sister go.

'What's got into her?' he wondered, then returned his attention to the bird. 'Is it one of the hunters'?'

'It must be.'

'I'll go and get Johari,' Mlicki decided. 'He can take care of it.'

Terrel nodded, still watching the falcon. She was ruffling her feathers and preening herself now.

'Make sure it doesn't try to peck Vilheyuna,' the shaman's apprentice said as he left.

Alyssa?

You need to see this, she replied.

What? See what?

Just let me show you. Close your eyes.

Why? What for?

Dreams are sometimes meant to show us things.

You saw Kala's dream?

It was real, she told him. *Watch.*

Terrel closed his eyes, and found himself in a different world.

The raid began at dawn, but Kalkara didn't know what was happening until later. She heard shouting and a lot of loud noises but, alone inside the family tent, she saw nothing. As the sounds outside grew louder and more frightening, she began to cry, calling for her mother. And at last she came, breathless and dishevelled, but trying to smile for her daughter.

'It's all right, little one. It's going to be all right.'

'Where's Dadda?' Kala sobbed. 'What's happening?'

'Shhh. Quiet now.' Her mother picked her up, then stood still, as if uncertain what to do next. Kalkara took comfort from the strong, warm arms around her, but the bad noises were still there; screams, running footsteps, the clash of metal.

'We're going to play a game, sweetheart. Let's play hide and seek.' Kala's mother carried the little girl over to the side of the tent, and put her down. Lifting the rug that lay there, she beckoned to her daughter. 'Crawl under here. Quickly. Then stay very still.'

Kalkara did as she was told, wondering how the game could work when her mother already knew where she was hiding. After giving the child a quick kiss on her forehead, her mother gave Kala her final instructions, then lowered the rug over her. Underneath it was darker than a moonless night.

Kalkara lay there, shivering even though it was not cold, and waited. She heard more screams, and voices pleading, but she couldn't make out what anyone was saying. Then, after a very long time, everything went quiet. That was good, but her mother still didn't come to find her, and she was getting cramped and uncomfortable now. She wondered when Mlicki would come back. He had been out night-hunting for snakes.

Eventually, the child could stand it no longer, and she crawled out from under the rug. The tent was empty. Timidly, she went outside. That was when she saw her father. He lay on his back, eyes staring at the sky, and his neck and chest were covered in blood. Kalkara shook his arm, then began to cry when he wouldn't wake up, the tears rolling silently down her cheeks.

After a while she began to walk around the ravaged camp. She was the only one left alive. All the men were dead, even the boys. Some of the women were dead too, mostly the old or the very young, but the others — including her mother — had vanished. All the tribe's camels were gone too.

Stunned with the horror of what she had seen, Kalkara had long since stopped crying. She went slowly back to her own tent, being careful not to look at the body outside, and crawled back under the rug. She would wait there for as long as she needed to. And she would hold on to the last words her mother had said to her, the words she would keep in her mind for ever.

'Remember, little one. Don't make a sound till I come back for you.'

Terrel returned to his own time and his own world, blinking away hot tears. His heart was breaking for the four-year-old girl who had undergone such a horrific ordeal, and who – four years later – was still obeying her mother's last command.

Look in the next room in the palace, Terrel, Alyssa told him, breaking the spell that the dream had cast over him. *I have to go now.*

Please stay, he begged. *I—*

I can't.

The ring around one of the bird's legs faded to nothing, and the falcon glanced around nervously.

'There you are, Qawra,' Johari said, as he approached the tent. 'How did you loosen your tether, my sweet?' He held out a gauntletted hand, and the bird hopped on to his wrist. The hunter left, and Mlicki set about the first tasks of the day, leaving Terrel to think about what he had learnt.

The reason for Kala's silence was painfully clear now, and he guessed that her dreams had reinforced her resolve in the years since the massacre. What was not so obvious was why Mlicki had claimed that *both* their parents were dead. Perhaps it had been easier to believe that than to accept that their mother had been carried off by the raiders. But the fact remained that there was at least a chance that their mother was still alive.

In a leap of faith that he could not have justified logically, Terrel realized something else. He finally knew the identity of the tattooed woman in his dream. And he knew why he had to find her. What was more, Alyssa had told him where to begin his search. Where else could the 'next room' be but at the great oasis of Qomish?

CHAPTER TWENTY-NINE

Even though he had been told what to expect, Terrel still found his first sight of the fabled oasis of Qomish awe-inspiring. His initial impression was of a huge valley full of greenery. Since he'd left Misrah's coastal plain he had seen no more than a handful of trees, but here there were hundreds – as well as a profusion of colours and scents that were in stark contrast to the desert landscape he'd become accustomed to. Most common were the distinctive date palms, but there were many other varieties too. The valley was also filled with cultivated fields, all irrigated by the many springs that were reputed to run ice-cold even in midsummer. Terrel had found that hard to believe, but now – as the caravan wound its way down from the surrounding hills – he felt the temperature drop as the air became more humid. He soon understood why the nomads regarded the place with such reverence.

However, the reactions of those around him indicated that not all was well in this seeming paradise. He saw several nomads frowning in consternation, pointing to various parts of the valley and muttering to one another.

'What's the matter?' Terrel asked Medrano as he fell into step beside him.

'The life is fading,' the artist replied.

'Really? It looks wonderful to me.'

'It is, for now. But compared to what it was three years ago, the change is obvious. We had hoped the decline of the last two years would be reversed, but it's got even worse.'

'The springs aren't flowing as strongly?'

'They're drying up, slowly but surely,' Medrano confirmed. 'If it goes on like this, in another ten years this place might be nothing but dust. And if Qomish dies, what hope is there for the rest of us?'

After the established routines of travelling within the close-knit community of the Toma, Terrel found the next few hours almost overwhelming. As the caravan made its way to their traditional campsite, he caught several glimpses of the city of Qomish itself. In many respects it was very similar to Triq Dalam, though on a huge scale. However, the permanent settlement was dwarfed by the expanse of temporary accommodation that had been erected in every available space around it. There were tents of all shapes and sizes, in tribal clusters, stretching up onto the outer slopes of the valley and forming a second, sprawling city. Herds of camels, each marked with a distinctive brand, were tethered in what little open ground was left and, most intimidating of all, there were people everywhere. After the quiet simplicity of the open desert, the noise, smells and sights of such an enormous gathering came as a shock.

'Looks like we're not the only ones to get here early,' Mlicki remarked as they began to set up camp.

To Terrel, that was an understatement of ridiculous proportions.

'Is all of Misrah here?' Terrel asked.

Zahir laughed.

'No. It just seems like that,' he replied.

The two young men were walking through the crowded streets of the city. Terrel's curiosity had overcome his nervousness, and he had asked Zahir to be his guide. The elder's son had agreed readily, more than willing to display his knowledge, and his ready self-confidence helped Terrel feel less out of place amid the hectic bustle of the vast markets, the alleyways full of eating houses and tea-sellers. The assault on the newcomer's senses intensified here, with a barrage of gossip, haggling and argument competing with the scents of mint, spices and qard – as well as many other, less pleasant odours.

'In fact,' Zahir went on, 'it's only the true nomadic tribes, like us, who bring everyone to the festival. Most of the others only bring their teams, their best traders and a few hangers-on. If they let everyone come it would be absolute chaos.'

'You mean this isn't chaos?'

'This?' Zahir queried in mock surprise. 'No. This is just a bit of fun. Before the real business begins.'

An impassioned quarrel had just broken out between two merchants, and as the heated words rose in volume, Terrel couldn't help staring.

'It's a good job there's the ukasa,' he commented. 'Those two look ready to come to blows.'

'No one defies the pact,' Zahir said. 'The Mehtar wouldn't stand for it.'

Terrel knew that the Mehtar was the elected leader of Qomish's ruling body, the Seyhim.

'Is he the one who settles disputes about water?' The two young men had already learned of some potentially explosive disagreements between tribes, which had come about because – for the first time ever – access to the various springs was being carefully controlled.

'Of course,' Zahir confirmed. 'During the festival, the Mehtar's word is law. There's only one man who would dare defy him – and then only for one day.'

'The King of the Desert.'

'Exactly.' Zahir grinned. 'I'm looking forward to that.'

The nomad's attitude seemed dangerously overconfident, but Terrel recognized that it was just in Zahir's nature to believe in his own infallibility. He had not been nicknamed 'the prince' for nothing. And such self-assurance might have its uses.

'Did you mean what you said at the gathering?' Terrel asked.

'Which gathering?'

'When we were discussing whether the Toma should compete in the Race of Truth.'

'What did I say?'

'You asked what would happen if for once the King of the Desert's decrees dealt with more than just trivial matters.'

Zahir pulled a face.

'You know what the reaction was.'

'But that was before the plague began, and before you knew the wells here are drying up,' Terrel argued. 'What about all the violence between the tribes, and what's happening to the refugees? Don't you think it would be an opportunity to do something positive, something that might make a difference?'

'I thought so once,' Zahir replied, 'but it's hopeless. Being king for a day is just a big joke, really.'

'That doesn't sound like you.'

'I've put things into perspective, that's all. You heard how all the elders reacted to my suggestion – and they were right. The winds wouldn't allow the king to do anything real.'

'How do you know that, if no one's ever tried?'

'But what could I do? I can't cure the plague by making some decree, and I couldn't bring the water back to the springs either, so what would be the point?'

'You could at least try to end the fighting,' Terrel suggested. 'The territorial wars are—'

'No one would listen to me, even as king,' Zahir cut in, shaking his head.

'What if I told you there might be a way to *make* them listen?'

'What are you talking about?'

'When we get to Makranash, I may be able—'

'You still think you can talk to the winds?' Zahir demanded.

'In a manner of speaking, yes. I could climb—'

'No!' The elder's son looked appalled at the idea. 'Only a champion can set foot on the sacred mountain. For anyone else it would mean death and dishonour. You'd be mad to even *think* of such sacrilege.'

Terrel was about to continue the argument, but then thought better of it. Zahir was already agitated, and the healer didn't want to give him a reason to ban him from the team. There would be time enough to broach his plans later – once they were in the Binhemma-Ghar, and there was no turning back.

'It was just an idea,' he said meekly.

'You're a foreigner. You don't understand these things.'

Terrel bit his tongue, forcing himself to ignore the condescending tone.

'Stick to what you're good at,' Zahir advised him. 'Healing.'

That's what I was trying to do, Terrel thought, but he said nothing – and at that point a familiar voice rising above the general hubbub distracted them both.

'Take your hands off me, you camel maggot!'

'I like a woman with spirit,' a man responded, laughing. 'But you should be flattered. Don't you know who I am?'

Zahir and Terrel pushed forward until they could see what was happening. Ghadira was confronting a man whom they both recognized instantly.

'I know you're someone with less manners than a billy goat in rut,' she spat.

At this the man turned and raised his eyebrows, to the amusement of several of his companions, one of whom wore the headdress of a shaman.

'You smell much the same too,' Ghadira added scornfully.

A space had opened up around the two adversaries, and as the man turned back to face her, angry now, the look in his eyes quietened the onlookers.

'Be careful you don't go too far,' he hissed. 'I am Kohtala, warlord of the Shiban.'

'That explains why you have no honour,' Ghadira responded acidly.

Kohtala moved forward, in a fury now, but he froze when Zahir stepped into the arena.

'Leave her alone,' he said loudly.

'Keep out of this, boy,' the warlord said, giving him a disdainful glance.

'I am no boy. I am a man, and my tribe's champion for the Race of Truth.' His voice was quieter now, but there was steel beneath the calm words.

Kohtala turned to look at him properly, temporarily forgetting the girl.

'Then that's another reason why I'm destined to win the race,' he commented.

'That is in the gift of the winds,' the nomad responded, his gaze fixed upon his opponent.

'I don't need your help, Zahir,' Ghadira claimed. 'I can deal with this oaf easily enough.'

Kohtala reached out, trying to grab the girl's arm, but she evaded him neatly. Her mocking smile only made the Shiban's leader even more angry. Terrel could see that he was on the brink of violence, and wondered whether that had been Ghadira's intention all along. If Kohtala broke the ukasa, his punishment would be her reward. Zahir was clearly thinking along the same lines.

'Leave her alone,' he repeated. 'Do you want to end up in the cages?'

'Best place for him,' Ghadira responded.

'Shut up!' Zahir snapped.

'Yes, Uncle,' she replied sarcastically, dropping in a mocking curtsey.

'She is your niece?' Kohtala said, his temper cooling

a little. 'Then her hand is in your gift. What do you want for her dowry?'

'You couldn't afford it,' Zahir replied evenly.

'I'm already taken,' Ghadira goaded. 'I'm promised to a better man than you.'

'Really? And where is this paragon of manly virtues?'

'There!' she replied, pointing.

Kohtala looked, and burst out laughing.

'That crippled idiot?' he exclaimed. 'The one trying to catch flies in his mouth?'

Terrel closed his mouth quickly, struck dumb by Ghadira's outrageous behaviour.

'She's lying, isn't she,' the warlord stated, still grinning.

Terrel looked from him to Ghadira, and saw the pleading look on her face. A mixture of emotions welled up in him – and uppermost among them was a sudden rage.

'Do not think to mock the Toma, Kohtala,' he said, stepping forward and glaring at each of the Shiban warriors in turn so that they got a good look at his eyes. 'Remember the last time you faced us? We can call down the darkness upon you and all your tribe.'

The smile vanished from Kohtala's face as he finally recognized the nomads. He was about to speak when another man intervened. He was wearing the Seyhim's insignia on the shoulder of his robe.

'Enough!' he commanded. 'The Mehtar would not be pleased to see how you honour the ukasa. Go about your business. Now.'

Kohtala seemed about to argue, then thought better of it and turned away, favouring Ghadira with one last venomous stare.

'And leave my woman alone!' Terrel shouted, before he too turned to go.

'I've put up with your teasing long enough,' Terrel said sternly.

'You think I was teasing?' Ghadira asked.

They were back at the Toma's campsite, and for once Terrel had sought out the opportunity to speak to the girl alone.

'Yes! Don't ever do anything like that to me again.'

'I won't,' she promised. 'But that animal deserved to be put in his place.'

'Maybe so, but you shouldn't have involved me. Now I've got to pretend we're betrothed for the rest of the festival.'

'Would it be so bad if we were?' she asked quietly.

'That's not the point!' he exclaimed in exasperation. 'It's a deception, and one you've involved others in too. That's not very honourable, is it?'

'I'm sorry,' she replied meekly. For the first time she seemed genuinely contrite.

'Look, Ghadira,' he said seriously. 'We both know it's just a game. You're not really interested in me. Even if you were, there could never be anything between us. I love someone else, and one day I'm going back to her.'

'One day?' she queried softly.

'There are things I have to do here first,' Terrel said defensively.

'Where is she?'

'On the other side of the world.'

Ghadira looked at him in disbelief. He could hardly believe it himself.

'Your love is obviously worth winning,' she commented.

'That's true of everyone, surely.'

'But some more than others,' she told him seriously. 'I'm grateful for what you did, standing up for me like that, but I won't presume on your friendship again.'

She turned and walked away, and Terrel's righteous indignation turned to regret at some of the harsh words he had used.

CHAPTER THIRTY

The Mehtar had taken the unsual step of calling an open meeting of the Seyhim. In addition to his fellow council members, he instructed each tribe to send two representatives so that they could discuss 'important matters'.

The gathering took place in the Great Circle, a large arena normally used for sporting events or entertainments. It provided ample space for the Seyhim and their guests, and also allowed a huge number of people to sit in the stone-carved terraces that encircled the floor and witness the debate. However, the demand for places in the stands was so great that Terrel and Medrano were only able to squeeze in near the back.

After he had come to terms with being part of such a large crowd, the first thing that attracted Terrel's attention was a jagged boulder embedded in the packed earth at the centre of the arena. The delegates were all sitting or standing near this stone – though none of them ever went too close to it. The rock was black, with marbled streaks of green, in marked contrast to the ochre and orange of the earth all around it.

'What is that?' Terrel whispered.

'The shaman's stone,' Medrano replied. 'It's sacred to all the tribes.'

'Why?'

'Legend has it that it fell from the dome, carrying messages from the winds. When the moons are aligned correctly, it breathes signals of flame and light that the shamen treat as oracles. We're forbidden to touch it, and even going too close is dangerous.'

Terrel studied the boulder, wondering whether it really had fallen from the sky.

'Some say the impact of its fall was so great that it carved the valley of Qomish from the land, and brought the life to the surface,' Medrano added.

'It doesn't look big enough to do that,' Terrel said. The stone only rose to half the height of a man, and was no more than twice that across.

'What you see there is just the tip of the whole thing,' the artist explained. 'What's buried underground is hundreds of times larger.'

There were more questions Terrel wanted to ask, but he saw that the Mehtar was holding up his hands for quiet. When the buzz of conversation died away, the Seyhim's leader began to speak.

'I asked you all to come here for several reasons.' His voice was resonant, and because of the remarkable acoustics of the amphitheatre, it carried easily to everyone present. Although he was speaking directly to the tribal delegates, it was clear that he wanted the entire audience to hear what he had to say. 'The first is to welcome you all to Qomish, and to the Festival of the Winds. Let me remind you that this is a time of celebration, for renewing friendships, as well as a time of competition. It has disturbed me to hear that there have been several incidents, where violence was only prevented by the intervention of my guards. Such behaviour will not be tolerated anywhere within my demesne. The cages await anyone who dares to offend the winds by breaking the ukasa.'

Judging by the expressions of some of the tribesmen, this lecture was not being received well, but no one was bold enough to interrupt.

'I know that in the world beyond this valley,' the Mehtar went on, 'some of you consider yourself to be enemies. That is a matter for regret, but there are no enemies here. Please ensure that all your people understand that fact, and that they are also aware of the consequences of ignoring it.'

He paused to look round at the circle of faces, then began to pace around the shaman's stone, glancing at each delegation as he passed by, before resuming his speech.

'The second matter of concern is the life of Qomish. As you all know, supplies are no longer as plentiful, and this is why we cannot grant unlimited access to the springs and reservoirs. Let me assure you that the oasis is still bountiful. There is more than enough for everyone – but Qomish must safeguard its future. Your use of our wells is a privilege, not a right. Please do not abuse that privilege. The Seyhim have devised as fair a means of distribution as possible, but if there are any disputes, I will settle them personally at the appropriate time. I trust you will find this arrangement satisfactory.' He swept the assembly with his gaze, but evidently did not expect any argument, and continued his address. 'This brings me to my final concern, the so-called plague that has begun to afflict our land.'

This, more than anything that had gone before, made the audience react. Glances were exchanged, and a low murmuring rose up. However, no one spoke out directly.

'As far as I can tell,' the Mehtar went on, 'this illness has not yet affected large numbers of people. However, it is a serious and extremely unpleasant disease, and I believe the best way for us to tackle the problem is to share our knowledge and resources. That way we are more likely to discover a remedy which will benefit us all. The first things we need to know are exactly how widespread the illness is, and whether anyone has yet identified either its cause or the way in which it spreads.'

'We already know that!' one of the tribal leaders claimed, his strident tone sounding harsh after the Mehtar's mellifluous voice. 'The unclean brought the plague from the north.'

This interruption caused another round of discussion among the crowd, and all eyes turned to the new speaker.

'Can you be certain of that, Ghasri?' the Mehtar queried. 'It's my understanding that there have been cases of the illness in tribes who have had no contact with the unclean.'

'They're everywhere,' the tribesman stated flatly.

'And again, there are some clans who have been in close contact with the unclean and yet who have not been infected at all.'

'That's nonsense,' Ghasri insisted. 'They're just hiding from the truth. The eyes of the Mgarr are not so blind.'

'The Toma are not blind either,' Algardi put in.
Together with Raheb, he was representing the nomads.
'We've been travelling with a group of orphan children
from the north for several months, and none of us has
caught the plague.'

'That proves nothing,' another delegate declared.
'You'll suffer for your stupidity in the end.' He sounded
pleased by this prospect – and Terrel recognized the voice
as belonging to Kohtala.

'Wait a moment!' Ghasri exclaimed. 'Are you telling
us you've brought these unclean children into the sacred
valley of Qomish?'

'Of course,' Algardi replied with equal fervour. 'The
alternative was to abandon them, to leave them to die.
The Toma are not murderers of children.'

'You would murder us all instead?' Kohtala shouted.
'This is madness!'

After that, even the Mehtar found it difficult to keep
the debate under control. Some people demanded that
the Toma and their refugees be expelled from Qomish;
a few even suggested that the children should be put to
death, to try to stop the disease from spreading. Algardi
patiently countered these wild protests with the assertion
that the northerners were in perfect health – as were all
his tribe. Eventually, the Mehtar ruled that the nomads
and their guests could stay, but that the children should
remain quarantined in the Toma's camp. This decision
was accepted – though many of those present were obviously reluctant. It was only when the Mehtar specifically
extended the ukasa to cover the refugees that the threats
and grumbling finally ceased.

Once that crisis point had passed, Terrel relaxed a

little, but for a while the debate continued to centre on the plague, and he followed proceedings with interest. It soon became apparent that the Mehtar's assessment of the situation was reasonably accurate. Almost every tribe had been affected, but in most there had been only a few cases – and there were disagreements over who or what was to blame. As well as the unclean, the malign influence of the Dark Moon was cited by some, while others blamed a new type of camel tick, or tainted water supplies, but no one could explain why the illness affected just a few people rather than whole communities. Finally, at the Mehtar's insistence, a grudging agreement was reached. All the shamen would work together, exchanging experiences and knowledge about the disease, in the hope of finding a way to combat it. At this point Terrel wondered whether – in Vilheyuna's absence – he would be involved in this exchange, and if so, how much he should disclose.

Later, the discussion turned to the water supplies once more, and from there it was only a short step to the plight of the country as a whole. It was clear to Terrel that the politics of Misrah were fearfully complicated, and he soon gave up any attempt to work out the numerous alliances and enmities between the various tribes. The smug indifference of those whose land still benefited from plentiful sources of water contrasted strongly with the evident desperation of others, and one speaker in particular painted an unpleasant picture of the country's future.

The man had introduced himself as Mizhieb, leader of the Rokku tribe, who lived on what had once been the shores of the Kullana River. Their land had been devastated by the disappearance of the river and, in spite of the newly-opened canyon, the Rokku still lived in hope that it would return one day.

'If the winds grant us that,' Mizhieb said, 'all will be well again, but until that time we need the help of those more fortunate than ourselves. That is the way of the desert,' he added, looking around hopefully. 'To aid the less fortunate.'

'The weak, you mean,' Kohtala remarked derisively.

'Bad luck is not a sign of weakness,' Mizhieb countered.

'Bad luck is a sign of the winds' disfavour,' the Shiban warlord replied. 'Why should we help you when they do not?'

'We all have problems of our own,' Ghasri added. 'The Mgarr do not come to Qomish in search of charity.'

'I'm surprised you're able to come at all,' Kohtala went on. 'If things are so bad, why aren't you at home trying to help yourselves?'

'The beacons will tell us if anything changes, for good or ill,' Mizhieb replied. 'My entire tribe agreed upon this visit. That is the measure of how desperate our situation has become. I do not beg. I merely ask for your aid.' Finding no response to his last appeal, he sat down again, his face a mask of proud despair.

Soon after that, following another appeal by the Mehtar for peace and cooperation during the festival, the gathering broke up.

The next day, after the teams for the Race of Truth had been publicly announced, Terrel found himself at the centre of a new dispute. Kohtala, as champion of the Shiban, had objected to the inclusion of a 'foreigner' in

Zahir's team, and the Mehtar had been obliged to call both parties to a meeting so that he could arbitrate in the matter. While the other members of their teams looked on, the two champions presented their arguments.

'He is not of the Toma,' Kohtala claimed. 'You only have to look at him to see that.'

'That's not true,' Zahir responded. 'Terrel has been admitted into my clan in an ancient ritual. For Kohtala to challenge that is an outrage.'

'But he's a foreigner!'

'Not any more.'

'To let such a person approach the sacred mountain is blasphemy. The winds will punish such an affront.'

'Then they will punish *us*,' Zahir retorted. 'I would have thought you'd welcome that. It's the only way you'll beat us.'

'This is an insult!' Kohtala shouted. 'This . . . this boy is hiding behind the ukasa. If it weren't for that—'

'We're dealing with realities here, Kohtala,' the Mehtar cut in sternly. 'Not pointless speculation. The ukasa *is* in place, and you will obey it.'

The Shiban's warlord glowered at this, but remained silent.

'I see no reason to usurp the winds' authority,' the arbitrator continued. 'If they object to Terrel's presence, they will make it plain. He is one of the Toma. Therefore there can be no objection to him being part of their team.'

'Thank you,' Zahir said, bowing.

'You may win the war of words, boy,' Kohtala snarled, 'but the race will be mine.'

'Cling to your delusions if you must,' the nomad replied coldly. 'You dishonour yourself by calling me boy.

I am a man – and a better man than you. I shall prove that in the race.'

'Would you care to take a wager on that?'

'Name it.'

The two opponents were facing each other now, oblivious to those around them.

'The winner gets to choose any unmarried woman from the others' tribe,' Kohtala said. 'To take as a wife, on payment of a single curd cheese.'

Terrel's sense of foreboding had been building for some time, and now his heart sank. He knew that marriages between two tribes were usually a matter of honour or politics, not often love. The ceremony itself was simple, but the arrangements leading up to it were complex – and the size of the dowry was often crucial. By proposing such a payment, Kohtala was making the match a deliberate insult to the loser's tribe, and to the woman in particular. And Terrel was in no doubt as to who Kohtala would choose if he won the bet.

Don't do it, Terrel urged Zahir silently, as the nomad hesitated. Don't let him goad you into this.

'Do you refuse the wager?' Kohtala asked, smiling now. 'Have you lost your tongue, boy?'

'I doubt there are any women in the Shiban worth that much,' Zahir replied eventually, 'but I accept your wager.'

CHAPTER THIRTY-ONE

Terrel spent most of the next day with Mlicki and
Kalkara, exploring as much of Qomish as possible. He
had invited them to go with him in the hope that they
might find their mother among the throng – though he
had said nothing of this to them. The strange trio
received many questioning glances, but knowing that
they were under the protection of the ukasa made them
feel bolder than they would normally have done, and
even though the city and its crush of people was intimidating, it also provided an endless flow of wonders.
They saw snake charmers, a man whose drums played
themselves, and a woman who danced barefoot on the
glowing embers of a fire. They listened to musicians and
storytellers, and watched jugglers and fire-eaters, as well
as witnessing the almost frantic trading of the streets
and market places. And everywhere they went, Terrel
watched for a woman with a tattooed face. He saw
several, but none of them matched the memory of his

dream – and neither Mlicki nor Kalkara showed any sign of recognition. Terrel's hopes faded gradually, and finally he was forced to accept the truth. Even if their mother *was* there, the chances of actually finding her in the next room of the palace were extremely remote. Alyssa's message had evidently not been as straightforward as it had seemed.

Eventually, for all her wide-eyed excitement, Kala grew weary and indicated that she wanted to go back to the campsite. Terrel was tired too – as well as disappointed – and his mood was not improved when, almost immediately on his return, Nadur accosted him with some unwelcome news.

'Where have you been? We've been looking for you everywhere.'

'In the city. Is someone ill?'

'No. It's not that. Zahir called a meeting of the team to discuss the initial stages of the route. He wanted you to be there.'

'Why?' Everyone was aware that Terrel knew next to nothing about desert navigation.

'All the team were supposed to be there,' Nadur replied simply. 'Come on.'

As the youthful captain led Terrel through the maze of tents, the healer began to wonder if he had somehow let the rest of the team down even before they set off for the Binhemma-Ghar. Nadur's next comment did nothing to reassure him.

'You should've been resting today,' the nomad said. 'The race starts tomorrow.'

Terrel was well aware of that, and he was beginning to regret having wasted so much energy on the day's fruitless expedition. Equally, he knew that he could not have left Qomish without at least trying.

The rest of the team were already at Zahir's tent, together with a few elders and some of the men who had taken part in earlier races and who were presumably on hand to offer advice. Terrel's late arrival – the meeting had apparently been in progress for some time – was accepted with relief, and any annoyance Zahir might have felt was dispelled by Terrel's apology. The discussion returned to the team's plans, but had not got much further before another arrival disrupted proceedings.

'Is it true?' Ghadira demanded, bursting into the tent and confronting her uncle.

'Is what true?' Zahir asked.

'Your wager with that pig Kohtala.'

Zahir had the decency to look abashed, and glanced round at his fellow team members to see who had betrayed his secret.

'Don't look at them,' Ghadira snapped. 'They're not the ones who told me. The Shiban are spreading the news all over Qomish.'

'Yes, it's true,' Zahir replied, belligerent too now. 'So what? We're discussing important matters here.' He clearly didn't want to talk about his bet in front of the elders, and was hoping that Ghadira would take the hint and leave. Terrel could have told him that that was not about to happen.

'You're an idiot!' she declared. 'How could—'

'Look,' he cut in angrily. 'I'm going to win the race. And even if I don't, Kohtala certainly won't. So you've got nothing to worry about.'

Ghadira considered this for a few moments, glancing

briefly at Terrel before returning her furious gaze to Zahir.

'If he *does* win, you'd better die of thirst in the Binhemma-Ghar,' she told him. 'If you come back here, *I'll* kill you.' With that she turned on her heels and stormed off.

'What was all that about?' Algardi asked quietly.

Zahir did his best to explain, but Terrel only heard his first few words before he was distracted by Alyssa's voice.

We need to talk, but there's not much time. Are you coming out, or shall we come in?

Terrel hesitated, knowing that if he were to leave now, so soon after his arrival, it was going to look very odd indeed. On the other hand, he wasn't sure he could cope with two meetings at once. He was confused enough as it was.

Before he'd had time to decide one way or the other, a small scruffy dog trotted purposefully into the tent and curled up next to him. A few of the nomads glanced his way, and smiled at the latest example of their healer's remarkable way with animals. In other circumstances they would have thrown the creature out, but Terrel seemed content to let it stay. They returned to their own concerns, just as – unknown to all but Terrel – three ghosts flickered into existence inside the tent. The newcomers were already engaged in what appeared to be a heated discussion.

—owe him that, at least? Elam exclaimed.

We're only trying— Muzeni replied.

Owe me what? Terrel asked, jumping to the obvious conclusion.

The ghosts looked startled, and glanced around at their new surroundings.

You might have warned us, my dear, Muzeni said mildly.

What for? Alyssa replied shortly. *I thought you were in a hurry.*

And you haven't answered my question, Terrel added. He was finding the whole situation very disconcerting. The nomads were still talking, and he was having to concentrate on the silent conversation while trying to ignore the words in his ears. It was hard to believe he was the only one who could see the ghosts. *Is there something you need to tell me?*

Who starts? Elam asked. *You or me?*

You, Shahan replied.

Terrel had the feeling the seer was still trying to regain his composure, and wondered if their abrupt arrival had been a deliberate ploy on Alyssa's part. He did not like the implication that his allies were at odds with each other.

The Emperor's ill, Elam said. *With the plague.*

These blunt words – about the father Terrel had never known – filled him with a confusing mixture of emotions. He realized that somewhere in the deepest recesses of his mind he had always believed that he would one day meet his father – and now it seemed he might never get the chance.

The court physicians are panicking, Elam went on. *They've no idea what to do, and everyone seems to think he's going to die.*

And if Dheran dies, Shahan put in, *Jax becomes Emperor. He's old enough now.* He didn't need to spell out the possible consequences of such a development.

There hadn't been many cases of the disease in Makhaya, Elam added, *but the plague's getting worse now, all through the islands.*

The only good thing about Dheran's illness is that it has brought Jax back to the capital from Betancuria, Muzeni said. *His meddling was getting out of hand. The people there have enough to cope with, without his wretched earthquakes and tornadoes.*

The plague is still worst in Betancuria? Terrel asked.

Muzeni nodded, and Terrel wondered if the same was true in the Maculian capital of Talazoria. Aylen and his comrades were hopefully in the process of rebuilding their ravaged country, and an outbreak of plague would be a terrible setback.

I tried to curb the prince's worst excesses, Elam said, *but it didn't seem to do much good.*

Terrel wasn't surprised to hear this. His twin brother was unlikely to listen to any advice – especially if it went against his own malevolent instincts.

Jax knows your name, doesn't he? he asked, recalling something that had puzzled him ever since an earlier encounter.

Elam grinned for the first time, and this helped lift Terrel's spirits.

He knows who I am, Elam replied, *but he's not sure what I am. There's already a connection between us, which is how I can still get at him even when he's in Betancuria. I've been annoying him for a long time, on and off. He kept saying, 'Who are you?'. I didn't see any point in not telling him.*

We don't have time for this now, Shahan stated firmly. *The point is, we can't afford to let Jax become Emperor.*

The seers will try to keep him under some sort of control,
but in reality he'll be able to do anything he wants.

You have to act quickly to stop the spread of the plague,
Muzeni said. *Even without Jax's efforts, too many people*
are going to die soon.

I can't go any faster, Terrel said defensively. *The race*
starts tomorrow. But it's going to take some time to reach
Makranash, even if we win.

There's a possibility you might be able to make contact
with the elemental before then, Muzeni told him.

How?

If our calculations are correct, Shahan replied, *there*
should be an eclipse the day after tomorrow.

The Dark Moon?

Yes. You don't need me to tell you that such times are
very significant. We're not sure exactly where you'll be,
but if you can, you've got to take the chance to talk to
the Ancient, at least try to persuade it to make the plague
less virulent. Apart from what's happening here, the
future of the Floating Islands may well depend upon it.

The seer's words weighed Terrel down once more.
Ever since his exile, one of his few consolations had been
that his homeland was not involved in the upheavals he
faced. But that had been an illusion. If he had not
prevented the great earthquake in Macul, the islands
would have been decimated by giant tidal waves. And
now, if he did not make peace with the third elemental,
the distant Empire would be ravaged by a deadly
epidemic. It seemed that, one way or another, the Floating
Islands would never be safe until he fulfilled *all* of his
fateful bargain.

I'll do what I can, he promised. *How accurate are your*

calculations? Do you know what time of day the eclipse will be?

It's all been done in rather a rush, Muzeni replied, *but we believe it will be in the late afternoon, about an hour before sunset. You'll have to be quick, though, because it won't last very long.*

Terrel nodded, storing the information away with everything else he had to remember. For a few moments none of the visitors spoke, and Terrel became aware that the nomads were still talking.

Is there anything else?

The ghosts had made no move to leave, and now they glanced at one another uncertainly.

Well, are you going to tell him or am I? Elam asked.

Tell me what? Terrel said, his sense of foreboding increasing still further.

Shahan and Muzeni remained silent.

According to the Tindaya Code, Elam said, *the Mentor dies at the mountain built of winds.*

It's not as simple as that, Shahan said quickly, before Terrel had the chance to react.

I can't die there, he was telling himself, numb dread warring with disbelief. I can't! He had seen the manner of his death, but that was a long time in the future, on the summit of Tindaya – unless he had somehow mistaken one mountaintop for another. I *have* to go back to Vadanis, he told himself. Otherwise nothing makes sense.

That's just— Muzeni began.

Was that what you wouldn't tell me? Terrel cut in. *The last time you were here?*

The Code is ambiguous, the ancient heretic replied. *We didn't want—*

You keep doing this! Terrel exclaimed angrily.

They wouldn't even tell me what they'd discovered, Elam added resentfully. *Until I pestered it out of them.*

The reason for the friction Terrel had sensed between Elam and the seers was clear now.

That's because we weren't sure what it meant, Shahan said patiently. *We still aren't sure which interpretation is correct.*

There's more than one?

As usual, Elam commented sardonically.

Yes. That's what I've been trying—

Tell me, Terrel ordered, then jumped as he felt a hand on his shoulder.

'Are you all right?' Medrano asked.

'What? Oh. Yes, I'm fine.' Terrel was horrified by the timing of the interruption, but knew he had to maintain at least the appearance of normality.

'Only you looked really upset,' the artist persisted. 'Don't you agree with Zahir's plan?'

'No. No. It's nothing like that.'

'Now's the time to speak up,' Zahir told him. 'It'll be too late tomorrow. I know it's risky, but—'

'You all know far more about the desert than I ever will,' Terrel said desperately. He could feel Alyssa nudging his leg with her paw, and sensed the ghosts' impatience. 'You carry on. I'm happy with whatever you decide.'

Thankfully, the nomads seemed satisfied with this response, and returned to their discussion, allowing Terrel to direct his attention back to his spectral visitors.

Tell me about the Code, he said quickly.

We've been studying the section concerning the

'mountain built of winds', Shahan replied. *It clearly describes one of the landscapes that doesn't exist on the Floating Islands, so it must stem from the observations of either the Guardian or the Mentor, or both. The problem is that the records are fragmentary, and several vital sections are missing. We've done our best to piece it together, but because no one's ever paid much attention to it before, we've had to start from scratch.*

The first and most literal translation seems to be that either the Guardian or the Mentor has to die at the mountain, Muzeni said, taking up the tale. *Neither of which makes much sense. But the more we studied the various texts, the more alternatives we came up with.*

That's why we didn't tell you about it earlier, Shahan claimed, glancing at Elam.

So what are these alternatives? Terrel asked.

One is that there are two *Mentors present,* Muzeni replied. *And that only one of them dies.*

Mlicki? You think he should go too? The idea appalled him.

We don't even know if he is a Mentor, Shahan pointed out.

Zahir would never agree to take him, Terrel said firmly. *In any case, I can't ask him to go just so he can die instead of me. That would be murder!*

The next interpretation is that the Mentor – or one of them – somehow splits into two.

What?

Maybe the oracle was correct, Shahan suggested. *Maybe you* do *become the double-headed man – and only half of you dies.*

Terrel thought this sounded utterly insane, but

nonetheless he tried to consider the idea rationally. He also had to try to keep his internal consternation from showing on his face.

There are some strange references to twins producing twins, Muzeni went on, *then becoming one again. We really don't know what to make of that, but you and Jax are the only twins we know about.*

How could I split in two? Terrel asked. *How could I become the double-headed man?*

We were hoping you might have some ideas about that, Elam remarked.

It could be symbolic, of course, Muzeni ventured.

Oh, that's wonderful, Terrel muttered.

What I mean is, your half-death might be symbolic, the heretic explained. *You wouldn't really die at all.*

Well, that's a relief, Elam commented.

There's one last possibility, Shahan said. *The 'death' that's referred to could also be translated as a 'long sleep'.*

I might become a sleeper?

It would be a kind of splitting in two, Muzeni pointed out. *Just like Alyssa.*

A separation of body and spirit, Shahan added.

But . . . All sorts of objections were crowding into Terrel's mind, most of them concerning how he was supposed to fulfil his bargain if his body remained in a coma in Misrah. And then he wondered about something else. *What happens if I don't die, or split in two, or whatever? What happens then?*

That, unfortunately, is all too clear, Shahan replied. *The trust between the Guardian and the Mentor will be lost, and a curse will fall upon all the world.*

In the shape of the plague, we presume, Muzeni added.

So this is another test, Terrel concluded, feeling utterly weary and dejected.

You passed all the others, Alyssa reminded him. *And I'll be with you.*

Terrel looked into her eager canine eyes, and felt a bit better.

And if you have to become a sleeper, she went on, *we'll be able to carry on together.*

That thought cheered him up a little more.

Moons! Elam laughed. *Just think of the havoc you two could cause if you both went round as camels.*

Let's cross that bridge when we come to it, Shahan said, but even he was smiling at the idea. *In the meantime, there are a few more things from the Code that could be significant.*

Could be? Terrel queried.

They're just fragments, Muzeni replied, *but they might give you some guidance. One talks about walking though forests of salt and stone. Another refers to 'dancing within the dreams of stone'. Both of these seem to be positive aspects of the prophecy, but there's another reference – mention of a great storm which is linked to 'a place where the ground trembles and the air turns to smoke'. The inference is that you should avoid this place at all costs.*

Beware the time of storms, Terrel quoted.

Sound advice, Elam muttered. The boy's ghost had lost his earlier smile and he was moving constantly now, the translucent form flickering as if he were agitated.

Are you all right? Terrel asked.

We're not meant to be here.

But I need your help. I couldn't do any of this without all of you.

That's not what I meant, Elam said quietly. *We're not even supposed to be in this world.*

We'll move on when the time is right, Shahan said softly.

I know. It's still unnatural, though.

On that unsettling note the three ghosts vanished, leaving Terrel feeling suddenly alone. He glanced down at the dog and knew, without having to search for the ring, that Alyssa had gone too. Their time had evidently run out.

'So that's it, then,' Zahir concluded, looking round at his team. 'Make sure you all get a good night's rest. We've got a race to run tomorrow!'

The whole of Qomish was bustling long before dawn the next day, as everyone made their way to the north of the city to wait for sunrise and the start of the race. The air of excitement was intense as each of the champions presented their banners to the Mehtar, then returned to their teams for their final preparations. All the competitors were dressed for protection against heat and dust, their loose-fitting robes leaving only their hands and eyes clear. Terrel felt constricted by the hood and the veil over the lower part of his face, but he knew that his pale skin made him especially vulnerable to the ravages of the sun.

After what seemed like an endless round of farewells, the sun rose and the champions strode forth proudly, followed – at a respectable distance – by their teams of men and camels. The initial pace was quite fast, making the best use of the early morning coolness, but Terrel was amazed to see that the teams were heading in several different directions, and were soon separated by considerable distances. When he expressed his surprise to Medrano, who was walking beside him – it was a matter of pride that no one rode at all on the first day – the nomad's reply was matter-of-fact.

'In the desert, the most direct route is not always the best. Each champion must follow his own instincts. And of course, everyone wants to be out of sight of the others as quickly as possible, so they don't give away their intentions.'

'No one seems to be following our route,' Terrel said.

'Zahir's strategy is a bold one,' the artist replied. 'Most people prefer to go around the Valley of the Smokers rather than cross it.'

Terrel felt as if someone had just forced a lead weight into his stomach.

'The Valley of the Smokers?' he repeated weakly.

'I've never been there either,' Medrano said cheerfully. 'It should be quite an adventure.'

That's not all it might be, Terrel thought, wishing now that he'd been able to take part in the team's discussion about their route. It seemed that they were heading directly towards the one place the ghosts had told him to avoid at all costs.

Like it or not, his own Race of Truth had just begun.

PART TWO

THE RACE OF TRUTH

CHAPTER THIRTY-TWO

By the time they set up camp that first night, Terrel had learnt all he could about the Valley of the Smokers. Although this was not as much as he would have liked – Okan was the only member of the team who'd ever seen the valley, and even he had never tried to cross it – it was enough to convince Terrel that it was indeed the place the ghosts had warned him about.

However, he also discovered that it would take them several days to get there, and this allowed him to hope that he might still have time to persuade Zahir to take an alternative route. During the day, their champion had walked ahead of the rest of the party, and the only way to communicate with him was by shouting – something the nomads tried to avoid in order to save their breath for more important tasks. It was therefore not until they gathered together for the evening meal that Terrel felt able to broach the subject.

'Do you think it's wise to try to go across the Valley

of the Smokers?' he asked tentatively.

'Wise?' Zahir replied, grinning. 'That's the first time anyone's ever accused me of being *wise*.'

'I think you'll find,' Okan remarked, 'that our healer is accusing you of being just the opposite.'

'Thank the winds!' Zahir exclaimed. 'Wisdom is for the elders. I'd rather be bold and adventurous, reckless even.'

The nomads were all smiling now, and Terrel was at a loss to understand their mood.

'I'm serious,' he said.

'Then why didn't you say anything yesterday?' Zahir asked. 'It's too late now.'

'What's given you second thoughts?' Medrano enquired.

Terrel had thought about how he should answer this obvious question, but had not come up with a satisfactory solution. He'd wondered about claiming to have had a dream or vision, but had discarded that idea as dishonest. In the end he had decided to try to exploit a tenuous connection to the oracle in the Hills of Senglea.

'Isn't it a place of storms? The oracle warned us against that.'

'Storms are no more likely there than anywhere else,' Fanari stated flatly.

'The valley does offer a lot of other possible dangers, though,' Cassar remarked, sounding as if he were almost eager to face these perils.

'A storm would be the least of our worries,' Okan agreed happily.

'You're not going to begrudge us a little excitement, are you, Terrel?' Korioth asked.

Terrel knew then that he was already defeated. When even the oldest – and most responsible – of the team shared the general sense of anticipation, there could be no chance of persuading them to change their plans. Any further attempts would only alienate him from the rest of the group.

'Of course not,' he replied, forcing himself to smile. 'Just make sure you don't let me get turned into smoke.'

'That's not going to happen,' Zahir declared. 'We may need your services before we're through.'

'The camels won't like it any more than you,' Luqa added. 'But we'll manage, you'll see.'

'Besides,' Okan put in, 'we've come too far now. If we tried to go around the valley, we wouldn't be able to replenish our water supplies this side of the Binhemma-Ghar. From here, Gantiya is our only choice – and from there, we've no option but to go across. We'd lose too much time, otherwise, and then we wouldn't stand a chance.'

'And by going this way we should get to Makranash in record time,' Zahir said.

'Record time?' Terrel queried.

'Didn't you listen to *anything* I said at the meeting?' Zahir asked, with an incredulous smile.

'He was probably too busy talking to that dog,' Fanari suggested, laughing.

'If all goes well, we'll reach the mountain in sixteen days,' Zahir went on, 'when the White Moon is new. No one's ever done it in less than eighteen before.'

'Here's to winning!' Cassar said, raising his small cup of water.

'And to breaking the record,' Fanari added.

'Together,' Zahir concluded enthusiastically.

Terrel joined in the toast, sipping his own meagre ration. This is what it must be like for a band of soldiers on the eve of battle, he thought. He had only experienced such camaraderie once before, when he'd been part of an acting troupe back on Vadanis – and the worst peril they'd ever encountered had been a hostile audience. This team was preparing to face much greater dangers.

That night, for the first time during his months in the desert, Terrel lay in the open, under the stars. He was wrapped only in his chilouk, but the darkness no longer brought such bitter cold. He listened to the continuing banter of the others for a time, but then was lost in his own thoughts.

As he waited for sleep under the serene gaze of the White Moon – which seemed almost supernaturally bright – Terrel found himself wondering about a simple puzzle, an antidote to the greater mysteries that surrounded him.

'Medrano?' he whispered.

'What?'

'How do the other teams know when someone's won?'

'The mountain tells us,' the artist mumbled.

'How?'

'It rings. You'll know what I mean when you hear it. Now go to sleep.'

By the afternoon of the next day, Terrel was already weary from having to match Zahir's fierce pace, and it was only when the temperature dropped unexpectedly that he realized the time of the eclipse was approaching. Fanari kept glancing at the sky suspiciously, as if he suspected the weather of trying to trick him. While the moon only partially covered the sun it was impossible to see what was happening – the glare was still much too bright – but the nomads had clearly sensed the sudden lessening of the sun's heat.

'It's an eclipse,' Terrel told them.

'Ah!' Fanari said, looking relieved. 'Vilheyuna would have told us about such things.'

'We can make better time while it's cooler,' Cassar observed.

'Zahir will see to that,' Korioth agreed.

'We'll have to be careful when it goes dark,' Terrel pointed out.

'It never goes *completely* dark though, does it?' Okan said.

'It might this time,' Terrel replied, wondering whether Misrah had ever experienced a total eclipse before.

The nomads were obviously puzzled, but by then he was wrapped up in his own concerns. The light was noticeably dimmer now, and part of the sky was changing colour. Several camels bellowed in alarm, and Luqa hurried to calm them.

'What's going on?'

'This is . . .'

And then a great shadow hurled itself across the desert, swallowing everything in its path, and both men and animals came to a halt, staring in awe. Terrel sensed that its course meant they would only just be inside the edge of the shadow, and that he would have very little time to make contact with the Ancient. As he was engulfed by the darkness he felt the amulet spring to life within him, shining from his left hand, and he reached out into the void.

Please. If you can hear me, you know I'm your friend. You have to stop us hating the magic. If you don't . . .

The massive shadow swept on, and as the sun returned, the spiral light of the talisman faded as quickly as it had arrived. Within moments, the brilliant circle of beads surrounding the moon became a blaze again, leaving Terrel breathless and appalled by the fact that he'd been granted so little time. He had felt no response from the elemental, did not even know whether it had heard his plea – but there was nothing more he could do about that now.

'Winds!' Okan breathed quietly. 'I've never . . .'

The nomads all seemed stunned by what had happened, by its enormity and speed, and they glanced at each other in amazement – until Zahir broke the silence.

'The winds have marked out our trail for us with their shadows!' he called back to them. 'It's an omen!' With that he turned and set off again – and the others reacted instinctively and followed his lead.

An omen, yes, Terrel thought, as he urged his aching legs into action. But for good or ill?

The next morning found the small caravan weaving its way through the streets of a bizarre 'city of demons' – as Medrano called it – which glittered in the sunlight and crackled underfoot.

'What is this?' Terrel asked.

'It's called yardang,' the artist replied. 'This was once the bed of a great saltwater lake.'

Terrel found it hard to imagine such a thing.

'When it dried out,' Medrano went on, 'what remained was a mixture of soil and salt, and the wind's been eroding it ever since, turning it into this.'

The tall columns and pillars of layered sediment had been sculpted into many strange and fantastical shapes, and for a time the travellers amused themselves by spotting miniature watchtowers, shining temples, a table fit for a giant's banquet, and other fanciful objects. But then one of the camels stumbled when its foot broke through the brittle surface, and gashed its skin on the sharp crystals. After that, for all its wonders, the nomads were wary of the yardang city, picking their way carefully, and watching Zahir closely to see that he came to no harm.

The area reminded Terrel of a smaller, brighter version of the jasper forest, the rocks he'd drifted among on the coast of Macul. He had come close to death there, and this place also filled him with anxiety – until he recalled that the ghosts had said the 'forest of salt' was a positive aspect of the Tindaya Code prophecy. After that, he wondered what benefit could possibly come from his visit there.

'You should be at home here, Terrel,' Okan remarked. 'Your eyes are a perfect match for this place.'

Not long after they left the strange salt-maze behind, the team came across a collection of even more ancient remains that, in some ways, were even more remarkable. Lying in a wide depression between two lines of dunes were some enormous tree trunks. Every detail of their structure was perfectly preserved – but they'd all been turned to stone. They had obviously been real trees at one time, but now they were as hard and lifeless as any rock.

Looking at the desolation all around him, Terrel found it impossible to believe that a forest had once stood there, but he took comfort from this second sign that the Tindaya Code was still predicting his path.

Both 'forests' had caused diversions to their planned route, and when Cassar checked on the heavens that night, it appeared that they were further from their course than anyone had suspected. He spent some time talking with Zahir and Okan about where they should head the next morning. At one point in the discussion their voices were raised in anger, and soon after that Zahir called the other team members to join them.

'This is my decision,' he said, 'but Okan and I don't agree, and I'd like to know what the rest of you think before I make my final choice. As you know, we're heading for Gantiya, but from here we have a choice of routes. The most direct is over soft sand, but the longer is on a proven trail, so they'd probably take about the same time. The direct route would be more strenuous, but it would give us an opportunity to visit Seckar's monument along the way and pay our respects. I want to do that. Okan doesn't.'

'I just think we need to preserve our energy at this point,' the scout said.

For a while no one spoke.

'What do you think, Cassar?' Korioth asked eventually.

'If it came to a vote,' the star-reader replied, 'I'd be with Okan.'

'I'm with Zahir,' Fanari said. 'We do well to honour the champions of the past.'

'I agree,' Medrano said. 'How else do we keep the memories of the heroes alive?'

'Luqa?' Zahir prompted.

'I'd rather give the camels an easy time,' the herder replied quietly, 'before the going gets rough.'

'Fair enough. Korioth?'

'I don't feel strongly about it either way.'

'Looks like you get the casting vote then, Terrel,' Fanari commented.

'This isn't an election,' Zahir pointed out. 'Mine's the only vote that counts.' Nevertheless, he looked at Terrel hopefully.

'I don't know,' Terrel said. He felt very uncomfortable at having been put in such an awkward position. 'I don't know enough about your traditions.'

'No one would even have suggested going to the monument if we hadn't been pushed off course by the yardang and those stone trees,' Okan said. 'So it's not really a matter of tradition, just practicality.'

'I think we should go to the monument,' Terrel said abruptly.

'Why?'

'Just a feeling. An instinct. I've been travelling a long time, and I've learned to trust such things.' Privately, he was thinking that if the 'forests of salt and stone' were trying to push them in one direction, then that was the way he wanted to go.

'We go to the monument,' Zahir decided – and there was no further argument.

The journey to Seckar's monument turned out to be just as arduous as Okan had suggested. Terrel was grateful that he was able to ride for at least part of the morning, as men and camels slogged over a succession of sliding dunes. At last they reached an area where the going was much easier because it had been scoured by the wind, leaving behind a bare stony surface that the nomads called 'desert pavement'.

It was on this plain that the memorial stood, a roughly-shaped monolith that rose out of a closely-packed stone obo. Carved into the surface of the tall menhir was a symbol that Terrel recognized from the oracle. It was the star and wavy lines that represented 'the river in the sky'.

The team stood in a circle, facing the monument, in a few moments' silent contemplation. Terrel found himself wondering about the desolate nature of such an end – to be buried amid such barren grandeur after a life-time of battling against the relentless elements. One day, when there was time, he would ask Medrano to tell him Seckar's story – but not now. Having paid their respects, Zahir led his team on towards Gantiya.

'This is bad,' Okan declared.

'How bad?'

'At this rate it'll take all night just to refill half our containers.'

The team had travelled for another day and a half to reach Gantiya, and now it seemed that the normally reli-able spring had been reduced to a trickle.

'All right,' Zahir said. 'Korioth, organize a rota. We'll all take turns to fill the skins through the night. Okan, have a look around. See if there's anywhere we might be able to dig, speed the process up a bit, or at least let the camels drink. One way or another I want to start across the valley tomorrow, so we'll just have to go with what-ever we've got by sunrise.'

The nomads accepted their leader's decision without question, working in shifts during the hours of darkness. Terrel took his turn, feeling like one of the team for the first time, and shared in their satisfaction when, as dawn came, all but two of their water containers had been replenished. It was only then that he remembered that the day that was coming would take him into the Valley of the Smokers.

CHAPTER THIRTY-THREE

During his many travels, Terrel had seen some extraordinary sights, but he'd never come across a natural phenomenon in his own world that unnerved him as much as the Valley of the Smokers. The closest he could think of was the wasteland outside Betancuria – but that had been a man-made nightmare, whereas here the smoke and fumes in the air came not from mines or smelting furnaces but directly from the earth itself.

Hundreds of circular hollow pillars had grown up from the floor of the valley, like a bizarre collection of grotesque chimneys, and every one of them was smouldering. At intervals they would each belch forth gouts of smoke, ash and steam, and sometimes even a few bright flames. And as if that weren't enough, the ground shook almost continually, with a sound that varied from a deep rumbling to a screeching roar. Terrel had been aware of this noise even when the team had still been some distance away. And even without the evidence of his ears, the tremors had reached him through the soles of his feet. But his internal warning system had been thrown into disarray; here he couldn't tell where one earthquake ended and another began.

Terrel saw that the valley stretched for many miles in either direction but, because of all the debris floating in the air, it was impossible to see how wide it was, how far they would have to travel before they reached the other side. Even on the edge, the air was hard to breathe. Down amongst the smokers it would surely be poisonous. Even without the warning from the ghosts, Terrel would have wanted nothing to do with such a place, and he understood now why Zahir's plan had been considered so risky.

At that moment, the team's leader was striding along the side of the valley, at the top of the steep and intermittently crumbling bank. Okan and Cassar followed at the proper distance, and they were shouting back and forth, and pointing. Terrel couldn't hear what they were saying over the uproar from the valley, but he guessed that they were discussing possible routes into the smoke-filled depression. Most of the others were occupied with trying to control the understandably fretful camels, but Medrano found time to come to join Terrel.

'Quite a sight, isn't it?'

'Yes.'

'They say it gets wider and deeper every year.'

'If you're trying to reassure me,' Terrel said, 'you're not doing a very good job.' To his surprise he found himself smiling, and realized that some of the nomads' bravado must have rubbed off on him.

'We'll be fine,' Medrano assured him. 'It's not as bad as it looks.'

'How do you know?'

'Instinct,' the artist replied, grinning.

Terrel thought back to the time when the two of them had first discussed the Race of Truth. Medrano had expressed the opinion that it was only in the pointless things men did that they proved themselves. The trouble was that, for Terrel, this race was anything *but* pointless and, even though the nomads might be looking forward to testing themselves, all that mattered to him was their eventual success. On this occasion, losing would have consequences far beyond the Toma's imagining.

'The valley's a border of sorts too,' Medrano remarked. 'Once we get across, we'll be in the real desert, in the Binhemma-Ghar.'

Terrel's attention was caught by a flicker of movement in the sky above. Looking up, he saw two large birds circling lazily on an updraft. He had seen similar creatures before, in pairs or larger groups, but he couldn't imagine why they should inhabit such a barren region.

'What are they?'

'Hubaras,' Medrano replied. 'One of the old legends says they're sent by the winds to watch over the race, and to make sure everything's done in an honourable manner.'

'I don't think they need worry about us with Zahir in charge,' Terrel commented. 'Why are they really here?'

'They're waiting to see whether we go into the Binhemma-Ghar.'

'Why?'

'They're scavengers,' Medrano explained. 'They live

on dead flesh, and they've learnt from experience that it's worth following anything or anyone who ventures into the real desert.'

'They assume we're going to die?'

'Exactly,' the artist agreed cheerfully. 'We'll just have to disappoint them, won't we?'

'Let's hope so,' Terrel replied, thinking once again about the Code's prediction of the Mentor's death.

'Cheer up, my friend,' Medrano said. 'This is where the adventures begin!'

Shortly after that, Zahir and the scouts decided on their route. As convention demanded, the champion led the way, slithering down the slope into the shrouded cauldron. The rest of the team followed as best they could, and it was a relief to both men and beasts when they all reached the bottom of the incline. However, even on level ground no one could be sure of their footing, because the earth vibrated constantly. The air was full of noxious smells and particles of ash and dust that burned their skin and irritated their eyes, and the noise was almost deafening. Even the normally sure-footed camels stumbled at times, their eyes wide and wild, and they complained loudly at each stage of their progress into the smoking forest. Luqa enlisted Terrel to help keep the animals from panicking, and he found that being set such a task enabled him to cope with his own fears more easily. On several occasions a small explosion nearby blasted out a mixture of fumes and smoke, but having to tend to one or more of the nervous beasts allowed Terrel to ignore just how close he'd come to being scalded himself. As it was, the heat within the valley was almost unbearable. Combined with the foul atmosphere, it made breathing an arduous chore, and turned every step into an act of willpower. Even so, Zahir made slow but steady progress, and none of the others was prepared to let their leader down by falling behind.

Terrel noticed that the soil in the valley was darker than in the surrounding desert – as though it had been stained by the fiery exhalations of the earth below – but occasionally drifts of lighter coloured sand were blown across their path by a sudden gust of hot wind. These swirls made sinuous patterns about their feet, weaving complex living shapes around the columns of ash and the legs of the intruders. In any other circumstances Terrel would have been fascinated by this almost liquid flow, but he was too concerned with simply escaping from this dreadful place to pay it much attention.

At last the dense air began to clear a little, and they were able to see ahead to the far bank. Buoyed up by the knowledge that their ordeal was nearly over, they pressed on, anticipating the joys of solid ground beneath their feet and clean air in their lungs.

By the time the main group reached the bottom of the slope, Zahir was already at the top, beckoning eagerly for them to follow. This proved to be easier said than done. The passage of the first camel seemed to make the ground unstable, setting off several minor landslides that left those at the rear floundering in the crumbling earth. As a result the team decided to move the animals up one by one, well spaced out, to avoid similar problems and to prevent the terrified beasts from running amok. For reasons he could not explain, Terrel volunteered to remain at the foot of the bank with the waiting animals, and to try to keep them calm, while the others coaxed each creature to the top.

The task was almost completed, with Luqa and Okan scrabbling down to collect the last two animals, when a new smoker erupted only two paces in front of Terrel. The earth simply buckled and split open, disgorging a boiling gush of bitter smoke that engulfed him in a single moment. Terrel fell, losing his grip on the camels' ropes, and would have screamed if there had been any breath left in his lungs. As he lay there, blind and terrified, the fog seemed to be inside his brain as well as all around him. The skin of his hands and face burned, and sharp stabs of pain were shooting up his right leg. He couldn't breathe, choking if he even tried to open his mouth, and his nostrils seemed to be clogged with ash.

As a more profound darkness began to close in upon him, the world lurched suddenly. He heard voices – though he couldn't understand what they were saying – and he felt hands gripping his arms as he was lifted to his feet. His unseen helpers half carried, half dragged him away from the smoker, then began the laborious climb out of the valley. Gasping for breath, Terrel kept his tortured eyes tight shut the whole time, his head swirling as if he were drunk. His limbs seemed to have a wayward life of their own. Eventually, he felt himself being laid on the ground, and knew that they had completed their escape. Relief made him weaker still as his breathing gradually became easier, and Medrano's voice, close to his ear, registered in his whirling consciousness.

'We're out, Terrel. Are you all right? Can you walk? We need to get away from the edge.'

Terrel didn't know if he *could* walk. He didn't know if he could do anything. He felt strangely detached, as if he no longer belonged to his own body.

'Terrel? Are you all right?' Medrano repeated.

But Terrel was hardly aware of the artist's words. He was listening, in horror, to another voice – a voice *inside* his head.

Well, brother, Jax said. *This is interesting. What shall we do now?*

CHAPTER THIRTY-FOUR

The nomads could hardly believe the speed of Terrel's recovery. After a brief coughing fit, he accepted a drink of water and then practically jumped to his feet. But then, instead of heading away from the scene of his misfortune, he looked down into the smoke-laden valley, with both curiosity and an odd glint of pleasure in his eyes. He ignored everything Medrano said to him, until finally, in response to the artist's renewed urging, he turned and joined the rest of the team as they went on their way.

Terrel watched all this from outside himself. He seemed to be floating in some sort of limbo, detached not only from his own physical presence but from the world in general. He could see and hear – and think – but apart from that he was helpless, an observer forced to watch as someone else usurped his life.

Whenever he had lost control of his body in the past, he had been unconscious, completely unaware of the havoc his twin was wreaking, until he woke up and was presented with the evidence of his crimes. It had been left to others to explain how he had burnt down Kativa's shrine, how he had killed Alyssa's snow-fox or, more recently, how he had become the voice of rain – and, on each occasion, he had been reluctant to accept the truth.

It was different this time, and he didn't know why. In a way it was even worse, watching as Jax took stock of his new surroundings, and wondering how the prince would take advantage of the opportunities they presented. Knowing his twin as he did, Terrel was in no doubt that he would not be content just to observe what was going on. He would want to make his own mark. And if he remained true to his nature, that mark would involve violence and destruction.

For the moment, however, the prince remained calm, and the mood among his fellow travellers was jubilant. For all their earlier bravado, the nomads were obviously relieved to have completed the crossing, and now that the healer was recovered, they'd come through their first real test unscathed. Their talk turned to the possibilities ahead, of breaking the record for the race, and of the celebrations that would follow. Even the fact that they were still being followed by a group of hubaras became the subject of defiant jokes. Terrel glanced at his fellow creatures of the air, noting that the original pair had been joined by two more birds, and for a few moments he thought of Alyssa. He had been assuming that she would join him in the guise of one of their camels, but the hubaras gave her another option. Either way, he hoped she would come soon – although not until after Jax had left and he had been able to reclaim his own form. He didn't like to think what torments the prince might inflict upon her if he was given the chance.

An hour passed, with Jax responding to any queries about his welfare with either a nod or a shake of his head. If the nomads were puzzled by his reluctance to speak, they did not show it, apparently assuming that the healer's throat was still sore from his ordeal. Terrel wanted to warn them about the danger they were in from his other self, but he had no way of doing so.

The air was clear now, the stench of the valley a fading memory, and even the heat of the day could not counteract the nomads' optimism, or reduce their new-found energy. Terrel began to hope that his head would clear soon, allowing him to evict his brother before any real damage was done, but his heart sank when Fanari fell silent in the middle of a conversation with Korioth and then, without offering any explanation, ran off up the side of the nearest sand dune. Once at the top the weather-reader stared into the distance for a few moments, then called ahead to Zahir.

'Turn to the right a little!'

Zahir came to a halt and swung around.

'What for?'

'Sarik-buan!' Fanari yelled back, pointing towards the horizon.

'Coming this way?'

'No. It'll miss us, but if you go a few measures to the right we should avoid even the tail end of the storm.'

The others had all been listening intently to this exchange, and now Okan entered the discussion.

'We can make up the distance easily enough,' he called. 'Better than being stuck in a whirlwind.'

'Agreed,' Zahir replied, then turned away and set off on his new course.

'What's a sarik-buan?' Jax asked.

Medrano glanced at him, thinking that the healer's voice sounded odd – though this was hardly surprising after his ordeal. It also seemed a little strange that Terrel would need to ask such a question, but the artist saw no point in not answering.

'It's a yellow sandstorm,' he explained. 'Nothing too bad, and Fanari will make sure we miss the worst of it. There's nothing to worry about.'

Oh yes there is, Terrel thought, caught on the edge of panic. He had seen – and felt – his twin's sudden interest, and knew that Jax would not be content to view the storm from afar. The only hope was that it would remain too far away for his skills as a weather-mage to be effective.

That hope was dashed as soon as the caravan crested the next ridge and the travellers could see the distant whirlwind. It was no more than a dull brown smudge on the horizon, a dusty cloud that clung to the earth rather than taking to the skies. But even as they watched, it seemed to expand, billowing up and out like the blossoming of a monstrous flower.

'That's not right,' Fanari muttered, bewilderment showing on his face.

'What's happening?' Korioth asked.

They had all come to a halt now, staring at the ominous spectacle.

'It's getting bigger, isn't it?' Okan said.

'It shouldn't be, but . . .' Fanari fell silent as a sepulchral light flickered inside the dull bulk of cloud, testament to the violence within.

'It's coming this way now,' Jax stated, with a small smile that told of his satisfaction.

The nomads glanced at him in consternation.

'He's right,' Fanari declared a few moments later. 'We've got to take cover.'

'I'll tell Zahir,' Cassar volunteered, and dashed ahead to warn their leader.

What are you doing, Jax? Terrel asked. *Are you trying to kill yourself?*

Shut up, the prince replied, still admiring his handiwork. *It's bad enough having to put up with this pathetic body without listening to your snivelling.*

'This doesn't make any sense,' Fanari said.

They could hear the storm now, a relentless rustling that was just on the edge of hearing, but which was growing steadily louder.

'Never mind that,' Medrano said. 'Where's the best place to—'

'Down there!' Okan shouted, pointing to a narrow hollow at the base of one of the dunes.

The team sprang into action, gathering the camels and leading them down into the dip. The six beasts were made to lie down in pairs, so that the men could take shelter between the two lines once they were in place. Cassar came back to join them as they were making the best of their improvised refuge.

'Zahir's found his own place, under a ridge of bare rock,' he reported breathlessly. Even in such circumstances the champion was not allowed to rejoin his team. 'He's more exposed than we are, but I think he'll be all right.'

'Just as long as he doesn't get buried,' Okan

commented. 'Do you know where he is, in case we have to dig him out?'

Cassar nodded.

'We might have to dig ourselves out,' he said, looking at the banks of sand surrounding them.

'Better that than being torn to bits up there,' Korioth remarked. 'That thing's turning into a karabura.'

Everyone turned to look at Fanari, but he merely shook his head, at a loss to explain what had happened.

'Where's Terrel?' Cassar asked abruptly.

In the confusion, the healer had apparently been left behind.

'There he is!' Medrano cried, and set off to retrieve the straggler. When he reached him, the foreigner's eyes were glittering, his pale face shining with excitement, even as the light was growing dimmer by the moment.

'What are you doing?' the artist asked, raising his voice above the muffled howl of the approaching storm.

'It's magnificent,' Jax breathed.

'Maybe so,' Medrano replied, 'but it'll squash you like a bug. Come on.' He grabbed the healer's arm and dragged his reluctant companion down into the shelter.

Terrel watched all this from another world. He knew that a karabura – a black sandstorm – could not touch him where he was, but he was drawn towards the others anyway, and saw it from their point of view.

Day turned into night. The sun became a dark red ball, lost in a thrashing, colourless sea. The howling erupted into an unearthly, piercing shriek that thrummed in their ears and made the dunes vibrate. As the sand-storm crashed in upon them, the scale of the violence was appalling. Sand and stones flew through the air, wind clutched at their clothes and hair and threatened to tear them limb from limb. The protective blankets they'd spread over their bodies were ripped away, disappearing into the deepening gloom beyond the trembling shadows that were all they could see of the camels. Lightning flickered overhead, adding another terrifying element to the storm's rage. Thunder roared, crushing the breath from their chests, and strange clashing noises rang out against the tumult, as if the winds were engaging in a ferocious sword fight.

In that inhuman chaos, where all normal senses had long been overwhelmed, each man lay alone, clinging to the ground in case they, like the blankets, should be hurled into the sky. All they could do was protect themselves as best they could, wrapping their arms around their heads, and curling up to make themselves as small a target as possible while they endured the buffeting of the furious air and the flying stones.

Even Jax was beginning to doubt the wisdom of his actions now. Terrel sensed his brother's fear, felt the pain that he felt, and wondered what would be left of his body when he was finally able to reoccupy it. *There's a price to pay this time*, he muttered venomously. *You stupid fool.*

Oh, stop whining! Jax said. *This was your idea!*

Mine?

That's why you stuck around, isn't it? the prince said contemptuously. *So you could watch. How was I to know* . . . He broke off, laughing, as another flash of lightning illuminated the tempest and another bombardment rained down on to the huddled group. *I have to hand it to you, brother. For once, one of your ideas turned out to be a lot of fun!*

You don't know what you're talking about, Terrel snapped, though the doubts were crowding into his mind.

Don't I? Jax mocked.

Why would I want—

How should I know? the prince asked. *You're the one that's here, not me.*

This was Jax's way of bidding his twin farewell. The unreality of his situation fell from Terrel like a dead skin as he found himself back in his own body, prey to the full terror of the karabura.

For what seemed like hours, he clung to the hope that it must end soon. He fought for each breath, wincing as each new impact stung his battered frame, and trying to block out the infernal roaring in his ears. Sand was everywhere; it filled his mouth and nostrils, worked its way into his clothes and hair, and scoured every tiny area of exposed skin. Even though he kept them tight shut, his eyes stung painfully, and he began to think that if he didn't die, then he would surely go mad. No one could withstand such an assault for so long and remain intact in body or mind.

Even when it seemed that the storm's fury was decreasing a little, Terrel did not trust his senses. He told himself it was just wishful thinking, that it was still dark, that he was going deaf and so could not hear the full roar of the whirlwind. Face down in the sand, he refused to move, determined to stay where he was until he could be sure it was really over. At length he heard voices, tentative at first, but then growing stronger, thick with pain but also containing an unmistakable sense of relief.

'It's over, Terrel,' Medrano said. 'We made it.'

Forcing his cramped and bruised limbs into reluctant action, Terrel rolled over onto his back. The effort nearly exhausted him and he groaned aloud, amazed that his own voice still worked. He felt the warmth of sunlight on his face, and knew that it was real. It *was* over.

Medrano spoke again, and this time his voice was full of astonishment.

'Dome's fire!' he breathed. 'Come on, Terrel. You've got to see this.'

Slowly, painfully, Terrel opened his eyes. But he remained in darkness. Realization came slowly, creeping through him like a horrible disease. With Jax gone, the true consequences of his accident in the Valley of the Smokers had become obvious at last.

Terrel was blind.

CHAPTER THIRTY-FIVE

'There shouldn't be a road here,' Okan exclaimed in disbelief. 'There's *never* been a road here!'

'Well, there is now,' Cassar replied. 'And this is no herder's track either. It's beautifully constructed.'

Terrel heard what they were saying, but he couldn't take it in. His mind was still reeling. I can't be blind, he thought desperately. Something must be blocking my eyes. But he knew that wasn't true. His whole world had become dark.

'Terrel?' Medrano called, suddenly anxious. 'Are you all right?'

'Not really,' he replied, his voice sounding hoarse and unnatural. 'I can't see.'

The nomads' concern was immediate and genuine, and they gathered round Terrel – although he couldn't tell who was there until they spoke.

'He must have been hit by flying stones,' Okan decided.

'Let me take a look at you,' Medrano said.

Terrel felt the artist's fingers gently probing his face and head, searching for any sign of injury.

'I wasn't hit,' he told them. 'I think it was the explosion from the smoker.'

'But you could still see after that,' Korioth said, sounding puzzled.

'That's right,' Medrano agreed. 'You walked with us and watched the storm approaching. I had to drag you away to take cover.'

'It's almost as if you *wanted* it to head our way,' Fanari added.

'Why would he want that?' Okan asked, dismissing the weather-reader's comment.

'I can't find anything,' Medrano reported. 'Are you sure it was the smoke?'

'I'm sure. It must have been a delayed reaction.'

'It'll probably wear off again soon,' Cassar said optimistically.

'Is there anything you can do about it?' Korioth asked.

'Heal myself?' Terrel shook his head, thinking for a moment about Talker, the blind healer in Fenduca, who had been able to help others but not himself. 'It doesn't work that way. If it did I'd have done something about this,' he added, holding up his deformed hand.

'Will you still be able to heal others?' Medrano asked.

'I don't see why not,' Terrel replied, then fought back the urge to laugh hysterically at his own choice of words. 'Is someone hurt?'

'Luqa got hit pretty badly on his arm. He's looking after the camels at the moment, but he'd get on a lot better if you treated him.'

'Bring him here.'

'We've all got work to do,' Korioth said apologetically. 'I need to know what supplies we've lost.'

'Go ahead,' Terrel told him. 'This doesn't change anything. We've still got a race to win.' His brave words took almost all the strength he had left, and he was glad when most of the team dispersed.

'Stay where you are,' Medrano said. 'I'll fetch Luqa.'

In the distance, Terrel caught a shouted exchange between Okan and Zahir.

'Is Zahir all right?' he asked quickly.

'He fared better than us. That ledge was more effective than our hollow.'

'That's good.'

'I'm sorry, Terrel. We've all been lucky, apart from you.'

'Did Okan say something about a road?' Terrel asked, not wanting to dwell on his own misfortune, or on the mind-numbing sense of despair that was threatening to overwhelm him.

'Yes. The storm uncovered a paved road, leading straight into the desert. It's incredible. No one had any idea it was here.'

'Are we going to follow it?'

'Why not?' Medrano replied. 'It heads in exactly the direction we want to go, and after what we've just been through, we'll all be grateful for a little easy travelling.'

'Are the camels all right?'

'I'd be surprised if some of them weren't injured, but they're all standing, so they can't be too bad. Luqa will be able to tell you. I'll be back in a moment.'

Terrel was left alone then, fighting back a wave of black misery that was now mixed with anger rather than disbelief. How was he supposed to complete all the tasks before him if he was blind?

An hour later, the caravan was on its way again. Terrel rode on one of the camels, his mood swinging wildly between bloody-minded determination and abject self-pity. In one sense, nothing had changed; he had proved his continuing worth to the team by utilizing his healing skills, finding that his blindness had not affected his ability to 'see' inside his patients' waking dreams. Having dealt with the human ailments – the most serious of which had been Luqa's arm, which was badly bruised but not broken – he had helped restore the wellbeing of some of the camels. Since then he'd learnt that although they'd lost some food and a little water to the storm, the majority had survived intact – and that Zahir, like all the others, was now keen to press on, to follow the new road that seemed to head directly into the heart of the Binhemma-Ghar. Terrel was frustrated at not being able to see the road, especially as his companions were so excited by its discovery. In fact, despite Terrel's misfortune and their concern for him, the general mood of the nomads was now very positive. The only exception was Fanari, who was subdued, evidently feeling that he had let his comrades down. Terrel could have told him that this was not the case, but he couldn't bring himself to do so. Explaining Jax's presence would have been impossible.

For his own part, Terrel was still trying to make sense of what had happened. His brother's words – *That's why you stuck around, isn't it? So you could watch* – had taken on an entirely new meaning in the light of his subsequent blindness. But the thing that really puzzled Terrel was the inference that the whole episode had been his own idea. The only possible reason he could think of for this was that it had been necessary in order to find the road they were now travelling. But he had not even been aware of its existence – and, in any case, were a few miles of easy travelling really worth risking the lives of all his companions as well as his own? And if it *had* been his idea, how had Jax known about it? Had possession of his twin's body given the prince access to what – at best – could only have been a subconscious desire? It was much more likely to have been a coincidence, with the accident allowing Jax in and letting his malevolent instincts take over. The fact that this had resulted in something beneficial – as the rain had been on an earlier occasion – was just a matter of luck.

It also occurred to Terrel that the prince's talent as a weather-mage, and specifically his ability to affect and shape the desert winds, would be seen by the Toma not only as potent magic but as truly divine power. If they credited the healer with such power, as they had already done to a lesser extent by dubbing him 'the voice of rain', then it would be a potentially dangerous misconception. However, only Fanari had even hinted at any such suspicion. The others had obviously shrugged off such a notion as absurd.

Thinking about all this helped keep Terrel from brooding on his own plight for a while, but dismal reality soon reasserted itself. With every step the camel took, Terrel raged against the fact that he could see nothing of the terrain about them. He couldn't even tell whether the hubaras were still following the caravan, and if there was another sandstorm, he would remain in ignorance until warned by others. He could still heal, which allowed him to retain some sort of purpose and self-respect. But in virtually everything else he was helpless, utterly reliant on his companions.

I can't be blind, he repeated, over and over again. I can't.

The reason for the ghosts telling him to avoid the Valley of the Smokers was all too clear now, but he'd had no choice in the matter – or at least it had seemed that way – and he'd paid a heavy price for it.

I can't be blind. It's not fair!

For a moment Terrel remembered Elam making the same complaint. 'It's not fair,' he had moaned. 'Why do *we* get lumbered with all the lousy jobs?' That had been during their time at Havenmoon, when Elam was still alive. He'd been protesting about their being forced to clean out the stables – which in hindsight seemed such a trivial hardship that Terrel had no choice but to laugh out loud. The half-strangled noise that came from his mouth was not a happy sound.

'Sometimes I hate the world so much I wish I could destroy it all,' Terrel murmured to himself, recalling another part of that same conversation. Those had been *his* words, not Elam's, and the way he felt now gave them a ring of truth.

'Did you say something?' Medrano asked from below.

'No.'

'Can I get you anything?'

'No.' At that point Terrel was doing his best not to cry, and wanted only to be left alone.

Medrano fell silent, recognizing the healer's distress, but a few moments later shouts from the other nomads alerted him to something – and astonishment forced him to speak again.

'Winds!' he exclaimed. 'I don't believe this.'

'What is it?'

'There's a city ahead of us. The road leads right to it.'

'A city?' Terrel queried, sharing his friend's disbelief. 'But—'

'It's a dead place,' Medrano added. 'The sandstorm obviously uncovered it as well as the road. It must be ancient.'

'It's a ruin?'

'Yes,' the artist confirmed. 'But it's no ordinary ruin. This place must have been three times the size of Qomish.'

Zahir was the first to enter the ruined city, but because their arrival coincided with sunset, the others were able to join him almost immediately. Terrel sensed their awe in the way they trod softly and spoke only infrequently – and even then in hushed tones. He wanted to ask them to describe what they were seeing, but he was reluctant to disturb the almost holy feeling in the silence of the place.

The nomads' urge to investigate the city was clearly very strong, and even though Zahir insisted that they set up camp first, he obviously shared his companions' curiosity and amazement. As soon as the most basic preparations for the night had been made, he gave them permission to go and explore, and – to his immense frustration – Terrel found himself alone.

Zahir had already stipulated that their stay would only be for that one night. In the morning, at sunrise, they would head off again. The team all accepted this readily, and so took advantage of the last of the fading light before continuing in the sombre radiance of the Red Moon, which was only a few days past full. They returned one by one, each bearing news of the wonders they had discovered, but aware that they needed to get some rest before dawn. Each of them hoped that they could come back another time.

Terrel listened to all of their reports, but it was left to Medrano, the last to return to the campsite, to sum up the place.

'This is the most remarkable discovery in the history of Misrah,' he said as he sat down and accepted his portion of the evening meal. 'There's not a single mention in any of our stories of a city this big anywhere near here.'

'It must be older than all the tales,' Korioth suggested.

'It's certainly been buried in the sand for centuries,' Okan remarked. 'The amazing thing is that so much of it's been left intact.'

'There was water here too,' Cassar said. 'Lots of it.'

'There must have been,' Korioth agreed, 'to support a city of this size.'

'You can still see some of the ducts and drains they used,' the scout added. 'They're huge!'

'Judging by the size of some of the storehouses,' Zahir put in, 'this whole area must have been fertile.'

'Hard to believe now,' Okan said.

'For me, the most astonishing thing is the way so many of the buildings are covered with carvings and inscriptions,' Medrano said. 'I've never seen anything like it.'

'Inscriptions?' Terrel queried, his interest piqued. 'Tell me about them. What do they say?'

'I've no idea,' the artist replied.

Terrel had immediately thought of Tindaya, another set of ruins that had carried messages from a distant past, but he was aware that the nomads knew no written language. Whatever was inscribed upon the stones of the desert city would mean nothing to the Toma – and Terrel couldn't even see them!

'Tell me about them,' he repeated, hoping to learn something anyway.

'There are just too many,' Medrano told him. 'I wouldn't know where to start.'

'They're everywhere,' Luqa confirmed.

'Just pick anything,' Terrel persisted. 'Anything you can remember.'

'Well, there are some symbols that reminded me of the oracle signs,' Medrano began. 'They're not exactly the same, but they have a similar feel to them. There are others that look as if they refer to the lunar cycles, and possibly the stars as well. Then there are whole sequences of marks and squiggles that look like the counting tablets merchants use to calculate their prices.'

'Writing?'

'It could be,' the artist admitted doubtfully. 'If it is, it's not like anything I've ever seen.'

'There are pictures too,' Luqa put in. Normally the quietest of the team, he became quite voluble for a while, describing the carvings he'd seen, most of which seemed to depict scenes of destruction – fires, earthquakes and storms. 'Whoever built this place had a horrible imagination,' he concluded.

'Maybe it wasn't just imagination,' Korioth said. 'Something destroyed this place, didn't it?'

*

After a while, when it became clear that there was nothing more the nomads could tell Terrel about the city, their talk turned to their plans for the next day. Cassar's reading of the heavens had confirmed that they'd made good progress, and even though they would no longer have a paved road to travel on, the scouts were confident of continuing success in the morning. Luqa and Korioth reported that both camels and stores were in satisfactory condition, which left only one member of the team to speak. Fanari had been virtually silent all evening, sunk in his own thoughts.

'Is there any weather coming up we should worry about?' Zahir asked.

Fanari looked up from his preoccupation and shook his head.

'Not as far as I can tell,' he replied.

'Good.'

'But then there shouldn't have been any today,' Fanari added. 'I don't know what happened. The winds must be angry with us.'

'No,' Zahir responded immediately. 'Who are we to judge their motives? The karabura didn't kill or seriously injure any of us – and it showed us the way forward. It brought us here.' He paused. 'Besides, you're the best weather-reader I've ever known. One storm doesn't change that.'

Fanari looked grateful for this vote of confidence, but he was clearly still shaken by what he saw as his own failure.

'This was meant to happen,' Terrel told him. 'I'm sure of it.'

'Just as you were *meant* to lose your sight?' the nomad replied.

'Perhaps,' Terrel said, taken aback by Fanari's harsh tone.

'He won't be blind for long,' Cassar asserted. 'Give it a few days, and the effect of the smoke will wear off.'

The healer could only wish he had the same faith in his own powers of recovery.

Terrel woke in the middle of the night to a flickering light that was too brilliant to be coming from any of the moons. Sitting up, he almost called out to his companions, to ask them what was happening, but then, as a reflex action opened his eyes, he found that he could see.

His joyful amazement was first compounded and then thrown into question by the fact that the city was bathed in sunlight. What was more, this was not the ruin Medrano had described; this was a living, breathing place, where trees and flowers grew and the sound of running water was all around him. Is this a dream? Terrel wondered, looking around for his team-mates.

A man strode out from behind one of the decorated buildings, and came to a halt in front of Terrel. He was dressed in some kind of military uniform, and carried himself with an unmistakable air of command. He was the most imposing figure Terrel had ever seen, and yet there was a sense of compassion, a deep sadness, in his dark, unblinking eyes.

'My name is Zorn,' the man said. 'Welcome to Y-Harah.'

CHAPTER THIRTY-SIX

Terrel blinked, wondering whether it might have been better for him to have remained blind. This had to be a dream or a delusion – and yet it *felt* real. The sunlight was warm on his skin, the scent of orange blossom was sweet in his nostrils, and the sound of running water was music in his ears. And yet Zorn was a legendary character from long ago, Y-Harah a lost city of myth. He had either been captured by some extraordinary magic, or he was going mad.

'Are you a storyteller?' Zorn asked.

'Not really.'

His answer seemed to perplex the hero.

'Then you are a messenger? You have the eyes for it.'

Terrel wasn't sure what to say to that.

'A traveller, then,' Zorn guessed.

'Yes.'

'Alone?'

'No. I am with friends,' Terrel replied, looking around.

'I'm just not sure where they are.'

'Is there a storyteller among them?'

'Yes.' He was thinking of Medrano, and his version of 'the oldest story of all'.

At this Zorn seemed to relax a little.

'Then tell your friend there is a new story to be told,' he said.

Are you a ghost? Terrel wondered. The man certainly looked solid enough. His clothes and even his beard were coated with dust, and the strong, scarred hand that rested lightly on the pommel of his sword looked like real flesh and blood. There was an indefinable air of dignity in the way he held himself, and pride in his stern face, but the eyes revealed another aspect of him – a glimpse of the man within the hero.

'On the night I was born, all the four moons came together,' Zorn began, 'and it was foretold that I would become a general, a leader of men. I believed in such things and, in due course, the prophecy came true. We fought for land, for wealth and power, but most of all for glory, because that was what we were meant to do.' Memories of those youthful days – of simpler, less troubled times – lit a fire within his eyes. 'But after a while,' he went on, the fire dying again, 'there were no honourable challenges left. Jealousy took us to Y-Harah. Jealousy and greed. Soofarah's tales beguiled us.' He paused and, even though his expression remained grim, Terrel could sense the pain behind it.

'She was aptly named "the Meddler", that one,' the general said, and for the first time there was bitterness in his voice. 'We learned too late that she was false. Hargeysa was guilty of nothing more than wanting his people to live well. His was a noble dream – and we destroyed it.'

'So the Sentinel was not a tyrant?' Terrel queried, remembering Medrano's description of the city's ruler.

'Far from it. He was generous and wise, a man of vision.'

'Did you kill him?'

The quietly spoken question seemed to shake Zorn's composure.

'With my own hand,' he replied harshly.

Terrel flinched at the shiver of steel as the general drew his sword. The blade was stained with blood.

'This is the mark of my shame,' Zorn declared, then sheathed his weapon again. 'By the time I discovered the truth, the deed was done. Hargeysa and his men fought bravely, but they could not match our relentless fury or our brutality in a fight. We were too strong, too experienced in the ways of battle. Evil triumphed in us that day.'

'And yet you are remembered as a hero,' Terrel said.

'A hero?' Zorn's surprise was apparently genuine. 'Hardly that. But for your coming I would still be the greatest fool who ever lived in Misrah.'

'You were misled,' Terrel protested. 'You couldn't have known—'

'I swore an oath that I have never fulfilled,' Zorn cut in, sweeping aside any excuses. 'I swore to go to the sacred mountain and confess my sins to the winds and, once I had done that, to tell the true story of Y-Harah and its Sentinel. That way Hargeysa's honour would be restored, and mine would be a little less tarnished.'

'Why didn't you keep your promise?'

'We were on the first part of our pilgrimage when we

were caught in the greatest sandstorm the world has ever seen. Even then, when much of Misrah was green and fertile, the Binhemma-Ghar was still a desert. We went in, but we never came out. We became part of the memories of sand.'

The memories of sand, Terrel thought. Is that what I'm seeing?

'So you weren't lost in the Race of Truth,' he asked, remembering another part of Medrano's tale.

'I know nothing of any race,' Zorn replied. 'I am held captive by my oath.'

'But this place,' Terrel said, indicating their surroundings. 'You said this was Y-Harah.'

'This is how it was,' the general told him. 'The winds punish us with unattainable perfection, while we languish in the wasteland. With water we cannot taste, flowers we cannot smell, soft beds we can never lie upon, music we cannot enjoy.' He shook his head sadly. 'Perhaps one day Misrah will produce another place like this, but I will never see it.'

'Is this the story that's carved into the stones of the buildings?'

'My story? No. That is an ancient prophecy, written long before I was born.'

'Do you know what it says?'

Zorn shook his head, as if such considerations were of no interest to him. Terrel was disappointed, but not surprised. He now believed that almost every aspect of 'the oldest story of all' was wrong – and that the version he'd just heard was the truth. In spite of his self-confessed crimes, Terrel had met no one on his travels who could match the general's weary nobility, and his healing instincts longed to release him from his torment. Zorn was clearly someone who, with his men, had been capable of carrying out acts of almost unimaginable violence – but only if he believed in the cause he was fighting for. He was a soldier, not a murderer, and the fact that his honour had been compromised had been enough to trap his spirit in Terrel's world long after he should have moved on.

'What do you want me to do?'

'Tell the true story of Y-Harah, and of our doom,' Zorn replied. 'That way, at least part of my oath will be fulfilled. Perhaps then the winds will forgive me. Will you do that for me?'

'I will,' Terrel promised. 'I'll make sure that in time all the storytellers of Misrah learn the truth.'

'Thank you.'

'What about the other part of your oath?'

'There is no remedy for that,' the general said. 'As I am, I cannot go to Makranash. A great gale holds me back.'

So you *are* a ghost, Terrel thought.

'I will have to rely on the mercy of the winds,' Zorn went on, 'but we will rest easier if you allow the real story to be told. And Y-Harah will be at peace at last.'

As he listened, Terrel saw a hundred small dust devils swirl up from the ground. They danced in the air for a few moments, and he remembered that the kwei were supposed to be the homes of lost souls.

'These men followed me everywhere,' the general said, recapturing Terrel's attention. 'With your coming, we are at least one step closer to going home.'

Sensing movement, Terrel looked beyond the general. The dust devils were gone, and in their place stood an army of ghostly warriors, each solemn face turned to look at him.

'One day we *will* go home,' Zorn added, and the longing in his voice was enough to break a soldier's heart. 'Farewell, Traveller. Remember us, and tell our tale.'

In the next moment, Zorn and all his men vanished – and Terrel saw that where each of them had stood, a shining crystal lay upon the ground.

The healer got to his feet and walked over to where the general had been. He picked up the stone and studied its fractured structure in the sunlight. Can the memories of sand be encased in crystal? he wondered, then smiled.

'You may not be able to go to Makranash,' he said aloud, hoping that somewhere Zorn could still hear him. 'But I might be able to *take* you there.'

When Terrel next awoke, he was blind again. Around him he could hear the bustle of the nomads as they broke camp.

'Good. You're awake,' Medrano said. 'We'll be off soon. Try to make up for lost time.'

'What lost time?'

'We missed the sunrise because of the mist.'

'Sand-mist?' Terrel guessed.

'Yes. A legacy of the karabura, no doubt. It's almost cleared now.'

'Did you see any visions?'

'Not this time. I was asleep most of the night. Woke up with a mouth full of grit.'

Terrel suddenly reached inside his robe and fumbled in the pocket of his shirt. When his fingers closed around the hard shape of the stone he'd picked up in his dream, he let out a long breath. It had been real.

'Are you all right?' Medrano asked.

'I think so. Will you stay close enough to talk when we set off?'

'If you like. Why?'

'I've got a story I want to tell you,' Terrel replied.

'I thought you meant one of *your* stories,' Medrano exclaimed, when Terrel had finished. 'I've never heard it told that way before.'

'This is the real story,' the healer said. 'The true one.'

'If you say so,' the artist responded casually.

Terrel realized that the nomad didn't believe him. In a sense, this didn't matter. What was important was that the tale be told. For the Toma, history and myth were indistinguishable.

'Will you tell it to the tribe?'

'The first chance I get,' Medrano replied enthusiastically, then hesitated. 'As long as that's all right with you.'

'It's fine with me. In fact I want you to.' Terrel knew that even if Medrano didn't repeat what he'd been told word for word, he would retain all the important ingredients – and the spirit – of the story. The first part of the healer's promise to Zorn would be kept.

'Who told it to you?' Medrano asked.

'Zorn.'

The few moments of silence that followed his answer made Terrel wonder if such a forthright response had been a mistake. Then his companion laughed.

'You're joking, right?' he said.

'No. It was Zorn. Or his ghost. I had a vision in the night.'

Medrano took a while to consider this.

'I bet that's not the only tale that place could tell,' he said eventually, his regret at having to leave the ruined city so soon clear in his voice. 'Do you think it really was Y-Harah? It's not supposed to have been anywhere near here.'

'I don't know,' Terrel admitted, glad that his explanation had been accepted.

'Was that the one day in ten thousand years?' Medrano asked, amazed. 'And we were there!'

'Who knows? It does seem as though we were meant to find the city.'

'It does, doesn't it?' the nomad said thoughtfully.

Terrel guessed that his friend was now considering some aspects of the earlier versions of the tale. Similar thoughts had already made the healer feel uneasy. In the earlier story, Zorn, the hero, had only appeared in 'a time of need' – and it had also been claimed that Y-Harah would only rise again 'when the world was coming to an end'. Neither of those possibilities was very comforting.

On the other hand, Terrel reminded himself that on two previous occasions he had been responsible for solving a puzzle from the past and thus allowing a beleaguered spirit to move on. Kativa and Aryel were gone from his world – and now, if his plans succeeded, Zorn and his soldiers would be able to leave too. And he would have passed another test.

'How far are we from Makranash?' Terrel asked.

'Ten days, if all goes well.'

'How far in miles?' the healer amended, thinking of the limit to the ghosts' approach, and wondering when Alyssa would join him.

'I don't really know,' Medrano replied. 'Okan might have some idea.'

'It's more than a hundred still, isn't it?' Terrel persisted.

'Yes. It must be.'

'Are the hubaras still with us?'

'No. I saw some of them flying over the city when we left this morning, but there's been no sign of them since. That's another good omen, eh?'

Terrel wasn't sure it was, but he said nothing about that to Medrano.

CHAPTER THIRTY-SEVEN

'We're in the lead,' Cassar declared. 'We must be.'

'I think so too,' Zahir said, excitement and satisfaction both evident in his voice. 'But that's no reason to be complacent. There's a long way to go yet.'

In the two days since they'd left the mysterious ruined city, the team had made excellent progress. Their only disappointment was that there had been no improvement in Terrel's eyesight, and hopes that it would return of its own accord were fading. Although no one had put their fears into words, the healer was aware that even Cassar was losing his characteristic optimism. For himself, he was growing more depressed and more accustomed to his condition at the same time. He could do some things for himself now, though he was still painfully aware of his dependence on the others. None of the nomads seemed to resent this extra burden on their time, and they made a point of reassuring him that he was still an important member of the team. He was grateful for their support, and glad that his healing skills had not been affected. Balanced against this was the realization that even if he was able to meet all the demands of his bargain in Misrah, he would still be a very long distance from home. The only way Terrel could begin to deal with the prospect of trying to make his way back to Vadanis as a blind man was to avoid thinking about it altogether. He told himself he'd deal with that when he had to, if and when he'd completed his tasks at Makranash.

Their camp that night felt slightly unusual, and for a while Terrel couldn't work out why. However, when Okan shouted for Luqa – who was presumably attending to his charges – to come and join the others for their meal, his voice sounded strange. It was something Terrel would probably never have noticed if he could still see, but his other senses were becoming more acute now.

'What's causing the echoes?' he asked.

'What echoes?' Okan queried.

After a few moment, Fanari gave a more considered answer.

'We're close to a small cliff,' he said. 'It'll shelter us from the wind overnight.' The weather had produced no more surprises, and the nomad was beginning to trust his instincts again.

'You remember the cliffs near Lebenzon, Okan?' Cassar asked.

'Where we found the paintings, you mean?'

'Yes. They were strange, weren't they?'

'Not strange,' Medrano said. 'They just looked at the world differently then.'

'Were they as old as the ones you showed me in the cave?' Terrel asked.

'Probably. We've no way of telling.'

'Do you think there might be any here?'

'We could go and look . . .' Cassar hesitated. 'And tell you about them, I mean,' he added awkwardly. 'If there are any.'

'I'd like that,' Terrel responded.

'Just don't take too long,' Zahir told them. 'We need our rest.'

'You especially,' Korioth said. 'At least we get to ride once in a while.'

'I'm fine,' their leader claimed. 'A bit stiff, that's all.'

'I can probably help you with that,' Terrel volunteered.

While the healer tended to the Toma's champion, Cassar and Medrano went to inspect the cliff. Their excitement when they returned was obvious even to Terrel.

'Did you find something?'

'We certainly did,' the artist replied. 'But it's not paintings.'

'It's dragons' eggs!' Cassar exclaimed.

'That's a rather fanciful description,' Medrano said, laughing, 'but it might be as good as any other. They're certainly eggs, but they're huge, and so old they've turned to rock.'

Like the trees in the forest of stone, Terrel thought, already intrigued.

'We've no idea what laid them,' Medrano went on. 'If it was a bird, it must have been huge.'

Like a caroc? Terrel wondered.

'Maybe it wasn't a bird,' Korioth suggested. 'Some types of lizards lay eggs.'

'I wouldn't want to meet the lizard that laid *them*!'

Cassar stated emphatically. 'It would have been a giant.'

'There's no telling what might have lived here once,' Medrano said. 'Whatever it was, it's long gone. There are some bones embedded in the base of the cliff as well,' he went on.

'They've turned to stone too,' Cassar added. 'Do you want to come and see them, Terrel? I mean . . .'

'It's all right. I know what you mean. I would like to touch them.'

'We'll all go,' Zahir decided. 'But we can't afford to spend the whole night looking at rocks.'

'Agreed,' Medrano said. 'There's not really that much to see. It won't take long.'

The artist took Terrel's good hand and pulled him to his feet, then allowed him to take his arm for the short walk.

'Shall I bring a torch?' Korioth asked.

'No,' Medrano replied. 'Those two should give us enough light.'

Even sightless, Terrel was sufficiently aware of the lunar cycles to know what he must mean. The White and Amber Moons were half full and waning that night, and he imagined them floating, almost together in the night sky, casting their dual radiance over the land below.

'Nearly there,' his guide told him a short while later.

'Hey! Clear off,' Okan shouted. 'Shoo!'

'Get away,' Cassar added. 'We're not dead yet.'

'What's going on?' Terrel asked.

'There's a hubara come to join us,' Medrano told him. 'It seems very determined.'

Terrel's heart leapt. Alyssa had come at last.

'Don't drive it away,' he said quickly. 'Please. Leave it alone.'

'Why?' Okan asked. 'They're nasty creatures.'

'I'll make sure it does no harm,' Terrel promised. 'Will you let it come closer?'

'Are you sure?'

'Yes.' He heard the nomads retreat, and then the shuffling footsteps of the bird and a faint rustling of feathers.

Alyssa? Terrel called silently – but the voice that sounded in his head was not the one he was hoping for.

She'll be with you soon, but we have work to do first.

Who are you?

I am the horned dancer.

What?

My name is Vilheyuna. Weren't you expecting me?

For a few moments Terrel was too confused to respond. Then he remembered that other sleepers had come to him on occasion – Lathan and, most memorably, Ysatel – and each time they had played an important part in his destiny.

What do you want? he asked, swallowing his disappointment.

Ask them to break open one of the eggs.

But they're made of stone!

Even stone can be broken.

Why? Throughout this silent conversation, Terrel had been vaguely aware of his companions talking about the discovery, exclaiming over the size of the eggs and speculating on the former owner of the bones in the cliff.

You'll see. If the shaman was aware of the irony in his words, there was no sign of it in his voice.

'Will you break open one of the eggs?' Terrel said aloud.

The nomads were obviously surprised by his request.

'What for?' Zahir asked eventually.

'I'd like to know what's inside,' Terrel replied simply.

'But it's just rock now,' Okan told him.

'How are we supposed to break it?' Cassar asked.

'Lift it high enough and its own weight will do it for us,' Korioth replied. 'Especially if we drop it here, where the ground is hardest.'

There followed a series of muttered instructions, scraping noises and grunts.

'Ready?' Okan asked finally. 'Now!'

Even though Terrel was expecting it, the crack as the egg smashed onto the rock below was so loud that he jumped. Moments later, the expressions of amazement from his companions made him wish – for the thousandth time – that he could see what they were seeing.

'That's incredible,' Okan breathed.

'It's so detailed,' Cassar added. 'Almost as if it was still alive.'

'Whatever happened here preserved it perfectly,' Korioth observed.

'It was never even born,' Luqa whispered sadly.

'What is it?' Terrel asked. 'Bird or lizard?'

'Lizard,' Medrano replied. 'But not like anything I've ever seen before.'

'Just imagine how big it would have been when it grew up,' Okan remarked. 'Look at those claws!'

'Can I touch it?' Terrel asked. He knew there must be some lesson to be learned from this relic of another age.

'Of course.' Medrano guided the healer's fingers to the

split surface of the egg, then left him to explore for himself.

At first Terrel couldn't make much sense of what his fingertips were telling him, but then he gradually got a sense of what the others had been looking at. The creature inside the shell had been frozen in stone and, given time, its entire structure could have been revealed. As it was, an outline of its skeletal structure, the shape of its muscles and skin, had already been laid bare.

You can dance now.

What do you mean?

There are memories here. All you have to do is seek them out.

Could anything so old retain the memories of the life it had once had? Terrel wondered. Of the life that had been stolen away before it had even begun? And if it did, how was he supposed to find them? There was no waking dream for him to explore as there was with his living patients.

Use the starlight.

It took Terrel a few moments to realize what the shaman meant. The amulet from Tindaya, the star he carried within him, shone in his mind, his own memories. Concentrating on that led him into a new inner world, a new realm of light. Terrel fell into the dreams of stone.

The sky was dark red, and fire burst from the earth as the ground shook. The enormous lizard roared in terror and anger, displaying rows of needle-sharp teeth that were as long as Terrel's forearm. Her claws raked the air, powerless against the forces that were tearing her world apart. But rage and bewilderment were not the only emotions surging through her primitive brain. Beyond them was an almost fathomless sorrow, a lacerating sense of failure, because she could do nothing to protect her clutch of eggs – the little ones who were the sole reason for her existence. The end of the world was less important than the loss of her children.

Terrel felt all this, seeing her through unborn eyes even as she died, choking on fumes and smoke, then being entombed by an ever-growing weight of ash and sand. His healer's instincts tried to reduce her final pain, but there was no cure for such agony, no antidote to such eternal grief. He could only pull his hand away, so that he could see no more.

'Terrel? Terrel! What's the matter?'

Someone was holding his arm, shaking him gently.

'I saw . . .' he began, but the words wouldn't pass the constriction in his throat. He realized that his face was wet with tears.

'Let's get him away from here,' Zahir said decisively. 'Back to the camp.'

Terrel was helped up and guided over the rough terrain.

Do you understand now?

What do . . . Terrel mumbled, then found that he *did* understand – in part at least. *I went beyond the winds again, didn't I? That's the true magic of the desert.*

Time, Vilheyuna confirmed. *There is wisdom in the past.*

And the future?

Perhaps. That's why you were expecting me to come, wasn't it?

Why should I have been expecting you? Terrel was lost again.

Follow the way of the shamen, Terrel, the sleeper told him, ignoring the question. *I have set you on the path.*

I don't understand.

There is healing in the tears of life, Vilheyuna said in parting.

Terrel knew the shaman was going before the hubara squawked in alarm at finding itself so close to so many living creatures.

'Is that rancid bird still following us?' Cassar asked, looking round.

'Not any more,' Zahir said. 'It's flown away.'

'Good riddance,' the scout muttered.

Once they were back at the campsite, Terrel assured the others that he was all right, and then wondered about what Vilheyuna had told him – and about what he hadn't. It was a good deal later when, as the nomads prepared to sleep, he got his first hint of what some of the shaman's enigmatic words might have meant.

'Shall I douse the fire?' Korioth asked. 'Or let it burn itself out?'

'Douse it,' Zahir replied. 'We—'

'No!' Terrel cried.

He sensed them all looking at him in the ensuing silence.

'Is the fire there?' he asked, pointing.

'Yes,' Korioth replied.

'Go and stand between me and the flames.'

'All right.'

Terrel's face broke into a smile.

'Now step away again.'

'Your sight's coming back, isn't it?' Medrano guessed.

Terrel nodded. He had 'seen' the fire only as a dull swathe of colour in the darkness, but it had disappeared when Korioth blocked off the light, and as he turned his head, it moved in his field of vision. It seemed that there had indeed been some healing in his tears.

CHAPTER THIRTY-EIGHT

Terrel's eyesight improved steadily over the next three days. It was a slow process, and at first all he could make out were patches of colour, but eventually he was able to see blurred outlines of various objects when the light was strong enough. His joy soon turned to impatience; he wanted to be able to see everything clearly, and his companions had to keep reminding him that not so long ago he hadn't been able to see anything at all. Cassar was particularly delighted by the healer's recovery, pointing out that he had predicted this from the start. Terrel was not sure whether he believed the scout's assertion that all he'd needed had been a little time and faith. It seemed to him that Vilheyuna must have had something to do with the process.

The shaman's visit had given Terrel much to think about. Now that he knew that the true nature of the desert's magic concerned time, he inevitably wondered about both past and future – but he still wasn't sure how he was supposed to obey Vilheyuna's parting advice and 'follow the way of the shamen'. He returned to one riddle more than any other – the fact that the sleeper had assumed his visit to have been expected. The only way that would have been possible was if Terrel had somehow been able to see into the future. But all his visions had taken him into the past. It was only when Fanari observed that night that the wind was rising, and likely to be stronger still the next morning, that Terrel remembered such visions were not the only means of prophecy.

'Do you think there are storms coming?' Zahir asked.

'I doubt it,' the weather-reader replied. 'There's nothing to indicate that yet.'

'We've already come through our time of storms,' Okan claimed. 'That was quite enough.'

This reference to the oracle set Terrel thinking. Instinctively, he looked up at the sky, but his vision still wasn't sharp enough to pick out the stars and, as far as he could tell, none of the moons was visible.

'Nothing much to see tonight,' Cassar remarked, following his glance. 'The Red Moon isn't up yet, and the other two are getting weaker.'

'The Dark Moon is full, though,' Terrel said. He could feel its pull.

'If you say so,' Okan said, 'but we can't see the Invisible, can we.'

A tingle of excitement ran through Terrel as he suddenly fitted some of the pieces of the puzzle together.

'Medrano, do you remember the oracle at Senglea?' he asked. 'How many red stones did the bird leave on the crooked arrows?'

'Four,' the artist replied, 'but one was much smaller

than the others. It looked as if it had been broken in half.'

'What phase was the Red Moon in when we were caught in the sandstorm?'

Predictably, after a few moments' silence, it was Cassar who answered.

'It was just past full. About two and a half days after its brightest point.'

'What are you getting at?' Medrano asked.

'What if four stones represents the full of the moon?' Terrel replied. 'Three and a half would indicate a few days on one side or the other.'

'You think the oracle predicted the karabura?' Korioth said.

'Yes.'

'The time of storms,' Cassar said. 'It fits.'

'It might just have been a coincidence,' Korioth suggested.

'I don't think so,' Terrel responded. 'The horned dancer had two white and two amber stones, didn't it?'

'Both of them half full?' Cassar reasoned. 'That would have been three nights ago.'

'When we came to the cliff where we found the dragon's eggs,' Terrel said, nodding. 'I think the way of the shamen led us there.'

'What for?' Zahir queried. 'Those rocks were amazing, but—'

'What I experienced there helped me regain my sight.' Terrel had decided not to confuse the issue by revealing Vilheyuna's presence. 'The shamen allowed me to heal.'

There was a pause while the nomads considered this theory.

'So what would the other signs mean?' Medrano asked

eventually. 'There were four amber stones on the river in the sky.'

'The Amber Moon was full the day after we left Qomish,' Cassar said. 'There certainly wasn't much rain then! And the next full is a long way off yet.'

'By which time we should be well on our way back to the oasis,' Zahir put in.

'We'll probably appreciate some rain by then,' Korioth remarked, half joking.

'What about the double-headed man?' Medrano said. 'One black stone.'

'And the picture was rubbed out,' Okan reminded him.

'I haven't worked that one out yet,' Terrel admitted.

'Let me know when you do,' Zahir concluded. 'It's a nice theory, but I'm not sure what good it does us.'

Terrel decided to leave it at that. His companions were clearly not convinced, and unless he could provide them with more evidence, this was unlikely to change. He would just have to work it out for himself.

'What is it between you and these birds?' Okan exclaimed.

'What do you mean?' The dawn light was spreading across the desert, but it was not yet strong enough for Terrel to make out much detail.

'There's another hubara stalking round the camp, and it won't go away.'

'Where?' Terrel asked, wondering if Vilheyuna had returned.

'Over there.'

Terrel got up and made his way carefully towards the spot Okan had indicated. He saw a flicker of movement in the gloom.

Are you there? he asked, then felt foolish. What if this was just an ordinary bird?

Of course I'm here, Alyssa replied. *Where did you think I was going to be?*

Alyssa! Terrel felt almost light-headed with delight and relief. *I was beginning to think you weren't coming.* Vilheyuna's reassurance that she would be with him very soon had restored his faith for a while, but the three days that had passed since then had raised doubts again – doubts he felt ashamed of now.

I don't break my promises, she told him.

Terrel wondered briefly what promise he might have broken, but there was too much he wanted to talk about for that to bother him for long.

I'm so glad you're here, he said. *I wish I could see you properly.*

No, you don't. This has to be the ugliest bird on Nydus, but it suits my purpose. Alyssa paused. *Why can't you see me properly?*

Terrel told her about his temporary blindness – and about Jax's interference.

That wasn't supposed to happen, she commented, her concern obvious.

Maybe it was, he replied. *If it wasn't for him, we might not have found Y-Harah.*

The ruined city?

Yes! Did you see it?

I arrived just as you were leaving. It looked interesting.

It was. He told her about meeting Zorn and about the promise he had made, and showed her the crystal. Alyssa stared at it suspiciously.

You think you're being tested again? she asked.

Probably.

The seers didn't set this one up. They weren't even aware of any other ghosts there.

Shahan and Muzeni were at Y-Harah too? he exclaimed. *Did they see the messages carved into the stones? Were they able to read them?*

They were there, Alyssa confirmed, *but not for long. They weren't able to decipher the inscriptions properly, but the parallels with the Tindaya Code were obvious. They managed to make out some elements, though.*

What?

References to the Dark Moon going off course, she replied, *which was connected to something about a pendulum – whatever that is – marking time. No one understood that bit. Muzeni said there was quite a lot about the White Moon, and Shahan found a passage that seemed to depict twins. Only here the double-headed man and the great hero seem to be one and the same.*

But I thought it was the Mentor who was supposed to split in two.

Maybe it's Zorn they mean, and not the elemental.

Zorn is the Guardian? Terrel asked in amazement.

He was born at the time of a lunar confluence, Alyssa said. *And he is going to Makranash with you.*

This was becoming much too confusing for Terrel. With Y-Harah's prophecy – if that was what it really was – the possibilities seemed to be multiplying alarmingly. Far from making matters clearer, the picture was becoming even more cloudy.

We'd have been able to learn more if we'd had longer to study, Alyssa added, *but I had to leave to catch up with you before you got too close to Makranash.*

Couldn't they have stayed there?

Not without me.

There must be someone who can read it, he complained. *What about Vilheyuna? He could go. Have you met him?*

The shaman? she asked.

Yes. He came to me as a hubara – like you – a few nights ago.

He's responsible for his own journey through the palace.

Terrel set aside his frustration and returned to an earlier concern, hoping for enlightenment from another source.

Have the seers learnt anything more from the Code?

Nothing they've deigned to tell me, Alyssa replied.

Terrel was dismayed by her response – apparently another instance of discord among his allies.

What about Vadanis, then? he asked. *Is the plague getting worse? Is the Emperor still alive?*

Dheran's alive, she told him, *and according to Elam the progress of the plague seems to have slowed a bit. It seems your appeal may have done some good.*

I wasn't even sure I'd made any contact, Terrel admitted, gladdened by the news.

At least Jax isn't Emperor yet, Alyssa concluded. *How's your race going?*

Well, I think. Everyone seems very confident. Have you seen anything of the other teams?

There are only two that still have a chance of catching you. The others have either turned back already, or are way behind, or are lost completely.

So we are in the lead. Do you know who the closest teams are?

You're ahead, she confirmed, *but not by much. One of the chasing groups is led by a man called Kohtala. I'm not sure about the others.*

Terrel absorbed this mixture of news as calmly as he could. That the Toma were in the lead was welcome; that the Shiban were one of their closest challengers was not.

I'll be able to keep watch on them as we go on from here, Alyssa added, *but it would be easy enough to make sure you stay ahead.*

How?

Being an unpleasant creature like this has its uses, she replied. *I could scare the dung out of their camels, if you like. Or try to peck Kohtala's eyes out while he's asleep.*

No! Terrel wasn't sure if she was joking or not.

I could do it, she insisted.

I don't doubt that, but sabotaging your rivals is cheating. We can't win like that.

Why not?

Because victory won without honour is worthless, he told her, repeating Medrano's axiom. *The winds wouldn't allow it.*

It's the people here who believe in the winds, Alyssa pointed out. *Not us.*

But we're here, in their land, Terrel began, then decided to put an end to the argument. *You* mustn't *do anything like that.*

Yes, master, she said, pretending meekness.

We can win anyway, he added, smiling.

Let's hope so.

'Time to go, Terrel!' Medrano called.

'If you can tear yourself away from your new friend,' Okan added.

The nomads were clearly amused by the healer's latest display of eccentricity, but they were prepared to be tolerant, even though it was plain they didn't like having the hubara around.

I won't be far away, Alyssa promised as she flew away into the sunrise.

'Do you talk to animals, Terrel?' Luqa asked, as he walked alongside the healer's camel.

'Only some of them,' he replied, trying to sound casual.

'I've seen the way you are with the camels,' Luqa added by way of explanation. 'Sometimes I seem to know what they're thinking, but it's never been that way with anything else. I can't imagine what a hubara would have to say.'

'You'd be surprised,' Terrel said, then laughed, hoping to conceal his awkwardness.

CHAPTER THIRTY-NINE

Terrel had not believed it could possibly get any hotter, but as they moved deeper into the heart of the Binhemma-Ghar, the temperature continued to rise. At midday the heat of the sun was like a physical force, threatening to crush their skulls and wither their overburdened lungs. As his eyesight returned to normal, the glare from the sky and sand was so intense that he was forced to squint all the time, and he became almost wistful about his recent blindness. The torment was made worse by the knowledge that, this far into the desert, there was no chance at all of finding any water – which meant that Korioth's strict and carefully measured rations were the only relief they would get for many days to come. A few mouthfuls of warm water was not nearly enough to stop his throat from becoming dry and sore, or his mouth from feeling as though it was full of grit. Even the wind that blew almost constantly now offered no comfort. The air itself was so hot that its movement had no cooling effect whatsoever.

In such conditions it was all the more remarkable that Zahir's pace never slackened. If anything, he'd accelerated as they drew closer to their goal, pushing himself to the very limits of his endurance. Terrel was staggered by the young man's courage and determination. Striding ahead, with the Toma's banner held proudly upright, Zahir was proving himself more than worthy of having been chosen as his tribe's champion.

Each night Terrel helped the elder's son to recover from the exertions of the day. He soothed aching muscles, enabled his patient to ignore the pain of blisters, and generally did what he could to ensure that Zahir regained as much strength as possible. After some of the ailments he had healed in the past, this was easy work, but Terrel knew just how important his contribution was. He also had no doubt that the shamen of the other tribes would be aiding their own champions in a similar fashion.

True to her word, Alyssa kept Terrel informed of the progress of the rival teams. On the evening of the day after her arrival, she reported that the closest challenger was Kohtala, but that he was a full day's march behind them. The third tribe were a short distance behind the Shiban, on a similar course. Terrel wondered whether to pass this news on to his team-mates, but eventually decided against it – mainly because they would obviously want to know how he'd obtained such intelligence. The nomads had grown used to the hubara's visits, calling it 'Terrel's pet', but he wasn't sure how they'd take the fact that the bird was the source of his knowledge.

The next day, Terrel witnessed a disturbing scene that reminded him of several unwelcome possibilities.

'I don't want it,' Cassar insisted.

'You have to drink,' Korioth said, 'or the heat will kill you.' The quartermaster was making his rounds with the afternoon's water ration. He was used to his colleagues grumbling about how little he would allow them, but this was the first time any of them had ever *refused* a drink.

'I don't want it,' Cassar repeated, with a quiver of distaste. 'Give it to someone else. Or save it for Zahir tonight. He'll need it more than anyone.'

'Don't be stupid.'

'I'm not stupid,' the scout retorted. 'I know what I'm doing.'

'No, you don't,' Korioth replied, but although he continued to berate Cassar, the younger man remained adamant that he wasn't thirsty, and in the end the quartermaster gave up.

Terrel – who had already accepted his own meagre portion gratefully – was left to wonder if the plague was about to claim another victim.

The confrontation was repeated that evening, with Cassar again refusing to drink, in spite of the protests of all his companions. However, as he seemed to be none the worse for his abstinence, no one wanted to force the issue. Terrel and Korioth tried to persuade Zahir to order him to drink, but their leader would not oblige. Instead, as a compromise, he decided that they should all be examined again by Terrel, to see whether there might be any potential problems with their health. The nomads submitted to this, under protest, but the healer could not be sure of his findings. The remote fear he'd seen earlier seemed a little stronger in all of them, but Cassar didn't appear to be any worse than the others – and in all other respects the team was surprisingly fit. No one tried to persuade the scout to drink after that.

The process almost exhausted Terrel, and he was glad when it was over and he could rest. As a result, when he saw the hubara swoop down towards the campsite, he was less animated than normal – though he was still very glad of Alyssa's company.

'Tell that thing we're not dead yet!' Okan called.

'And there's no way it's getting any of our food,' Korioth added.

Terrel ignored their comments, and the ensuing laughter, and went to talk to his friend. Until that moment he hadn't thought about what the hubara might be able to eat. The bird had to survive somehow. It was an uncomfortable thought, but Alyssa gave him no chance to broach the subject.

The third team has turned back, she told him.

Good, Terrel responded. There was only one team to beat now.

Maybe not.

Why? What do you mean?

They gave up because they woke this morning to find all their waterskins empty, she explained.

Terrel took a few moments to absorb the implications of her words.

Completely empty? he queried. *Just like that? Surely they'd have known their supplies were running low.*

Apparently not. The chances are they'll never make it out of the desert alive now.

What happened?

I'm not sure, Alyssa replied. *But I don't see how it can have been an accident.*

Neither do I. Terrel paused as an alarming possibility occurred to him. *Do you think one of them might have come down with the plague? Would that make them mad enough to throw their water away?* He was wondering whether their own precious reserves might be in danger from Cassar.

It's possible, Alyssa conceded.

Did any of them seem ill?

Not in any obvious way. But then none of them looked too happy either.

Hardly surprising, Terrel commented grimly. He could only pity the other team – and hope that their plight would not befall his own.

There is another possibility, Alyssa said.

What?

The water could have been stolen.

'Shouldn't we think about setting a guard overnight?' Terrel suggested, later that evening.

The nomads all looked at him in surprise.

'What for?' Okan queried. 'There's nothing out here.'

'There's the other teams.'

'Nobody moves at night,' Zahir said. 'You know that.'

'Besides, we're well ahead of the others,' Cassar added. 'I'm sure of it.'

'What are you suggesting, Terrel?' Korioth asked. 'That someone might try to raid our camp?'

'Don't be ridiculous!' Zahir exclaimed before Terrel could respond. 'No one would dare do that.'

'Even if it's Kohtala's team?' the healer asked pointedly.

'Not even he would be so dishonourable,' Zahir said, after a short, doubt-filled silence. 'I don't want to hear any more of this nonsense. It's shameful to even think such things.'

Having received that unequivocal answer, it was left to Terrel to do what he could alone. He tried his best to stay awake during the night, with the result that his sleep, when he could hold out no longer, was light and restless – but there was no disturbance of any kind.

The next morning Terrel thought that Cassar's eyes seemed unnaturally bright, but the nomad was still in good spirits and, even though he would not take any water, this didn't seem to affect his work in any way.

Exhausted from both his healing efforts and his relative lack of sleep, Terrel rode all that day in a kind of stupor, gazing almost unseeingly at the unending vistas of burnished sand. But he was roused when a sudden and ominous noise brought the entire caravan to a halt.

It began like a distant rumble of thunder, a deep grumbling in the air, then rose in pitch to a keening that made their ears ache and their chests vibrate. For a few moments the same appalling thought flashed through all their minds – that this was the sound of Makranash ringing. Unbelievably, someone had beaten them to the sacred mountain. But they soon realized that this was not the case.

'It's coming from over there, not ahead,' Okan said, pointing. 'It can't be Makranash.'

'It isn't,' Medrano confirmed. 'I remember the sound the mountain made when we lost the last time. This is different.'

'It's the singing sands,' Korioth told them. 'You don't
hear it very often. The wind makes some dunes vibrate
as if they were hollow.'

By the time he'd finished speaking the noise had died
away, and the team went on, their earlier fears forgotten.
However, their progress for the rest of that day was slowed
by a series of mishaps, most of which stemmed from the
ground underfoot. Okan's usual skill at finding the best
route through a line of dunes seemed to desert him, and
– although his advice to Zahir always seemed to be good
– when the camels came to follow in the champion's footsteps, both the animals and their handlers often found
themselves slipping on the treacherous slopes. At one
point the side of a dune collapsed inwards, as if it really
were hollow, causing one animal to fall and tossing Fanari,
who was riding, to the ground. Fortunately the soft sand
broke the nomad's fall and he suffered no serious injuries,
but it took Luqa some time to calm the terrified camel
and rearrange its load. As a result of this, and other delays,
Zahir was often forced to slow his pace so that he did not
get too far ahead of his team – something that left them
all feeling frustrated and irritable.

The mood in their camp that night was tense. Zahir
hardly spoke at all, and no one else was willing or able to
lift their spirits. There were only two days left if they
were to meet Zahir's target of reaching Makranash by the
new of the White Moon, and they didn't need Cassar's
reading of the stars for them all to realize that they were
now unlikely to get there so quickly. By the time they
settled down to sleep, exchanging muttered comments
about having a better day tomorrow, Terrel was already
feeling drowsy, but he was nervous too. To make matters

worse, he'd seen nothing of Alyssa since that morning, and he was keen to learn the whereabouts of the Shiban. In the end sheer fatigue overcame his anxieties, and he slept.

Terrel awoke with a start before dawn the next day, with the echoes of a horrified yell still ringing in his ears. Before he had a chance to put his fear into words, someone else did it for him.

'What's the matter? What's wrong?'

'I don't believe this!' Okan replied, his voice choked with outrage and dismay. 'The waterskins have been slashed open. It's all gone!'

CHAPTER FORTY

It was difficult to take in the enormity of the disaster, and their first disbelieving exchanges centred on how such a thing could have happened.

'This is insane!' Zahir declared. 'Are you sure they didn't split open accidentally?'

'All at once?' Okan said.

'No. This was a deliberate act,' Korioth said, picking up one of the ruined containers and showing them the straight incision that had been made in the skin. 'It was done with a knife.'

'But who would do something like that?' Zahir cried.

'And why didn't any of us wake up?' Fanari added. 'Whoever it was must have made *some* noise.'

It was only then that the nomads realized one of the team was missing.

'Where's Cassar?' Zahir asked.

'Still asleep,' Luqa replied.

It was true that the scout was still wrapped in his

chilouk, but he was not asleep – as Terrel soon confirmed. Even without his own talents, Cassar's darkened complexion and staring, sightless eyes would have been enough to show that all was not well.

'Is he dead?' Okan asked.

'No. He's still alive,' the healer replied, 'but he's very ill. He has the plague.' The fear was rampaging through Cassar's waking dream now, defying all reason and all of Terrel's efforts to counteract its pernicious effects.

'But you said—' Zahir began, then fell silent.

'I don't know how the disease starts,' Terrel said, defending himself against the unspoken accusation. 'Or how it progresses. Elodia was already ill when I saw her. I had no way of telling this was coming.'

'Then what was the point of those tests?' Okan asked.

'I hoped to see into the future. Obviously, I failed.'

'Terrel's a healer,' Zahir said. 'Not a prophet.'

'Do you think it was him?' Fanari asked abruptly.

There was a short, uncomfortable silence while everyone worked out what he meant.

'What are you talking about?' Zahir said.

'It could have been Cassar. Think about it. If he's become terrified of water, he'd want to get rid of any that was near him.'

'And risk killing us all?' Korioth asked.

'If he's got the plague he wouldn't be rational. His fear would have taken over.'

'It makes sense,' Okan commented.

'No it doesn't,' Medrano stated firmly. 'Correct me if I'm wrong, Terrel, but surely his fear of water would have been so strong that he wouldn't go anywhere near it – let alone cut open the skins and have it splash all around him. He'd be more likely to run away into the desert to get *away* from it!'

'Are any of his clothes wet?' Zahir asked.

'No,' Terrel replied. 'They're quite dry.'

'And there's no moisture on his blade,' Korioth added, having picked up Cassar's scabbard and removed his knife.

'That doesn't prove anything,' Fanari claimed. 'They could have dried by now.'

'Did *no one* see or hear anything in the night?' Zahir asked.

Nobody had.

'Terrel was right,' Okan remarked. 'We should have set a guard.'

'Against whom?' Zahir exclaimed in exasperation.

'The Shiban,' Terrel said.

The elder's son had clearly not expected an answer to his rhetorical question, and a few moments passed before he responded.

'I don't like Kohtala any more than you do,' he told the healer, 'but even he would never do anything like this. It's unthinkable. In any case, we don't even know they're anywhere close.'

'Three nights ago they were a day's march behind us,' Terrel said. 'They're probably even closer now.'

Zahir stared at him.

'How do you know that?'

Terrel had known this moment would come eventually. Now that it had been forced upon him, he felt a sense of relief.

'The hubara that's been visiting me was sent by the winds to watch over the race. I don't understand how, but I'm able to talk to her.'

'I knew it,' Luqa whispered.

The others simply stared in disbelief, but Terrel's use of their own legend prevented them from dismissing his claim out of hand.

'She's been telling me about the progress of the other teams,' the healer added. 'It seems we're not the only team the Shiban have sabotaged.'

'This is nonsense,' Zahir said, but there was no longer any conviction in his voice.

'Why didn't you tell us this sooner?' Okan demanded angrily. 'If we'd known the Shiban were so close we *would* have set a guard.'

'No, we wouldn't!' Zahir exclaimed. 'I still can't believe they'd flout the honour of the race so flagrantly. And there's no point yelling at Terrel. What's done is done.'

Terrel was amazed to find that the rest of the team had accepted his being able to talk to the bird at face value. He had been prepared to offer proof when Alyssa next appeared, but it didn't seem as if that would be necessary. Okan's outburst had seen to that.

'There's still no proof it *was* them,' Fanari said. 'How could they have got so close without disturbing us?'

No one had an answer to that.

'Look at this!' Korioth called. He had gone back to the spot where the waterskins had been stored, and was now returning with one of the containers. Pinned to its neck was a small scrap of bright orange cloth.

Zahir's face instantly suffused with rage. He threw his arms in the air in a gesture of despair and let out an impotent bellow of fury.

'What is it?' Terrel asked, not understanding what had provoked such an extreme response.

'That's the colour of the Shiban's banner,' Medrano told him quietly. 'It's a message. Taunting us.'

'The winds will punish them!' Zahir shouted. 'It's . . . It's . . .' Words failed him, and he sat down on the ground and put his head in his hands.

It was the first time Terrel had ever seen Zahir totally at a loss, and it was a disheartening sight. No one else seemed to know what to say or do, until Korioth spoke quietly.

'Leave him with me for a few moments.'

Recognizing the authority in the older man's voice, the others drifted away, though none of them really knew what to do with themselves. The realization of what the loss of their water meant was beginning to sink in now, and each man was having to come to terms with the likelihood of his own death. Terrel had the additional burden of knowing that he alone might have been able to prevent the catastrophe, and even though Zahir had defended him, he still felt wracked with guilt. For once, the prospect of his own failure to reach Makranash took second place when confronted with the thought that his friends were going to die because of his own lack of conviction.

A short while later, all such morbid thoughts were temporarily set aside when Zahir called the team to rejoin him. The champion had regained his composure now, and there was determination in the set of his jaw and a new fire in his eyes. Terrel couldn't help wondering what Korioth could have said to bring about such a transformation.

'Feeling sorry for ourselves won't do us any good,' Zahir told them briskly, 'and we're wasting time here.

The sun will rise soon. Korioth has told me that not all our water supplies have been lost. He kept some reserves, concealed from the rest of us, in case of some emergency like this, and luckily the raiders missed them. It means we're not completely without life, but there's not nearly enough to sustain all of us for the journey to the nearest water supply.' He paused, looking round at his team, as their new-found hopes faded again. 'So we have to decide now whether we go on or turn back.'

'We go on!' Fanari declared immediately and with fervour.

'We have to,' Terrel agreed quickly.

'Even if we all die?' Okan queried. 'We may well win, but there's no way we'd ever get out of the Binhemma-Ghar again.'

'I won't ask anyone to come who doesn't want to,' Zahir said calmly. 'But I tell you now, I'll go on alone if necessary. I won't leave the Race of Truth at the mercy of someone so dishonourable. I would rather plant the Toma's banner at the summit of the sacred mountain, knowing I was going to die, than risk Kohtala making a mockery of all I hold dear. Each of you must decide for yourself. We can divide the camels and supplies now. It's your choice.'

Zahir had never sounded more mature. There was an echo of his father's natural authority in his voice.

'I'll go on,' Luqa said quietly.

'So will I,' Korioth volunteered.

'The story of this race will live on, even if we don't,' Medrano claimed. 'The winds will see to that. I'll go on too.'

'Oh, well,' Okan responded, grinning. 'We can always

ask Terrel to be the voice of rain again if we get *really* desperate.'

'Then we go on?' Zahir said.

'Together,' Okan confirmed.

Alyssa arrived shortly after the caravan moved off, and flew in slow circles above Terrel to match his camel's more ponderous pace. Even from the air she was able to tell that the nomads' reaction to her presence was different from before.

Why are they looking at me like that?

They know I can talk to you.

You told them? Was that wise?

I had no choice. Terrel described what had happened, and asked if she had seen anything in the night.

No, she replied. *Even I have to sleep sometimes. But I'll keep a closer watch on them from now on.*

After a few moments, she flew off to check on the whereabouts of the Shiban.

'Any news?' Medrano asked.

'Not at the moment,' Terrel replied. 'But she'll be back.'

At their camp that evening, Okan declined his tiny measure of water.

'Don't worry,' he told the others. 'I haven't got the plague. I want the water, but it should go to Zahir. He needs it more than me. The rest of us will just have to become more like camels.'

Korioth glanced uncertainly at their leader and offered him the cup. Zahir took it, but made no move to drink.

'This is yours, Okan,' he said. 'Unless you drink it, I'll pour it into the sand right now.'

'Don't be stupid.'

'We do this together, or not at all.'

'But—'

The cup began to tilt in Zahir's hand.

'All right,' Okan conceded hurriedly. 'Give it to me.'

As his team-mate drank, Luqa spoke up, picking up on his earlier comment.

'Even the camels are going to start suffering soon,' he told them. 'They've been on minimum rations for some days now, and they can't go on indefinitely. Many more days like this and they'll simply be too weak to carry us or the equipment.'

His grim warning was greeted with silence, and the diversion caused by Alyssa's arrival came as a welcome relief.

'Here comes the winds' spy,' Korioth noted.

'Will you ask her if the winds are planning to punish Kohtala for his treachery?' Zahir requested.

'She's just their servant,' Terrel replied. 'I doubt she'd be told such things.'

Who's just a servant? Alyssa enquired as she sidled towards the group of men. For once she seemed to enjoy being the centre of attention.

Did you find them? Terrel asked.

Yes. They're still behind you, but gaining fast. It's going to be close.

'What's she saying?' Okan asked.

'I'll tell you in a bit. Let me talk to her first.'

You could wait for them, you know, she told him.

What? Why would we want to do that?

It would be easy enough to set up an ambush. We could make sure they walk right into a trap. You could dispose of your only rivals and solve your water problems. The Shiban have plenty.

I bet they do, Terrel thought bitterly.

We can't do that, he told her.

Because you're honourable men?

Yes.

They weren't exactly honourable when they hid themselves in the shaman's cloak and slashed your waterskins, were they?

No, Terrel admitted. *But that's no reason to stoop to their level. The race—*

The race means nothing, she cut in. *Have you forgotten why you're here?*

Of course not, but the two things aren't separate. Makranash is the home of the winds as well as the Ancient. I can't afford to offend them.

Then can I at least slow the Shiban down a little?

No! He had no doubt that Alyssa would be capable of devising a way to do just that, but it would still bring the manner of their victory into question.

Your obstinacy might kill you all.

That's the way it has to be, he told her, weary of the argument now. *Maybe after we've won the race and I've talked to the elemental, the Shiban will see some sense and share their water with us.*

You're clutching at straws.

What did you mean about the shaman's cloak? he asked, finally catching up with the import of her earlier statement.

That's how they were able to sneak into your camp. Their shaman's a nasty piece of work called Sansunak, and he was the one who rode across in the night, then cast some sort of spell over the two men who came with him so that none of you could see or hear them as they did the dirty work. They've been laughing about it all day.

Terrel absorbed this latest example of the Shiban's duplicity with some difficulty.

Still feel like treating them with honour? Alyssa asked.

The next two days were torture for both men and camels. The brutal heat was unrelenting, and without adequate water any form of physical exertion had become a nightmare. Terrel could only marvel at the fact that Zahir was able to keep going. It was a superhuman effort that spoke volumes about the young man's bravery and determination, but for all Terrel's efforts each night, their champion was weakening fast.

The healer had tentatively raised Alyssa's suggestion of an ambush but, as he'd expected, the idea had been rejected instantly and angrily, and he had not mentioned it again. The only good news was that, even though he was still unconscious, Cassar was clinging to life, and no one else was showing any sign of succumbing to the plague.

That night Zahir decided to camp on top of a large dune. Medrano told Terrel that he'd chosen the place because it was high up, and with an unobstructed view to the east, it would mean that sunrise would come a few moments earlier. But as it turned out this was not the only advantage of the site. When they were all at the top, Zahir pointed into the distance and smiled.

It was Terrel's first glimpse of Makranash. As its summit caught the last few rays of the setting sun, the mountain seemed to float above the plain like a jewelled cloud.

'We'll be there tomorrow,' Zahir stated.

The team soon discovered that the sacred mountain was not all they could see from their vantage point. When they saw the light of a nearby fire, they knew that the Shiban had caught them up. They would start level on the last day of the race.

Even that illusion of fair play was shattered the following morning. When the Toma rose, well before sunrise, to prepare for their final effort, Okan pointed to something he'd seen in the feeble light of dawn.

'It's the dust from their camels,' he said. 'They're already on their way.'

CHAPTER FORTY-ONE

'We've no chance of catching them now,' Okan groaned.

'I won't accept that,' Zahir snapped. 'We can overtake them, and we will. The winds won't let them get away with this, and nor will I.' So saying, he went over to Korioth, who was holding one of the few remaining waterskins. 'Give me that.'

'But it's supposed to last you several days,' the quartermaster warned.

'I don't care. Unless I get to the mountain before Kohtala, this will all have been for nothing. I need it now. One way or another, it won't matter if there's nothing left for me by the end of today.'

Korioth still hesitated.

'Give it to him,' Okan said quietly, and the older man obeyed.

Zahir drank deeply, then gave the container back.

'Catch me up when you can,' he told them. 'I'll see you again when the race is won.'

Without waiting for any response, he turned away. As the sun rose over the horizon, he began to stride towards Makranash.

Zahir set a suicidal pace. Even after a hurried departure – when much of their equipment was abandoned so that the rest of the team could each ride one of the camels – they were barely able to keep up with their champion. And yet, to their collective dismay, the dust cloud from the Shiban's caravan remained ahead of them.

In the distance, the sacred mountain changed colour with the varying light of the day. Its grey silhouette became a delicate shade of purple, and then, as the sun reclaimed its sovereignty over the sky, Makranash turned brown, becoming brighter and more jewel-like as the heat made the desert air shimmer. At one point, a mirage effect made the mountain look as though it was an island rising from the waters of a calm, glittering ocean. When Terrel made this comparison to Medrano, who was riding alongside him, the nomad replied that he'd have to take the healer's word for it. He had never seen the sea.

For several hours, the team seemed to get no closer, but eventually Terrel began to see variations in the appearance of the mountain. From far away it had looked like a single, separate peak, striking up from the flat plain around it, but from closer to he saw that it was made up of many slopes and folds, small ramparts below the main fortress. He also realized just how big it was. The thought of Zahir having to climb to the summit after the agonizing journey of the day was too appalling to contemplate.

During the afternoon Zahir's pace slowed a little, and he staggered occasionally. Each time this happened Terrel wondered helplessly if they would have to stand at a distance and watch him die. But the champion always managed to recover, and never once looked back at his followers. His eyes were fixed firmly on his goal.

He's gaining on Kohtala, Alyssa reported when she returned from one of her flights. *But not fast enough.*

Terrel had reached much the same conclusion. He expected Alyssa to try to persuade him to let her find a way of delaying their rival, but she did not.

At least he seems to be obeying the rules for once, she went on. *He hasn't had a drink since sunrise.*

Maybe he thinks the winds might notice his cheating now that he's actually in sight of Makranash, Terrel muttered cynically. Kohtala's hypocrisy was galling, but he knew that Zahir would never forgive him if he tried to do anything about it. The injustice of the situation made him want to scream.

Still, whoever wins now, you're going to get to Makranash, she replied. *So you should be able to make contact with the Ancient.*

Terrel realized that this was why Alyssa had apparently abandoned the idea of sabotaging their opponents, but he was not sure it was as simple as she made out. In his mind, the Race of Truth and his mission had become inextricably intertwined.

You might even be close enough now, Alyssa added.

Terrel took the hint, and tried to let his thoughts expand, reaching out towards the strange creature that lay somewhere beneath the mountain's imposing bulk. But he could sense nothing, and soon stopped trying.

Not yet, he told Alyssa. *There was no response at all.*
Oh, well, she replied. *It was worth a try.*

As she flew ahead once more, Terrel wondered how many people had already died from the plague – and whether his own father was among them – and felt a renewed sense of urgency.

The border that marked the end of the desert and the beginning of Makranash was quite clearly delineated, just as if it really had been an island rising from a surrounding sea. Terrel realized that this was because the bare rock that formed the mountain was different from that which encircled it. It was lighter in colour, and more angular in its formations – as if it was harder and more resistant to the constant erosion of wind and sand. Although its crags and gullies looked very steep, Terrel could see that, for the most part, it should present no real difficulty to a determined climber – always assuming that the climber had the necessary strength to make the ascent.

Because they had approached from a slightly different direction, it was not immediately clear when the Shiban had reached the base of the mountain. However, by the time Zahir got there, Terrel had already spotted Kohtala well on his way up to the summit. His dismay at this discovery was compounded when he saw that Zahir was standing still, looking up but making no attempt to begin the climb. The healer was trying to work out what was going on when a voice from the other side of a nearby ridge made him realize that the Shiban were closer than he'd thought.

'You're late!' the voice called, amid the sound of

mocking laughter. 'The hubaras are already waiting for your corpses.'

The Toma ignored the taunting, but Terrel looked to the sky, and saw that Alyssa had been joined by a second bird. By then, the nomads' camels had come to a halt the usual distance from their champion. Zahir had still not moved, and the mood of his team-mates was sombre. Glancing round, Terrel realized that they had finally given up. The dejection on their faces was hard to bear.

'The race isn't over yet!' Terrel called to Zahir.

The elder's son turned to face him, and the healer saw from the uncoordinated movement of his limbs that he was fighting to stay on his feet.

'Yes, it is!' he shouted back, his voice hoarse and full of disgust and pain. 'There's no way I can catch him, and besides, only the king is allowed upon the sacred route to the top.'

Terrel wanted to argue, but realized that it would be of no use.

'We did our best,' Medrano told him quietly, confirming the nomads' acceptance of defeat. 'We did well to get this far.'

The world seemed to come to a halt. The only one who moved was Kohtala, who was becoming an ever smaller figure as he made his way towards the summit. After so long on the move, the constant travelling during the hours of daylight, the stasis seemed unnatural, but Terrel found himself caught up in its enervating spell. He simply didn't know what to do. For so long, he had been assuming Zahir would win the race, and that he'd be able to deal with his own concerns once that had been achieved. Now that those hopes had been dashed, he seemed to have been robbed of the ability to do anything – or even to think.

Zahir had slumped down to sit on the ground now, and several of the nomads had dismounted. They were debating whether to go to their leader's side now that the race was over, or whether to wait until sunset. Terrel was about to join them when Alyssa flashed by, so close that the camel shied away and Terrel almost fell.

Don't let them go to Zahir! she said urgently.

Why?

It's coming. Don't let them break the rules.

What's coming?

That doesn't matter, she retorted angrily. *Just stop them!*

Okan and Korioth were beginning to make their way towards their desolate champion.

'Stay where you are!' Terrel yelled. 'Don't go any closer!'

To his relief, the nomads stopped and turned back to look at him. He was struggling to come up with a reason for his outburst when everyone's attention was drawn to the western sky. There – against all expectation – a thick black cloud had just drifted across the sun. The sudden cool shade brought Zahir back to his feet, but it did not last for long. The dark mass was moving at an incredible speed, far greater than the wind, and was apparently heading straight towards the mountain. As it came closer, the cloud bulged and writhed as if it was being tormented by some unimaginable force and, in spite of the strong afternoon sunshine, it remained dark and opaque.

'That's no cloud,' Fanari whispered.

'No, it's not,' Luqa said. 'It's a swarm.'

'Insects?' Medrano queried in disbelief. 'Here?'

'I don't believe it either,' Korioth said, 'but that's what it is.'

Terrel watched, mesmerized, as the enormous swarm flew on. They could hear it now, still no more than a whisper, but terrifying nonetheless. The rustling of millions of wings turned to a constant angry thrumming as the insects approached Makranash, flying even higher than the mountain itself. The human onlookers had all fallen silent, but Alyssa had not.

You'd better take cover, she advised. *This could get messy.*

Terrel now knew what she had seen coming, and wondered whether it had simply been her airborne position that had allowed her to do so. He had the feeling that she'd known about the swarm before she could see it.

Why? he asked. *What's going to happen?*

The swarm had come to a halt now, whirling round in a great undulating mass, directly above the summit of the mountain. Before Alyssa could respond, the answer to Terrel's question became obvious. The insects began to descend, flying vertically downwards, and then spreading out and flowing down the sides of Makranash like a living avalanche. Even then no one realized the danger they were in, and it wasn't until they spotted Kohtala, plunging downhill in a vain attempt to outrun the buzzing horde, that any of the nomads reacted. Even as they scurried to gather the camels together, to try to provide some cover at least, they kept glancing back up the slope. Although he was still a considerable distance above them, Kohtala's screams as he was engulfed came to them clearly above the whirring roar of his attackers. The Shiban's champion vanished into the darkness and was lost from view. The living avalanche swept on, but Zahir remained where he was, standing in the open.

'I was right!' he yelled in triumph. 'The winds couldn't stomach such a dishonourable man winning. He has been punished.' He seemed oblivious to the fact that he was about to suffer the same fate.

'Zahir, get over here!' Korioth called. 'You must take shelter!' The nomads were making the best of the situation, huddling down between their animals and covering themselves with whatever came to hand.

'No!' Zahir called back. 'I need to stay here. I can still win the race. The winds have no reason to punish me.'

The others were about to argue when something even more remarkable happened, something that made them think their champion's faith might well be justified. Starting at Zahir's feet, a small swirl of dust rose up. Within moments it expanded and grew more powerful, until a strong wind was blowing around them all in a circle. The sun went dark – just as if they had been caught in a sandstorm – but the air inside the circle remained clear and relatively calm. The Toma were all enclosed inside a dome of flying sand, while the swarm remained outside, held back from their prey by the whirlwind. Even the sound of their droning was muffled as an eerie quiet settled upon the group in the darkness.

'It's as though it's protecting us,' Okan whispered, gazing about in awe.

'It is,' Korioth agreed. 'Zahir was right. The winds have no reason to punish us.'

'It's impossible,' Fanari breathed.

'I wonder how Kohtala and the rest of the Shiban are faring,' Okan said. 'I wouldn't like to be in their shoes.'

'This is what Mlicki saw, isn't it?' Medrano said suddenly.

'What?'

'His vision,' the artist explained. 'When the Shiban came to us and demanded a tribute. He showed them – and us – the future, beyond the winds.'

'The darkness!' Fanari exclaimed, remembering.

'Theirs was a swarm of insects. Ours was a sandstorm,' Medrano confirmed. 'This is what he saw.'

'So the boy really is a shaman,' Okan commented.

At the time, Terrel's impression of the darkness in Mlicki's vision had been that it was caused by an eclipse. But there was no sign of that now, and what was going on around him was full of enough wonders.

In the wavering gloom, a new sound came to their ears. It was one they hadn't heard for a long time, and at first no one could be sure what it was. Then they realized it was coming from their champion. At the centre of the whirlwind, Zahir was laughing.

The miraculous storm did not last long, but when it died down – clearing from the air as fast as it had arisen – there was no sign of the swarm. Either the insects had scattered as they flew away, so that they were no longer visible as a single mass, or the swarm had flown on at incredible speed. Either way, the nomads were delighted by their absence.

Zahir immediately picked up his banner and began to climb.

'I'll see you after I've set this in its rightful place!' he called over his shoulder.

The others watched him go, following his careful progress over the first of the ridges.

'Any sign of Kohtala?' Okan asked.

'Not that I can see,' Fanari replied.

An hour later Zahir was almost out of sight, obviously very weary but still moving purposefully upwards, when another figure crawled over a spur and half fell, half slid down towards the plain. Kohtala's clothes were in shreds, and his face, arms and feet were covered in blisters and welts from hundreds of insect bites. His eyes were swollen shut, and he was bleeding from several nasty cuts. When he tumbled down the last slope and lay whimpering in pain, the nomads gathered around him and watched without sympathy. He tried to speak, obviously aware that someone was near him, but his lips and tongue were too distended for anything other than an inarticulate gurgle.

'Not such a great champion now, are you?' Okan observed coldly.

Kohtala flinched at the sound of a strange voice. He had presumably been hoping to be found by his own men. Now he knew he was in the hands of his enemies, at the mercy of those he had wronged.

'You've paid dearly for casting honour aside,' Korioth told him.

'I would kill you,' Fanari added, 'but you're not worthy of my blade. We'll leave you for the hubaras.'

At this mention of the birds, Terrel looked up, wondering how Alyssa had fared in the recent upheaval. But there was no sign of her, or of her partner. Looking down again, he saw that Kohtala had curled himself into a ball, shivering in spite of the day's heat. He looked so pitiful that Terrel felt a stab of compassion. Much as he despised the man and his ways, and understood the contempt his friends felt for him, he found himself wanting to ease his suffering. Pain was something he instinctively wanted – and needed – to fight against. He stepped forward, but hesitated when Okan caught at his sleeve.

'What are you doing?'

'I'm going to help him.'

'*Help* him?' Fanari exclaimed. 'He—'

'Don't waste your time,' Okan hissed. 'He tried to kill us.'

'And he's paid for that,' Medrano said. 'Terrel's right. By helping him, we prove ourselves to be the better men.'

'I don't need proof of that!' Fanari spat angrily.

'I'm a healer,' Terrel said simply. 'It's what I do.'

'Then save your energy for someone who deserves it,' Okan advised him.

'There's room for both,' Medrano argued. 'For myself, I would rather he survived to answer for his crimes before all the tribes at Qomish. He will have true justice then.'

'I wouldn't want to see an animal suffer like that,' Luqa put in quietly.

'Do what you must, Terrel,' Korioth decided, ending the debate. 'We should go and see what's happened to the rest of his team. If they're all as bad as him, they might be glad to share their water with us in return for our help.'

*

As Terrel learnt as he treated them, the Shiban had scattered in panic at the coming of the swarm. Three men and two animals were dead, and one camel was lost, but the rest – four men and three beasts – had survived. They had all been badly bitten by the insects, but none was as tormented as Kohtala. Terrel suspected that those who had died might already have been weakened, possibly by the plague. This impression was reinforced by the fact that Sansunak, the shaman, while still alive, was in a coma very similar to Cassar's.

The other three survivors were pathetically grateful for the healer's help, and when they were able to talk, they were quick to disavow any part in Kohtala's treachery, blaming all the law-breaking on their champion and the shaman – though the Toma regarded this version of events with some scepticism.

By the time Terrel had finished doing what he could for the Shiban, Zahir had been out of sight for more than an hour. The nomads kept glancing up at the mountain, but they could only imagine their leader's agonizing journey to the summit, and the waiting was beginning to prey on their nerves. The sun was less than two hours from setting, and no one wanted Zahir to have to spend a night alone on Makranash.

Terrel hoped that Alyssa's continued absence meant she was keeping an eye on their champion, but when she next appeared it was to demand that he try to contact the Ancient again. Her aggressive approach worried Terrel, but he did as she asked without demur. Once again there was no response. On this occasion, however, he sensed some sort of barrier between them, which prevented his efforts from even getting through. When he reported this to Alyssa, her response was typically oblique.

Too many walls, not enough windows, she remarked, then flew away before he could ask what she'd meant.

The only explanation Terrel could think of was that the winds – the god-like winds that only the Toma had believed in until now – were not yet convinced that he was worthy to speak to the strange entity who lay beneath their sacred home. This made as much sense as anything that had happened recently – and Terrel could only hope that when Zahir won the race, being a member of the winning team would allow him access to the protected realm. Because of that, as much as his concern for Zahir, he waited as anxiously as the rest of his companions for the signal of victory.

That signal eventually came in dramatic fashion. Even though Terrel had been told what to expect, nothing could have prepared him for the reality. The ground shook, but this, he knew, was no ordinary earthquake. The sound that filled his ears, his head, his entire being, was much more than a sound. It was a moment of pure joy, of celebration, transformed into a noise so vast that it reached beyond all normal human senses. For an instant the sun shone brighter than it had ever done before, the sky was a deeper blue, and the desert laughed aloud. Terrel knew that the ringing of that bell would stay in his memory for all time, because it belonged not just to his world, but to *all* the worlds. That bell was the size of a mountain.

'He's done it!' Okan yelled, leaping into the air like a madman. 'He's done it!'

Soon all the team were dancing, hugging each other and smiling idiotically as the titanic reverberations died away. Terrel was swept up in the wild celebration, finding tears in his eyes even as he laughed.

'Our flag is in place!' Medrano told him ecstatically, as they clasped each other in yet another embrace. 'And the signal will have been heard all over the Binhemma-Ghar. And all the way to Qomish!'

CHAPTER FORTY-TWO

The nomads' euphoria faded with the day when there was still no sign of Zahir's return. Their champion's situation was the Toma's primary concern, but Terrel had worries of his own. He had tried to make contact with the Ancient again, but with no success. That this was the case even after Zahir had won the race dismayed him, and he wondered what more could possibly be needed. To make matters worse, he hadn't seen Alyssa for hours. He wanted to know what she was doing, in part because she might be able to tell him what was happening with Zahir, but mostly because he wanted to be sure that she was all right.

As the shadows lengthened, Terrel watched both the mountain and the sky, but saw no movement. And then – just as he was wondering whether it would be possible to get any sleep that night, the mountain rang for a second time. This was a different sound, and one that no one had heard before. The nomads were as baffled as he was.

The noise was nowhere near as loud, nor did it shake the ground, but the most significant change was in its tone and in the emotions it evoked. There was no joy, no celebration in this tolling. Terrel felt sadness, tinged with anger – and something else, too fleeting to pin down. It affected his companions in a similar manner, and although no one could explain what had happened, they were all left with a vaguely ominous sense of disquiet.

By then the sun was only just above the horizon, and Terrel was becoming more and more agitated. He sought out Medrano as the one most likely to put his mind at rest.

'Zahir should have been back by now. Shouldn't we go and find him?'

'We're not allowed to set foot on the mountain itself,' the artist replied.

'Even though the race is over now?'

'The champion has to return with last year's banner as proof of his victory,' Medrano explained. 'We can't help him till he's done that.'

'But he could be injured. He might have collapsed,' Terrel protested. 'He could die up there. Why would the winds want that? He won the race.'

'We can't break the laws, Terrel. You saw what happened to those who did. Don't worry. Zahir will get down. He wouldn't have made it this far if he didn't have the heart of a champion.'

'Even if he's reached the end of his strength?'

'If that's true, then he'll sleep, recover and return in the morning. The nights are mild now. He won't come to any harm.'

'Without water?'

'He drank well this morning. And he's dealt with thirst before.'

All Terrel's objections were set aside one by one, and eventually he gave up. Schooling himself to patience, he scoured the twilight, thankful at least that he was able to do so. If he'd still been blind, the waiting would have been unbearable. He saw nothing of Zahir, though he did catch a glimpse of a small dust devil, spiralling up into the air from a ridge on the side of the mountain.

'There's a cave there,' Medrano told the healer, when the kwei was pointed out to him. 'Just at the top of that cliff. It's called the prophet's lair. The winds often send signs from there.'

'What did this one mean?'

'Kweis can be omens for good or ill. It's said they call to the souls of the newly dead. Perhaps it was for the Shiban.'

Terrel thought he knew better. Even as Medrano spoke, he'd realized who the mountain was calling – and the knowledge renewed his determination to climb it himself – at least as far as the prophet's lair. Remembering the mines of Betancuria, he wondered whether the cave might provide him with an entrance to the *Ancient*'s lair.

Darkness came swiftly after the sun set, and the camp settled down to wait out the night, making the most of their enforced rest. A watch was set, in case Zahir was still trying to complete his descent, but the team didn't think this was likely. The mountain was too dangerous in the dark, and for all his youthful recklessness, their champion was no fool.

*

In the morning there was still no sign of Zahir, and Terrel's patience was beginning to wear thin. He had slept very little, and was now gripped by a feverish restlessness. He tried once more to break through the barrier that surrounded the elemental, but he no longer believed there was any point in the attempt – and his intution proved correct. Alyssa had apparently abandoned him, without any explanation, and the prospect of sitting around – doing nothing – for several hours was more than he could bear. He couldn't wait any longer. Whether Zahir needed help or not, he had to go.

Trying to appear as casual as he could, Terrel strolled over to the base of the mountain, then – moving as quickly as his stiff and mismatched limbs would allow – he clambered onto the bare rock. Ignoring the shouts from behind him, he went on, before finally turning to face his team-mates. He found it hardest to look at Medrano. Although the artist's expression did not echo the outrage shown by most of the others, the bitter disappointment of betrayal in his eyes was much worse. Some of the others were shouting, but Terrel could ignore their threats and insults. Medrano's silence was much harder to answer.

'I have to do this!' he pleaded, knowing that the only way they could prevent him from leaving was to cross the invisible boundary themselves. 'I have duties I have sworn to perform here, and this is the only way.'

After another round of protests, Medrano spoke for the first time.

'I had thought you a man of honour, Terrel.'

'I am!' the healer claimed. 'I'm doing this for honour. Let the winds judge me. If they disapprove and punish

me as they punished Kohtala, I will accept my fate as
the price I have to pay. I have no choice in this,
Medrano.'

'Are we going to let him do this?' Okan exclaimed.

'What choice do we have?' the artist replied. 'His
beliefs are not ours. Do what you must, Terrel. I hope
the winds will be kind.' With that he turned his back and
walked away.

One by one the others all did the same, without another
word being spoken. Terrel had never felt more alone in
his life.

The climb up to the prophet's lair was exhausting and
occasionally terrifying. From below, Makranash had
seemed relatively benign; from within its borders, the
mountain was full of pitfalls. The bare rock reflected the
growing heat of the sun and, with no water to sustain him,
Terrel began to question the wisdom of his decision. The
crags and gullies that had seemed mere undulations from
ground level proved to be considerable obstacles, and on
several occasions he had to backtrack, having reached the
point where a vertical drop or an overhanging climb made
further progress impossible. Finally – and to his immense
relief – he found himself crossing a reasonably flat ledge
that took him to a small plateau at the top of the sheer
cliff he'd seen from below. From there the cave was in
full view.

Terrel crossed to the entrance, keeping well away from
the edge of the precipice, and peered inside. It was not
what he had expected or hoped for. He could tell at a
glance that this was no entrance to the mysterious centre
of the mountain. Although the opening was tall and wide,

it narrowed very rapidly to a tiny black tunnel, too small
for a man to navigate. Ironically, when Terrel went to
investigate, he felt a breeze blowing from this hole, like
the 'spiral wind' that had guided him into the mines of
Betancuria. But there was no way he could follow this
wind to its source.

Backing out of the cramped inner cave, Terrel turned
and noticed something he'd missed on the way in. At
once his disappointment turned to delight, and he knew
then that he had indeed come to the right place – for one
of his tasks, at least. The rock table stood no more than
a handspan above the cavern's floor, but its surface had
obviously been levelled and polished by hand – though
Terrel couldn't imagine who had done the work. It
reminded him of the jasper stones in the fog valley, but
the sign that had been engraved on the table was more
recently familiar. It was almost identical to the stylized
representation of a bird Medrano had drawn for the oracle
in the Senglea Hills. The symbol was known as 'the eyes
of the wind' – which was appropriate enough for
Makranash – but more importantly, it had been the sign
on which a translucent crystal had been placed by the
white hawk. It had been the only stone that had not corresponded to one of the moons, and until now Terrel hadn't
known what it meant.

He took Zorn's crystal from his pocket, and saw the
light glowing in its fractured depths as he placed it on
the table. At once a restless zephyr swirled the air in the
cave, sending up many tiny dust spirals. Terrel half
expected the general to appear, but he did not. No ghost
could come to Makranash in that form. But there was
something in the atmosphere that made the healer's skin

tingle and his pulse quicken. He caught a few snatches of conversation, and knew that – at long last – Zorn was talking to the winds. Terrel smiled, then heard the general's voice inside his own head.

I owe you an even greater debt now, Traveller.

You owe me nothing. I only did what any man would have done, given the chance.

You're too modest. That you stood the test of blindness to enable you to see into our realm and to release us is proof of a great heart. I hope we meet again in the next world – but not for a while!

I hope so too, Terrel said. *But there is much I have to do in this world yet.*

I'm aware of it, Zorn replied. *Take care when you choose your resting place of memory.*

Terrel was still wondering what to make of this strange piece of advice when the general spoke again, his deep voice full of emotion.

We salute you, Traveller, he declared, and there came a sound like a hundred clenched fists thumping onto a hundred breastplates. *My oath is fulfilled and honour satisfied. Now, at last, we can go home.*

The air around Terrel was suddenly empty. In his mind's eye he saw again the massed ranks of the forgotten army as they followed their general on one last journey, and left the world for ever.

For once the eclipse came without warning. The darkness simply arrived, turning day into night a few moments after Terrel left the cave. Stars glittered in the purple sky – and in the healer's hand – and the connection was made. He had not even reached out; the elemental had come to him.

Terrel sensed confusion, discomfort and animosity, but underneath the negative emotions there was a curiosity, a yearning, that gave him hope. He had been taken by surprise, and there was no time to plead his case. He simply tried to bring the appropriate thoughts to the surface of his mind, knowing that the Ancient would be able to read them there. His first concern was the plague, and he could only hope that the elemental would respond to his wordless appeal. There was much more he wanted to say, but he knew it would have to wait.

In the next moment he realized that this was a two-way process, an *exchange* of thoughts. Terrel suddenly understood *all* the meanings of the oracle, and was even able to make sense of some of the incomplete messages from the Tindaya Code. At last he knew what he had to do. He just wasn't sure *how*.

The eclipse ended as suddenly as it had begun and, with the returning light, Terrel found that he was not alone. Zahir was standing only a few paces away, looking exhausted but proud, a sun-faded banner clasped in his hand. For once his youthful face was haggard, but his expression was one of utter astonishment.

'You shouldn't be here!' he exclaimed. 'The laws—'

'The winds made an exception in my case,' Terrel said.

Two hubaras flew down and landed on the plateau, distracting Zahir for a moment.

'You must leave at once,' he declared, turning back to the healer.

'No. I have to stay. I have work to do here.'

'That's impossible.' Zahir looked bewildered rather than angry, and he kept his distance, presumably trying to ensure that his victory would not be tainted by any suggestion that he had received any unlawful help. 'We must get back to Qomish. The longer we stay here, the less chance we have of surviving.'

'You must go,' Terrel conceded. 'I understand that. But I can't.'

'You'll die.'

'Maybe not. I now know everything the oracle was trying to tell us. I'm going to become the double-headed man.'

'What are you talking about?'

'I have a star inside me. I talk to ghosts. I have a twin brother who lives inside me too.' Terrel was almost laughing now. 'I once even played the part of someone who was literally two-faced. Who else *could* I be?'

'You've been in the desert too long,' the nomad told him. 'It's driven you mad.'

'Does that matter? If I succeed here, by the time you get back to Qomish, the plague will have ended.'

'The plague? What . . . This is insane!'

'Is it? When you're crowned king, you can take credit for curing the plague. And you can do so much more.'

'Not that again,' Zahir groaned.

'Your decrees could change the whole future of Misrah.'

'They'll never accept anything serious, you know that.'

'What if I told you we could restore the Kullana River?' Terrel asked. 'Would that help them take you seriously?'

Zahir did not respond and, for a few moments, Terrel thought he might have convinced him.

'You still think you can talk to the winds?' the champion asked eventually.

'I know I can.'

'This is sacrilege, Terrel. They would never . . . You *must* come with me. I don't want to force you, but I will if I have to.'

But Terrel was no longer listening. He'd been thinking of all the things he wanted to achieve, and had realized that he'd never win Zahir over. And then he saw the way to evade the nomad's insistence. He knew what he had to do – though the idea terrified him.

This is the only way, Terrel, Alyssa told him. *The Ancient will never accept you as a man. Trust me.*

She's right, Vilheyuna added. *You will join us. You have to do this.*

Terrel still wasn't sure he had enough courage, but then he heard Zorn's advice again – *Take care when you choose your resting place of memory* – and felt a little of the general's boldness fill his spirit.

'The oracle held an omen for you too,' he said, knowing he had one last message to pass on. 'You must return to Qomish the way you came.'

'Are you crazy?' Zahir exclaimed. 'That would mean crossing the Valley of the Smokers again! And besides, Gantiya's dying.'

'Go to Seckar's monument,' Terrel went on. 'In seven days' time, when the Amber Moon is full, there will be life there. Will you take my word for that, as the voice of rain?' As he spoke he lifted the cord that hung round his neck over his head, and held the pendant in his left hand.

Zahir looked confused and worried now. He clearly didn't know what to think.

'This is important,' Terrel told him earnestly. 'I don't

know how much water you'll have, but this is the only way you'll all survive the journey. You've got to believe me.'

'Even if I did, I'm not going without you.'

'Then you leave me no choice.'

Terrel turned away and, quite deliberately, stepped over the edge of the cliff.

CHAPTER FORTY-THREE

When Zahir finally reached the foot of the mountain, he was greeted joyfully by his fellow nomads, but he was still shocked by what had happened outside the prophet's lair. He had been dreading telling them what had happened, but he realized almost at once that they already knew. In fact, the healer lay on the ground near the campsite, and although Zahir was surprised that his team-mates had ventured onto the mountain to recover the body, he was glad they'd be able to give him a proper burial, rather than leaving him for the hubaras.

'I was there when he jumped,' Zahir told the others, as they all gathered round the prone figure. 'I don't know why he did it.'

'He jumped?' Okan queried. 'We thought . . .'

'We thought the winds had punished him for trespassing on sacred ground,' Medrano finished.

'No. It was deliberate. He was saying all sorts of crazy things, but I never thought he'd kill himself.'

For a few moments no one spoke.

'He's not dead,' Korioth said eventually. 'He ought to be, but he isn't.'

'But . . .' Zahir was stunned. 'Are you sure? I saw him fall!'

'We all saw him fall,' Luqa said. 'There was no way he could have survived, but he did.'

'He's deeply unconscious,' Medrano reported, 'and we can't rouse him, but there are no broken bones, no sign of any injury. There's not a mark on him. Look for yourself if you don't believe me.'

'It's impossible,' Zahir whispered, but as he looked down at the healer, he could see what Medrano meant. Terrel appeared whole and unharmed – and the expression on his face was serene.

'It's even stranger than that,' Okan said. 'After we saw what happened, we went to see if we could find him. He was lying there, looking just like he does now, *outside* the mountain's boundary.'

'Which made no sense at all,' Fanari added. 'I mean, the slope below the cliff is steep, but not *that* steep. How could he have rolled so far after he hit the ground?'

'And he looked as if he'd just laid down and gone to sleep,' Korioth remarked, 'rather than fallen halfway down a mountain.'

Once again Zahir found himself at a loss for words.

'Do you think the plague could have driven him mad?' Okan asked. 'Then left him like this?'

'No. This is deeper,' Medrano replied. 'You can see Cassar twitch in his fever sometimes, even now. Besides, how could catching the plague have saved him from such a fall? In some ways this reminds me of what happened to Vilheyuna.'

'He's become a sleeper?'

'That's what it looks like.'

'Maybe that's his punishment,' Korioth suggested.

'Did he tell you what he was trying to do up there?' Medrano asked Zahir.

'No. He just said he had work to do.'

'He told us much the same,' Okan said.

'Well, he's not going to do any now,' Korioth concluded.

'There was one other thing he said,' Zahir added reluctantly, then told the others about Terrel's insistence that they return to Qomish via Seckar's monument. 'The question is, should we take any notice of someone who was acting like a madman?'

'He was – is – the voice of rain,' Fanari pointed out. 'Perhaps he knows something we don't.'

'But you said yourself he was crazy,' Okan countered. 'It could just as easily be a delusion.'

'On the other hand, Gantiya *is* the closest possible source of water, isn't it?' Zahir said.

'Yes,' Okan confirmed, 'providing the spring hasn't failed – and I wouldn't want to stake my life on that.'

'And we all know the extra risks involved in going that way,' Korioth added.

'Tell me what's happened down here,' Zahir said, becoming suddenly businesslike. He had already noted the extra camels and the injured members of the Shiban's team in the distance.

'As far as water's concerned, we're much better off than before,' Korioth said, 'but we still have less than I'd like. No matter which way we go, we'll definitely need to find more before we get back to Qomish.'

'The Shiban's surviving camels are in decent shape,' Luqa reported, 'but ours need water soon.'

'Food isn't a problem,' the quartermaster went on. 'We can butcher one of the dead camels if necessary.'

'We'll be able to travel at night now,' Okan stated confidently. 'Even without Cassar, I'll be able to get us home.'

'And if we arrange the loads properly,' Luqa added, 'we'll all be able to ride.'

'So we should make good progress,' Zahir concluded. 'Can we get to Gantiya in seven days?'

'We'd have to travel almost nonstop to have any chance of doing that,' Okan replied. 'Only rest in the hottest part of the day.'

'If we go that quickly we'll use more water,' Korioth warned.

'But there'll be less days to survive,' Zahir countered.

'It's a balancing act,' the quartermaster agreed. 'A risky one.'

'And not having a healer of any kind will make it harder,' Medrano commented. 'Kohtala's shaman is in a coma.'

Zahir scowled at this mention of his treacherous rival, but kept his mind on the task in hand.

'So, do we follow Terrel's advice?' he asked.

'He'll be with us,' Fanari replied. 'If he's wrong, he'll have been putting his own life – or what's left of it – in danger. Why would he do that if he didn't believe what he said?'

'He may well believe it,' Okan said. 'But that doesn't make it *true*. It could have been a desert dream.'

'I think we have to take the chance and trust him,'

Luqa said quietly. 'Anyone who's done all the things he has must have some link with the winds.'

'I think so too,' Medrano said. 'I still don't know what he was trying to do when he went on to the mountain, but he must have had his reasons. He's never let us down before.'

'So, are we agreed?' Zahir looked round, and the team all nodded their assent. 'Then let's go. We're wasting valuable time.'

Some time later, as the expanded caravan moved off – with the various sick and comatose travellers carefully strapped in amongst the baggage – two hubaras were perched on a rock a short way up one of the lower slopes of Makranash. The birds watched as the humans departed, leaving them in possession of the sacred mountain. Dangling from the beak of one of them was a pendant marked with the sign of the river in the sky.

PART THREE

MAKRANASH

CHAPTER FORTY-FOUR

Watching 'himself' being carried away on a camel was one of the oddest sensations Terrel had ever experienced. As the caravan began to make its way back across the desert, the healer was sitting on a rock next to Alyssa and Vilheyuna. He saw the two sleepers as the birds they were inhabiting, but saw himself as a ghost. Rationally, he knew that couldn't be true, because no ghost could come this close to one of the Ancients. To do so would be to risk annihilation, not only from his own world but from the next – and from whatever came after that. He looked down at his hand now, seeing through its faintly luminous shape to the rocks beneath. He had found himself in a similar state – though in completely different circumstances – at another mountain, Tindaya, on Vadanis. On that occasion he had left his body on a stage many miles way, amongst his fellow actors, while the ghosts transported his spirit to the ruined temple. This time he was responsible for his own fate – though the elemental had played a part in it too.

Terrel truly had become the double-headed man. One half of him was on its way back to Qomish with Zahir and the others, while the other remained at Makranash. Two Terrels. Two heads. And yet if he could have seen his own head now, it would have been transparent. What else *could* he be but a ghost?

You're not a real ghost, Alyssa told him, with her customary insight into her friend's thoughts.

Then what is this? he asked, waving a spectral hand in the air.

What you see is just the shape your mind's constructed around your spirit, she explained. *It's easier for you if at least some aspects of your appearance seem familiar. If you wanted to, you could change it to anything at all. But your own form is the easiest, and the most comforting.*

Is that how you see yourself? he asked, curious now.

No. It's different for the sleepers. We borrow the shapes of other living creatures, but we can't wholly replace them. Their shape becomes ours. Where you are, yours is the only life. She shook her beak, making the pendant swing from side to side. *You can shape your perception of it however you wish.*

Terrel stared, wondering how his essential being could possibly be confined in such an insignificant container. The choice of the pendant to house his spirit had been an obvious one. Zorn's crystal had given him the idea, and the general's advice had confirmed his own intuition. He had cast it aside as he jumped into the abyss, to make sure it stayed at Makranash when his body was taken away.

The fall itself had been initially terrifying. He'd been convinced he was about to die. The cliff he had leapt from was far higher than the one where Ysatel had become a sleeper, and there had been no water below to break his fall, only unforgiving stone. However, in the next instant everything had changed. The normal forces of his world, which were propelling him towards the rocks below, had been negated. He had slowed and then floated sideways, without really being aware of what was happening, before coming to rest on level ground a considerable distance from the precipice. His landing had been so soft that the soil might have been a feather bed. By then he was no longer inhabiting his body, but was watching it from above, where he was as light as air.

Terrel had often tried to imagine what it would be like to be a sleeper, to separate spirit from physical form. He'd had a taste of what it entailed after crossing the Valley of the Smokers, when Jax had usurped his body, but now he was experiencing the real thing – or something similar, at least – and it felt very strange.

All his senses seemed to have remained with him – sight, smell, hearing, even, to an extent, touch. In an abstract way he could 'feel' the rock beneath him – though he already knew he couldn't affect the world around him. He could still think, he was still prey to the full range of emotions and, within limits, he could still act. Moving from one place to another was no longer a question of actual physical movement, even though he still found himself picturing it in those terms. He was dependent on Alyssa to move his 'resting place of memory' over long distances, but he had some degree of freedom within a limited range of the pendant. Even now, after only a little while, he was beginning to feel constricted, and understood something of what Alyssa went through when she stayed in any one animal for too long.

The caravan was almost out of sight, and Terrel bid his friends a silent farewell, sending his blessings for a safe journey – and hoping he'd be able to make their return to Qomish a memorable occasion. He had watched the nomads discuss their route, and on several occasions he had longed to interrupt, to make sure they came to the right decision. It had been a great relief to him when, in the end, they had chosen to heed his advice. And he was glad that even Medrano seemed to have forgiven him. But now that they were gone, it was time for Terrel to turn his attention to other matters.

Ready? Alyssa asked.

I suppose so, he said, all his doubts resurfacing.

You have work to do, remember? she reminded him.

They flew back to the prophet's lair. Alyssa laid the pendant on the rock table, next to the empty crystal, then went back out into the open air to join Vilheyuna. Left alone in the cave, Terrel realized what he had to do. Now that he had no body to hold him back, the mountain's secrets were open to him.

I'll be waiting for you when you return, Alyssa told him.

Remember the path, Terrel, Vilheyuna added. *I'll follow it with you as far as I can, but there are others who may need me as a guide.* With that the male hubara turned and swooped from the ledge, diving first to gain speed and then soaring into the sky.

Where's he going? Terrel asked as he watched the bird fly away.

To follow his path, Alyssa replied. *He'll be back when we need him.*

Need him for what?

How should I know? she demanded irritably. *You're the one with the oracles. Do you know what you've got to do?*

I know what I want to do. I'm just not sure how to go about it.

Well, you'll never find out unless you start, she told him.

Terrel turned and made his way to the back of the cave. He felt the spiral wind blowing gently through him and shivered, nervous about taking the final step of his journey.

I'll wait for you, Alyssa reassured him again.

Still hesitant, Terrel would have replied – but at that moment the wind reversed its flow. Makranash breathed in, and he was sucked inside.

At first the darkness was absolute. Distance and time meant nothing here. Even when a faint glimmer from his left hand helped Terrel to see his own ghostly outline, it showed him nothing of the void. He couldn't see the elemental, but he felt its presence all around him, infused into the very fabric of the place, indivisible from Makranash itself. Realizing that he was entirely at the mercy of the Ancient was unnerving, but Terrel could sense none of the enmity he'd encountered in their earlier brief contact. Instinctively, he knew that the creature was much more at ease with him now he was no longer made of flesh and blood. The form he was taking was much closer to the elemental's own.

Terrel's second impression was much less encouraging.

There was sickness here, an imbalance that his healer's insight recognized. He wanted to put it right, to cure the illness, but it was too alien for him to combat immediately. He didn't understand its symptoms or its cause; all he knew was that something was wrong. Even as he recognized this, he sensed the Ancient's suspicion, and hurried to reassure the creature that his only concern was to help, not harm.

Just being regarded with suspicion made him feel guilty – though there was no reason for it – and his reputation as the voice of rain floated, unbidden, into his consciousness. He immediately sought to justify himself, explaining that water – which the elemental regarded as an evil, magical substance – was not only welcome to human beings but absolutely vital. He sensed incomprehension and revulsion, but persevered, knowing he must convince the Ancient of this if it was ever to agree to end the plague. He tried to explain that he had never intended to threaten the creature with his supposed talent, and certainly hadn't meant to break any tenets of their bargain. His honesty evidently made its mark, even if his reasons were not yet accepted or understood.

Terrel was about to continue the process, hoping to make a rational argument that might lead to a renewal of cooperation between him and the strange entities, when all conscious thought flew from his mind. A flame sprang into life from nowhere, flickering in the void just a few paces from him. After the darkness its orange glow seemed uncomfortably bright, and Terrel squinted, only to find in the next moment that the fire died down a little. He couldn't imagine where it had come from, but he was hypnotized by its liquid dance. After a few moments, he realized that the flame was cold; it gave off light, but no heat. Even as this thought crossed his mind, he felt the warmth reach him – though the fire wasn't burning any more strongly – and he suddenly realized what was happening. A real flame, he thought, is not a single colour like that. There are many shades of yellow, orange and red, depending on how hot it is and what is burning. In that instant the flame became a riot of colour, making it look even more unnatural. No, he prompted gently. Like this. He conjured up the memory of his last campfire, and immediately saw it before him, perfect in every detail. He could not only see it and feel its heat, but he could also smell the smoke and hear the faint crackle of its burning.

The fire vanished then, and was replaced by a whirl of sand, like a nascent karabura. Without conscious thought, Terrel remembered his own experience beneath a sandstorm – and suddenly found himself in the midst of a hurricane. It didn't affect him – he had no substance to be affected – but the swirling disorientation made it seem very real indeed, and he was glad when it stopped.

For the first time, Terrel truly understood the implications of his encounters with the elementals. As he learnt more about them, they learnt more about *him* – and thus about humanity in general and the world they lived in. With each meeting the Ancients were growing more skilled at presenting themselves as part of that world. The first, in Betancuria, had been a shifting pattern of energy, quite out of place in its surroundings, and anyone who saw it knew instantly that it was unnatural, stranger than anything they had ever known. The second, in Talazoria, had been able to disguise itself as a rock, a simple, dry substance which allowed it to remain hidden, except when it moved. The creature in Makranash was able to produce much more sophisticated imagery; flame – a moving process that mimicked life – and a sandstorm, a large-scale representation of the natural forces of the desert. As Terrel had just proved, it was learning all the time. Curiosity, it seemed, was one of the creature's foremost characteristics. And the images it was showing him now were not just images. In a very real sense, they *were* the elemental.

Terrel was about to follow up that discovery, in the hope that knowledge would help dispel the Ancient's fear of water – and of the men who brought it with them – when he was stunned by the next vision presented to him. Delicate, brilliantly-coloured blooms burst into short-lived glory before his eyes, spreading out all around him as they had done on the night when he'd first earnt the title 'the voice of rain'. He knew that these images must have been the hardest of all for the Ancient to create, because they sprang to life through water, with all its fearful magic. He watched as they faded again to a desiccated field of tinder.

And then, just as he thought the display was over, he saw his own unnerving, crystalline eyes looking back at him from the darkness. In a moment they too were gone, but the sight had sent shivers down his spine, and he knew the image would haunt him for as long as he lived.

The false night returned, recalling another memory, an emptiness Terrel could not even begin to comprehend. He saw a swirl of stars, and the moons all out of place, as if their orbits had become unstable. Then they vanished, and he was left with a sense of awe and longing that soon gave way to a tense nervousness. This was because the predominant sensation surrounding him now was one of expectancy. The elemental had shared some of its memories. Now it wanted to see some of his.

CHAPTER FORTY-FIVE

At first Terrel tried to control the flow of memories. Deliberately thinking about specific incidents that seemed most likely to gain the elemental's trust, he recalled his encounters with its 'brothers' – he could think of no better to word to describe the distant relationship. Emphasizing what he had done to help the creatures in both Betancuria and Talazoria – by ensuring, among other things, that water was kept away from them – he described how he had acted as mediator between them and the local human populations, and expressed the hope that he could play the same role here. He also recounted the details of the bargain he'd struck – the bargain that drove him still, and which he hoped to renew. However, he realized after a while that the Ancient had no interest in what he was describing. Either it already knew these stories, through its contact with the others, or it had learnt all it needed when he'd been thinking earlier about the elementals' developing skills.

For a few moments Terrel despaired – what was he supposed to do now? – but then he realized that their communication was meant to take the form of an involuntary – and therefore honest – exchange of memories. He was not supposed to pick and choose what he presented, but let whatever rose naturally to the surface of his mind speak for him. Trying to calm himself, to relax enough so that this could happen, was not easy, but eventually he managed to clear his thoughts and start again.

The problem then was that so many memories crowded in, clamouring for attention. So much had happened to Terrel in his short life, and especially in the last four years, that he was hard-pressed to keep his recollections in any sort of order. And if *he* couldn't make sense of them, how was the Ancient supposed to cope?

The major turning points of his life were jumbled up with apparently trivial events; landscapes of all kinds blurred and overlapped; he saw hundreds of faces, heard countless voices, and felt the echoes of every emotion he'd ever known. Moons waxed and waned; the seasons changed in their endless cycle; the ancient words of generations long dead came to life again to taunt him with their riddles. Dreams were as real as his waking experiences, and he talked to animals and ghosts.

Terrel was trying – unsuccessfully – to bring some harmony to this expanding chaos, when he found that he no longer needed to worry about making sense. The Ancient was perfectly content to survey the deluge of memories, accepting them all as a whole or selecting specific thoughts for further scrutiny. He sensed the creature's reaction to his revelations, and was astonished to find that, although its range of feelings ran from disgust to wonder, and from fear to incredulity, its overriding emotion was one of envy.

For all its extraordinary powers, the elemental had actually experienced very little, and intimate knowledge of the life of just one human being had aroused in it a jealous curiosity and a deep need to learn more. It was voracious, forcing Terrel to relive many moments that had been terrifying or traumatic, as well as other more pleasant events. Gradually, he was able to identify the memories that were chosen for special study, and in doing so he found that the creature's interests – and its reactions – were not always what he would have expected.

His discovery of Muzeni's telescope at the observatory in the grounds of Havenmoon, the comet that had been seen over Vadanis, the dark star mosaic at the hilltop ruins near Tiscamanita, and the shaman's stone at Qomish were all considered important, but Terrel's ability to foresee earthquakes was dismissed as commonplace. The moon ceremony at Betancuria seemed to annoy the Ancient, as did the sharaken's collective dreaming. The birth of Parina's baby in the fog valley hospice provoked disgust and fascination in equal measures, and the fire-opal that Aylen had found in Fenduca caused a sudden interest that was subsequently set aside with some disappointment. The moon mosaic that had mysteriously been decorated with swirls of bright crystals on the night of Terrel's 'voice of rain' was regarded with both excitement and an empty yearning, neither of which Terrel could comprehend. However, he did understand the elemental's response to his memory of the oracle. The creature saw the obliteration of the double-headed man, together with the black pebble, as a prediction of an eclipse – something that didn't fit with the rest of the augury, but which made perfect sense now.

During this process, Terrel realized that certain trends were becoming apparent. The Ancient could sense Terrel's emotional reactions to various memories, and although its own responses were often different, it was curious about his feelings. Through him, it was also apparently gaining a faint appreciation of beauty. Very occasionally it was so taken with something that it reproduced the image in the void with astonishing accuracy. Terrel saw again the almost metallic sheen of a polished jasper stone, the vivid plumage of a bee-eater, the glory of the red flowers at Kativa's shrine, and the flare of green light that preceded a desert sunrise. At one point, acting on a sudden inspiration, he tried to interrupt the flow of memories, to get the elemental to satisfy a yearning of his own. Since he'd left the haven, he had not once been able to see Alyssa's face, not even in his dreams, and he hoped that by thinking about her now, he might be able to *see* her at last. But all he got was an image of the hubara. No! he thought indignantly. That's not what I want. I want— He broke off, realizing that he was antagonizing the Ancient.

After that there were no more images, only the continuing barrage of abstract memories and the elemental's responses to them. It clearly liked fire, and was comforted by the presence of sand. Animals and plants provoked mixed emotions, with doubts and fears outnumbering instances of amusement or appreciation. With humans, the response was very different. The problem – as always – was water. Not only did men carry this sorcerous substance inside them, but they also sought out new supplies whenever they could, pouring the evil into their bodies. The elemental found such behaviour inexplicable and abhorrent, and it jaundiced its whole view of humanity. Terrel knew he couldn't change that. Instead, he had to try to convince the creature that it was safe where it was, that there was no source of water for many miles, and that there was no need to persecute men with the plague, because they represented no threat. The elemental's reaction to these deliberately planted ideas was unnerving.

Terrel sensed an enormous agitation, and he was glad he was in an incorporeal state, knowing from experience that being inside the entity when it was confused or angry could be extremely uncomfortable. There had been times in the past when he'd feared being torn limb from limb by the swirling, apparently random forces of its frenzy. The violent nature of its current response seemed quite out of keeping with its earlier curiosity – almost as though the Ancient had more than one identity within its peculiar existence. What was more, Terrel now sensed both pain and enmity in its regard for him, which made him wonder about the real nature of the connection between them. If it hated him so much, even without bodily encumbrances, why had it turned him into a sleeper – in effect saving his life – and initiated their contact?

Once again, Terrel was almost overwhelmed by a sense of illness, an imbalance that reminded him of the terror that lay at the heart of the plague. It was irrational, but no less real for that. *What is it?* he asked, trying to use psinoma to provoke a direct response. *What's making you ill?* His question went unanswered, and the atmosphere of menace intensified. Sparks of light flickered briefly in the void. *I'm a healer*, he tried desperately. *If you tell me what's wrong, I may be able to help you*. He could feel the spiral winds blowing through him, and feared that he would be expelled – exhaled – from the mountain before he had the chance to achieve anything. After all he'd been through, he couldn't stand the thought of failure now.

You were trying to make yourself safe, weren't you? he said. *When you diverted the Kullana River?* The reply came in the form of a brief flash of memory, of the desert cracking open and the torrent disappearing into the canyon. The whole scene was filled with horror and revulsion, but there was another emotion too, something Terrel couldn't identify at first. It was overlaid by desperation, and a degree of recklessness, even madness, but its true nature only became clear when the image was gone and had been replaced by the endless darkness once more.

It didn't work, did it! Terrel guessed. *You diverted the river to keep it even further from you, but it didn't make you feel any better.* He was convinced now that water was at the heart of the creature's sickness, though he still had no idea what had caused it. But in a sense that was irrelevant. The most important thing was to find out whether he could use his healer's instincts to help remedy the effects. If he could, then the prospects of their being able to renew their bargain would be greatly improved.

But Terrel didn't know how to look for the creature's waking dream. He didn't even know if the elemental was ever awake or asleep. As far as he could tell, such terms had no meaning for a life form such as this. So how was he supposed to search for the disease? And even if he

managed to find its centre, would he really be able to treat
it? He knew so little about the internal structures of these
strange entities; perhaps he would make things worse
rather than better.

Terrel was just about to try to probe the elemental's
mind once more when he realized that he was alone. The
Ancient had gone. He'd experienced no sensation of
movement, and the darkness was just as complete, but
their exchange was over. What do I do now? he wondered.
Go in search of it? Go back outside to Alyssa? Or stay
here and hope it comes back?

He soon realized that he had no idea how to even
attempt the first two possibilities – which was in itself
a frightening admission – and so, by default, he chose
the third option. He couldn't tell how many hours had
passed since he'd been inside Makranash, but he was
suddenly exhausted. Resigning himself to the inevitable,
he slept.

The dream was an old one, yet he remembered it all too
clearly. A city of glass and crystal rose from the waves,
but this time the waves were made of sand, not seawater.
The city was not real, of course, but as before, it was
important. It was beautiful but flawed, with obvious frac-
tures running through the delicate patterns of light.
Terrel had tried to mend these flaws – to *heal* them –
once before, but had only been partially successful. What
was more, he'd been unable to prevent the destruction of
the place when radiant meteors smashed into its fragile
surface, shattering it to glittering fragments that sank
down into the darkness of the ocean. Alyssa's eyes had
been trapped inside the city, but later, in another version

of the dream, she had appeared as a raven, and had been protected by glowing lines of light – light which had also enabled the city to survive.

This time Terrel's need to heal the cracks in the crystalline structure was more urgent than ever. He had learnt a great deal since the first time he'd had this dream. He was a healer now. Instinct allowed him to recognize what was wrong, and to adjust the complex patterns to remedy the defects – though some of the flaws were too deeply ingrained for him to reach them. He tried, again and again, making progress only in tiny increments, until exhaustion forced him to step back and rest, hoping to recover his strength for another attempt.

The dream faded and returned so many times that he lost track of his efforts, and became engulfed in a permanent haze of fatigue – often having to begin a task all over again because he'd simply forgotten where he'd got to. Eventually, he knew he had done all he could. It was not enough, but he'd reached the limit of his skills. For anything more he would need help.

Terrel awoke to darkness, and to the certain knowledge that his connection with the elemental had been renewed. The air of curiosity was back, accompanied this time by a new and encouraging sense of gratitude and relief. The Ancient's illness was still present, but it was less malignant than before, and Terrel knew that his efforts within the dream had not been in vain. The creature's pain was more manageable now, and it was no longer on the brink of insanity. What was more, Terrel believed he knew what had caused its suffering in the first place – and how to end it altogether.

Can we talk now? he asked hopefully.

The answer did not come in words but in a sudden certainty. It was all around him, a force so powerful that it was as terrifying as it was welcome. The elemental was finally willing to discuss anything Terrel wanted – but it also had some very definite ideas of its own. The healer's skills had only earnt him a hearing. And even though nothing was ruled out for the future, some of the Ancient's demands made his blood run cold.

Alyssa? Alyssa! Are you there? Can you hear me?

Terrel! Thank the moons! I thought . . . Although her voice sounded muffled and distant, she was obviously very relieved. *Are you coming out now?*

No, not yet.

Why not? Her disappointment was plain.

There are still things I have to do here. Terrel did not like to tell her that he was effectively the elemental's prisoner.

Has the Ancient agreed to end the plague? she asked anxiously.

No. But it's promised not to make it any worse.

That's no good. People will still die—

I know, he cut in. *But if I can convince it of a few things, it will end the plague. I'm sure of it.*

What things?

I'll tell you in a moment. Is Vilheyuna still with you?

Yes. He's anxious to be gone.

We need to get a message to Zahir, Terrel told her. *When he reaches Qomish. Vilheyuna's the only one who might be able to do that.*

How? Alyssa queried.

I'm not sure. Perhaps we can find a way together. Can he hear us now?

I can hear you, the shaman responded.

What do you think?

There might be a way, Vilheyuna replied thoughtfully, *but I'll need help.*

What can we do? Alyssa asked.

An hour later, Vilheyuna flew off, beginning the long journey to Qomish. Terrel had told him exactly what to say to Zahir, but was still worried about whether the shaman's plan would work.

It sounds very complicated, he commented doubtfully. *Do you think he'll manage it?*

I don't see why not, Alyssa replied. *He's resourceful enough, and you have many allies there.*

I hope you're right. If he can't do it, I don't want to think about what might happen. And all this is assuming Zahir actually makes it back to Qomish.

He will, she stated confidently. *If there was ever a man born to be King of the Desert, he was.*

Terrel smiled to himself in the darkness.

You're right, he said. *His friends have called him 'the prince' for years now.*

My main worry is whether Zahir will be able to convince the other tribes, Alyssa said. *It's a huge undertaking.*

If it works as we hope, we'll be giving him some pretty effective bargaining tools. I don't think he'll let us down.

Well, we'll know soon enough.

It'll be a long time yet, surely.

Not so long. He should be at Seckar's monument tomorrow, for the full of the Amber Moon.

That can't be right! Terrel exclaimed, then made a rapid calculation. *How long have I been in here?*

Six days, she replied. *That's why I was so worried.*

Terrel was astonished. He simply couldn't believe that so much time had passed in the outside world. And then something else occurred to him.

Are you all right? He knew Alyssa had been inside the hubara for a long time now.

I'm fine. Vilheyuna was fretting, but he's not as used to this as me.

I wouldn't mind if you wanted to leave too, he said, not really meaning it. *You could always—*

Don't be stupid. Someone's got to carry you back to Qomish when you've finished here.

I know, but I wouldn't want anything to happen to you.

Don't worry about me, she told him. *Just make sure the Ancient gets what it wants. We can't afford to let the plague get any worse.*

Terrel didn't reply immediately. He was aware that Alyssa's prolonged incarceration in a single bird was not the only peril she faced. The elemental was suspicious of the hubara – which it knew was somehow more than flesh and blood – and it had left Terrel in no doubt that it wouldn't hesitate to destroy her if anything happened to endanger its new-found, partial recovery.

I'll make sure I keep it happy, he said eventually.

Good. Then all we have to do is wait.

And then what? he asked abruptly. He had just realized that there was another gaping hole in their plan. *How will I know what happens in Qomish? I've got to know, so I can tell—*

I've already thought of that, Alyssa cut in.

You have? Will Vilheyuna come back here?

*No, that would take too long. I've got another idea.
You probably won't like it, but I don't see any other way.*

Terrel's heart sank.

Tell me, he said.

CHAPTER FORTY-SIX

'Three days into the return journey we picked up the trail of Fgura's team.' Zahir looked around the Great Circle, knowing that each person there was hanging on his every word. He was telling the most important story of his life – one that would either make him a figure of legend or a laughing stock for all time.

'Theirs was an honourable race,' he went on. 'Until they were betrayed they had been only a short distance behind the Shiban. But then they were forced to turn back, and their plight was desperate. When we caught up with them, they'd reached the point where they couldn't go any further. Their animals were useless, four of their number were already dead, and the three who had survived were also close to death.'

His audience listened in silence, the throng crowded onto the terraces and spilling across the arena itself so that Zahir's 'royal' podium was completely surrounded. The only open space in the entire amphitheatre was around the shaman's stone.

'We shared our life with them,' Zahir continued, 'even though this left our own supplies perilously low. As most of you know, Fgura himself died in spite of our efforts, before we were able to leave the Binhemma-Ghar, but his two companions survived and are recovering now with their tribe. The Mehtar has spoken to them, and they have confirmed their part of my tale.'

Zahir had been speaking for some time now. Even before the Toma's victorious return to Qomish, people had realized that this Race of Truth had been no ordinary contest. Several teams had got back much earlier, telling strange stories about misleading desert dreams and the sudden inexplicable inability of their scouts to navigate properly. For a while it had seemed possible that, for the first time in living memory, no one would reach Makranash. But then they had heard the mountain ring, and a welcome sense of normality was restored – at least temporarily.

That all changed when Zahir returned. The rumours began almost immediately, fuelled by the fact that several of his party were ill. The champion's entry into Qomish had not been the traditional triumphal procession into the city. Instead, he had gone straight to his own tribe's camp-site and sent a message requesting a visit from the Mehtar. That had taken place the previous evening, and during the night the oasis had been awash with speculation about the reasons for such a request. The following morning, after a brief ceremony to honour those who had died in the Binhemma-Ghar, Zahir had been crowned King of the Desert and 'enthroned' on the platform where he now stood, delivering the customary speech.

This was normally a time of good-natured banter and

boasting about great deeds, but this year it was different. Zahir's podium was surrounded by his team-mates, including two who were comatose, lying on portable pallets. There was nothing unusual in the team's presence – the winners usually wanted to share in their leader's glory – but the fact that they, like Zahir, were all solemn and grim-faced at what should have been a festive gathering told its own story. Tension in the Great Circle had already been running high by the time the champion began to speak, and when he reached the part about the Shiban's sabotage of the race, a hush had fallen over the entire audience. In spite of their astonishment, they remained quiet and subdued while Zahir told them what had happened at Makranash, and now, as the tale neared its conclusion, they were riveted by his words.

'We'd hoped to see the ruined city once more,' Zahir went on, 'but we could not find it – and we had no time to stop and search.' In truth, there had been no sign of either the city or the paved road, and Zahir wondered privately whether they had ever really been there at all. Either way, it didn't matter any more.

'We went on, crossing back over the Valley of the Smokers. When we reached Gantiya, the spring was dry. All the life was gone. Our remaining camels were weakening rapidly, and we were all close to death. We had no water left, and we were down to the last of our food, but we pushed on to Seckar's monument. We stopped there, knowing we could go no further without aid. That night, at the full of the Amber Moon, it rained.' Zahir paused as a ripple of disbelief ran around the arena. 'I have never seen such rain in winter, let alone in the dry season. It came down in sheets, filling every hollow and washing away our dread. The oracle was proved correct. And it saved our lives.'

Once again, a low murmuring filled the Great Circle, as the listeners at the outer limits of the gathering passed on what they had heard to those who'd been unable to get inside and who were clustered in the streets around the stadium.

'Five days later,' Zahir concluded, 'we reached Qomish. But that is not where this story ends.'

He looked around once more, aware that he was the focus of several thousand pairs of eyes. He knew he was about to take the greatest gamble of his life, and that this was his last chance to back down, to renege, on his unspoken promise. As the crowd held its breath, waiting for him to go on, Zahir thought about what had happened the previous evening.

Mlicki had come to see him after the Mehtar left, when all Zahir had wanted to do was sleep. The meeting with Qomish's ruler had been difficult for a number of reasons – not least because the story he'd had to tell was so outlandish – but the main area of disagreement had been Zahir's insistence on using his 'coronation' the next day to reveal everything to the other tribes. The Mehtar had believed that the presumed guilt of Kohtala and the other Shiban would be better dealt with in a less public manner. Murder was a heinous crime in any circumstances, but what they had done was so horrendous that they were likely to face harsh reprisals. The Mehtar was anxious to see justice done, but he also wanted to avoid the possibility of any rioting. So it had been agreed that Kohtala and the surviving members of his team would be incarcerated in secret, and not in the cages at the Great Circle – whose place in general view represented their main value as a deterrent to ordinary wrongdoing. However, Zahir could not be dissuaded from speaking out. He wanted to tell the truth – all of it – and the Mehtar finally approved, recognizing the young man's evident determination and genuine sincerity.

Zahir's family had tried to prevent Mlicki from disturbing him, but the shaman's apprentice had been insistent, and eventually Zahir had shouted to them to let the visitor in. Mlicki's first words made him wonder if he'd done the right thing. He was already surrounded by enough madness.

'I have a message for you. From Terrel.'

'Terrel's a sleeper. He's not sending messages to anyone.'

'Not directly,' Mlicki agreed, 'but there's a part of him that *isn't* asleep – and that part's still at Makranash.'

'You're as crazy as he was!' Zahir exclaimed.

'I know it seems that way,' Mlicki said earnestly, 'but I can explain. Terrel's become the double-headed man.'

Zahir remembered that this was one of the things Terrel had claimed while he was on Makranash. But he still didn't know what it *meant*.

'The double-headed man is just a symbol,' he said. 'A sign for the oracle. How could he *become* that? It's absurd.'

'We already call him the voice of rain,' his visitor pointed out. 'That's almost the same as one of the oracle's signs too.'

'Yes, but—'

'Look, I don't know how it happened, or what it

means,' Mlicki cut in, 'but I do know the message is important, and I believe it's genuine. What harm can it do to hear me out?'

Zahir's hesitation was all the encouragement Mlicki needed.

'There were two hubaras with Terrel on the mountain, weren't there?'

'How do you know that?' He'd instructed his teammates not to say anything about their journey.

'They were there to make sure he jumped off the cliff,' Mlicki added. 'That was when he became the double-headed man.'

By now Zahir was beginning to doubt his own sanity.

'Even if this is true,' he said slowly, 'and part of Terrel *is* awake, how could he get a message to you if he's still at Makranash? And what have the hubaras got to do with anything?'

'One of the birds is here. In Qomish.'

'Here? How do you . . .' Zahir paused in disbelief as the implication of Mlicki's words sank in. 'Are you seriously telling me that a *bird* brought this message?'

'Yes.'

'What did it do? Carry an inscribed stone in its beak?'

'It's not as simple as that.'

'You think this is *simple*?' Zahir exploded.

'The bird isn't just a bird. It contains Vilheyuna's spirit.'

The elder's son laughed then, wondering just how much more nonsensical Mlicki's explanation could get.

'So Vilheyuna gave you the message?'

Mlicki knew that he was being ridiculed, but he remained serious and intent.

'No. He can't talk to people in this world – apart from Terrel – but he brought some ghosts with him.'

'This gets better and better,' Zahir muttered, more disconcerted than ever now. 'And just who *are* these ghosts?'

'I don't know, but they're Terrel's friends. And Kala was able to talk to them.'

'Your sister? She doesn't talk to anyone!'

'Not with words. In here,' Mlicki said, tapping the side of his head. 'She could see them too, even though no one else could. But of course she can't speak, so she had to find another way of telling someone.'

'You?' Zahir guessed.

'Me,' Mlicki confirmed, recalling Kalkara's frustration until he'd realized what she wanted. 'I've always known a lot about what she's thinking. This time she just made the intuitive connection more deliberate. I had a vision.'

'Beyond the winds?'

'I'm not sure. All I know is I heard Terrel speak, and he told me what I must say to you.'

'And what's that?' Zahir asked, deciding to humour his visitor one last time.

Mlicki told him.

When he finished, Zahir was too stunned to do anything except ask to be left alone to think. The messenger had gone – albeit reluctantly – but solitary contemplation had brought Zahir no comfort. Part of him had wanted to dismiss the whole thing as a ludicrous fantasy, the product of delusions, but there were too many aspects of the tale that he couldn't explain away. In the end he had tried to sleep, hoping that rest would clear his mind, and to his surprise he had not lain awake for long.

Towards dawn he had dreamt about a hubara. It wore a shaman's headdress and spoke to him in Vilheyuna's voice, telling him that truth came with the White Moon and that the way of the shamen was not always easy to follow. The dream ended with another oblique piece of advice, which held echoes of an earlier conversation.

'You defeated one set of fears,' the shaman told him, 'with Terrel's help. He's asking now that you do the same for him. Accept his fears, and you can conquer them – together.'

At that point Zahir had woken to find a hubara – a real one – inside his tent, staring at him from no more than two paces away. What he'd thought was just a desert dream had become reality.

He had almost expected the bird to speak, but it did not. Instead, as he watched, it lowered its ugly head and scratched at the ground with its curved beak. When Zahir got up to see what it was doing, he saw that it had outlined two overlapping symbols in the dry earth. Even though the representations were crude, he recognized them easily. They were the river in the sky and the double-headed man.

Returning to the present, Zahir became aware of the restlessness created by his prolonged silence, but he still couldn't bring himself to speak. He had spent the rest of the night and the early part of that morning wondering about what he should do. Terrel had been right about the rain at Seckar's monument. Zahir knew that if he had not accepted the healer's advice, he would not be alive now. But did *this* advice really come from Terrel? Was he really the double-headed man, the mythical character who brought wisdom from his people's ancestors? 'I talk to ghosts.' Terrel had said that on Makranash, before . . . And he had not been killed when he should have been. Surely that meant something. And if the message – which certainly *sounded* like Terrel – had not come from him, then how could Mlicki have known about the birds, and about the healer's fall from the cliff?

Zahir cleared his throat, looking round at the expectant crowd.

'The only way to overcome your fears,' he stated clearly, 'is to confront them. There are many things to be afraid of in Misrah, but I believe we have the means to change that.'

He paused, noting the bewilderment and consternation on the faces that surrounded him. He had confounded their expectations once again – and that thought gave him a small jolt of pleasure. No one would forget this day in a hurry, whatever happened from now on.

'All we need is the courage to begin,' he declared. 'And the winds will look upon our efforts kindly.'

He glanced up, and saw a hubara perched atop a nearby building. The sight gave him the impetus to confront the first of his own fears – the terror of being the object of mockery and scorn. There was no way he could avoid that – and possibly even worse – if he went ahead. This was the moment of truth.

'I am the King of the Desert!' he cried. 'And for this day, my word is law.'

This traditional announcement was greeted with obvious relief by the majority of his audience. Here, at last, was something they understood. Everyone knew that the king's decrees would follow – a chance for some fun and laughter now that the serious business was over and done with. Zahir knew what they were thinking – and found himself able to smile. If you discounted Mlicki, and presumably Kala too, no one – not even the Mehtar – knew what he was about to say.

'These are my decrees!' he called, raising his voice so that no one could be in any doubt about what he was saying. 'First, we must ensure that the Road of Hope is reopened, so that anyone who wants to can travel freely and in safety.'

The onlookers muttered at this. They were no longer smiling.

'Second,' he went on quickly, counting the points off on his fingers. 'All the wars between the tribes of Misrah must end immediately.'

The resulting uproar was no more than he had expected. The sense of outrage was palpable. The Mehtar, who was standing near the podium, was trying to say something, but Zahir couldn't hear him over all the noise and was quite prepared to ignore him anyway. He held up his hands, asking for quiet, but it was some time before he was able to make himself heard.

'I don't say this lightly. I know many of you have genuine grievances against other tribes, but killing never solved such problems. It only makes them worse.'

'Zahir, this is hardly the time—' the Mehtar began.

'Are you mad, boy?' Ghasri roared. The leader of the Mgarr was almost apoplectic with rage. 'You can't—'

'I am the King of the Desert!' Zahir shouted, over-riding his accuser. 'Hear me out! Elders from neutral tribes can be appointed as arbitrators, to settle disputes peacefully. With justice, not swords.'

'You can't tell us who we can or cannot fight!' Ghasri yelled. 'You're making a mockery of this festival, and of the race itself!'

'No!' Zahir replied, with equal force. 'It's what the race has *become* that's a mockery, with all its jokes and pointless boasting. They only last for a day, and they mean nothing. Why can't we try to do some lasting good instead? That's how it used to be. This festival, this place, draws us together. It's not just the ukasa that allows us to meet here in peace. If we can do that here and now, then why not for the rest of the year, and in all of Misrah? The Race of Truth used to mean something. It can again. I am only king for one day, but what we decide during this one day can make a difference – a *real* difference.' As he spoke, he was aware of the irony of his repeating Terrel's argument – the same argument he himself had rejected out of hand.

'This is outrageous!' a voice shouted.

'An abuse of trust,' someone added.

The noise level rose to a tumult as a thousand separate arguments filled the air. Many people obviously could not believe what was happening, while others were incoherent with anger. But a few were apparently taking Zahir's side. He was helpless against the barrage of noise, and waited for one of his opponents to suggest removing him from the platform by force. The fact that no one did was evidence of the status of the King of the Desert. Zahir was grateful for that, because he was uncomfortably aware that his friends and the few Seyhim guards nearby would not be enough to protect him if the mob turned ugly. Even so, he had not finished yet. There could be no turning back now.

'Third!' he cried, when there was a brief lull in the din.

'There's more?' someone cried incredulously.

'There's more,' Zahir confirmed. He was certain now that at least some of the onlookers wanted to hear what he had to say. The prospect of peace was attractive to many, however it might be achieved. 'All tribal boundaries must return to the way they were when the Kullana River dried up. And . . .' He paused until he could make himself heard again. 'And all the women and children who have been taken in raids must be allowed to return to their own tribes.'

'Mehtar!' Ghasri demanded furiously. 'Put a stop to this now!'

'Let me finish,' Zahir insisted. 'Then let everyone decide.'

For a few moments the old man seemed unsure, but then he climbed part of the way up the stairs to the platform, stopping short of the king's 'throne'. He held up his hands in the way Zahir had done earlier, and the noise gradually subsided.

'I think we should hear the rest of what the king has to say,' he declared, to the consternation of many and the approval of some. 'Then we may judge if his decrees are honourable.'

'Thank you,' Zahir said softly, as a grudging silence fell.

'I hope you know what you're doing,' the Mehtar told him.

So do I, Zahir thought, then steeled himself for the final confrontation.

'My fourth and final decree is the most important of

all. From this day forth, no man may enter the Binhemma-Ghar. The Race of Truth must end!'

The uproar that had greeted his earlier pronouncements was nothing compared to the frenzy that erupted now. A storm of noise threatened to shake Qomish from its foundations. His other decrees had all found some supporters among his audience – though they had been in the minority – but even the most broad-minded of the spectators found this unacceptable. The rage Zahir saw on some faces was horrifying – and yet he could understand the reaction. How could he use the spurious authority of one day's rule, which had been gained by winning a race of legendary standing, to attempt to destroy that same competition for ever?

'This is too much!' the Mehtar cried, shaking his head.

'I do not ask for these things lightly!' Zahir shouted. 'But if we can accept them, the winds have promised us much in return.'

He waited while his words were passed on by those few who had heard them to those further away, watching as the ripples of intrigue spread until the whole of the Great Circle had grown quiet again.

I've done my bit, Terrel, Zahir thought nervously. Now it's your turn.

'If all the tribes will swear an oath to uphold these decrees,' he called, 'then the winds have promised to end the plague. And they will restore the Kullana River to its original course!'

CHAPTER FORTY-SEVEN

'How can you know of these promises?'

'Are you claiming to have spoken to the winds?'

Even though the debate was now being conducted in a more civilized fashion, the questions were coming thick and fast, and Zahir wished that Terrel was able to answer them with him. He glanced down at the healer, who still lay, unmoving, on his pallet.

After the king's final claim, the gathering had threatened to degenerate into chaos. Only the intervention of the Mehtar, and the persuasive presence of the Seyhim guards, had gradually brought the proceedings under control. Qomish's ruler had argued that if they were to respond to the champion's decrees in a sensible manner, then the best way was for each tribe to speak through a chosen representative. This suggestion had eventually been accepted, and the crowd grew quieter again as the elders gathered around the podium. Everyone wanted to hear what Zahir had to say.

'I cannot claim to have spoken to the winds directly,' the nomad replied, 'but they are speaking *through* me.' He was all too aware that he was treading on dangerous ground. The line between reverence and blasphemy had become very thin – and many of his inquisitors obviously thought he'd already crossed it. But he had no choice now. He had to go on. 'Our shaman, who should be dead but who lies here sleeping, was given the information by the winds when he was at Makranash.' By referring to Terrel as a shaman rather than as a healer, Zahir hoped to make his demands more acceptable, but because his team-mate's climb to the prophet's lair had been an act of sacrilege in itself, he wasn't sure whether drawing attention to that part of his story was such a good idea. On the other hand, he had to justify his claim somehow.

'So all this has come from the *foreigner*?' Ghasri said, stressing the word to emphasize his disgust.

'He's one of us, no matter where he was born,' Zahir replied. 'And his talents speak for themselves.'

'They seem to be speaking for the winds,' someone commented, provoking some sarcastic laughter.

'Is it so surprising that the winds should want a return to justice in Misrah?' Zahir asked, deciding to go on the offensive. 'We all know times have been hard recently, but for some of us to benefit at the expense of others' suffering is against all the laws of humanity and common sense. It insults the winds. Is war a good thing? Is the enslavement of women and children just? Have we abandoned the customs of hospitality and fairness when it comes to the unclean? We must remedy these things, or Misrah is doomed.'

'That's all very well,' Raheb stated, 'but you said the most important of your decrees was the one stopping the Race of Truth.' The elder had taken Algardi's place as the Toma's spokesman, because Zahir's father had not felt able to interrogate his own son. 'Would you care to explain that? Why destroy a tradition that has served us so well for so long? What do you hope to achieve?'

'Apart from ensuring your place in history as the last ever King of the Desert?' another elder added cynically.

Zahir took a deep breath before answering. He knew that what little support he'd won with his earlier decrees might well have been lost by his apparent attack on the race. Many people could see the advantages of peace, of the restoration of lost lands and people, and some even had sympathy for the refugees who travelled the Road of Hope, but no one saw any point in ending the annual contest. Even Zahir's own team-mates had been visibly shocked by the idea. If he was honest, Zahir wasn't even sure of the reasons himself. All he could do was try to explain what little he had gathered from Terrel's message.

'The winds chose Makranash as their home in this world because it's a place of purity, remote from the distractions and troubles of this land.'

'Remote from all of us, you mean?'

'If you like,' Zahir conceded. 'For a long time all was well. Until the race began. At first, our invasion of the holy place was no more than a slight irritation to the winds, but each year they grew more and more vexed. Over the centuries this grew to anger and resentment, until finally they felt the need to take their revenge. That's why they sent the plague, why we lost the river of life. For years now, many springs and oases have been dying.

The winds have been trying to drive us away, so that they could be left in peace.'

'This is utter rubbish!' someone cried, and several people nodded their agreement.

'Can you deny that things have grown progressively worse over the last few years?' Zahir countered. 'Even Qomish is less green than it was.'

'These things go in cycles. The life will come back.'

'Can you be sure of that? The Kullana hasn't come back. Without the help of the winds, it never will.'

'That's different.'

'Why? It's a symptom of the same malaise.'

'But you say the winds promise our salvation if we abide by your decrees?' Mizhieb queried. As leader of the Rokku tribe, he had a particular interest in the restoration of the river.

'Yes.'

'Are you saying we can *bargain* with the winds?' Ghasri asked incredulously.

'No. There can be no haggling. Their terms are set. We either accept them or we don't.'

'The boy's mad,' Ghasri growled. 'Let's end this farce now.'

'No. Zahir acted honourably – both during the race, and on his return. He deserves better than to be dismissed this way.' The latest speaker was Fgura's father, his face painted white in mourning for his son, and even Ghasri fell silent in deference to his grief. The elder turned back to the champion. 'Can you offer us proof that what you say is true? How do we know the plague won't end of its own accord, whether we do as you suggest or not?'

'I have no proof,' Zahir admitted. 'Only my faith in the vision I was shown.'

'A vision?' Ghasri scoffed. 'This would be laughable if it weren't so callous. How can you offer hope when there is none? We know where the plague comes from, and we know that the river now falls into a great canyon. Are we to—'

'The winds do not honour a liar,' a new voice cut in. The audience murmured their surprise and disapproval at this intervention, because it came from a man who wore an orange badge on his shoulder, marking him as one of the Shiban. After their disgrace had become public knowledge, few people thought the tribe would dare show their faces in the arena, let alone speak in the debate.

'My name is Takarna,' the man said. 'Now that Kohtala has been cast out of our clan, and Sansunak has fallen, I speak for the Shiban. Despite what you have heard today, some of our tribe are honourable men. We did not agree with the way our chieftain or his shaman were leading us, and we were deceived by them during the race. Now that they have been punished, we will do all we can to restore the dignity of our people.' Having got that off his chest, he returned to his original point. 'That the winds spared Zahir and his team, when Kohtala was attacked, seems to me to be proof of the king's worth. We should at least grant him the courtesy of a fair hearing.'

Zahir was grateful for the support, though he wished it had come from a different source.

'The fact remains that it is intolerable for Zahir to presume to speak for the winds in this manner,' another elder said. 'How can we accept such sacrilege?'

'Exactly!' Ghasri exclaimed. 'He offers us no proof, other than the word of a foreigner who cannot speak for himself, and he promises us the impossible. The King of the Desert was never meant to get involved in such things. His authority, such as it is, lasts only one day. What he's proposing will have effects far beyond that.'

'Isn't that the point?' the Mehtar enquired mildly.

'The *point* is, we're being asked to yield our freedom, our lands and possessions, in return for nothing.' Ghasri was determined to make his position clear.

'Can it be that you are so opposed to this because the Mgarr have stolen more in the last two years than any other tribe?' another spokesman asked.

Ghasri glared at his accuser with contempt.

'If it weren't for the ukasa, you would die for those words.'

'Some have more to lose and some more to gain from my proposals,' Zahir said. 'But that should not sway our judgement.'

'Easy for you to say. The Toma have no land.'

'And we would *all* lose the Race of Truth,' another elder pointed out.

'And yet if there is even a chance of the Kullana being restored—' Mizhieb began.

'You're deluding yourself!' Ghasri snapped. 'These promises mean nothing.'

'Then make your oaths conditional,' Zahir declared, moved by a sudden inspiration. 'Swear to do as I ask, but only if the promises are met.'

This suggestion met with a thoughtful silence, each man calculating his options. Zahir knew that most of them would never have agreed to his decrees without this offer. Now the decision hung in the balance.

'You have nothing to lose by agreeing to such an oath,' he added. 'And if it helps to convince you, I'm prepared to be locked in the cages here until the winds prove me right.' As soon as the words were out he gulped, half wishing he could take them back. He was committed now.

The elders remained silent, glancing at one another, until eventually, Ghasri laughed.

'Under those conditions I will take such an oath,' he stated. 'If only to see this charlatan rot in his prison.'

After Zahir's fiercest opponent had agreed to the terms, there was never any doubt that the rest would follow.

You have to do something now! Terrel pleaded. *To convince them.*

The elemental did not respond.

Please, the healer went on. *We've done all we can for now. You heard what happened. You must convince them that you'll keep your promises. Do you understand?*

Are you talking to another monster? Jax asked.

Shut up! Keep out of this.

I don't seem to have much choice, Jax grumbled.

Terrel had been listening to the debate in Qomish through the ears of his sleeping body, using his twin as an intermediary. As Alyssa had predicted, it had been easy to lure Jax away from Vadanis. It had only taken the pointless use of the glamour, and a false intimation of Terrel's vulnerability. But it had been much harder to confine Jax within the comatose body. The prince had naturally wanted to get up and take a look around, assuming that he'd be able to wreak havoc as he had on previous occasions. This time, however, Terrel had been ready for him. He had allowed his brother to animate those parts he himself needed – his brain and ears – and built a shield around all the rest. But maintaining that barrier was putting a huge strain on his resources, and now that he had to communicate with the Ancient once again, he could feel Jax testing his bonds, looking for a way to escape. The prince's defeated tone was a ruse, as he tried to lull Terrel into a false sense of security, but there was no time to be concerned with that now. The time had come for Terrel – and the elemental – to fulfil at least part of their side of the bargain.

They need a sign, he told the Ancient. *Zahir risked everything to do this. Now you have to help him, or the oaths won't mean a thing. They need proof – and quickly.*

It seemed that the elemental was either oblivious to his pleas, or was entirely unconcerned. It had shown no surprise at Terrel's being able to talk to a distant twin – and now, it seemed, the creature was similarly unconcerned about events in Qomish. There was no way of telling what it was thinking, and Terrel was becoming impatient.

Come on! he shouted. *We agreed on this. Give them a sign.*

You mean there's finally going to be some action? Jax asked.

Terrel ignored him.

You could at least let me open my eyes, the prince said, sounding pathetic. *That way you'd be able to see what was going on.* His reasonable words were undermined by the fact that, at the same time, he was surreptitiously testing Terrel's strength again – but to no avail. Jax was doing a good job of concealing the fury he felt at being used in this way and not being able to respond, but Terrel knew his brother well enough to know what he was feeling.

I can heal you, if you'll let me, Terrel told the Ancient, *but if you don't help us now, men will still come here every year and you'll grow ill again.* He had come to recognize the annual invasion by the Race of Truth as the cause of the creature's imbalance. Zahir had claimed that it was the winds that had been affected, but Terrel knew better. He'd just amended the story for the champion's benefit, to make it more acceptable to the people of Misrah.

Listen. They're all swearing to obey the decrees, but only if you help them in return. The healer was aware that no one had yet done anything to convince the elemental of their good intentions. That would come later. All they had for now was words. And words, as he knew only too well, could be false. The creature's response – if there ever was one – would have to be an act of faith.

You don't have to grant them everything at once, he suggested, *but you must give them* something. *Why don't you end the plague? Or make it less severe? You can leave the river until later.*

He sensed a change in the elemental's mood, and wondered what that presaged. Was it a good sign, or bad? A few moments later he had his answer. Something undefinable shifted all about him – and in the world as a whole – and a great weight was lifted from Terrel's shoulders. At the same time he felt Jax nearly slip from his grasp, but even that couldn't overcome his new feeling of optimism. It had begun!

*

In the Great Circle, Jax fought to open his eyes, and eventually succeeded.

On the pallet next to him, to the astonishment and joy of his fellow nomads, Cassar sat up. Looking around, he was obviously surprised to find himself back in Qomish and surrounded by so many people.

'Winds! I'm so thirsty,' he croaked, his voice hoarse. 'What's going on?'

CHAPTER FORTY-EIGHT

Zahir couldn't help thinking that it was too good to be true. He had hoped and believed that accepting Terrel's message had been the right thing to do, but such obviously dramatic results made him nervous. Although he was too astonished to proclaim Cassar's sudden recovery from the plague, others were not so reticent.

A clearly bewildered Cassar became the centre of everyone's attention. His fellow nomads were ecstatic, not just because one of Zahir's predictions had come true, but because their friend and colleague was well again. Their cries of joyful disbelief were echoed by many around them, and the news spread rapidly through the crowd.

Not everyone shared the Toma's delight. Some people were quick to decry the whole episode as a sham.

'This is a trick,' Ghasri declared. 'He was never ill!'

Zahir knew the allegation was untrue, but he couldn't blame his adversary for thinking that way. Cassar's revival was too convenient, too obvious. Several people took up the Mgarr's cry, and the newly-woken nomad became the eye of a fresh storm of protest and accusation. The furious argument threatened to get out of hand, and even the Mehtar and his guards were unable to restore order. Watching the commotion, Zahir felt equally helpless, but then he caught a glimpse of his father's stern face amid the throng, and wondered what Algardi would have done in this situation. *Stay calm.* That would have been his father's first piece of advice, and imagining him saying those words helped Zahir to think clearly again. Once he'd regained his own wits, he knew he had no choice but to take advantage of what had happened. No matter how suspicious the timing of Cassar's recovery might seem, he *had* been ill. And now he wasn't.

'The winds have spoken!' Zahir cried, spreading his arms wide to increase the impact of his announcement. 'They have heard our oaths, and honoured the first of our promises.'

'This deception is beneath contempt!' Ghasri yelled back. 'You're not fooling anyone.'

'Then check on other victims of the plague,' the king replied, his confidence growing, 'and you'll see I'm right.'

Others had already had the same idea, and it was not long before the first reports came back.

'It's true!' a man called from the outer edge of the terraces. 'My brother was close to death. Now he's taking water, and says he feels fine. It's a miracle!'

No sooner had the gathering absorbed this news, and the arguments began to turn in Zahir's favour, than another cry went up from the opposite side of the arena.

'Our two girls are no longer ill.'

'The plague is ending,' one of the Seyhim declared. 'My daughter—' The rest of his words were lost as he hurried away, disappearing into the crowd.

Zahir was exultant. Deep down he had always believed that Terrel would be able to deliver on his promises – otherwise he would never have embarked on this perilous endeavour – but he hadn't expected anything so spectacular, or for it to happen so soon. There had only been time for a few of the tribal representatives to swear the oath after Ghasri's patently insincere recitation, but the champion was now in no doubt that the others would all follow suit. It was left to the leader of the Mgarr to snuff out his jubilation and bring him back to the volatile reality of the situation.

'This is not the winds' doing,' Ghasri asserted, taking up a new argument now that the proof he'd demanded had been supplied. 'This is sorcery. Zahir's shaman has not recovered,' he added, pointing to Terrel's body.

'He never had the plague,' Zahir protested, glancing at the healer and wondering whether that slight smile had always been on his face.

'No. But he may have caused it!' the Mgarr retorted.

This wild accusation left Zahir speechless.

'It's nothing more than an elaborate hoax,' Ghasri claimed, 'set up to make us think—'

'To what end?' Zahir interrupted. 'What would I possibly gain by such a deception?'

'Perhaps *you're* the one who's being deceived. You're under his influence.'

'This is absurd,' Zahir replied, but he could sense the mood of the crowd wavering again.

'These oaths have been taken under false pretences!' Ghasri roared. 'They are not valid.'

At this point the Mehtar tried to intervene, but could not make himself heard. Ghasri's righteous anger overrode all about him.

'The king is false. I take back my oath.'

Zahir had hoped that the apparent ending of the plague would have brought at least some of the elders – and the crowd – to his defence, and indeed there were some who seemed to be arguing in his favour. However, none of them could match his opponent's fervour, and if Ghasri was allowed to renege on his oath, then there was nothing to stop the others from doing so too. It seemed that all Zahir's efforts – as well as Terrel's – were being undone, in spite of the wholly spurious nature of their adversary's arguments. He braced himself, determined to avert disaster.

'It is Ghasri who dishonours this meeting with his lies and self-serving deceit!' he cried. 'I have kept the first of my promises. The plague is gone! The rest will follow. Your oaths are binding,' he went on, looking at the elders. 'To take them back will bring shame to us all and anger the winds.'

There were some shouts of support from the crowd, but there were many who were still to be won over.

'We've seen through you, boy,' Ghasri responded. 'What do you really want?'

'I want peace and prosperity for all Misrah, but that will only come if—'

'So you're still willing to sit in a cage until the Kullana returns?'

'Yes.'

'Then come down off your throne,' Ghasri said contemptuously, 'and we'll put you there.'

Zahir hesitated for only a moment, then nodded and began to make his way down from the podium.

Terrel was close to despair. It had all been going so well – better than he could have dared hope – until this latest setback. He couldn't believe that Ghasri had been able to twist the facts in such a malicious way, or that anyone had taken any notice of him. Now it seemed that they had been forced back to the beginning again, and he had to try to persuade the elemental to restore the river before the oaths had been formally completed. Even if he succeeded, it would be several days before the news reached Qomish, and with Zahir stuck in one of the cages, there was no telling what might happen in the meantime. Terrel could not help but feel that he'd let his friend down, even though what had happened had not been his fault.

He consoled himself with the thought that at least the plague was at an end now. He had achieved one of his objectives, and for the moment, at least, the Floating Islands were safe. But he was uncomfortably aware that the Ancient could restore the fearful illness at any time. It could even make it much, much worse.

Don't worry. You did the right thing, he assured the elemental. *This will all work out.*

In spite of his brave words, he knew the creature could sense his doubts and fears. He could only hope it would also see the truth behind them, and recognize the necessity of fulfilling its other promise. It was obvious now that the fate of the Kullana River would decide the fate of his quest – and the future of all the people of Misrah.

The Ancient remained ominously quiet, watching and waiting as if nothing important was happening. And the more Terrel tried to persuade it to his point of view, the harder it became to maintain the barriers that kept Jax imprisoned. Then Terrel realized that the prince had also been silent for some time, and a spasm of terror ran through him as he wondered just what his twin brother might be up to.

The crowd's attention had switched from the king's podium to the cage where Zahir was now installed, and so no one had realized what Mlicki was intending to do until it was too late. He scrambled over the jagged surface of the shaman's stone until he reached the top. Once there he stood with his arms spread wide, then threw his head back and screamed. His hair was standing on end, and his rose-pink eye seemed to glow with the brilliance of a jewel within its pale setting.

After all the extraordinary events of that day, the boy's actions still had the power to shock the gathering. It was forbidden to touch the shaman's stone, or even to approach it too closely. To clamber over its sacred surface was an appalling crime, a blatant defiance of the most revered laws and customs of Qomish. No one could quite believe what was happening, least of all Zahir, who had no idea what Mlicki was trying to achieve. The last thing they needed now was another distraction, another reason for Ghasri and his allies to deride the conduct of the Toma.

'He's one of them, one of Zahir's clan!' someone cried, breaking the whispering spell of shock that had fallen over the arena. Shouts of protest rose from all around the Great Circle.

But none of this had any effect upon Mlicki, who remained where he was, oblivious to the outrage he was causing. He was still staring at the sky, where the full White Moon floated as serene and remote as ever, a pale disc in the azure heavens. Although he did not utter a single word, or move his outstretched arms, his whole body trembled, as if he were in the grip of some great secret he was powerless to contain.

'More sorcery?' Ghasri shouted, and his angry cry was taken up by several other onlookers.

Hurried discussions were taking place about how to remove the miscreant from the stone without anyone else having to trespass upon its surface, when all thoughts of such action were swept aside in the most extraordinary manner. White flames sprang from the rock itself, making its facets glitter and its marbled streaks flash like green lightning. The unnatural fire surrounded Mlicki, seeming to cause him untold agony, but still he did not move. For once, everyone could see that Ghasri had got it right. This was sorcery indeed.

'Mlicki! What are you doing?' Medrano had pushed through to the front of the crowd surrounding the shaman's stone. 'Get—'

He was interrupted by a small figure that suddenly burst out of the throng behind him and tried to hurl herself at the stone. It was only Medrano's reflexive grab at her arm that halted Kalkara's progress, but as it was they both fell to the ground. She struggled, but the artist held on tightly.

'You can't go up there,' he gasped, half winded by the fall.

Kala did not reply, of course, but the terror in her bright blue eyes was eloquent enough.

'You'll only make matters worse,' he told her, pulling her towards him and edging them both away from the burning rock. Kalkara stopped struggling, but turned back to stare through the flames at her brother.

The fire seemed to grow brighter then, but only because the day had grown dark. The reason for this soon became apparent to everyone, and the entire gathering came close to panic. Qomish had been surrounded by a ring of massive clouds rising up from the land at colossal speed, each one bulging and swirling as though powered by a tornado within its grim bulk. The clouds were a mixture of grey and brown, promising rain as well as sandstorms, and their presence was enough to induce both awe and fear in everyone who saw them.

'This is what the winds *really* think of this sorcery!' Ghasri bellowed above the rising shriek of the wind, as he pointed to the sky. 'Now we shall all pay the true price of Zahir's treachery!'

Jax? Jax! Stop this! As soon as he'd realized what was happening. Terrel had known who was responsible. He had forgotten that Mlicki was susceptible to the enchanter, and even though the prince was still being forced to lie on his pallet, he had been able to reach out and make another create his mischief for him.

Why should I? Jax replied, sounding pleased with himself. *This is fun!*

Hasn't it ever occurred to you to use your talents for good instead of evil?

Mlicki's doing this, not me, Jax said innocently.

Don't lie to me. He would never—

Then don't lecture me, the prince snapped back. *You think you know everything, don't you? This will teach you to try and trap me. Let's see how all these people like their winds now. And the thunder and lightning. And the rain. I don't think your friend's going to like* that much.

For a moment Terrel didn't know what he meant. Then, as it became clear who his 'friend' was, he was horrified. The elemental was indeed becoming fretful, watching the coming storm as if it were a concentration of all the evils in the world. Trying to reassure it was pointless; Terrel wasn't even able to reassure himself. All he could do was watch the disaster unfold through Jax's gloating eyes.

The storm broke over Qomish with the fury of a hurricane. It came upon them so suddenly that few people had time to take shelter. Most simply flung themselves to the ground, where the wind tore at their clothes and pelted them with sand, pebbles and – incredibly – pellets of frozen water. Many of them had never seen hail before, and took the icy stones for another sign of sorcery. Lightning flashed, and thunder crashed and echoed above the city – while Mlicki screamed again in pain or triumph.

In the pandemonium, no one saw the large bird labouring through the flying debris as it headed towards the shaman's stone.

CHAPTER FORTY-NINE

The hubara had been buffeted by gale-force winds and battered by the flurries of hail. At times it had barely been able to stay airborne and, at the last, it was assaulted by the white flames – which did not scorch its feathers but caused it enormous pain nonetheless. And yet it never once faltered in its determination.

Alighting on the shaman's stone, close to where Mlicki stood, the bird was engulfed by a fresh spurt of fire, but it held firm. Alone among the cowering multitude, Kalkara looked up to see the hubara shuffle forward, moving clumsily now that it was on the ground. She watched as it stretched out its ugly wrinkled neck and pecked savagely at her brother's calf. The attack did not dismay her. Kalkara knew what the bird was doing.

The sudden stab of pain in his leg startled Mlicki from his intoxicating dream. His eyes came into focus, and he looked around at the flames, the people and the storm. It was only when the hubara's beak caught him again, less viciously this time, that he glanced down and realized where he was. He could remember nothing since the time when he'd been standing in the crowd, watching as Zahir was locked in the cage. He had no idea how he had come to be on the shaman's stone, or what was happening now. Some power beyond his comprehension had been released – and the idea that he might be responsible for it was horrifying. The fact that he had broken the taboo about touching the sacred rock was in itself appalling, but there was nothing he could do about that now. There was no way he could escape. The white fire imprisoned him just as surely as the cage held Zahir.

Listen to me. You have to find your way back to the true path.

The voice that sounded in his head was familiar and he looked down at the bird again, making the connection at last.

Vilheyuna?

The way of the shamen is not always easy to follow, but you have the strength and the will to manage it. This is a false road, forced on you by another. Turn back and end this storm.

I can hear you! Mlicki exclaimed. He hadn't been able to communicate with the hubara earlier, and had had to take Kala's vision as proof that it was Vilheyuna.

Listen to me, the shaman repeated. *This is wrong. Turn back.*

There was another voice in Mlicki's head now, fainter and further away, but it had a strangely compelling tone. He tried to hear what it was saying, but it faded too quickly.

Ignore him, Vilheyuna said urgently. *He has no power*

over you now that I'm here. You're a shaman, Mlicki. Prove to him what that means. Truth comes with the White Moon.

The boy looked up, and glimpsed the pale disc through the whirling sand.

There is power here, Vilheyuna added. *That's why you can hear me. Use it for truth, not for this mockery.*

Once again Mlicki felt the tug of another purpose — but he set it aside.

What should I do?

The hubara was trembling now, its beady eyes almost closed, and when Vilheyuna spoke again his voice was thick with pain and a stifling weariness.

I can't . . . much longer. Take them . . . beyond the winds. Take . . . them . . . all.

Then the bird collapsed, and Mlicki felt a sudden surge of fear. He wanted to go to the shaman's aid, but he was still unable to move more than a tiny amount. And he still didn't know what he was supposed to do.

Who should I take beyond the winds? he queried. *What am I supposed to show them?*

There was no answer, and he realized that he would get no more help. It was up to him now. Take them all? he wondered, looking round at the gathering. It was a daunting prospect, but his master had granted him the chance to do something worthwhile, and he was not about to let Vilheyuna down.

The storm raged on, but Mlicki saw it now for the unnatural phenomena it was. The unknown voice had created it through him, and he could stop it if he tried hard enough. The shaman had broken the connection between Mlicki and whoever had been controlling his actions. That realization was enough to start the process. He sensed a slight lessening in the hurricane's fury, and sought to hasten its decline. Gradually, the true nature of the winds, of the air and sand, began to re-establish itself. The storm soon died away, leaving Qomish covered in silt and melting hail but otherwise undamaged. In the Great Circle, people got to their feet, not quite believing that the tempest was over – and saw that the flames were still burning on the shaman's stone, with the disfigured boy in their midst. However, there was something different about him now. Only Kalkara knew what it was.

Our shaman lives in spirit, Mlicki thought. Through me. Those were the words he had used to the Shiban raiding party months earlier, when he had brought the darkness down upon them all. He didn't have Vilheyuna's headdress now, but he had something more potent. He had the shaman's blessing.

'My eye sees beyond the winds!' he cried. 'I can see your past and your future.'

Many of the faces in the crowd were hostile, but no one dared speak out against him. Closing his good eye, Mlicki looked up at the White Moon and asked for her help.

'Darkness comes,' he intoned.

And the noonday sky went black.

Afterwards, no two people could agree on the vision that had enveloped them. Once the darkness relented, they had each been swept back to some incident in their past, a significant moment or a trivial one. For every man and woman, it was as if they were experiencing those moments again in every detail. Then a series of brief images, too fleeting for them to recognize, brought them to the present, spiralling inward until they were all back in the Great Circle, where the tribes' elders were taking the oath that Zahir had demanded. The curious thing was that in *this* arena there was no boy on the shaman's stone, no flames, and Zahir was still on the king's podium. When all were committed to the decrees, the vision swirled out again, separating into a thousand different strands. Some saw the Kullana flowing again, the music of life chiming out in all the old familiar places. Others visited dying springs to find that they were running strongly again. For the citizens of Qomish, their oasis became verdant again, their fields more fruitful than ever. Many nomads saw parts of the desert blooming where before there had been only arid desolation. A few saw the Road of Hope, paved again and open to all, but strangely it was empty. Almost everybody witnessed joyful scenes of shamen dancing, marriage ceremonies being celebrated, and children being born. And they heard a thousand stories being told.

Just as everyone had seen this new world it was swept away, and they were back in the Great Circle once more. This time the scene was one of chaos and fear. Zahir lay unmoving on the floor of his cage, and there was fighting in several parts of the amphitheatre. Furious arguments raged back and forth, but it was clear that Ghasri and his allies had won the day. The king's decrees had been refused.

Once more the vision splintered into individual paths. But this time they led into horror, into a world where violence and terror were commonplace. Scenes of carnage, of blood soaking into the sand, were mixed with images of vast clouds of insects ravaging land already parched from a lack of water. The bed of the Kullana was now a desiccated gully, its music forgotten. Qomish was reduced to ruins, with only a few broken hovels left amid the devastation, its trees now blackened stumps and its fields no more than bowls of wind-blown dust. Other oases had simply vanished, reclaimed by the desert's shifting sands. And worst of all, blackened corpses lay everywhere, victims of hideous pestilence and disease, left to rot where they fell, their flesh too vile even for the hubaras.

The sky turned blue again, the sun blazing down on the stupefied throng. Only its pale cousin, the White Moon, remained serene, watching over her domain.

The flames had gone, their purpose fulfilled, and Mlicki was released at last. He had caught glimpses of what the others had seen, but hadn't been able to make sense of any of it. It was too complex, too *big*, for him to comprehend. He had no idea whether he'd obeyed Vilheyuna's command, but he knew there was nothing more he could do. Stooping, he picked up the lifeless bird and stumbled down from the rock, then fell to the ground. A moment later Kala was at his side, holding him, tears shining in her eyes. Medrano was there too, but Mlicki was hardly aware of the artist's presence. As he closed his eyes and sank into a darkness all of his own, he heard a voice begin to speak.

'Truth comes with the White Moon!' Zahir shouted, remembering the advice from his own dream. 'You've all seen beyond the winds now. What else do you need? You must agree to the terms of the decrees. You know now what good will come of that. But if you rebuff the winds, our plight will be worse than ever. Even Qomish will die.

And the new plague will make the one that's just ended seem like nothing!'

'This is an illusion, another trick,' Ghasri replied. 'The boy is one of them.'

'Do you doubt the shaman's stone?' the Mehtar asked.

'Its power has been corrupted,' Ghasri claimed, though he was obviously taken aback by the elder's intervention.

'Impossible!' the Mehtar declared. 'The boy would have died if what he showed us was not true.'

'Besides,' Medrano put in, 'what does Mlicki have to gain from such a delusion?'

'The decrees—' Ghasri began.

'The decrees do not benefit him or any of the Toma,' Zahir cut in. 'We have no land. We have lost no people or property. *Our* motives are not in question.'

'And we've already seen how the king made good on his promise to rid us of the plague,' Mizhieb said. 'I believe we have been shown the choice of our futures, and that there is only one way forward. I will swear the oath.'

Some of the onlookers shouted their agreement. Others were still dubious.

'You're deluded,' Ghasri told him. 'The river will never come back.'

'It won't if you don't join us,' Mizhieb replied. 'We must *all* swear the oath.'

'No! The Mgarr will never be dictated to by lesser tribes. We choose our own path.'

'Even if that path leads to the destruction of all Misrah?' the Mehtar asked.

The tide was turning against Ghasri, and he knew it. Even some of his own tribesmen no longer seemed happy with their leader's stance.

'If the Kullana does not return, then no one will hold you to your oath,' Zahir pointed out. 'If you're so sure it will never come back, you have nothing to lose.'

For the first time, Ghasri was at a loss for words, but he was saved from having to reply by a sudden commotion near the arena's main entrance. A group of men, armed with swords and short hunting bows, were forcing a path through the crowd, yelling at the onlookers to get out of the way. This open display of weapons was contrary to the laws of Qomish, and a breach of the ukasa, but the newcomers were clearly beyond caring about such matters. The group was led by Kohtala, his face and hands still pocked and scarred from insect bites, and by Sansunak, his shaman's headdress swirling around his snarling face. As the throng fell back before them, Kohtala saw that the king's podium was empty and that Zahir was in one of the cages.

'So, you've come to your senses at last!' he roared. 'I am the true King of the Desert!'

In the chaos that followed, no one noticed that the pallet next to Cassar's was empty now.

CHAPTER FIFTY

Terrel cursed himself for a fool. In ending the plague he had released Sansunak from his coma, thus allowing the shaman to return to his foul work. No doubt it had been his arcane powers that had released Kohtala and the other Shiban from their prison cells. After all, anyone who could allow men to creep undetected into Zahir's camp would surely find it easy to free himself and his friends from jail. And the timing of the Shiban's intervention in the Great Circle could not have been worse.

Terrel had seen and heard most of what had taken place through Jax's borrowed eyes and ears, and been able to deduce the rest from the reactions of those around him. He had witnessed the twists and turns of the debate with fluctuating emotions, had been shocked by Mlicki's intervention and by the storm – even though he knew who had really been responsible – and had been awed by the subsequent visions. And then it had seemed as though everything was going to turn out as he'd hoped – in spite of the Mgarr's obstinate opposition – until Kohtala had introduced a further element of chaos and violence to the scene.

What was worse, the Ancient now seemed to be in a state of great agitation. The storm – especially the flying pellets of frozen magic – had disturbed its composure, and subsequent events had done nothing to comfort it. The fact that a hubara had been involved had deepened its animosity towards the birds, and Terrel was now genuinely concerned for Alyssa's safety. The elemental had not yet taken any action, but Terrel could sense the build-up of tension within its patterns, and knew the potential devastation it could unleash upon those who it believed were betraying its trust. If the Ancient was pushed too far, all of Qomish could be destroyed by earthquakes and fire from beneath the earth – making the fate that had befallen Triq Dalam seem almost mild by comparison.

Terrel tried to keep the Ancient calm, attempting to explain what was going on and what the hubara had been doing, hoping all the while for a change of fortunes in the Great Circle. There didn't seem to be anything he could do about the outcome now. All he could do was wait helplessly, and pray.

Given everything that was happening, the fact that Jax had managed to slip from his control and was now free to wander inside the city seemed almost irrelevant.

Sword in hand, Kohtala limped towards the king's podium, intent on claiming his crown. He was about to mount the steps when the Mehtar moved in front of him, barring his path.

'Get out of my way,' Kohtala snarled.

'Does your banner fly at the summit of Makranash?' the Mehtar demanded.

'It would, but for the sorcery of the Toma!'

'It is *your* deeds that have dishonoured the race,' Mizhieb put in. 'Zahir has told us—'

'He's lying,' Kohtala snapped.

'That's what I've been telling them all along,' Ghasri said, seizing the opportunity to side with his natural ally. 'Zahir, the Toma, that boy – they're all charlatans. And these decrees are madness.'

'What decrees?' Kohtala asked angrily. 'I am the one—'

'That is not for you alone to decide,' the Mehtar stated firmly. 'By bringing weapons here, you sully your own standing even more. Stand back and we will discuss—'

'The time for talking is over,' the warlord cut in. 'I am the rightful King of the Desert. Out of my way.'

But the Mehtar did not move. He believed that the universal reverence for both his position and the ukasa would prevent violence, though there were many among the onlookers who could have told him that he was foolish to cling to such a belief. Kohtala was not behaving rationally. Imagined wrongs burned in the mad eyes of the Shiban leader. Several guards edged nearer, but none of them dared make any sudden move, and they weren't close enough to protect their commander.

'Can't we—' Mizhieb began, but his plea was cut off by a roar from Kohtala.

The Shiban's sword was raised and swung down in a deadly arc in the next instant. The only reaction came from one of the elders who had been standing beside the

Mehtar. Algardi dived across, shoving Qomish's ruler aside just as the Shiban's blade sliced through the air. The blow missed its intended target, but caught Algardi at the junction of neck and shoulder, sinking deep into his flesh.

'No!' Zahir screamed, shaking the bars of his cage in a rage of pain and frustration.

A fountain of blood flew into the air as the two old men crashed to the ground in a tangled heap. Kohtala ignored them and tried to climb the steps, only to be set upon by a combined force of nomads and Seyhim guards. As he was overpowered and dragged down, he went on shouting in fury that he was their king, but no one took any notice. Then he glanced around wildly and caught sight of his shaman.

'Sansunak!' he yelled. 'Kill the impostor. Kill Zahir!'

Sansunak grabbed a bow from the nearest tribesman, and took aim at the imprisoned champion. Several people cried out in warning, but Zahir was too shocked to move, still grasping the bars and staring aghast at the spot where his father had fallen. Others moved to try to disrupt the shaman's aim, but they weren't quick enough. There was a sharp snap as he fired and the arrow sped on its way, a deadly blur in the sunlight. But, like Kohtala's blow, it too was destined never to reach its intended target. Takarna had leapt into its path, his hands held out defensively in front of him, but the shaft flew through his fingers and slammed into his chest with a sickening thud.

As he fell, the scene degenerated into pandemonium. Some people were trying to flee from the violence, while others were intent on overwhelming the invaders, and everyone seemed to be shouting at the top of their voices.

Having seen their champion fall – and having witnessed
the murder of one of their elders by their own shaman –
the Shiban warriors had no real stomach for a fight, and
they were soon disarmed and captured. Only Sansunak
evaded his pursuers – by jumping onto the shaman's
stone.

His desperate ploy worked. No one dared follow him,
and the crowd was suddenly convulsed with fear. They
had already seen what an unknown boy had been able to
do from there, and Sansunak was a fully-fledged shaman.

'Release Kohtala, or it'll be the worse for you!' he
shouted, pointing into the crowd. 'This is—'

But his demands were abruptly cut off as the power
of the sacred rock burst forth once more. This time the
flames were real. Sansunak's clothes caught alight immediately and he screamed, twisting round and beating at
the material with his hands. His ineffectual efforts became
more frantic when he realized that his feet were rooted
to the spot. The relentless flames grew fiercer and more
concentrated, scorching his skin and turning his headdress into a writhing swirl of sparks. Before long the
stench of burnt flesh made it all too obvious that the
conflagration was to be the shaman's funeral pyre. He
collapsed in a charred heap, but even then the fire raged
on, and his screams died away to nothing.

With three people dead and several more injured, it took
a considerable time to restore order to the Great Circle.
Eventually, however, this was achieved and the Mehtar,
though shaken and appalled by what had happened, was
able to quiet the crowd and speak to them calmly. As
Kohtala and the rest of the prisoners were led away, the

Mehtar told the gathering that the winds had spoken, that Zahir's claims were ratified, and that Kohtala's disgrace was confirmed. Standing there, his clothes stained with another man's blood, the ruler of Qomish was clearly moved.

'I owe my life to the sacrifice of another,' he went on. 'His tale will live on long after we have all joined him in the next world. But let us not forget that one of the Shiban also acted with courage and honour,' he added, glancing down at Takarna's body. 'Let that be a sign that all is not lost, that hope for the future can spring from even conflict and tragedy. And our greatest hope now lies in the decrees of our King of the Desert. Guard, unlock the cage and restore Zahir to his rightful place on the podium. We will all take the oath now.'

No one, not even Ghasri, made any attempt to argue with the Mehtar's decision.

'Is that it, then?' Jax asked, sounding disappointed.

'Is that *it*?' Ghadira exclaimed. 'What more do you want?'

'Oh, I don't know,' he replied casually.

Ghadira looked at him with a puzzled expression on her face. She had found him wandering aimlessly through the crowd, heading towards one of the exits. When she'd asked where he was going, he had just shrugged – and then Kohtala had arrived and they'd watched together as the final drama was played out.

'It's amazing the Mehtar wasn't killed,' Ghadira remarked. 'Did you see who saved him?'

'No. Pretty stupid thing to do, really.'

'It was a very brave thing to do,' she retorted.

'Same thing.' He turned to face her, aware of the effect of a direct gaze from Terrel's crystalline eyes. 'Well, the show's over here. What shall we do now?'

'Are you all right?' she asked. 'When did you wake up?'

'I'm fine.' He reached out with his good arm and pulled her towards him, kissing her forcefully on the lips. She was startled, and resisted at first, then relaxed and returned his ardour. When they finally drew apart, she was grinning.

'That was a surprise.'

'I'm not always feeble,' he told her, smiling.

'What now, then?'

'What do you have in mind?'

Ghadira's expression changed as she stared at him.

'You're not Terrel, are you?' she said quietly.

'Does that matter?'

'Yes,' she whispered. 'Yes, it does.'

'Why?' he asked, grabbing at her again. 'Is kissing all you want to do?' He grinned, but the expression froze on his face as he felt the tip of a knife blade touch the underside of his chin.

'I think you'd better leave,' she said softly. 'Don't you?'

'That's a shame.' He shrugged carefully, correctly judging the menace in her eyes. 'Still, it's your loss. Goodbye, my sweet.'

Terrel's eyes closed, and he slumped to the ground. Ghadira had to pull the dagger away quickly to avoid hurting him. She knelt beside him, fearing that he was dead, but he was still alive – back in the deep coma that had held him prisoner since his fall from Makranash.

CHAPTER FIFTY-ONE

Because he'd been unable to prevent Jax from wandering off in search of his own amusements, Terrel had had a limited view of later events in Qomish. It had been enough to know that Kohtala's last-ditch attempt to usurp Zahir's crown had failed and that, at long last, the oaths had all been agreed. But the jubilation he felt at the final outcome was tempered by regret at some of the things that had happened earlier. Although he wasn't aware of all the details, Zahir's survival, Sansunak's spectacularly unpleasant end, and the Mehtar's subsequent determination had all been cause for celebration – or at least for grim satisfaction. But Terrel's remote encounter with Ghadira, which had followed these momentous events, had left him with quite different feelings.

He was embarrassed by what had happened – even though he knew it had not been under his control – and wasn't sure how he'd be able to face her when he returned to Qomish as himself. He was glad that Ghadira had seen through the prince's imposture, and had not allowed things to go any further, but he dreaded having to explain what had happened. His relationship with the girl was confused enough already, and this could only make matters worse. For one thing, he knew he wouldn't be able to look at her without wondering where she concealed her knife. Her defeat of Jax had been admirable, but Terrel did not want to be the victim of a repeat performance.

He realized that he was dwelling on what was after all a relatively trivial matter when he discovered that the elemental was apparently fascinated by Jax's meeting with Ghadira. Terrel couldn't tell whether it found the experience repulsive or amusing, but it kept returning to the kiss, studying the contact in detail. The feeling of curiosity had returned, but Terrel shied away from any explanations, and sought to divert the creature's attention by going back to infinitely more important affairs.

You're safe now, he assured it. *They've all agreed to stop the race. They won't come here any more. All you have to do is bring the Kullana River back to where it was, and you'll never be disturbed again.*

Terrel was assuming that the oaths were still conditional on the return of the great river.

Will you do that? he asked.

The elemental did not respond directly, but one question dominated its thoughts. How could it be sure that the tribes would all honour their oaths? The Ancient knew – because Terrel knew – that words were sometimes unreliable. It wanted proof.

The only way I can prove it to you is to wait a year, until next summer. Then you'll know that the race isn't being run. He suggested this in the belief that it would seem as ridiculous to the creature as it did to him, but to his horror it accepted the suggestion at face value – and decided they would do just that.

No! Terrel exclaimed. *I can't wait that long.* The idea of spending a whole year away from his own body, constricted by both the mountain and the pendant, was too appalling to contemplate. And he knew that Alyssa would have to leave soon, with no guarantee that she would be able to return – which might mean he'd be stuck in Makranash for ever.

In any case, Terrel went on desperately, *you have to bring the river back* now, *not in a year's time, or everyone will assume the oaths are meaningless. Don't you see, if you wait all that time, the race* will *be run again and you'll get sick.* And everything will be lost, he added to himself. *You can't do it like that. You can't!*

The Ancient remained implacable. It wanted proof. And a year seemed a very short time to wait.

No. No, Terrel pleaded. *This is ludicrous.* After everything he – and his friends – had been through, to falter at this late stage, because of a simple misunderstanding, was unthinkable.

He was about to try again when Makranash rang, making Terrel feel as though he was inside a giant bell, and he knew that the elemental was angry. The antagonistic side of its character had come to the fore again, and he saw the unbalance – the illness – that had caused such malice in the past. He still had work to do.

Terrel, what's going on? Alyssa asked, breaking into his thoughts. She sounded as worried as he was. *What was—*

I've no time to explain now. I'll tell you later. He wanted her to pull back, not to draw attention to herself. The last thing he needed now was for the Ancient to attack *her*.

When? Alyssa persisted.

I don't know yet, he replied, then paused. *Thank you, my love. Don't worry. I think I know what to do.* He'd been about to tell her that he couldn't foresee the future when he realized that – perhaps – the desert *could*.

With some relief, he felt Alyssa withdraw. He knew that she was puzzled and hurt, and promised silently to explain everything later. But now he had to concentrate on the task in hand. The true magic of the desert dealt with time. He needed to summon that magic and show the elemental the proof it needed. But just how was he supposed to do that?

A memory came to his rescue, and he brought it to mind, recalling the exact sensations, all the feelings of the time when he'd been enveloped by the sand mist, the chilouk ta'kwei. The Ancient was instantly intrigued. It liked sand, and was comforted by the thought of being wrapped in such a dry, dusty blanket. The visions came then, but instead of being carried by them, this time Terrel directed their course.

Following Mlicki's pattern, he saw the past, with its seemingly endless procession of teams making the annual pilgrimage to the heart of the desert; then a brief glimpse of the present was followed by a new succession of images, where each year the tribes came to the borders of the Binhemma-Ghar, but did not cross over. Each time they remained on the far side, paying tribute to those who had ventured forth in earlier times, but honouring the oath

that their leaders had taken at Qomish. The Race of Truth
had run its final course. And the elemental was left in
peace.

The vision faded. Terrel waited for a reaction, and
then realized that it had already happened. The creature's
hostility had vanished. It was open to him now as it had
never been before. And he knew just what he had to do
with the gift of the Ancient's trust. He would heal the
last of the imbalance in its structure, and seal their bargain
once and for all.

Terrel had no way of knowing how long it took him to
complete his self-imposed task. All he could be sure of
was that, at the end, he was exhausted – and the crystal
city was whole and perfect once more. He wanted to sleep
– he didn't even have the strength to call out to Alyssa
– but he wasn't given the chance to rest just yet. And the
Ancient was repaying its side of the debt – and taking
Terrel along for the ride!

Swirling crystals glittered below him. Then the light
became dazzling, and he saw rainbows and heard the
rumble of distant thunder. Terrel was flying over the
great canyon that had been called the Sorcerer's Mouth.
And this time he knew it was real.

The huge ravine was full of spray, and decorated with
a single glorious rainbow. Terrel knew that for all the
disgust and fear the Ancient felt at the substance that
created this colourful wonder, it was able to look at it now
as a thing of beauty as well as an object of terror. Terrel
could also see two birds flying below him, and he felt the
Dark Moon above, half full now and waning, conceding
precedence to its opposite, the White.

And then, just as he'd known it would, Nydus creaked and groaned, drawing in its sinews and grinding rock against rock. The opposing cliffs slowly drew together, crushing anything that stood in their way to dust or vapour. At the last, the mighty waterfall that vanished into the depths was squeezed into a smaller and smaller crack until it could no longer be contained. Water spilled over to the other side. The Sorcerer's Mouth closed, and the Kullana River began to flow again.

Thank you. It seemed a wholly inadequate response, but Terrel couldn't find any better words. And the Ancient already knew how he was feeling.

Its response came in the form of an image – Terrel's pendant, with the sign of the river in the sky upon it. The emotions that accompanied this were indefinable. The closest Terrel could come were gratitude, respect and a little sadness – though he knew that only skimmed the surface of what the creature was trying to express. He took the message to be both a blessing and a farewell.

Goodbye, he said softly as the image disappeared.

Makranash exhaled, and Terrel found himself back in the prophet's lair. Alyssa was waiting at the entrance, and when she saw him, they did not need any words to express their joy. She lumbered forward, and picked up the pendant in her beak.

As they flew away together, Terrel allowed himself to look back at the mountain. His last sight of Makranash was of the Toma's banner fluttering proudly at the summit – where it would fly for the rest of time.

CHAPTER FIFTY-TWO

Terrel roused himself, and found that he was lying at the foot of Seckar's monument. The recent rains had left the stone clean and bright, and the symbol of the river in the sky looked as though it had been carved only that day. There was still some greenery there too. He glanced around, looking for Alyssa, but there was no sign of the hubara. He knew that she had to rest every so often and, if possible, scavenge for food, so he was not unduly worried by her absence. The pendant lay beside him.

For most of their flight, Terrel had been unaware of the passage of time. He had been asleep – or what passed for sleep in his present state – for much of it, and so had seen little of the desert from the air. There had been no sign of Y-Harah – though he had never expected to see any – but he had been able to observe the Valley of the Smokers from above. It had looked comparatively harmless. The smoke-mist concealed most of what lay below, and Terrel had been unable to sense the constant succession of tremors. Nevertheless, he'd been glad when they'd completed the crossing. It meant they had left the Binhemma-Ghar behind, and that Qomish was only a short distance away.

Once they were outside the hundred-mile limit, Alyssa had told him that he could now return to his own body if he wanted to – she would show him how it was done – but he had decided to stay with her until they got to Qomish. He wanted to keep her company.

Alyssa returned now, landing with the large bird's customary lack of grace and then shuffling over to where the pendant lay.

There's still water here, she remarked. *That's a good sign.*

Let's hope that's true for all the springs and oases too, he replied. *Now the river's on its way back, it should make life easier for a lot of people.* And if Zahir's decrees are obeyed, Misrah will be much safer too, he added to himself.

So you passed another test, Alyssa concluded. *All your aims have been fulfilled.*

All except one, he corrected her.

Knowing him as she did, Alyssa didn't need to ask what that was.

Things have a way of working out, she told him.

I hope so.

And if they don't, we'll just have to find a way to push them along a bit, she added. *It was the same at the end of the race. The winds didn't mind us giving them a little help then.*

Terrel took a few moments to realize what she meant.

You were responsible for the swarm?

Not me personally. Are you ready to go? She stooped to pick up the pendant.

Terrel nodded, recognizing that she wasn't going to tell him anything more.

Alyssa flew on for the rest of that day and well into the night, anxious to complete the journey. For the last few miles she was guided by the lights of the city itself. Many lamps and torches still burnt there, but in the surrounding encampment the fires had long since been banked down and it was comparatively easy for her to enter the Toma's site without causing any disturbance. Terrel's body lay, as expected, in the shaman's tent. Looking down on himself after such a long absence felt most peculiar, and when Alyssa gently laid the pendant on his chest, Terrel didn't know what to expect. Leaving his physical form had involved a violent act; rejoining it was the opposite. He felt himself seeping slowly back into the real world, finding comfort in the familiarity of his reclaimed body. It was impossible to identify the exact moment when he ceased to be a disembodied spirit and became human once more. It was a process of osmosis, a gradual re-establishing of an infinite number of connections that felt both natural and welcoming. His consciousness shifted, and the double-headed man was no more.

If his reabsorption was painless, his first real breath was not. It was a tortured, shuddering gasp that seemed to go on for ever. A reflex action made him sit up, and every muscle in his body instantly cramped, objecting to their sudden reawakening. By the time the excruciating pain had faded to a bearable level, he was aware that both Mlicki and Kalkara were staring at him from their respective beds.

I have to go now, Alyssa told him.

Terrel barely had time to say goodbye when her ring – which had been looped around one of the bird's legs – vanished, and the hubara ran out of the tent in a sudden panic and flapped away. He was sorry to see Alyssa leave, but knew that she needed to rest.

'Terrel?' Mlicki's bleary-eyed astonishment was replaced by joy. 'Are you awake?'

'I'm awake,' Terrel confirmed in a hoarse whisper, then fell back on his pallet as Kalkara collided with him, her thin arms flung about him and an ecstatic smile lighting up her usually solemn face. In spite of the dreadful tingling sensations that were plaguing every part of his body, Terrel found himself laughing at the welcome.

'I think she's glad to see you,' Mlicki commented dryly. 'Take it easy, Kala. He's only just woken up.'

A short while later, after Terrel had taken a drink and eaten his first meal in many days – finding in the process that he was ravenously hungry – his desire for news became even more pressing.

'Where's Vilheyuna?' he asked, noting the shaman's absence for the first time.

Mlicki's face fell.

'He's dead.'

The bread he was eating stuck in Terrel's throat in mid-swallow, and for a few moments he thought he was going to be sick.

'As far as I can tell,' Mlicki added, 'he died at the same time as the bird collapsed on the shaman's stone. I suppose his spirit . . .' He shrugged.

In that moment Terrel knew that Vilheyuna's death would haunt him for a very long time. It was not just the loss of Mlicki's former mentor that dismayed him, but also the implication of such a death. He knew now that sleepers *could* die. Alyssa had told him many times that she was protected – and he knew this was true – but it was clear that such protection was not infallible. He'd already known that in theory, of course. Whenever Alyssa took the form of an animal she was vulnerable, especially when close to one of the elementals. But theory was one thing; an unequivocal demonstration was quite another.

'I think, in a way, it was what he'd have wanted,' Mlicki went on. 'He helped me get back to the true path. There's no telling what damage the storm would have done if I hadn't stopped it. I still don't know what possessed me to create it in the first place. And without the visions that came afterwards, none of the rest would have happened. We all owe him a great deal.'

Terrel nodded. There was some truth in that, at least – and it *was* some consolation. Vilheyuna had probably been in the hubara for too long, weakening himself, and in that state he'd been unable to escape from the fire-magic. It had simply been too much for him, and because he couldn't return to his own body in time, he had perished. His efforts to save them all had cost Vilheyuna his own life. Terrel could only hope that the shaman's spirit had been able to move on – and that Alyssa would never be put in the same position. His sole reason for going on with what he was doing was that he expected to be with her again in *this* world.

'When I saw that hubara just now,' Mlicki said, 'just for a moment, I thought . . . but it wasn't him, was it?'

Terrel shook his head.

'Of course, Vilheyuna wasn't the only one to die that day,' Mlicki said.

'Sansunak,' Terrel said, remembering the second fire.

'You saw that?' The shaman's apprentice had begun to appreciate how much Terrel already knew from earlier exchanges. Although he didn't really understand *how* Terrel had seen events in the Great Circle, the extent of his knowledge was impressive. 'But that's not who I meant. Algardi's dead too.'

Terrel was appalled by this news, and Mlicki realized that there were some things about which the healer knew nothing.

'Algardi?' Terrel paused. 'He was the one who . . . Moons! That's terrible.'

'He died with honour. That's all he would have asked for. The storytellers will remember him.'

'Yes, they will,' the healer agreed sombrely. 'They'll remember you too.'

'I suppose so,' Mlicki said, looking uncomfortable. 'I still can't believe I did any of those things.'

'You're a shaman,' Terrel told him. 'The headdress is yours by right now.'

At first light, Terrel made his way to what had been Algardi's tent. He was greeted joyfully, and was embraced by everyone there, but the air of mourning hung like a pall over the family, and the void left by the one person who *wasn't* there was one that no visitor could ever fill. Terrel found himself sharing hugs and shedding tears with all the elder's family, and the wordless emotion with which he was greeted by Zahir spoke volumes. Bubaqra did her best to welcome him as usual, but the loss of her beloved husband had extinguished the light in her eyes, and Terrel's stumbling words of condolence could not touch her inner grief. And yet it was his reunion with Ghadira that Terrel found the most difficult. She held him tighter and for longer than anyone else, and in that clasp the awkwardness he had feared faded into insignificance.

Later, both Zahir and Ghadira went with Terrel to visit the graves. Algardi and Vilheyuna had been buried a short way from the city, where the desert reclaimed its dominance. In accordance with nomad tradition there was no monument to mark the place, only small mounds in the dusty soil. Their memories would be kept alive by storytellers rather than by stonemasons.

'Who's buried there?' Terrel asked, indicating a third grave nearby.

'That's Takarna,' Zahir replied. 'He was the Shiban elder who took the arrow meant for me. He at least was honourable.'

The impact of the gesture was not lost on Terrel. In allowing the body of their supposed enemy to lie alongside their own heroes, the Toma had taken a step towards reconciliation – the first step on the long road towards lasting peace in Misrah.

'What happened to Kohtala?' Terrel asked as they walked back to the campsite. He already knew that the ashes which were all that was left of Sansunak had simply been left where they were, to blow away and scatter gradually – and then be forgotten – but Mlicki hadn't said anything about the fate of the Shiban's former warlord.

Zahir's face became a blank mask at the mention of his nemesis, and it was left to Ghadira to answer.

'He was condemned by the laws of Qomish to rot in one of the city's gaols for the rest of his life,' she said. 'But as it turned out that wasn't very long.'

'He's dead?'

'He was found with a rather unpleasant knife wound in his throat,' she replied, and the satisfaction in her voice made Terrel wonder if she had been the one to wield the blade. There was still a small nick on the underside of his own chin.

'Oh, it wasn't me,' Ghadira said, reading his mind. 'I almost wish I could claim it was, but the general belief is that it was one of his own tribe. The Shiban's sense of justice is not as humane as the Mehtar's.'

They returned to the camp to find the entire place buzzing with a new excitement.

'The beacons have spoken!' Medrano told them. 'The Rokku just got a message that the Kullana has returned to their territory. Mizhieb's shouting the news from the rooftops!'

After that, the good tidings came thick and fast. Messengers arrived from various places along the course of the river, bringing reports that the music of life had come back. News from other oases spoke of wells and lakes returning to earlier levels, and it was soon plain to everyone that even the springs of Qomish itself were flowing faster again.

Finally, a lone rider appeared from the desert, a mirage making it seem as if his camel was walking in the sky. He brought the astonishing news that the great canyon, the Sorcerer's Mouth, was gone. It had simply closed up again, he told them, so that now it was impossible to tell it had ever been there.

Having seen it happen, Terrel was the only one who was not surprised.

Ordinarily, the visiting tribes would have begun to leave Qomish on the day after the king's coronation, but because of the special circumstances, the festival had been extended for several days. Now it seemed that it would go on even longer. With the Kullana back, and no sign of the plague returning, Zahir's promises were fulfilled, and the oaths concerning his decrees were declared valid and binding by the Mehtar. As a result, it was formally announced at another massed gathering that the Race of Truth was to be abandoned. No man would ever venture into the Binhemma-Ghar again.

In addition, the Mehtar offered his services to any of those tribes who needed help to re-establish boundaries, to agree exchanges of displaced people, or to discuss treaties designed to ensure peace. It was the beginning of a mammoth undertaking, which would entail a huge amount of work, as well as patience, courage and tenacity. Even if all those qualities were present in every one of the negotiations, it would not guarantee peace for the future – but at least it was a start. Hope had returned to Misrah.

*

The new mood of optimism had even reached the orphan children from the north, a fact that was demonstrated when Hamriya and Luleki came to speak to Terrel.

'We've come to ask your advice,' Hamriya told him solemnly as they sat down.

'I'm not sure I'm the best person to ask.'

'Yes you are,' Luleki said. 'Zahir told us you knew all this was going to happen.'

'Not all of it,' he corrected her, smiling at the girl's evident confidence in him.

'And you're the voice of rain,' Hamriya added, as if this was conclusive proof of his worth as a source of guidance.

'All right. I'll do my best.'

'We've decided we don't really want to go on down the Road of Hope.'

'Even if it is open again,' Hamriya said.

'We want to go home, now that things are better. Do you think that's the right thing to do?'

At first Terrel did not know what to say. He didn't feel remotely qualified to answer such a question.

'Do you all agree on this?' he asked eventually.

'Yes. It's too hot here,' Hamriya explained. 'And we miss the mountains.'

'Do you know where to go?' He was worried by the thought of a group of children – even one as resourceful as the northerners – setting out alone into the desert. Even if that was truly what they all wanted.

'One of the tribes have said we can go part of the way with them,' Luleki told him.

'And once we get so far, we'll know what to do,' her partner added. 'Some of our own people will still be there, and maybe *our* rivers are back to normal now.'

The idea of an escort was a point in their favour, but Terrel thought the children seemed unduly optimistic. The canyon couldn't have had any effect on the rivers further north. But then perhaps the elemental had changed other water courses too.

'Don't you want to stay with the Toma?' he asked.

'They've been very good to us,' Hamriya admitted, 'but we're not really nomads.'

'If you like,' Luleki added hopefully, 'you could come with us.'

Until that moment, Terrel hadn't really thought about what he would do next. In the back of his mind he knew he'd have to move on eventually, but for the time being he'd been content to leave that decision for some indeterminate point in the future.

'We'd really like it if you did,' Hamriya told him earnestly.

For a moment Terrel pictured himself leading a gaggle of children into the unknown. It was a ridiculous image, but it made him smile.

'Will you?' Luleki pleaded.

'I'm not sure I'll be able to,' he replied, to their obvious disappointment. 'But I will think about it. When are you planning to go?'

'The day after tomorrow.'

'Then I'll let you know tomorrow,' he told them.

Later that day, Terrel had another visitor wanting advice.

'Are you busy?' Zahir asked.

'Not really.'

'Can we talk, then?'

'Of course,' the healer replied, glancing at the nomad's unusually anxious face. 'Are you all right? You look nervous.'

'I am,' Zahir replied. 'I'm getting married tomorrow.'

CHAPTER FIFTY-THREE

When the suggestion had first been put to him, Zahir had refused point blank. He'd kept his temper, and been polite, but he'd made his opinion very clear. He did not want to be reminded of any of his dealings with Kohtala, and certainly not a stupid bet. The Shiban elders had tried once more, claiming that honour demanded the wager be fulfilled, but also implying that their offer was more than that. It was a peace offering, another step down the road of reconciliation. Zahir had refused again, unable to forgive either the murder of his father or Kohtala's treachery during the race – even though he realized now that most of the tribe were guilty of nothing more than having been beguiled by the wrong man. A further emissary had come to plead the Shiban's case, telling Zahir that the girl chosen was Takarna's youngest daughter, and that her name was Chiara. Zahir had turned them down once more, telling them he didn't even want to meet the girl.

Then Chiara had come herself.

*

'She's so beautiful, like a desert flower.' Zahir shook his head in wonderment. 'I . . . Am I a fool?'

'I can't answer that for you,' Terrel told him. 'But surely you want more than just a pretty face in a wife?'

'Of course. She's very intelligent too, though I think she sometimes tries to hide that. She can sing and cook, and tell stories as well as any man. And she's strong, but graceful at the same time.'

'You seem to have learnt a lot about her in such a short time,' Terrel commented, smiling.

'We talked for hours,' Zahir replied. 'And she seems so wise – and brave, too. Even though she's sad, she wants to look ahead. She said that's what Takarna would have wanted.'

Terrel realized that Zahir and Chiara, in sharing their grief at the loss of their fathers, could forge a bond of compassion and comfort that would help them both look to the future.

'My mother's already taken Chiara under her wing,' Zahir went on. 'I think it'll be good for her. They've both lost someone, and they can help each other. Even Ghadira seems to like her – or at least she said she couldn't find any fault with her.'

Terrel grinned, imagining what even grudging approval must have meant coming from such a source.

'Then from a practical point of view, there's no problem,' he said. 'But what about love?'

Zahir looked down at the ground.

'I *could* love her,' he said eventually. 'It would be very easy, I think. But who can tell with these things? No one ever loved each other more than my parents, but theirs was an arranged marriage. They didn't even meet till their wedding day.'

'And could Chiara love you?'

'Why not?' Zahir asked, with a trace of his old arrogance. Then his head dropped again. 'How can I know that?' he asked plaintively.

Terrel was silent for a while, not knowing what to say next.

'Well, I've agreed to it now,' Zahir said staunchly. 'The elders all thought I should at least consider the idea, and it certainly has advantages from a political point of view. I can see that.'

'It will mean a lot,' Terrel agreed. 'Not just to your two tribes, but to all the others as well. Even if the marriage is only symbolic, it will send a very powerful and positive message.'

'That's what Raheb said.' Zahir looked up at his friend. 'But I can't help wondering if I'm deluding myself. I don't want it to be symbolic. I want it to be real.'

'That will be up to you and Chiara,' Terrel concluded. 'You're the ones who'll have to try to make it work.'

That night, Terrel dreamt of a blue-white desert, which turned to the colour of blood when the night came and the Red Moon rose to dominate the sky. Both sun and moonlight made the surface of the land glitter, but it was nothing like the desert he was familiar with. And it was colder than any place he had ever known.

He felt the elementals' presence rather than saw them. All three were there, remote and powerful yet benevolent. Terrel sensed they had a message for him, something linked to the icy landscape around him. There was madness here.

Far ahead of him, beyond the frozen desert, a mountain exploded in a crimson sheet of flame.

When Terrel awoke, he was certain that the next stage of his journey along the unknown road had been chosen for him. He had to go north to the mountains. He got up and went to look for Hamriya and Luleki.

Zahir and Chiara were married in the Great Circle, in front of their own clans and hundreds of guests drawn from all the other tribes. Initially, the atmosphere was very tense – especially when, with due ceremony, the bride's dowry was handed over to her brother. The single curd cheese, as specified by the ill-fated wager, was accepted graciously enough, but when – at Zahir's request – it was cut open, and found to contain a quantity of gold jewellery generous enough for any match, the mood improved dramatically.

The simple ritual of joining was carried out by the Mehtar, and was followed by feasting and drinking that lasted all day. Musicians played, and the arena was filled with people dancing. Among them Zahir and Chiara were tireless, graceful and energetic by turns, serious at times, laughing at others. Watching them together, Terrel thought that if he was any judge at all, they seemed to have every chance of making their marriage real.

As evening drew in, the time for storytelling arrived. Zahir decreed that for this night they should have only old stories and, as the arena settled down and prepared to be entertained, the groom called upon Medrano to begin. The artist got to his feet and climbed onto the king's podium, which had been pressed into service again for the occasion.

'This is the oldest story of all,' he began, looking round at all the eager faces. 'The true story of Y-Harah.'

Much later, as the fires burnt low and another tale meandered to its close, Terrel was feeling more relaxed than he had done for a long time. When Ghadira came to sit next to him, he felt a surge of affection for her. Her face was flushed, and he guessed that she was slightly drunk.

'You're leaving tomorrow, aren't you?' she asked.

'Yes.'

'Then I have a favour to ask.'

'Anything.'

'I want a kiss,' she said. 'From you, not . . . Well, you know.'

For once Terrel didn't try to analyze his feelings, or even to think at all. He simply acted. Even though his twisted arm made him clumsy, he took her head in both hands and kissed her, more gently than Jax would have done, but with a great deal more tenderness and feeling. When they finally drew apart, Ghadira's eyes remained closed for a few moments, then she opened them and sighed.

'I don't suppose you'd like to honour your promise and marry me?' she asked.

'I didn't—' he began, then realized she was teasing him. 'You made that up, remember? Besides—'

'Well, it's your loss,' she said, pretending indifference. Then she smiled, relenting. 'What is it about you? I can't even dislike you when you reject me.' She paused, gazing up at the stars. 'When you get back to that girl on the other side of the world, tell her from me how lucky she is.'

'Is she?' Terrel asked quietly.

Ghadira gave no sign of having heard him.

'It's a shame, though,' she said. 'Our children would have been something special.'

Before Terrel had recovered enough of his wits to respond to that, she was gone.

The next morning, as he was gathering together his few belongings in preparation for the journey north, Terrel was surprised to see two sleek falcons fly down and alight on the ridge of a nearby tent.

There's something you ought to see.

Alyssa! he exclaimed in delight. *Are you all right? I didn't expect you back so soon.*

It's only a short visit. Come with us.

Us? Terrel queried.

You'll see, she replied, and the two birds took to the air again.

Terrel followed them to the edge of the encampment, where he saw Mlicki and Kalkara studying the flowers on a chirkewa plant that had sprung up recently. They were intent on what they were doing, but when the second falcon flew past, Kalkara looked up and followed its flight out towards the desert. Terrel did the same, and saw a caravan making its way towards Qomish. Although there were only a few camels, there were a large number of people walking beside them.

A few moments later, a lone figure broke away from the main group and began to run towards Mlicki and Kalkara, who had both stopped to watch the newcomers.

Suddenly Kala broke into a run too, though her brother remained rooted to the spot.

The woman was dressed in ragged clothes, and her face bore the signs of suffering, but her tattoos matched those Terrel had seen in his dream long ago, and Kalkara was in no doubt as to who she was. The little girl had been rescued at last. The two of them met in a fierce embrace, the woman kneeling to take her daughter in her arms.

The other falcon, Terrel said to Alyssa. *It's their father, isn't it?*

Yes. He stayed for this.

And you just found a way to help them, to push things along a bit?

Alyssa didn't answer, but she didn't need to. Watching now with tears in his eyes, Terrel went to join Mlicki.

'Don't you want to go and say hello to your mother?'

Mlicki did not say anything, even though Kalkara and the woman were only a few paces away.

'Mlicki!' the newcomer cried, getting to her feet. 'My beautiful boy!' Her daughter was still clinging to one of her hands, but she held out the other, inviting her son to join them.

'Is it really you?' he whispered.

'It's me,' she replied seriously. 'After all this time, they just let us go. I don't know why. I had a feeling I ought to come here first, but I never thought that you and Kala . . .'

Mlicki finally moved then. Although his sister still held tight to her mother's hand, she used her other arm to hug her son to her.

'I've dreamed about this for so long,' she said. 'So long.

You've both grown so much. Are you well?'

Mlicki could only nod.

'And what about you, little one?'

Kalkara turned her face up to look at her mother, and the expression on her face – one of the utmost concentration – made Terrel want to weep.

'Ma . . .' she tried. 'Mama.'

'What's the matter with your voice, Kala?' her mother asked. 'Why's it so hoarse?'

Mlicki began to laugh and cry, all at the same time.

Terrel looked round for the falcons, but they had already flown away. He knew why. Trying to take part in the reunion would have been too complicated. It was enough to know that it had taken place.

He turned away, deciding to leave the reunited family in peace. Thanks to Alyssa, the last of his aims had been fulfilled. He was finally free to go.

EPILOGUE

'I see them sometimes, in the air,' Hamriya said.

'So do I,' Luleki claimed, not to be outdone. 'They used to fly over our tent when we were in Qomish.'

'Protecting us,' her friend agreed sagely.

The two girls were discussing the legends of the north, but Terrel recognized the creatures they'd described. They were what the nomads called erlik, watchful spirits of the night. After all he had seen, he would not have been surprised to find they really *had* guarded the refugees while they'd been at the festival. They had certainly been in need of protection then – at least for the early part of their stay. But hopefully those times were over. No one called them the unclean now.

'Of course, we might meet a tiarken instead,' Luleki suggested brightly.

'Then we'd catch it and make it grant us wishes,' her companion said.

'What would you wish for?' Terrel asked, smiling.

'To go home,' the two girls said together.

A median month had passed since they'd left Qomish, and the children were still some way from reaching their goal. However, it now seemed as if it really would be possible. The tribe they'd been travelling with had passed them on to others who were equally sympathetic, and who were headed in the right direction. Unfortunately, it was the wrong direction for Terrel, and he knew that the time had come for them to part.

'Is that what *you* would wish for?' Hamriya asked.

'To go home?' If I had that choice, would I take it? Terrel wondered. The thought of returning to Alyssa's side made his heart ache with longing. She was still so far away. 'No,' he said at last. 'I can't go home yet.'

'Are you really going to the other side of the mountains?' Luleki asked.

Terrel nodded.

'That's where my road leads,' he explained.

'Your Road of Hope?' Hamriya queried.

'That's as good a name as any,' he said.

ICE MAGE

Julia Gray

The remote and wild land of Tiguafaya is on the edge of chaos. The menacing volcanoes that dominate the landscape grumble and threaten destruction. The repulsive fireworms, the marauding pirates and the ancient dragons grow bolder by the minute. The corrupt and ineffectual government is paralysed and helpless in the face of all the dangers.

The country's only hope for survival lies with a group of young rebels known as the Firebrands. Led by the lovers, Andrin and Ico, and the half-mad musician, Vargo, the Firebrands are desperately fighting back. Using the once-revered but now lost arts of magic against the overwhelming odds, they are all that stand between Tiguafaya and total destruction.

Rich and exciting, powerful and engrossing, _Ice Mage_ marks the arrival of a thrilling new voice in fantasy adventure.

FIRE MUSIC

Julia Gray

The stunning sequel to *Ice Mage* is a fast-paced fantasy adventure of war, magic and romance. The new government of Tiguafaya has finally brought peace to a people long suppressed by its tyrannical rules. But it may not last, for now a much greater power threatens the Firebrands – the mighty Empire to the north, whose emperor will not tolerate the Tiguafayans heretical belief in magic. However, the attempts to resolve the dispute by diplomacy will all count for nothing if the fire and lava shaking the ground cannot be controlled.

'A spellbinding storyteller' *Maggie Furey*

Orbit titles available by post:

❑ The Dark Moon	Julia Gray	£6.99
❑ The Jasper Forest	Julia Gray	£6.99
❑ Ice Mage	Julia Gray	£6.99
❑ Fire Music	Julia Gray	£6.99
❑ Isle of the Dead	Julia Gray	£6.99
❑ The Empire Stone	Chris Bunch	£6.99
❑ Transformation	Carol Berg	£6.99
❑ A Cavern of Black Ice	J. V. Jones	£7.99
❑ The Eye of the World	Robert Jordan	£6.99
❑ Colours in the Steel	K. J. Parker	£6.99
❑ Thraxas	Martin Scott	£5.99

The prices shown above are correct at time of going to press. However the publishers reserve the right to increase prices on covers from these previously advertised, without further notice.

ORBIT BOOKS

Cash Sales Department, P.O. Box 11, Falmouth, Cornwall, TR10 9EN
Tel: +44 (0) 1326 569777, Fax: +44 (0) 1326 569555
Email: books@barni.avel.co.uk.

POST AND PACKING:

Payments can be made as follows: cheque, postal order (payable to Orbit Books) or by credit cards. Do not send cash or currency.

U.K. Orders under £10	£1.50
U.K. Orders over £10	**FREE OF CHARGE**
E.E.C. & Overseas	25% of order value

Name (Block Letters) _____

Address _____

_____

Post/zip code: _____

❑ Please keep me in touch with future Orbit publications

❑ I enclose my remittance £_____

❑ I wish to pay Visa/Access/Mastercard/Eurocard

Card Expiry Date